Sam,

Survival of the Fittest: Metamorphosis

Be prepared.

Volume 1 of the *Survival of the Fittest* series

Be very prepared...

Johnny Pearce

Survival of the Fittest: Metamorphosis
Copyright © 2016 Johnny Pearce
Published by Loom
Printed by Lightning Source International

All rights reserved. No part of this publication may be reproduced, stored in a retrieval system, or transmitted in any form by any means, electronic, mechanical, photocopy, recording, or otherwise, without the prior permission of the publisher, except as provided for by UK copyright law.

This is a work of fiction. Names, characters, businesses, places, events and incidents are either the products of the author's imagination or used in a fictitious manner. Any resemblance to actual persons, living or dead, or actual events is purely coincidental.

Cover design: Jules Bailey and Loom

Trade paperback ISBN: 978-0-9926000-7-5

LM 02/16

About the author

Johnny Pearce is a philosopher from Hampshire, UK, who is taking that background and applying it to fiction. In this case, zombies. He thinks that fiction can be pure escapism, but also escapism with thought. One should be able to think a little about existence…before getting one's face ripped off by a zombie.

Acknowledgements

I would like to thank Rebecca Bradley, my editor, for being pretty damned awesome. Check out her own brilliant books! I am also grateful to my guinea pigs: Andy Loneragan, Glenn Andrew Barr, Alan Kennedy, Geoff Toscano, Pete Black and Rachael Easton. They were early testers and tested well. Maybe they can feature in a future instalment. They might get eaten, though. Jules Bailey did a great job with the cover—I might save him for a particularly grisly death! Big thanks to him.

As ever, I need, should and want to thank my beautiful partner, Helen, for all of her support.

Praise for this book

"A frightening and credible zombie apocalypse. This *is* the way the world would end—not with a bang or a whimper, but with a snarl and the gnashing of teeth…" Rebecca Bradley, author of *Cadon, Hunter* and *From Hades With Love*

"Pearce's rollicking suburban adventure begs to be consumed and it won't let go until life is sucked from the final pages." Glenn Andrew Barr, author of *Skin of Them*

"Johnny Pearce has written a shockingly good zombie story with a literary quality unfamiliar to the genre. Don't let the slow build fool you—the growing tension plays a vital role in allowing everything to snap with a most satisfying sort of frayed devastation. Once all hell breaks loose it's a no holds barred gore fest!" Tristan Vick, author of *BITTEN: Resurrection* and *BITTEN 2: Land of the Rising Dead*

"The secrets of evolution are death and time—the deaths of enormous numbers of lifeforms that were imperfectly adapted to the environment; and time for a long succession of small mutations."
— Carl Sagan, Cosmos

*To those who sacrifice
much of themselves
for the greater good*

PROLOGUE

I remember the days of using power without any second thought. The glory of a guilt-free consumption of an abundant and painless resource. To think that listening to music is now such a guilty pleasure, and one that involves blood, sweat and tears. Literally. How easy life was! No, really, how easy... Everything is so close to being normal, and yet so far. I can see a television in the corner of the room, and yet it is useless. A sewing machine—redundant. An empty packet of biscuits—like gold dust. A dated newspaper—a stark reminder of Before.

"Hey, are you up there?"
Pause.
"Aha."
"Food's ready!"

It's easy to be nostalgic. Everything in sight, inside and out, shouts of Before. Every day is full of wishing for the past; of moving around living museums; of memories that ebb and flow and then slowly begin to fade. That's why I want to write this. I've crossed the bridge from Before to Post. I've lived them both, and there's not too many left who can claim that. Well, not many who can write.

"Are you coming?"
"Two minutes."

I'm not angry. Not any more. And who do I have to be angry with? I just find it a little bit annoying that those without the Stain are the ones carrying all the pain. We were, each of us, hoping that it would all be over with. But with this time that has passed, the Stain has only slightly faded.

He lifted the pen from the paper, a crisp pad of lined A4 sheets. His wrist was certainly not used to the arduous task of committing ink to paper. He hadn't written this much since he had been at school and that was... He calculated some fourteen years previously. This then triggered a wave of memories of laptops and electricity, cups of tea and endless hours spent surfing the internet. Memories of normality.

Waggling his hand and fingers, he proceeded to look at his watch, something which still worked thanks to the stash of batteries he had requisitioned from a jeweller's last year. Five-thirty and almost dark. He had been struggling to see his writing as it was. It was time to stop, before They arrived. Which they would if he had a lamp up here to light up any more of his penmanship. Food waited for him in the cellar. Safe, if not particularly warm.

He put the lid back on the rather elegant fountain pen. *I wonder when another new fountain pen will get made. Fifty, a hundred, two hundred years?* Placing the pen next to the now-closed pad of memories and cascading thoughts, he stood up, pushed in the chair and moved to the stairs. He had been in the study on the top floor of the house. A large window provided quickly dimming light which burnished the top of the stairs with dying hope, losing out to the creeping darkness of the lower floor. He managed a furtive yet habit-driven glance out on to the field outside the house, checking for anything untoward. There were always untoward things to check for. Most of his days were spent giving sideways glances, life-saving looks behind him. Everyone did it. You had to. To survive. Those who didn't, didn't. A perfect example of an evolutionary behaviour. The fields were safe, it seemed: no sign of movement, only the dying sun giving off its final shards of light, slicing through the naked trees, before resurrecting on the morrow. It had forced its way through a break in the low-hanging grey clouds which blanketed the countryside for most of the view. It would rain soon.

He trudged downstairs, building up enthusiasm for a meal of tinned vegetables and tinned meat. Once at the bottom, he walked to the front door. It was a homely wooden front door, since the house was an old farmhouse set on its own amongst a number of fields to one side and a small wood to the other side. The woods to the right of the front door, as he looked out of the window next to the door, unnerved him somewhat. It was never good to have so much of your field of vision blocked by a dark gathering of trees. The fields offered ample warning of anything approaching. The farmhouse stood at the top of a gentle rise in the undulating landscape, and the several fields to the left rose to another hill some half a mile away or so. But the woods—so close, even if they weren't the biggest to negotiate. Anything coming out of there would offer the farmhouse little in the way of advance warning.

He checked the lock. Secure. Moving down the low-ceilinged corridor, he walked past the living room and dining room to the kitchen. Next to the kitchen door was a low door that led to the cellar. Everywhere else in the house was near-dark. From the cellar, without windows, candle flickering escaped. He closed the cellar door behind him as he stepped down the wooden stairs to be greeted by the simple dining room table, which had emigrated to a safer environment, set with meagre plates of food. He looked to the two other people sitting at the table expectantly.

"You okay?" asked the woman, a frown of concern on her face.

"Sure. Thanks for doing the food. Sorry, I was getting into my writing there."

"A right Ernest Hemingway or even Jack Kerouac there!" added the third person in the room, a man in his middle forties, balding, with wire-rimmed glasses.

"We'll see. Actually, it's hard to see what kind of writer I'll be with an audience of two."

"You never know, the others know where we are, they could arrive at any moment. You might over double your audience," said the woman, brushing aside her shoulder-length, newly cleaned hair. The benefits of a stream running alongside the farmhouse. Shampoo doesn't go out of date.

"Hope springs etern—" but the spectacled man's voice was cut short by the sound of an urgent banging on the door. Banging with a purpose. All three stood up immediately, the woman moving to the side of the cellar and picking up a shotgun and a satchel, throwing the satchel hastily over her shoulder. The balding man grabbed a motorbike jacket off the back of his chair and fastened it tightly, as quickly as he could. He patted the thick padding reassuringly. Meanwhile, the man who'd entered the room last spun on his heel and jogged back to the stairs, picking up on his way a baseball bat that was lying against the wall.

As they ran quietly on the balls of their feet, the frantic banging continued. *Cut the noise down, for Chrissakes!* The writer, first in line, opened the cellar door with minimal sound, turning to see the woman following him and the other man moving into the kitchen to get his motorbike helmet. As the writer reached the door, the banging surged. He knew that the banger would be Normal, with that kind of purposeful behaviour. He pulled the curtains aside at one of the windows which conveniently banked the door. A shower had started and the window was spattered with heavy drops of winter rain. However, he could still make out the person on the other side.

"It's her!" he hissed to the woman behind him, who already had her gun raised, a panicked look on her face. He unlocked the door quickly, to be greeted by a distraught and dishevelled woman of about thirty in jeans, combat boots and a thick, black leather jacket. Her hair was matted and wet, though he could not tell whether it was with rain or sweat. She had her head turned partially to the back, and to the side, showing a cut to her right cheek, almost from her eye to her mouth, in a vicious crescent. It wept dark, viscous blood. The writer followed her gaze through the gathering rain. Towards the woods.

"Holy fucking shit!"

1
Jason

They say that necessity is the mother of all inventions. Well, in the case of Jason Newton, stasis was the mother of all inaction. Nonchalant comfort had sanctioned a rather monotonous life.

The summer, so far, had been a hot one. A really hot one, as far as the records were concerned. Well, as far as everyone was concerned. With several fairly dry years and particularly dry winters, water levels were low and reservoirs were struggling. Hosepipe bans were running for a second consecutive year, meaning that suburbia couldn't water its gardens or wash its cars with the normal thoughtless ease. Neighbours had started acting in un-neighbourly fashion (perhaps it was the heat) by shopping each other to water companies for flouting the rules. The fines were high, and tempers flared. Consistently hot days seemed to drain people's energy and good humour. In a typical manner, people complained to each other constantly, whether down the shops in casual "weather conversations", or on the radio and TV. Typical, because had it not been warm enough, they still would have complained. And had it been just right, they would have complained it still wasn't warm enough. Such is the way with human nature: one is never satisfied.

Jason, however, realised with newfound glee that he had bucked the trend by thoroughly enjoying the languid summer so far, mainly due to the fact that he had already come to terms with his midlife crisis, handed his resignation in to his boss in the City, and gone to help his friend set up a surf and kite-surf shop in Devon on the southwestern coast of Britain. A win-win of having amassed a decent sum of disposable income, having few outgoings, and dealing almost exclusively with scantily clad people, had returned a smile to Jason's face that had been sadly absent for too many years. He felt he had really landed on his feet. Okay, so he couldn't surf for toffee, and he was almost literally a fish out of water in the shop, selling and renting equipment to people who often knew infinitely more about the equipment than he did. But that couldn't dampen his spirits. In his late 30s, Jason had finally taken one of his first big risks; although, compared to half the world's population, it was a fairly comfortable risk afforded by someone in a particularly fortunate position. But, hey, he had thought, everything's relative.

"The Shack" was adorned with all sorts of water sports and beach paraphernalia, liberally attached to any spare area of wall so that one couldn't tell what colour the shop interior actually was. There were surf boards, rash vests, kites of all shapes and sizes, Frisbees, wetsuits, alternative jewellery and anything else that could fetch a few pounds for his lifelong friend, Danny.

"Alright, fella?" asked Danny as he came out of the workshop at the back of the shop with a freshly waxed board in his hands. He nestled it into a spot between another board and a kite after deliberating for some time, as if calculating the feng-shui consequences of such an important placement. He turned and ran his hand through his sandy-coloured mop of sea-washed hair and stood with his other hand against the board as if in some kind of surf magazine photo shoot.

"You prima donna prick," replied Jason, who spent much of his day watching Danny in various poses, usually around sun-bleached and tanned female clientele. "You know, it's hard to believe we're in the UK and not some Australian beach Mecca. Olding Bay may not be Surfer's Paradise, but it puts up a good fight this year."

"She's a beaut today, yet again. Scorcher!"

"I swear I can actually see you evolve on a daily basis into more of a stereotypical 'surf-dude'. It's like the Evolution of Man picture, but in your case, Man has started regressing with the help of a surf board."

A group of three people, two men and a woman, walked into The Shack. Two of them rested their shades on top of their heads whilst the first man rested his on his forehead above his eyes. Jason took an instant dislike to him. What a dick. People who did that were on a par with people who played their music full volume in their cars with the windows wound down just so others could hear them being cool. Of course, Jason took it as fact that it was acceptable to do so in *his* case since *his* musical taste was exemplary.

"Hey guys, can I help you?" Jason chimed.

"Yeah, we're looking to hire some boards. We've had a few lessons and want to practice," said Forehead-shades.

"No worries. Danny can help you with that. He's the pro."

The three turned to Danny and started chatting. Jason checked out the girl with the two men. They were all in their early twenties, probably university students, or graduates enjoying their last piece of extended freedom before shackling themselves to the prison of corporate whoredom. Jason smiled wryly. The girl was a petite brunette, not too dissimilar to his previous girlfriend in height and build. Memories flooded back — flashes of life together for five and a half years; of going through the ups and down; of going through the down and out. Slave to the City, no time for anyone else, he remembered.

He finally moved his eyes off the girl and on to the second man. He was pretty pale. Actually, very pale. With dark brown hair, short and spiky, he looked out of place in The Shack, partly because he was wearing some pretty terrible sandals and shorts, and partly because he simply looked uncomfortable. Jason examined him a little more closely. He'd always been an observant person, noticing all the signs around him when driving, or reading everything that was in front of him, whether it was a cereal packet or the active ingredients in a tube of cream for thrush. No, there was something uneasy about this guy. He was sweating, but then everybody was at the moment. This sweat looked different, though — heavy beads were rolling down from his temples, and his nose was pretty red. What a time to get the flu! Man, Jason thought, summer flus were worse than winter ones — they were so incongruous. Then he couldn't believe he had just thought of the word 'incongruous'. *What a loser! No, that was just anti-intellectualism. No, I can't believe I've just thought those words in The Shack...*

Jason had a propensity to lose himself in banal ramblings of thought. He looked at his watch. It was just past two.

"Sorry to interrupt, Danny, but I gotta dash. Surf's up." He shook his head imperceptibly: he couldn't believe he had just said that. Who did he think he was?

"Sure, fella. Thanks for today. Don't drown, like normal!" Danny replied, making sure Jason's surf image was destroyed in front of the three would-be surfers.

"Saves me showering. See you at the pub later. Don't forget I'm shooting off tomorrow for three or four days," Jason said, referring to his imminent sojourn with Bevan in his campervan. Which would have been all the more pleasant had Bevan been someone whom Jason had much time for. He wasn't.

With that, Jason nodded his goodbyes to the clientele and their grinning expert customer service representative, turned around, picked up his bag, and walked through the back and into the workshop. There were boards everywhere. Half of them, Jason was sure, didn't even belong to anybody. Some had damaged fins, others were being waxed or cosmetically improved. Jason moved over to a yellow long-board and picked it up. He was already in his boardies. He grabbed his rash vest from the side, threw off his T-shirt and replaced it with the vest. Sporting bare feet, he was now ready to assume his new role as surf-dude. He already had the shark's tooth necklace, as if to indicate to anyone who met him that he was at one with the sea. Like a tiger shark, except not so good at moving through the sea.

Jason had worked pretty hard to get to being a top surf shop customer services representative. A three year economics degree at the University of Bristol and approaching two decades of working in financial institutions in London. He often had the feeling that he was over-qualified. He couldn't wax a board very well, but he could develop a three-stage, five-year business plan for The Shack. Perhaps, in some ways, he was woefully under-qualified.

The great thing about The Shack was its proximity to the bay. The quaint Olding Bay was in the process of being exploited commercially. The Shack was part of that, if Jason would care to admit it. The bay was small, and acted as the mouthpiece to a nestled community of old cottages and houses with one pub and a newly built bar, as well as assorted tea rooms and typical shops. The land rose fairly sharply behind the village, with the road curving round above the west to enter it on the east. This gave panoramic views of the small bay and the chocolate box surroundings as you drove into Olding itself. The Shack sat at the western end of Olding so that it was nearer the start of the break as it moved across the bay and one had to go through the village in order to access the shop. It was a short walk down the quiet road, across the promenade and then onto the sand of the beach. The day was hot, the sky clear, a comfortable breeze was strong enough to signal some decent enough waves, and a broad smile adorned the face of Jason Newton as the sand eased through his toes.

He always smiled when his feet hit the sand. He couldn't help it. The idea still excited him, of leaving London and the world of corporate conformity to begin a new life whereby he could do what he wanted and when — even if it did sound like a cliché to all of his friends.

Jason looked down the sandy beach to the other end of the bay where, in the distance, there stood a beachfront café. "The Crab Shack", despite its simple, homely name was obviously designed for upmarket tourists. Not the sort associated with run-down seaside has-beens of resorts, which had never moved on from the heyday of staycation tourism of the fifties and sixties. No, the sort with middle-classed disposable income. This was a modern, stylish beachfront café-restaurant appealing to a more current clientele with money and predilections for swanky food and clean lines, or a good cup of quality fresh South

American coffee with biscotti and a generous price tag. The confusion of there being two shacks in town didn't affect Jason; he'd turned his back on modern commercialism, at least when it suited him. There was only one shack for him—*The* Shack—and the dress code was definitely damp board-shorts and shark-tooth necklaces.

Moving across the sand, carrying his not-insignificant board, he thought about surfing. He was not a great surfer, not by any stretch of his imagination, but he was getting to be a little more than a rank amateur. Jason felt that his level descriptor (as if he had been playing some kind of surfing computer game) was "indistinctly average". He loved the idea of slowly being able to commandeer nature, in all its rapturous power; of being able to harness its energy and drive for his own ends, using a man-made device and a little bit of skill and knowledge. He was also all too aware of how powerful nature could be and, as a result, he was mindful of the danger that always lurked under her every swell. One mighty wave could be the crest of his experience or the very end of his experience, and he was savvy enough to be cognisant of the limits to his abilities. Playing with nature could be fun, until you lost.

The swell was average, which suited his abilities and he had a good hour or so paddling about and surfing the odd wave with a few other near-beginners. Even a short session was tiring, so he wandered back across the beach with a feeling of weary satisfaction. He had only swallowed a few litres of seawater today. That was a result. He shivered with cold, having risked the sea in merely a rash vest and boardies today—a little unusual.

Jason had been living in a one-bedroom flat in a house a few doors up the hill from The Shack, which suited him down to the ground. Wet with the delights of a more outdoor existence, he placed the board against the garage wall after letting himself through the back gate. He took a key from under a flowerpot, and opened the door that stood opposite the garage, on the side of the house. His flat, overlooking its back garden, occupied a small portion of a large, detached house covered in a wizened wisteria. A small lounge-diner, impeccably tidy, greeted him as he entered, with the tiny kitchenette to his right. He walked through the bijou lounge and through to his equally unblemished bedroom, off of which was a small bathroom.

Washing under a steaming hot shower, Jason relished the joy of rinsing the briny residue off his now fairly tanned skin. He was successfully losing much of what he liked to call his "city-fat", the recognition of which was cemented by a narcissistic rub of his stomach. It was no washboard, but there were some bumps attempting to push through the remnants of late-thirties blubber. He quickly washed his hair, eager for something to eat and a trip down the pub. Even his hair was starting to resemble the hair of a younger, more carefree man. Although straight in nature, the sea was giving it a few light waves of its own, though he could still only manage a rather teenage set of brown curtains at the front.

Drying himself roughly, he threw on a surf tee, some cargo pants and a pair of Reef sandals, and made himself a decent sandwich. He opened the fridge again for a cold beer. *Whatever did they do before fridges? Man, before beer?* Nothing like an early start. It was about quarter to six so Jason flicked on the television. He scrolled through the tripe that was late afternoon TV until he got to the news channels. Even though he was changing into a new and more happy-go-lucky man, he still had his habits, and one of them was a mild addiction to news programmes.

After a few inane stories and headline recaps (*it must have been a slow news day*) about the Middle East peace process (*never going to happen*), the Home Secretary trying to introduce new immigration laws (*middle-class vote winner*) and a large number of flu cases across Britain (*whinging Brits*), he finally got to the business news. However, he never quite got the wholesome edification he was hoping for out of knowing the stock market rises and the latest telecoms market buzz. Maybe he *was* changing.

One thing that didn't change was his early-start Friday night down at the local pub, the *Bull and Barleycorn*. And tonight, *The Bull* it was.

Jason put on some aftershave, grabbed his wallet, rinsed his mouth with mouthwash, and left the flat. He strolled down the road to the beach and ambled happily along the promenade to the other end of the village where the pub was situated. It was a sort of ritualistic walk where he always noticed the same things as he walked the same exact route.

The pub was several centuries old and retained its character well, meaning it was still a popular destination for locals and tourists alike. An old coach-house, it had a large garden to the side, replete with picnic tables and parasols, and it was already beginning to fill. Jason took one last look out to sea to view the calming waters lap gently against the sandy shore, and smiled to himself. Life couldn't get too much better. Well, maybe a girlfriend. All good things come to those who wait...

Turning his back on the bay, he stepped through the covered porch and into the pub.

"Well, if it isn't Mr Newton himself. Good evening to you!" called the landlord from behind the bar. David Bentley always worked Fridays and Saturdays behind the bar. He felt it kept his fingers on the pulse of Olding. Things couldn't easily get under his radar. He was a typical landlord: portly, ruddy-faced and red of nose, with a bald patch ringed by greying hair. In his mid-sixties, he had owned the pub for as long as anyone could care to remember, and he was a veritable cornerstone of the Olding community.

By the time Jason had got to the bar, the landlord had half-pulled his usual pint. Jason used to be a wine drinker, and still was on occasion in his flat. Now, though, he had adapted to the local environment in making himself appreciate the finer nuances of cloudy Devon cider.

"Cheers, David. Put it on the tab," nodded Jason towards the check-shirted man, whose bulging belly overhung his dark green corduroy trousers. Jason took the pint of musky looking "apple-heaven" (as he now liked to coin it) and sauntered through the main lounge, nodding to a few acquaintances, before taking himself into the beer garden to find an empty table. He may only have been here for the summer and the end of spring but he had got to know a fair few people. He felt so much more alive and relevant in Olding. Everyone was someone. In London, he felt that nobody was anyone.

He had sunk half of his pint by the time Danny got to the pub.

"Mate!" Jason grinned at his advancing, equally beach-casual friend.

"Hey buddy! Good sesh?"

"Yeah, not bad. Caught a few, missed a few, drowned in a few," was Jason's fairly accurate summary.

"Hey boys!" It was a brash West Country accent from across the garden, rural and loud. It could only mean one thing.

"And enter Bevan…" was all the excitement Danny could muster as he sat down after giving Jason a friendly pat on the back.

Jason could never quite work out whether Bevan was a bit of a fool, annoying but with a handful of redeeming qualities; or whether he was simply an idiot. Either way, he was about to spend the best part of four days holed up in a campervan with him. The more he thought about it, though, the more he realised it was the latter.

Bevan, a short man in his early forties, strutted through the garden swinging his arms in some kind of urban fashion that was out of place both in an essentially rural pub garden, and on a balding man of a certain age who hadn't been near a big city for the best part of three years. And even then that was Plymouth, which one could hardly recognise as an urban heartland. Clumping along in his combat boots, grey camouflaged combat pants and tight black T-shirt, Bevan swung past a table of pretty young girls— holidaymakers staying at the campsite over the hill.

"Evenin' ladies," he attempted to charm, quite ineffectually, with a wink and a tobacco-stained grin, "Life is short, don't waste it. I'm over here all night". He was short-changed (or adequately-changed) with dismissive looks and eye-rolling from the intended quarry.

Danny leant over the table to Jason. "Why is he such a social fucking leper?"

"And why are we the charity leper colony?" Jason replied, rolling his own eyes.

"Boys, boys, boys!" Bevan sat down with a thud next to Danny.

"Why don't you come and join us, Bevan?" said Jason.

"Don't mind if I did." Bevan, having already put his pint of cider down and taken out a tobacco tin from one of his several pockets, began rolling himself a cigarette. He had a few days growth of stubble on his tanned and weather-worn face, a stud in his left ear. "So, Jace, you looking forward to our little trip in my camper, day after tomorrow?"

"Er, yeah. Exactly what have I let myself in for?"

"Well, I know a few places on the moor where we can secret ourselves, and live a few days in quiet bliss. You know, have a few walks, make some fires, smoke some weed, listen to some music—"

"Eat beans on toast for eight meals in a row?" Danny interrupted.

"Sounds good to me!" Bevan grinned.

Jason had felt that he should do something a little different this weekend and coming week. Danny had been fine when Bevan had offered, and Jason (to his own surprise) accepted. Danny could cope with The Shack for a few days on his own. Quite what Bevan was supposed to be doing, Jason could only guess. He seemed to get by with doing the odd job here and there, mainly helping one of the local builders, but he must surely have had some money banked to support a life of relatively few responsibilities. In fact, Bevan had hinted at having been left a small house in the next village together with a little pot of money. Jason had seen him cope with only doing what he had to, and this was precious little, evidently.

Jason broke out of his reverie. "Early start, is it?"

"I'll pick you up at nine. Ish," Bevan said.

"Sweet. A day of polishing boards tomorrow and then Exmoor here we come!"

Jason turned to see that Danny had lost interest and had started surveying the pub garden like an anthropogenic prospector, looking for a golden-skinned treasure. His eyes narrowed as he caught sight of a pair of holidaymakers seating themselves at the next table. The man accompanying them had his shades, even in the lower evening sunshine, propped on his forehead.

"Hi guys. Where's your mate?" asked Danny.

"Oh, hi there. You're the guy from the surf shop," answered the petite brunette, whom Jason remembered from their brief encounter earlier that day. "Pete didn't feel like coming out. He was feeling pretty dodgy when we saw you. Now he's really taken a turn for the worse. Proper flu symptoms. He's aching all over and pissing sweat."

"A few pints'll sort him out!" said Bevan.

Danny added, "Hope he didn't give me anything. I've got a surf comp up in Croyde next weekend!"

"Well, I hope he gets better," was as polite as Jason could be, but then a thought came to him. "It's probably that flu that's going around. It was even on the news."

Forehead-shades, chewing some gum, furrowed his brow, making the sunglasses move magically. "My parents are ill too. You could be onto something there! I left them in Southampton last night."

"It's amazing that a bit of poxy flu can get on the news," said Danny. Jason thought this was a good attempt at trying hard to care.

Bevan, wearing his doctor's hat, was somewhat academic in his approach. "That's the problem with city types. Don't get enough Vitamin C. Who's up for another pint of cider?"

METAMORPHOSIS

2
Fran

Every day, Fran knew a little bit of her life was slipping away. She wasn't dying. To be fair, she was in pretty good shape, if a little on the thin side; but that was to be expected after the best part of a year without any exercise. Anxiety had kept her metabolism up and her weight down. Her flat, comfortable enough, was her solace. A sufficiently nice place in the heart of Bristol, it had two bedrooms, a kitchen, fair-sized bathroom and a separate lounge and dining room. There was even a hallway leading to all of the rooms. On the right, as you entered the door and a few paces down the hallway, was the lounge. Painted a calming blue, it welcomed in the daytime sunlight or the cooling breeze in the height of summer through its French doors. The balcony, reached through the French doors, looked down from the top floor of the five-storey block on to a lawned area which sat between Fran's and two similar blocks. The dining room, a deep burgundy, was a darker affair, though tastefully decorated with abstract paintings, which sat opposite the lounge.

The lounge and dining room were the places in which Fran spent most of her day, regulating her moods with changes in surrounding colour. In combination with the other rooms in the flat, they were where she spent *all* of her day.

Fran sat down at her laptop in the dining room. She liked to do this because if she didn't make herself use the dining room, she would spend all her time in the lounge, and she recognised that this wasn't healthy. Clearly, using two rooms was more varied and showed at least a little effort. The burgundy made her feel warm, too.

Sitting at a wooden dining chair laden with her favourite embroidered cushion from the market, Fran opened her internet browser and loaded up her own blog page. *Diary of a Prisoner*. Her blog title for the day was "When your Mum is ill". She sat rubbing her face for inspiration, and then the words started to flow. Her fingers tapped with their compulsive haste, so much so that she kept having to backspace to rewrite misspelled words. She was well used to it.

So my Mum has got bronchitis. That's not too bad in and of itself. It was touch and go as to whether it was pneumonia. Either way, she is none too well and all the way over in London. And I am here. In my flat. As much as I love her, and as frail as she is, I'm not sure I've got it in me to go and see her. Well, as you all know, I'm not sure I've got it in me to get to Bristol Temple Meads train station; or down the road. In fact, I'd be lucky to get out on the lawn in the next few days.

And so prison continues. It's not like I'm getting beaten or that the food is crap, or that I have to sleep in the same stark room as my toilet bowl. Okay, so I beat myself up emotionally, and I am being tortured by boredom, but I could go out. Couldn't I?

I just don't feel like I'm getting any better. And nor is my Mum.

The buzzer rang. Fran's heart started beating a little faster at the mere thought of opening her door to someone strange. Her rational mind overcame the anxious moment, reasoning that it was clearly going to be the supermarket delivery service. Sainsbury's home delivery service was a real life-saver for her. She relied on it. In fact, she relied on internet deliveries for most of her solitary existence. And there was never any chance of her missing the delivery slot—she was always in. That was the bonus to being agoraphobic.

I must do that as a blog post.

The buzzer rang again. She hit the button by her front door.

"Hi there."

"Hello, is that Fran Peters? It's Sainsbury's," said the distorted voice.

"Yup, I'll buzz you through. Fifth floor, flat B," Her heart fluttered again. What if she were to panic in front of him? *Oh come on, sort yourself out.*

Fran patted down her hair a little too manically, which was redundant given that her hair was neatly restricted into small micro braids, falling down past her shoulder. She looked in the mirror by the front door. Her dark skin had a mild sheen to it. When the knock at the door broke her momentary trance, she watched her own eyes widen before she finally shook herself and opened the door.

"Hi there. Fran Peters?"

She nodded. The gap-toothed man grinned at her and turned to start unloading his box trolley, which was stacked high with large trays of plastic bags, each filled to differing capacity with groceries. To be honest, the grin was more of a grimace. As Fran looked more closely, she could see that the man had a sheen of his own. He caught her looking at him.

"It's a long way up here. Er, even in the lift...I'm not feeling too good today. Don't worry, I'm not contagious," he joked, handing her some plastic milk bottles. "You're not going on holiday, I see! Enough food here for some time!"

"I like to keep stocked up. Saves me going to the shops and lugging it back." Fran hustled the first load of bags to the kitchen, dumped them on the floor, and went back for more. It was soon over, after a couple more forgettable interactions with the delivery man. She signed the paperwork and closed the door on the world again. Things went back to normal and her heart rate slowed to a regular beat.

Fran unpacked the groceries with no particular haste. There was no need to hurry, especially since this was one of the highlights of her week.

As she unpacked, Fran pondered her predicament, her agoraphobia, and what she wanted out of life. She had had to give up her newspaper job some months back when her condition deteriorated to an unworkable level. Luckily, she had her flat to fall back on, paid up courtesy of her father dying from cancer some years ago. Silver linings, she often thought. Now she confined herself to the flat, and blogged. She had written some pieces for newspapers and magazines about her situation and condition, about her self-imposed imprisonment, and she was hoping to get a publisher for a book she had already almost finished. Things were moving quickly, of that there was no doubt. But money was tough at the moment. She was relying on loans from her mother and on the welfare state, but at the age of thirty-two, she was beginning to feel that this wasn't ideal. She was getting no younger, and her mother only had finite resources, and even less time if her track record of health was anything to go by. Fran realised that she needed to do something about her agoraphobia: either she submitted to it and accepted a very difficult and solitary life, or she overcame it and achieved something in doing so. She could take up her journalism again, or writing, or both, even, she was hoping.

Having unpacked her groceries and put the kettle on for a cup of tea, she moved into the lounge and switched the television on. The default channel was always the news. That's where she often left an evening's television viewing, and that's where it remained until the next day. It was what kept her interested in, and connected to, the world

"...thinking that this could be a little more serious than our usual cases of flu?"

[John Durham, Department of Health] "Well, it does seem to be spreading fairly rapidly, though not, from what we can tell, through airborne means. That

means that the flu spreads through exchange of fluids and the like. But yes, we are a little concerned that the numbers of people off work are higher than they normally would be."

"We have heard rumours that a few cases are a little more serious. Is there any truth to these claims?"

"There is nothing to suggest that there is anything to worry about..."

Fran changed the channel. She was avariciously fascinated with the news, all aspects of the news. All, that was, apart from health. For some reason, talk of hospitals, healthcare and illness, as important as it was, did not ring any of her bells.

That Sainsbury's bloke must have had that flu, she thought. She didn't get near enough to him to have caught anything, she was sure. However, on the rare occasion in the last few years that she had caught a cold, the feeling of illness had given her a sense of justification for remaining indoors.

The kettle had boiled and Fran returned to the kitchen via her laptop to check, as was habit, whether she had any messages. Her facebook page showed a message from one of her friends, Sharon, in London.

Hi ffran. Hope your ok. Sorry, won't be able to visit you this weekend. Im proper illl at the moment with this flu thats going around. I cant tell you how shitty I feel. heads pounding and all that. Ive started feeling pretty delirious 2= in the last hour. So thought i wd sendd you this message sooner rather than later. Going 2 bed now for a very long time methinkss! Sorry honey!!1 Ws looking forward 2 seeing u.

How topical, Fran thought, but she was disappointed. The garbled message wasn't quite what she had wanted to read.

Sharon was an old friend from London who had moved to Bristol some years back and then recently back to London, and who acted as one of Fran's vital lifelines to the outside world. She visited up to a couple of times a month, which was amazing. Oh well, Fran would see her soon enough, no doubt.

3
Vince

Two years is a long time inside. It's boredom that punishes. And Vince got bored easily. He always had and he figured he always would. School was tough, not least because he struggled to read and do maths, which meant that when he had hit secondary school he couldn't access most of the curriculum. The only method of communication he felt he had was to misbehave. He would get sent out of class and spend time in the nurture unit—a much preferred place to spend one's time. Unfortunately, with no real qualifications or aspirations to write home about after leaving school, and rather a lot of run-ins with authorities, Vince had little chance to evade the trouble he ended up getting into.

Home Detention Curfew was a pretty fancy name for electronic tagging, but it served its purpose. Vince passed his risk assessment—he was deemed safe enough to have an electronic tag around his tattooed ankle. The aesthetic quality of the Maori-style design of sharp curves was rather wasted, as a thick black strap with a grey face boldly covered it up. It felt uncomfortable, both physically and otherwise. Vince's curfew was from seven o'clock in the evening right through until six o'clock the next morning. A black box sat, connected to electricity, in his dingy lounge. He couldn't move it, turn it off or cut the tag strap, otherwise the shit would hit the fan.

It wasn't as if Vince had much to do anyway. He had to go to the Job Centre and sign on, on a regular basis, to show he was looking for work. Other than that, he had taken to sitting at home. He was wanting to turn his life around, but found he didn't quite know how, nor even what he wanted out of his life. A couple of years for assault, out early and tagged, he felt adrift on the seas of society. He knew he didn't want to go back inside. Not that it was horrendous—it wasn't really all that bad. It was more about control, he reckoned. He just didn't like not being in control. And that's why this tag pissed him off. He wished he had had a false leg, like that other guy in the news, and tricked the taggers into putting one on his false leg so that he could change legs, leave his first one at home, and go where he pleased! No such luck, his legs were fully functional.

Instead, Vince was becoming something of a hermit. He had enough food. His parents, for what they were worth, had taken a little pity on him and stocked him up every few weeks. Vince was the sort of young man of whom people walked out of the way, on the streets. He looked lean and fairly mean. Your typical youth that the right-wing newspapers used as cannon-fodder. He had his latest Playstation, the internet and cable TV. That was enough to keep him occupied. The only thing he missed was the gym, so he kept himself fit at home with a variety of exercises.

Even his hair was getting a little too long. *Head needs a shave. I look like a fucking hippy,* he thought, as he looked in the mirror at his still remarkably short, mousy hair. He'd never been a fan of hair, feeling he looked harder with only a minimally shaved amount; anything more than a grade one was a sign of weakness. But he admired how great his body looked in the mirror, another set of sharp curved designs slicing out from under the strap of his grey vest, and lancing up the side of his neck. *I look dangerous!* Vince rubbed his short hair, touched his bent nose, a remnant from an altercation in a pub several years previously, and went through to the lounge to pick up his Playstation controller and slump onto the couch.

All was not lost since Col was coming round that night to bring over some pirated films and games, and have a smoke. It was the highlight of Vince's week at the moment.

Vince's phone vibrated to some loud dance tune in his pocket. He leant over and took his phone out from his loose grey jogging pants.

"Col, my man!"

"Hey Vinny. Mate, I can't come round tonight, no. I'm feelin' well bad," Col replied.

"You sound like shit, man."

"Yeah. Look, once I get over this bangin' headache, I'll come over, yeah?"

"Sure, man. Take it easy," said Vince.

"Laters, bruv." The inner city London talk was filtered through a heavy Bristolian accent.

Vince returned the phone to his pocket and settled down to shoot some zombies in the face. After a minute or so, he paused the game, stood up and went through to the tiny kitchen, complete with microwave and very old gas cooker, towards the dented fridge. He opened the door, retrieved a can of lager, gratifyingly lifted the tab to be greeted with a refreshing *phizz* and returned to his seat. Vince took a long hard swig from the can of lager, let out an *aaahh!* and planted his can on the small table at the side of the couch. Fleetingly, an image of his dad passed through his mind, slouched in the same way, in the middle of a similar day, with a vest of the same grey.

"Shit!" Vince shouted and slammed his fist on the arm of the sofa. He slammed it again. And again. And some more, quickfire. Blood pumped and raged through his temples, as anger took control. A small trigger in a corner of his brain stopped him, and he settled back down. Panting, he took another long draft from his lager and picked up the controller.

METAMORPHOSIS

4
Jessica

"Jess?"

"Hi baby!"

"Jess, where are you?" Mike asked.

"Er, at home, where I always am these days! Galen's playing up. You know what he gets like..."

"Sure, I know. Look, I'm still at the hospital. I know I should be on the way, but you know this flu thing. Well, it's serious." Mike sounded worried. She could tell when he was worried—his tone had that edge.

"What's happening?" Jess asked.

"Well, loads of people have it, and I mean loads. We can't really cope. The A and E is rammed with people. Worse than that, though, is that guy. You know I said we had someone in almost a week ago who had it, and that he got really ill a few days ago? Well, they've taken him away."

"Who?" Jess interrupted.

"The HPA—The Health Protection Agency, or whatever it's now called... Public Health England. You should have seen him. I caught a glimpse of him before he left. It was bad Jess, really bad. The guy looked properly bad."

Mike's voice had moved from worried through to unnerved, with elements of the hysterical lurking around the edge.

"What's going on?"

"I don't want to freak you out, but I think everyone might have this. The news has been cagey, hasn't it? Well, we've had remits that we need to stay in or around the hospitals and work some serious overtime to clear the backlogs. The NHS are announcing on the news just now for people *not* to come to hospital if they have flu symptoms as we have too many here already. This has gone from like a bit of an issue yesterday morning to totally mental now. From nought to sixty in a day and a half." Mike was talking really quickly now.

"So you've got to stay there, in Bristol? How long for?" she replied, starting to worry too.

"Jess, it's bad. I think all these people have got a worse illness than they think. The guy who was taken away? He's never coming back, I'm sure of that. And, Jess?" Mike paused.

"Yeah…"

"Jess, I think I've got it too. I think a few of us have. Well, maybe most of us. I don't want to worry you, but I won't be back tonight—I have to work. Can you do me a favour?" Mike didn't give Jess time to answer. "Don't go into the village. Don't go into town. Don't go anywhere. Just stay at home. I'm probably overreacting, but there are memos and messages flying everywhere, and the consultants are looking worried. We have a meeting we have to attend in ten minutes and I think there might be bad news. I think there is genuinely some kind of outbreak, only the horse has already bolted."

"Oh my…Just come back, sweetheart," Jess implored.

"I can't, I've got to stay here, and I've got a job to do. And… Look, I'll call you later, okay? I've got to go now, they're calling me. Promise me you'll stay at home, yeah?"

"Okay. I love you."

"You too, honey," and Mike put his phone down. Jessica kept the phone to her ear for half a minute simply trying to decipher everything and order her thoughts. Then she moved, quite suddenly, a rapid patter from the kitchen to the television in the lounge. The lounge was covered in baby toys and apparatus which she had to dodge, a skill she had honed in the last seven months of life with Galen. The TV was on a baby channel. She flicked over to the BBC news channel with an urgency that had sprung up like a geyser from the pit of her stomach.

For the next twenty minutes, she stood transfixed, absorbing everything. It seemed that the nation was starting to go a little off the tracks. Literally within a day or two, a seemingly routine bout of flu was now being described as most probably some avian flu mutation. Rabies and ebola were even thrown into the mix with scant regard for evidence. What was clear was that large numbers of the population had contracted flu-like symptoms, with the added murky idea that there were perhaps some older cases that had deteriorated to a worrying level. However, sources were hard to come by and there was little official statement to defend such a rumour. Such a rumour as Mike had himself now verified.

The official government line was to follow standard hygiene procedures—washing hands, using alcohol handwash after touching doors and suchlike, keeping hands away from mouths, not kissing anyone with the symptoms and so on. But there was yet no explicit recommendation that people stay at home, that people not go to work. It was a strange mix of admitting that something serious was going on, with a denial that this could be a potential epidemic of sorts, with all the financial and logistical implications. If people could go to work, well then the whole country was fine, no?

Some time later, Jess's phone rang. She retrieved it from her faded jeans' pocket and looked at the screen. It was Ankita, friend from her days at the University of Nottingham in the Midlands. They had read philosophy together, which made for long and interesting nights, or dull and endless ones depending on who was listening, spent in their shared house over a bottle or three of wine.

"Jess?"

"Hi, Kita."

Ankita rattled into startled conversation without any delay. "What's going on Jess? This looks pretty crazy!" Her voice was slightly panicky, and as such was taking on a more-than-typical Indian thickness.

"Kita, I'm really worried about Mike. He says it's really serious and he has to stay at the hospital. I'm not going to lie to you, Kita, but I'm pretty scared. We watched a film about this just the other week, and it could be happening now!" Jess was starting to work herself up as her mind recalled a movie in which an epidemic spread rapidly throughout the world. The movie didn't really have a happy ending either, which added considerably to the anxiety that washed over her like a thick, impenetrable ocean.

"Okay, calm down. It could just as easily be some flu-thing—"

"Mike told me they took an early victim away to some kind of government agency. It really sounds bad," interrupted Jess, keen to pass on her nugget of information, which raced through the telephone network to Kita like a virus on speed.

"Oh." Kita sounded knocked off guard. "What, like quarantined?"

"Mike said he was *really* ill. I think it's supposed to be hush-hush."

"What...what did he think *exactly*?"

Jess frowned. Kita had sounded desperate. "Why do you ask?"

"Well, I'm not feeling a hundred percent myself, you know."

"Hey, it's probably just working too hard or something—"

"No," Kita interrupted, "it's not. I'm pretty sure, with my job and everything, that I have what loads of other people seem to be getting, Jess."

Jess thought for a second. "Look, Kita, they're working on what to do with this. They'll have the best people, the best scientists working everything out. Anyway, the guy they took away was probably weak and old..."

All the while that they were talking, Jess's mind was reeling with panicked thoughts, flitting from idea to idea with manic energy.

After a few more worried exchanges, Kita rang off with the intention of relaying the information from Mike to her family, spreading the *good news*. She was audibly upset and Jess had made her promise to phone back if anything changed, and if she heard any more news.

There was that never-too-infrequent cry from the nursery—Galen was awake and he wanted the whole world to know about it.

Jess ignored him.

The news rolled.

5
Jason

"Bevan, I've been wondering this for some time now: why are you such a dick?"

Jason stared hard at the pathetic excuse for a campfire, and looked in barely hidden contempt at the can of beans that had been badly balanced on some small burning logs, only to fall, like Judas, spilling its guts onto the ground.

"I mean, it seems abundantly apparent that you are unable to cook even the simplest of things," continued Jason, aware that his words were undoubtedly falling on deaf ears.

"Mmm? You what?" The reply oozed from under a thin blanket, from a worse-for-wear Bevan as he woke from a drink- and drug-induced slumber. His camping seat had a cup-holder containing a can of lager, which Bevan used to further arouse his mind to post-slumber clarity.

"Well, while you've been dreaming of Alvin and the Chipmunks, I've been hunter-gathering. To no avail."

Bevan looked too smug for a man with a hangover. "It seems 'abundantly clear' that you are unable to buy the simplest of things..."

"Very good. Actually, the shop and garage down the road — our connection to reality — is closed 'due to illness'. Weird. Anywhoo, we've got enough beans, despite your ineptitude; it's just beer we've got to watch out for."

The pair were camping on Exmoor, a sometimes bleak but always beautiful stretch of moorland covering part of the south-western corner of England. They'd purposefully tried to get away from it all — to "get in touch with nature". Which more accurately involved getting drunk and talking rubbish, and in Jason's case, watching Bevan smoke himself into a fountain of gibberish and strange sounds, which *he* seemed to mistake for common language.

They had been away for over three days, walking around their makeshift campsite, reading books for the first time in too long. Bevan's idea of reading was securing a copy of the modern erotic classic *50 Shades of Grey* which elicited the occasional childish guffaw or guttural murmur of appreciation, a puerile grin smugly stealing its way onto his small, round face.

Jason, on the other hand, had a slightly more cerebral approach to literature. Slightly. Having struggled with Jack Kerouac, he had settled for a few Stephen King classics picked up from the charity shop. He had read *It* and *The Stand* as a kid, and had forgotten how enjoyable they were.

However, Jason had come to realise over the four days that spending too much time with Bevan was not good for his sanity. Bevan was best in small doses, like a herbal, tar-tasting cough mixture, and with the same dubious medicinal qualities—for all Jason knew, he would feel worse after the whole experience. Perhaps this jaunt into the countryside, Jason mused, was his attempt at charity.

Staring at the fire, he recollected his last engagement with charity. His previous girlfriend (*Girlfriend? Or partner? What is it for people in their mid-30s?*) had a grandmother who worked in an Oxfam charity shop. It was there where he and Annette had had their last big argument. In front of a pair of bad cords.

Jason remembered now. He hated charity.

"So what's going on?" asked Bevan.

"Well, we've got a bit further to go for our beer today. We might have to take the van out of this field and down the road, later," he replied.

"We have been here three days. Best go out with a bang. I vote we get to the next shop sooner, rather than later," Bevan said.

"Let's do it! Come on, it's half eleven and we've accomplished the square root of fuck all today. Put the fire out, mate, and let's get on the road."

With that clarion call to action, Bevan promptly remained slumped in his camping chair whilst Jason busied himself clearing up the ramshackle campsite.

"No offence, but I'm driving," stated Jason, not willing to put his life in the sluggish hands of a half-inebriated fool.

Bevan threw him the keys. "Offence taken."

Leaving most of the camp furniture there (the seats, cooking utensils and a small fold-away table) the two loaded themselves into the turquoise VW campervan to set off for the store. The van wheezed a little and then kicked into life, the distinctive sound of the air-cooled engine cutting through the otherwise still and silent late-morning ambience.

Jason drove the van from behind a copse in the large field of moorland where they had been clandestinely camping, and approached a wooden gate. Bevan fell out of the van to do the duty, before closing the gate again behind the van and jumping back in. The van turned out of the field's entrance and rumbled off down the country lane.

After a mile or so, the van passed the garage to which Jason had earlier walked, and Bevan could see, at a distance, the notice up in the doorway. Continuing down the road, they passed the odd farm house and country cottage before seeing signs to the next village a few miles further.

"I like the country. Quiet roads," observed Bevan.

"And exactly when have you ever been caught in a rush hour traffic jam?"

"Well, last Tuesday, I was caught behind some sheep being moved field..."

Jason snorted. "Very good!"

Houses started dotting the roadside and then the village appeared, a random settlement surrounded by moorland. A post office which doubled as the local shop was the only commercial outlet other than the pub, both of which sat at the centre of the village. The village was small and had only one short cul-de-sac off the road they were on. Jason pulled up by the shop and the two men alighted, eager to replenish their beer and cider stocks for their last night.

Bevan pushed through the wooden-framed glass door first, to the tinkle of the attached bell.

"Afternoon!" he chimed in his West Country accent.

"Hello, there." The middle-aged lady behind the counter eyed the two men with the suspicion of a shopkeeper who was expecting to be burgled.

The two men headed straight for the small alcohol section and retrieved more beer and cider than they really had any need for. Bevan waddled over to the refrigerated sandwiches and randomly grabbed a pair.

"Pot-luck sandwich day today! Woo hoo!" he exclaimed.

Meanwhile, Jason was hovering around the newspaper section. Scanning the tabloids and broadsheets, he looked pensive. It seemed that all of the newspapers' headlines were pretty similar. All of them reported "flu deaths" of sorts. In big letters.

"What's all this?" Jason asked of no one in particular, pointing at the papers.

"Do you not know?" asked the shopkeeper incredulously. Jason shook his head and shrugged his shoulders.

"Where have you been? Do you really not know what's been going on?"

"The joys of sitting in a field for three days. So, people have been getting a bad case of the flu? I saw that on the news almost a week ago."

"Aah, that explains it." She grimaced and, in Jason's eyes, visibly relaxed. "It's worse than that. In three days, the hospitals have been inundated. They even say that some of the earlier victims have died and been taken away—well, that's the rumour. It's spreading like wildfire. The message from the government is that people who contract it should stay at home and avoid contact with others. You wouldn't believe it, but in three days this country has become not a little panicked! I was wondering whether to close for a week or so—"

"So hang on, love, are you telling us that this flu thing is possibly dodgy? That if we get it, we might end up in hospital?" Bevan chimed in.

"Well, I'm only going on what the news and newspapers are saying. Some people around here are saying it's birdflu, others that it's something brought in from Asia. Either way, I bet it's come from outside. I'm not racist, but I bet it was brought in by some asylum seeker."

"Well, I think I'd better grab one of these," Jason said, picking up *The Independent* (he liked to think he was neutral in matters of information). He picked up *The Sun* tabloid paper for Bevan—partly to match his persona, partly because he knew Bevan would appreciate the utterly anachronistic topless model on page three of the most popular national newspaper.

The two men coupled together their gatherings of beer, pork pies, sandwiches and newspapers. Bevan added an assortment of chocolate bars and crisps.

Saying their goodbyes to the lady, Jason and Bevan returned to their campervan with interests piqued to the point that they turned on the radio immediately after hastily dumping their supplies in the back. Jason sat in the driver's seat and adjusted the radio to *5Live*, the national AM radio station for news from the BBC.

And the latest from-

"Turn it up, mate!" Bevan barked.

-the weather centre...

"Ah bollocks."

Jason and Bevan took their respective newspapers and opened up a chocolate bar like a pair of builders on their lunch break in their van. *The Independent* ran the headline "Will Flu Be An Epidemic?" whilst *The Sun* ran "Hospitals Full: Britain In Health Crisis".

Jason avidly took in everything that he read, whilst also listening to the news. It appeared that a flu virus that was particularly virulent had hit the UK, as well as elsewhere in Europe, quickly spreading amongst the population. The incubation period appeared to be very short, only a matter of one or two days between being infected and exhibiting symptoms of the virus. Some clinical tests suggested some avian flu mutation (with special emphasis being placed on the testing of blood and blood groups), but other sources suggested otherwise. It seemed there was a large degree of uncertainty. Sufferers had quickly become ill with serious flu-like symptoms, soon becoming at least house-bound, and in many cases bed-ridden. Of course, with a particularly infectious strain with a large infection rate, supply chains to businesses had become very quickly affected. In short, in a couple of days, the economy was already showing signs of difficulty.

Jason texted his parents to check they were in good health and was relieved to receive a call back immediately to confirm they were fine, though worried. After a five-minute conversation, he returned to the papers.

"Well, fuck me!" exclaimed Bevan, shocked.

"What's that? What've you read?"

"Sharon Osborne's been asked to judge on the X-Factor *again*. I never thought we'd see her on do *another* comeback!" replied Bevan, with no false seriousness.

"God, you're a dick."

"He'll strike you down for calling him that!"

And the pair laughed, before returning their attention to the news. And the not-so-news.

METAMORPHOSIS

6
Fran

Fran put her mobile phone down. She had been trying to reach her mother's phone even though mobiles were not usually welcomed on the wards. Her mother definitely had it with her because Fran had received the odd text message and one phone call providing her with bronchial updates. Now, however, the phone merely rang. It was frustrating, but not really unusual. Fran's mother, being the age and generation she was, was never, and would never be, proficient with mobile phones. Or any other *standard* technology that most people took for granted.

Fran, though, wanted to hear those familiar broad West Indian lilts and tones (even though her mother was second generation) which characterised her accents and warmed Fran's heart.

The last few days had been productive for Fran, full of the modern orchestral sounds of keyboard button tapping: the harsh QWERTY clicks interspersed with space bars and backspaces, punctuated with pauses of soft, almost silent, caressing of fingertips across the buttons as the mind was caught in pensive deliberation. Her draft for the final chapter was progressing apace: *And Where To Now?* The book charted her experience of agoraphobia, how she was dealing with it, and what she was doing about it. In the case of the latter, *not enough!* Perhaps this whole project was premature. Perhaps she needed to have improved more before writing so much. Perhaps the whole feeling of the book was not hopeful enough. Perhaps, though, this project might inspire her, as she really hoped, to *actually* do something about her predicament. The status quo wasn't anything to feel positive about.

A welcome cool breeze wafted in through the French doors, ajar in the heat of a decent summer's day. Fran stood up from her writing position at the dining room table and stretched in emphatic fashion. Feeling a little warm from the dry daytime heat, and from being indoors for its duration, Fran made towards the lounge and the French doors. The net curtains billowed softly. She pulled them aside and opened the doors to let herself on to the balcony. The sky was blue and cloudless, as a fine summer day should be—a poor, wan blue that hazily stretched over the surrounding blocks, from East to West.

The lawn below was empty. In fact, Fran struggled to see anyone walking around the block complex, and the roads were quiet. Mind you, the country seemed to be in a bit of a tiz about this whole flu thing. Fran had been alternating between writing and checking the news channels and was somewhat hooked on finding out as much as possible about the epidemic. She had even heard words like *pandemic* and *outbreak* being used with casual abandon. Well, not so casual and rather fraught, if truth be told. She figured that now was a good time to be agoraphobic. She was quite well stocked on food since her delivery and had no real need to leave her apartment, let alone her block. The only thing that really worried her was how her mother was doing.

The lawn was bordered on three sides by the apartment blocks, about ten storeys each, her block being the middle one. Dark red-brick ugly things, dating back some fifty years or so, these blocks housed a wide mix of people, stretching over most of the socio-demographic spectrum. The rich and the not so rich, the not so poor, and everyone in between. It made for interesting and colourful noises, interactions and events. Sometimes, Fran would while away the hours merely staring down at the lawn and various benches and paths, which presented a free-to-view soap opera of sorts.

But it *was* quiet today, bar a number of hurried figures moving to and fro on what appeared to be important errands. As she scanned the vista, one such figure caught her eye. Rather than being purposeful, though, this person, a man in his mid-twenties or so, was stumbling about in what looked like pain. He fell to the path, convulsing with clear discomfort. Fran glanced around to see if anyone was there to help him, but there was no one. Only a few cars passed on the road on the far side of the large lawn, past the privet hedges.

Of course, had Fran been in a different headspace, she would have called out to him, whether to reassure the man or get him some other help. But she wasn't in that space; she wasn't that person.

Instead, the man was positioned on his knees, genuflecting to the god of pain, unnoticed by everyone but Fran. After a minute of jerky bodily movements, he seemed to calm. And with that calm, Fran's heart rate eased. He slowly picked himself up and continued to stumble along the path and shambled over its edge when it curved to the left, almost tripping on the low concrete ridge. He was not a well man, Fran thought, that much was sure!

The man stumbled off out of sight below her. Fran thought for a second, and then turned to enter her apartment. Now was a good time to try and get hold of Sharon. Her friend had not answered any of her emails, or indeed the phone, and Fran was worried, what with this flu thing in full swing. Picking up the landline phone, she dialled a number stored in the handset and listened as it connected and rang until the answer phone kicked in. The recording told her that the memory was full and that she was unable to leave a message for her ill friend. *Do I phone the police? I mean, it's been some time since I was able to get hold of her.*

Fran decided to just see what the latest was on the illness hitting the country and so she moved to the sofa to re-familiarise herself with her television, and the news. After switching the set on, the news channel flashed up at her.

"Breaking News from..."

METAMORPHOSIS

7
Jessica

It had been a day now since she had heard anything at all from her husband. Mike had phoned her again half a day later. The news channels had filled her in that there really did appear to be a flu pandemic. It was getting to a rather serious level too, and people were panicking, which wasn't helped by the plethora of rumours that spread like digital wildfire in the internet age, the dry kindling of *Facebook* and *You Tube*, of *Twitter* and *Tumblr*, and other social media platforms heating up—and being stoked by—an already jittery public.

What was now evident was that this was not confined to the island nation of Great Britain. The world was soon seen as a map that quickly overtook the pinks of Victorian British Empire maps. The planet seemed unable to evade the flu. Unsurprisingly, the rumours were rife that the bug had piggy-backed into the country on an Eastern Asian host, or some other Johnny Foreigner. The "blame the *others* game" hadn't taken long to materialise, tapping into the wells of fear in pretty much anyone.

Mike's call had been a blow. A blow to Jessica's very existence. To almost everything she was. He had insisted she keep it all to herself. Mike was adamant that this was an outbreak of the most serious kind. Indeed, he had it himself, he was convinced, as did most of the staff he was working with at the hospital in Bristol. But, as he had told her, he knew he couldn't leave. He couldn't leave because he was in the best place for any potential developments in helping *him*, but more to the point, because the only place he could go and wanted to go was home. It was where his family were; but his family were fit and well. And he wasn't. He knew better than most the ramifications of coming home, despite what they both wanted.

Mike was worried enough about the whole predicament, based on memos and snippets of genuine information, together with rumour and hearsay, to be honest enough with Jessica. Honest enough to say, in the worst-case scenario, that he might, might, *might* not be coming home. And that sent the walls tumbling down that built up Jessica's life. Even the remote chance that he might not be coming back, that this may indeed be a pandemic the likes of which had never been seen since the days of the Spanish influenza or the Black Death, was enough to send her into a blind panic. Usually a calm person by nature, patient after years of careful, rational thought, after years of arguing laboriously over minutiae in her philosophical capacity, Jessica had been nothing but a mixture of shellshock and nervous hysteria. All this had exploded exponentially over the shortest conceivable period of time.

Ankita had even phoned her to say that she was definitely feeling ill in a pandemic sense and that many of her own family had come down with what she thought was this very same flu. Several video calls across the internet to her parents in London had confirmed that people were starting to get genuinely panicked in the capital. Thankfully, her parents appeared to have stayed free of the flu and were staying safely at home.

It had been some nine days since the first person taken away from Mike's hospital had been admitted, and now the numbers were so high that the government had requested that people not go to hospital unless desperately necessary. Indeed, most hospitals appeared to be staffed with those who had the flu themselves as it was spreading so freely amongst the population, acting in a particularly virulent manner. The hospitals were understaffed to the point that they were requesting volunteer retired nurses and doctors to assist, and were providing proper equipment for them to wear. But even seeing television footage featuring doctors in protective gear was enough to send the population into near panic. There must be a whole lot more that the government organisations knew but weren't letting on.

Jessica sat holding a sleeping Galen—luckily the baby was still in a period of sleeping a lot during the day, which was a blessing in this most stressful of times—watching the news. There seemed only to be news on at the moment.

"In the last twenty-four hours we have noticed a step-change in what the government is saying and doing" said a reporter camped outside one of the hospitals, white material mask strapped on and sitting around her neck whilst she spoke. *"As we have reported, the hospitals are struggling hugely under the immense load of the patients seeking care and help. And earlier today, the government called a one-week forced holiday. Again, as we reported, all employers and employees are being ordered to stay at home to allow for what is now officially being called a pandemic to settle down. Only emergency services together with essential utility provision will continue uninterrupted. We are presently trying to find out whether journalists will be allowed to continue working and whether, given the rumours, we deem it in our own best interests. Rumours are sweeping the world that there is no sign of this outbreak calming down, and that with reported (though uncorroborated) deaths, we could see our*

country enter some sort of curfew. This was unimaginable even two or three days ago."

The news anchor, with his grim tone, took over. *"Thank you, Sarah. Tell me, what is the feeling amongst journalists out there? Is there an appetite to continue working through this?"*

"Well, John, this is nothing any of us have experienced. There is a mixture of panic amongst our own ranks, and looking to get back to our families, but also gritty determination to do what people need us to do—to disseminate vital information. It's reminiscent of wartime spirit. At the end of the day, John— Hey!" And all of a sudden the camera swung downwards to point at the grass as if it had been knocked or someone had fallen into it or the cameraman. It was buffeted with a few bangs as something went on off camera.

"What the…?" Jessica breathed with a furrowed brow, tense. At that, point, the world according to Jessica, and perhaps almost everyone else, took a big step backwards.

METAMORPHOSIS

8
Vince

Vince had only been out a few times over the last week, to pop to the local shop to get a few beers and other essentials. He wasn't one for keeping abreast of topical affairs, but he couldn't help but notice the change—fewer people on the streets, the overheard conversations in the shop. Oh, and the change to the TV schedule.

Being stuck inside for unwelcome amounts of time meant that Vince had got himself into a bit of a routine, which was something that had always suited him (and why he hadn't minded prison too much). So television, playing a large part in his life in all its formats and opportunities for providing minimal-effort entertainment, had supplied the skeleton to his daily routine, fleshed out with exercises, simple food preparation, preening and smoking.

Vince recognised the irony of spending so much time exercising and so much time smoking and drinking. However, the exercise was for aesthetic outcome since he knew he couldn't very well run to his folks' house and back without some serious lung expulsions.

But to make matters worse, he had run out of weed and needed a restock of beer. Together with the increased proportion of repeats on TV and news interruptions, his last few days had provided something of a headache.

Leopards do change their spots, though, and Vince was capable of taking on new interests. The news, it seemed, was becoming more like his regular pulp-TV diet. In fact, he had seen the news more times in the last week than in all of the rest of his life. He had it on now, whilst munching on a packet of crisps, and he was staring at the screen with a strange sort of newfound interest.

"So with the first confirmed deaths of the flu pandemic, there are disturbing reports afoot that the virus might be mutating such that it is starting to have more serious affects more rapidly than with the earlier cases. Only yesterday afternoon we saw one flu victim crash through the camera crew and journalists outside St Thomas Hospital. It is in this context that the government has called this state of emergency. As you have heard, people are not to leave their houses for any reason. We repeat, you are to stay at home. A bare-essentials team will be reporting from Broadcasting House in London to communicate the latest important news. There will be a military and police presence on the streets.

However, we have also heard reports that the flu is rife within the whole cross-section of society. The police and the armed forces, it seems, are just as much victim as the general population. As the Prime Minister has declared, the scientists at Public Health England and elsewhere are working to find out what this virus is, exactly, and how best to deal with it..."

Vince left the TV streaming its news and walked to the kitchenette. He opened the fridge to be met by a blank stare. Nothing but some margarine and a hunk of cheese in all their dairy glory.

"Shit. Shop time."

Slipping on his light blue hoodie, Vince picked up his keys and walked to the front door.

"Again, we repeat, please do not leave your houses, for your own safety and for the safety of others..."

Hands in his pockets, his door slamming behind him, Vince wandered off down his street. He lived in a maisonette on the side of a launderette, courtesy of the Council. Just over the last couple of days, there was suddenly more rubbish floating around the streets. It looked like the street cleaners and refuse services were some of the first whose absence had taken effect. A few people scuttled around the streets.

Vince looked ahead to the shop, some twenty metres or so down the road. Drayton wasn't the most desirable place in Bristol to live, but that didn't worry Vince one iota. It was a little way out from the centre, Vince's road being a mixture of residential houses with a few shops. Normally, Vince would expect to see a few of the lads hanging outside the store, but today, no one was there. Just a feeling of quiet emptiness.

He arrived at the newsagent's to find a closed and locked door. On the inside of the window hung a scribbled sign, "SHOP CLOSED UNTIL FURTHER NOTICE". Then he heard a screech behind him as a white van with "Locke and Sons, Plumbers" on the side pulled up. A couple of men jumped out of the front, dressed in jeans and dark jumpers, with large backpacks on their backs, and hastily made balaclavas (by the look of them) disguising their faces. *Either that van is stolen, or those guys are stupid.* He quickly moved to the side, standing some five metres to the left of the door, still with his hands nonchalantly in his pockets. The men wielded a baseball bat and a crowbar, which they put to clumsy use against the reinforced glass of the top half of the door. Eventually, the pane gave in and after some fumbling and swearing and glass clearing around the frame, the first man struggled through it. When he was finally inside, the alarm sounded its shrill cry. The other man followed him in quickly.

Were these guys robbing the place of money? Raiding the tills? Vince moved over to peer through the broken door window, wincing at the irritating sound of the alarm. The men were at the back of the shop, filling bags with the items that they were indiscriminately sweeping off the shelves.

"What the hell are you guys doing? The till's over there!" Vince called to them, pointing at the untouched object, which was undoubtedly empty anyway.

"Getting what we can!" came the muffled reply. "The world's going to hell in a handcart, mate. I suggest you do the same!"

"What, this flu thing?"

The other man turned to him whilst continuing to denude the shelves of assorted goods, from tuna to teacakes, shouting "Do you not watch the news? You been online at all? Mate, people are *dying*! And there ain't no cure. Not yet anyway. I don't think we'll be going back to work any time soon. So we need stuff for the long haul. Now get in here, or piss off!"

Vince hovered there, deeply confused. He had had a niggling feeling there was more to this than the news or government were letting on, and today's bulletins had registered with him, even though he refused to let it get the purchase it deserved. But he was tagged. Then again, he had no food, and if shops were closing... Like a donkey stuck equally between two piles of carrots, he stood there, unmoving. A door opened on the other side of the road a little way up. A man ran out, glanced up and down the street, then darted across the road towards Vince. He was a Chinese man who looked distinctly like the takeaway owner. Arriving at the door, the takeaway owner looked at him with an expression of anxiety and desperation, holding a backpack, open and full of other bags, and then jumped into the shop through the broken door window.

Vince looked one way, and then turned and looked the other, and then back again, bouncing on his feet.

"Shit, shit, shit." Would this send him back down? But these other guys had started it...

There was no one else around bar a couple of shifting curtains. Taking his hand out of his pocket, he slapped his forehead in frustration, something he was inclined to do, something he had started doing in frustration in lessons at school.

Spinning once more on his heels, he carefully grabbed the jagged side of the window frame so as not to cut his hands, and jumped into the shop. *No way back now!*

METAMORPHOSIS

9
Jason

The flames flickered and danced to an unsung nocturnal tune, lurching and thrusting off ample logs and sticks. Sitting around the fire in their camp chairs, drinking slow and silent drafts from their beer cans, Jason and Bevan stared into the incandescent middle distance, lost in their thoughts.

A moth circled the fire, and both men followed its apparently random and twitchy moves. Every time it fluttered too near the flames, it seemed to feel the heat and pull back to a safer distance, though not too far, attracted as it was to the fiery sirens.

"That moth has a death wish. I mean, what's with that flying into the depths of hell malarkey?" Jason said. "What a stupid creature!"

Bevan continued staring, thinking. Then, "Maybe not. Maybe it's got something else in mind, it's just confused."

"What, it thinks those flames are a tasty bit of moth food?"

"No, dummy, maybe it thinks the fire is something else. Something it usually uses for something else. Or something. You know, evolution and that. If it couldn't do that, then it wouldn't survive. It's a good skill, used badly. I mean, I didn't evolve fingers to play Xbox, right? I didn't evolve eyes to watch porn...I don't think. Although those are good skills used well. I bet it's got something to do with survival. Or something."

"Wow, Bevan. That's deep. For you." Jason paused and thought. "I'm sure I read somewhere that people really do actually know why moths fly into light, so I guess you're right. Maybe. Ish."

The two late-night thinkers gazed on as the moth continued to circle, feint one way then the other, until, like Icarus, it just flew that bit too close. Singeing its wing, the moth plummeted into the depths of its fiery grave, like a crippled Hephaestus returning to his forge. Jason's childhood love of Greek myths had been oddly rekindled.

He snorted, "What was that about survival?"

* * *

"Okay, mate. We've stayed an extra few nights, and we've even weathered some rain. What now?"

"Have you got through to Danny yet?" asked Bevan.

Jason had phoned Danny on the evening that they restocked from the shop. He wished he hadn't had so much to drink because the phone call had rocked him. Danny sounded like death warmed up, and told him that most of Olding Bay had either caught the flu or locked themselves away in self-imposed quarantine. What was worse, Danny had warned him to stay away; he'd closed The Shack. It seemed that the tourist industry was being affected; people had returned home as shops, pubs and restaurants struggled to get staff or clientele. This had prompted Jason to phone his parents that night, too, to speak to them again. They reckoned they were fine, but that his father and sister had taken some impromptu holiday time, just to be on the safe side. They were having a proper staycation, planning to remain not just in the country, but in their house. Jason had promised to stay in touch. Danny, though, had most certainly caught the flu virus.

"Well, I keep trying him, but nothing. I'll give him one more go, though I've hardly any battery left. Better get my hand charger on the case in a minute."

Jason dialled again and put his phone to his ear. He was pretty pleased with his phone—the newest iPhone, which had set him back a pretty contract, but then it could do most things short of make the tea. He had always liked his technology, being interested in gadgets and not being afraid to spend out on securing the latest top-notch piece of kit. He felt like a peacock adorning itself with flash digital apparel, hoping to attract the finest robot this side of the Fembots. There were some aspects to the consumerist lifestyle he once led that he couldn't shake off.

"Eh? There's no signal any more...But I'm sitting in exactly the same place as earlier!" Jason stood up and moved around, lifting his mobile phone to catch some higher signal waves. To no avail.

"It says there is no network available," he said, a perturbed edge to his voice.

"You don't reckon it's all connected, do you? You don't reckon society is falling apart around our very eyes, except we're stuck illegally in some farmer's field without the first clue about what's going on?" Bevan replied.

"Bevan, it would be kind of funny if you were actually right. Well, not so much funny, as fucked up." Jason continued searching for a signal before sitting back down in his camping chair.

"What now?"

"Put the radio on, sunshine," Bevan advised with a smile.

They had exhausted all of their supplies and most certainly needed to do something today. Jason moved over to the van, opened the door and turned on the radio.

"*...message. All listeners are advised to stay in their homes until further notice. Under no conditions are they to leave, for their own safety. The pandemic is still an unknown quantity and there is no known cure or relief from the symptoms. Victims are advised in the event of a death to please call 101 which has been co-opted as the new national line for reporting flu deaths. Please be aware that the armed forces and the police are doing all that they can to help...*"

"What the f—"

"Shut up!" shouted Bevan, listening intently.

"*The police 999 number is not presently working due to personnel shortages but will be up and running as and when possible. Please take care to look after yourselves, and do not leave your houses until further notice. Live broadcasts are restricted to one hour from 21:00 tonight. This is a national emergency message. All listeners are advised to stay...*"

Both men remained where they were, unable to move, their brains digesting what they had just heard, trying to distinguish fact from wild fiction being concocted in their minds. The only problem being, there appeared to be no wild fiction.

Jason turned slowly toward Bevan, who was slumped in thought in his chair, long-finished empty can in the holder. "So, I actually think, unless I am dreaming, that the country, or even the world, has fallen to pieces in less than a week. Literally fallen to pieces."

Bevan looked up. "Well, it hasn't *literally* fallen to pieces. I mean, the van is in one piece and the field—"

"Dick. Look, we need to get out of here, but what if we go back to Olding and everyone's got the flu? What then?"

Bevan looked at Jason anxiously, "Well, we can't just drive around forever. Actually, we haven't got enough petrol to get Annie back home, even." Bevan indicated his beloved van.

"Bollocks. Well, we need food, we need petrol and we need to know what the hell is going on."

The men agreed to clear up and head back to the shop where they had bought their refreshments. After packing everything away, they said their goodbyes to the field, and with Jason driving, crept along the road back toward the village post office.

Whilst they were navigating a slow rising bend, a BMW screeched past them in the other direction.

METAMORPHOSIS

"Jeez, mate, slow down. D'you know how hard it is to get parts for Annie?" Bevan bellowed to the long-distant car.

After a few more bends and turns, Jason said, "The shop should be up here on the left somew—SHIIIIT!"

With a crunching thump, Annie hit what looked like an old man who had wandered on to the road from his front gate, which directly opened on to the narrow country lane. Jason jammed on the brakes, and both men flew forward and then slammed back into their seats like rag dolls being thrown around by a young girl. Annie was rough with her toys, it seemed.

"Did you just hit a man? Have you just run someone over? Jason what the hell have you done, mate?"

Jason had never been in an accident before. Well, unless you count the night in his nineteenth year, in a beachfront car park, when he reversed his Austin Metro, with its steamed-up windows, into a parked minivan. The owner had got out of his van in his boxer shorts, of all things, surveyed the limited damage, and had proceeded to tell Jason not to worry about it. Jason had been disbelieving at the time, and very grateful, since his young driver's insurance would have skyrocketed. It turned out, some years later, on talking to a friend who had worked in the café to the side of the car park, that the owner of the café used to sleep with his mistress in his van of the odd evening, parked next to the café. Jason was delighted thinking he had got away with his accident on account of a man wanting to keep his dalliance under wraps.

This, though, was threatening to be in a whole new league. The two men unbelted themselves and got out of the sky-blue and usually gleaming van. Bevan looked at his left hand passenger-side corner. The damage was plain to see: a smashed headlight and dented corner, liberally spattered with dark blood.

"Oh Jesus, mate, this is bad," groaned Bevan with his hands clasped to the side of his balding head.

Jason looked back down the road to where he could see, lying to the side, a crumpled and distorted body. "Call an ambulance!"

"You've got the phone, and remember, 999's buggered!" retorted Bevan.

Jason jogged towards the man and almost stumbled when he caught a flicker of movement. "He's still alive, Bevan. Get the first aid kit out of the van!"

The man's body was slightly twitching, lying on its front, with one of the leg bones jutting its jagged end through polyester trousers. "Are you alright, mate?" Jason stammered.

There was an odd, choking groan, nothing more.

Jason flipped the old man onto his back, realising that he was probably not helping the man's back or legs, and yet the casualty gave no hint of resistance. Jason looked at his face.

"Jesus!" The face was battered from the impact, bloodied all over, possibly carrying a broken jaw, and his wiry white hair was matted with dirt and dark red blood. His eyes, though, appeared odd to Jason. Thin and darkened bloody capillaries infused his eyes like spider's silk; in the middle of the webs sat large irises-cum-pupils, milky and dark. To Jason, the old man had some serious cataract issues. Tearing his stare away from those eyes, he positioned himself behind the man's head, resting the battered skull on his thighs as he knelt on the road.

The thin and aged body started to moan in pain. Jason grasped his head to pull it back into the recovery position, to clear his airways. He stared in the man's odd and somehow disconcerting eyes.

Suddenly, the head moved to the side to where Jason's hand was. His mouth, with its thin, wan skin (even under the dirt and blood) started stretching back over his teeth. His mouth was full of congealed and muddy saliva. It snapped toward Jason's hand, the teeth making awful clacking sounds.

"What the hell, old man!?" exclaimed Jason in disbelief, yanking his hand back. The head flopped to the other side and snapped at Jason's other hand, saliva, dirt and blood dropping liberally from his mouth onto the ground, and dribbling down the side of his face. "Are you mental?" Jason let the head fall the short distance to the concrete, giving a dull thud to which the old man paid no attention. The body was now twitching energetically.

Bevan slid to a breathless stop beside Jason. The old man, his spittle spattering, growled at them both through his snapping teeth.

"Here you go, mate," Bevan said, gasping for air, and he held out a small green first aid kit, replete with plasters and safety pins. "First aid kit."

METAMORPHOSIS

10
Fran

Okay, so things weren't good, Fran thought. And they didn't seem to be getting better.

She had taken serious measures after the delivery from Sainsbury's. She had washed every single item, thinking of how ill the delivery man looked—and then she washed them all again, in hotter water. Only then did she feel secure. Blogs and news channels had been awash with rumour; claims had gone viral, spreading from person to person, house to house, infiltrating minds with distracting and destructive ideas or half-truths and perhaps-accurate guesses. People were dying; no, they weren't. This was a government conspiracy; no, it wasn't. It was the Americans; no, the Chinese; no, the Islamic radicals. This was an outbreak; no, we don't like to use such strong language. And on it went.

But there was no doubt about it, society was severely hamstrung. Services were cut as people in their masses were unable to go to work, the forced holiday and then the curfew. But even then, rumours abounded that the authorities couldn't cope themselves, being hit by the illness like everyone else. She had seen the occasional police car drive past her block, sirens on, and she was sure one of the drivers was wearing a gas mask.

Fran went to sit down at her laptop on the dining table, lifting it out of its digital slumber where perhaps it was dreaming, filing its memories into the correct places after days of multitudinous frantic connections. The screen flashed up, her internet browser open, with a series of tabs. She clicked her blog tab open with the deftest of finger swipes.

Fran thought for a moment, and then clicked the cursor on the "New Post" hyperlink. The browser thought for a while and then returned the message, "Server cannot be found". Fran repeated her request, only to be confronted with the same message.

"You've got to be joking."

But there was no "Ha ha! Fooled you!" message in reply.

Fran selected the BBC News website and found a message at the top declaring "Limited web services available," which, it turned out, meant that only the news site was in any way working.

Fran ran through her repertoire of forums and websites to find only a select few still operational past cached posts and information. She was unable to get on Facebook or Twitter, but found one of her less-used forums available. Perhaps they had servers in different places, she thought.

However, it did not make good reading.

"*I feel like I am dying, help me!*"

"*I think my Mum has died!*"

"*Where are the police?*"

And, scarily enough, similar messages were emanating from people in a number of different countries. As the media of communication were shrinking, more people congregated at the loci which were still functional, like tadpoles writhing in a slowly shrinking muddy waterhole.

Until many stopped wriggling, their Google accounts and Yahoo avatars falling silent.

Scraps of genuine information were hard to come by as the hours went on. Was it because the government didn't want to obviously lie and say all was well, but didn't want to crush people's hope by saying what was *actually* happening?

After some time, Fran stood up. She had had her fill of what would normally seem like wild and improbable claims—but in this context, given what she had seen and heard from so many different outlets, they were, she guessed, pretty accurate portrayals of life around the country. Heck, the world. Fran was genuinely upset at what was going on, but she felt in no way inclined to set foot out of her apartment, feeling about as safe as one could where she was.

Putting her laptop to sleep, Fran moped to the kitchen, took a few slices of bread out the packet and slotted them into her toaster: a nice pastel green number to match her kitchen design and accompanying utensils and appliances.

The toast popped and Fran applied some butter-but-not-quite-butter spread and a thin layer of marmalade to the pieces before dejectedly plodding through to the lounge and turning on the television. There wasn't really much else *to* do. Sighing, she planted herself down onto the brown faux-leather sofa and fixed her gaze on to the window into the world.

"*...been able to get hold of a government representative who is on board a naval vessel in the Solent, moored off Portsmouth. Alex Frome is a junior minister in the Ministry of Defence, working under Secretary of Defence Peter Duggan. Mr Frome, these are incredibly uneasy times with deaths now being reported in large numbers, and we've heard nothing from the Prime Minister or* *anyone else for the last twenty-four hours. Can you explain this? Where is the PM, or the Deputy PM, or Peter Duggan, for that matter?"*

The camera switched to a thin man in his mid-forties wearing an open-neck blue shirt and a sailing jacket, standing on the deck of a frigate. Behind him was a grey wall of metal, naval steel grey. The overcast Portsmouth day added to the grim hues. A light breeze ruffled the dark brown hair of the minister, who stood looking exhausted, ready to answer the newsreader.

The minister, undoubtedly a product of a private education, nodded to someone off camera and replied in his well-spoken tones, *"Well, as you can see, things are difficult, both for you and the general public, and for us in government, trying to get things sorted. We are facing fundamentally serious challenges. It seems that this virus is lethal and that there is little we can do to quarantine it since it has spread too far, too quickly, for anything effective to be put in place. Our logistical teams, and our decision makers have been equally as affected as the general public—"*

The newsreader interrupted. *"Do you mean to say that the Prime Minister, as rumours suggest, has caught the virus?"*

"Yes. Yes I do, and we are hoping for, er, a speedy recovery. We are in a state of some emergency."

"Are you suggesting that we are without the PM for the foreseeable future? What about others?"

The minister looked distinctly uncomfortable. *"Look, I will be as honest as I can here. Things do not look good for dealing with this outbreak. We have been crippled in every department. The virus spread so quickly, and seemed to have spread before people showed outward symptoms. The armed forces, the government, the authorities had to deal with family members and colleagues contracting it, and faced tough decisions about where their loyalties lay."*

"Can you promise that essential provision such as power, electricity and gas, will be secured?"

"We have some provision, but there will be inconsistent power distribution and generation."

"Hang on, is there a chance that our nuclear power stations are in any kind of jeopardy?"

The minister shifted his eyes repeatedly. *"We are confident that our nuclear sites will be safe."*

"Minister, there has been little to no advice or assistance from the government whatsoever. If the population weren't so largely debilitated, they would be seriously up in arms about this."

"If the government weren't so debilitated, we would be seen to be doing so much more. Look, what we have said and what we continue to say is that all people should stay in their houses. I mean this with utmost seriousness. Everyone must stay in their houses. It is contact with others which will spread this virus, and it is self-imposed quarantine which will stop any further spreading."

"But what about a cure? Surely this should be top priority. And what about a safe public quarantine area or areas for people to congregate?"

"We are working tirelessly with every available resource on finding a cure. In the meantime, stay at home. As for quarantine areas, these will only help to spread the virus more quickly around those who have not yet caught it. We have considered these, but without instant diagnosis, and with limited resources, this has been deemed unworkable. The problem is the speed of this virus and it only seems to have picked up its pace."

And with that, a naval officer briskly walked into shot and ushered the minister away.

Fran sat shell-shocked as the newsreader kept up his commentary. How could this happen so quickly? How could things fall apart in the blink of an eye? What should she do? Questions and worries, thoughts and confusions, buzzed around in Fran's head like multiball in a pinball table. Of course, if things continued to get worse, and if the worst-case scenario came to pass, then, Fran considered, she would need a long-term plan. But surely things would get better!

Surely?

11
Greg

The weather had been incredibly calm, and the seas with it, for a good week as a high pressure system had advanced on the British Isles via the North Atlantic. Skies had been clear of cloud and the sun had been strong. In fact, Greg's tan was improving, as he had even had a chance to lie on deck, soaking up the rays like a sun-loving seal on a sea-surrounded rock.

Which was where he was now, though the weather had turned a little and he was doing no sunbathing, instead adjusting some of the lines on deck. The boat was rocking a good deal more today than yesterday, and he was having more trouble keeping himself steady as the wind was whipping up around him, making his coat flap around under his life vest. Greg bent his large, almost bulky 6'1" frame down to tie a rope around a cleat, before he turned back toward the stern and wobbled his way unsteadily with the generous help of the lifeline which skirted the perimeter of the yacht. Greg returned to the helm, where the bearded Peter stood intently staring forward through his glasses, past the bow and into the distance. Towards the land which was not yet in sight. There was something about Peter, on this trip, which reminded him of Richard Dreyfuss in the movie *Jaws*. The smaller frame, the beard and wavy hair, though somewhat greyer, and his round spectacles. Whenever he thought this, though, Greg had to give a quick glance over the side of the boat to make sure that there was no monstrous shark just about to break the surface and gouge man and boat. So far, so good.

Greg clapped Peter on the back, "Great job, Peter!" before returning to the cabin. "Rains a-coming!" he stated loudly to a diminutive man hunched over a small wooden desk, surrounded by only the most essential of technology.

The three men were navigating the Atlantic from the States to the UK. They had met through church, some years back, in the town they lived in near Charleston, South Carolina. Dale owned the 38-foot sailing yacht named *Grace*, of which he was very proud. They had cooked up the idea of sailing "the Pond" after Bible studies one evening, and the idea gained momentum as the weeks went by. Dale had the yacht and was a competent sailor, Peter had some experience, and Greg didn't know his mainsail from his halyard, but was willing to learn. Peter was retired,

Dale self-employed, and Greg had decided to take six weeks out from his summer vacation as a teacher in Lennox, South Carolina. The idea was to spend some time bonding, both with each other and with God. They had kept themselves to having minimal technology and contact with the world, such that on the journey they had the radio only for emergency or navigational reasons, but any communication with friends and family was virtually impossible. Just them and "God's own ocean," as they said.

They had whiled away particularly the calmer days and evenings, when not at the helm (or with them all sat at the stern), discussing all manner of things theological and philosophical, strengthening their beliefs, shoring up each other's confidence in their worldviews. Some of their work colleagues looked at them oddly when they discussed their intentions to have a break away from society, on the oceans, getting back in touch with the world and its Creator. At times, they had enjoyed some cards and the odd tumbler of imported single-malt Scotch whisky, saved for those special occasions. God certainly would have approved...

And so far they had loved the brotherhood of the whole journey; not so much a Road to Damascus as a Shipping Lane to Clarity, for them.

The weather was turning, though, now they were approaching the British Isles. Dale, white cap still on, tongue moving inside the top lip of his mouth, moving his wiry grey moustache in concentration, was scrutinising the map. Greg had once grown a moustache in his thirties, way back when, but it had not suited him. He had come to the conclusion recently that moustaches were just not reflective of the new millennium. He was not one to be concerned in the slightest about image, it was just that moustaches were definitely something which evoked the seventies or eighties. Or being in the fire department. Why that predilection remained was beyond him.

"So, we're all in agreement that mooring off Olding Bay on the northern coast of Devon is the way forward?" Dale asked, seeking confirmation.

"Yup, suree. Gotta use that dinghy for something!" Greg replied, referring to the small dinghy stored just in front of the mast, before the bow, with its pontoons deflated to allow for greater visibility when at the helm. Dale had chopped and hinged the transom so that the tiny engine folded into the tender and it provided less of an obstacle.

"I think we can check out some of the places in Cornwall once we're there, but it would be nice to see my cousin in Olding first. So I think we should be there, by my calculations, in just over two days. In other words, we've done a darned good job, so far!"

"Aye aye, Cap'n. You proved quite seaworthy, and so has *Grace*! I'm looking forward to some wonderful British hospitality, courtesy of your cousin and his wife," replied Greg, genuinely starting to look forward to some home comforts, and a damned good shave. His sun-browned face was covered in a healthy grey stubble, befitting his fifty-two years of age.

"And no more night watches! Oh, the joy of a real and steady bed beckons!"

Greg smiled. "They *do* have enough spare rooms and beds, right?"

"So they tell me. Look, they own a hotel, so either way, we should be well catered for!"

Dale's cousin had married a British woman many years back and had moved to the north Devon coast to buy a hotel with his new wife. Over time, they had renovated the *Bay View Hotel* to a good standard "three and a bit" star hotel with some sought-after views. The plan for the three men was to moor up to the side of the bay on one of the buoys for a short while before setting back off up the Devon and then Cornwall coasts. Dale was due to stay whilst Peter and Greg were to catch flights back from Bristol to Orlando. It was all going to plan.

The three men had made a good team, though they were all fairly different people. Dale was a meticulous man, both in thought and detail; he was the organiser, which was what they needed to be well prepared for such a project, fraught undeniably with risks as it was. He was a more serious man than Greg, who was at times jolly in his general disposition, being a natural optimist, having faith that "things'll be all right in the end, just you see." Greg taught high-school mathematics, and one might have expected him to be more like his friend Dale. That is not to say he wasn't organised (he was), or that he wasn't meticulous in his thinking (he could certainly be), but his classes were perhaps more lively than one might have expected for high-school maths. Peter was more dry-humoured, which could at times be mistaken for being gruff. The stocky man ran his own small building company, which was taking care of itself (well, his son, Nathan, was running things) in his absence. He had an abrupt manner (and this was where he departed from Dreyfuss), perhaps born of decades running his own show, playing foreman to his various workers. It had taken the other two men longer to get to know Peter, but once they had, they recognised that the three of them worked as foils for each other, balancing their own foibles with different ones. This trip had built a unity between them, a modern day Trinity.

And so the Three Horsemen of the New Age, as they sometimes called themselves, continued their undulating traverse toward the Devon coast, looking forward to a nice cup of English tea and perhaps a crumpet, or some such other delightfully quaint refreshment.

12
Jessica

It was not *her* face. Lines etched with worry, light olive-tinged skin dry with neglect, dark bulging bags beneath her usually bright but presently dulled green eyes. Her eyes were normally the part of her body which she liked the most, particularly as they were framed with delicate lashes. Not now. Everything was not how it should have been and the only delicate thing around here was her mental state. No, the face staring back was foreign to her; the mirror was lying, or had turned into an ugly portrait. Jessica's mousey shoulder-length hair was dank and limp, hanging in unwashed clumps, and her oval face held within harboured her thin and drawn lips, lacking in colour. Thirty-three had become fifty-three.

Jessica looked down at the sink and gathered her thoughts. Turning the hot tap, she waited until it ran warm and then plunged her hands in, giving her face a welcome blast of cleansing water. She rubbed her face vigorously, before returning her gaze to the mirror. *Nope, no improvement.*

Giving up, she turned and moved through the large house to the lounge window which looked down the gravel drive and out over the road at several other of the village houses. No cars on the road, no human sounds to be heard.

Ever since that camera incident on the TV, things had gone from bad to desperate. Jessica had not heard from her husband and she feared the worst. The hospital was not answering calls. No one seemed to have the first clue what was going on, and no one (at least no one in Jessica's village) had any inclination to leave their houses and risk contagion in the outside world. She had spoken to her parents, who by some sheer joss had escaped catching the illness to date. However, they had told her of some scary scenes which they had witnessed on the streets of London from the safety of their own home. They were too afraid to leave the house themselves and had no intention of risking catching what was clearly a troubling virus. She had failed to get hold of some of her friends, and others returned a scary verdict of ill-health.

Jessica couldn't stop thinking about Mike, though. Indeed, she had spent the last few days in tears, overcome by emotion and worry, confusion and disbelief. Grief came in waves. She held out little hope, being a fairly realistic woman who, certainly introspective, could flag up when she was lying to herself. Internal honesty, Jessica had felt for some years, was an important principle. Her philosophy degree and following two-year Master in Philosophy degree had taught her the rigours of critical thought and more than a passing grasp of psychology. In dealing with arguments and rational discussion, she had learnt to be aware of her own biases, separating out what she wanted to be true from what was actually more likely to be true.

She wanted her husband to be alive and well but that wasn't enough to make it probably so. No, she was realistic enough to understand that he was probably holed up in one of his own wards, and possibly even…well… And that's when she usually contented herself with seeing to Galen, or switching on the television, or busying herself with some such distraction, rather than breaking into floods of tears, unable to fully grasp the totality of everything going on in the world around her.

Jessica continued to stare down her driveway and onto the road beyond when, like the surprising first strike of lightning and thunder, she heard a high-pitched screech and subsequent crash. She could see nothing; whatever it was, and it sounded to her like a crash, was close but not in sight.

Panicking, heart rate galloping, Jessica ran to Galen's room to make sure he was fine and still sleeping, before running to the hall and putting on her red Converse baseball trainers. Hurriedly tying the laces and pulling her blue jeans over the high tops, she opened the wooden front door, with its rectangular central viewing window, and ran out on to the gravel. She ran to the end of her ten-metre driveway and looked out to the left and then the right, along the road. There, some twenty metres away, with its front thrusting through her neighbour's brick wall, was a black Audi estate. The engine was steaming through the crumpled bodywork; the windscreen was shattered, as were the two front windows. Her neighbour, a widow in her late sixties, turned up at her own driveway entrance, which was now partially blocked by the Audi. The car had, judging by the tyre marks, screamed to a sudden stop, swerving to the right and off the road, hitting the wall with some force. Bricks lay scattered.

Jean, her neighbour, dressed in maroon trousers and a thin light green jumper, looked at Jessica as she ran out on to the road and then returned her attention to the car, and who might be inside. This was the first real person Jessica had seen for days, at least since the curfew had started. Jean edged cautiously to the side of the car and halted. Jessica could make out the driver inside and also, perhaps, someone in the passenger seat. She jogged to see if she could help.

"Oh, dear God!" called Jean, her hand going to her mouth. She stumbled back, a look of profound horror and confusion on her wrinkled face.

Jessica warily approached. Perhaps she could help. She was first aid trained and liked to think that — being married to a doctor — she had more than a rudimentary understanding of things medical.

That didn't prepare her for what she saw.

The long-haired female driver was groggily moaning, blood streaming from her face. And yet the airbag had deployed, though it was now deflated. Spread across the front seat and lying on the driver, facing her, was a man who must have been propelled over the front seats from the rear seat. He seemed to be cuddling the woman. But, on closer inspection, the man wasn't just lying there. The scene was coming together for Jessica as she slowly gained on the car. Now she could see where the blood was coming from. There
 were nasty fresh and oozing gashes on the side of the woman's face and down her neck. These were not impact injuries, though; the cause was evident. The man lying across the front was undeterred by what must have been considerable force on his body. *He's...no...surely not! He's bloody eating her!*

The erstwhile passenger was, by all accounts, ripping at the driver's face and neck with his own mouth. Just then, the woman, victim to this ferocious insanity, came to and opened her eyes. She screamed, her almost equally pallid and sickly face spattered in its own blood where it hadn't already been torn. The man seemed to be entering into some kind of frenzy.

Jean was trembling on the other side of the car and otherwise incapacitated with shock. Jessica could only scream, drowning out the hideous sounds of the other woman. "Get off her, you bloody sick bastard!"

The man reacted to Jessica's outburst by turning to her. Her heart stopped. He looked like nothing she had ever seen before, save for films which she watched from behind a cushion or from between protective fingers. This, though, was worse. This was *here*. The face was drawn, stretched over veins and ligaments, tendons and bone. Its eyes were milky and bloodshot, like marbles suffused with spidery cracks of burgundy. Blood, that of the poor driver, smeared the chin and cheeks of this wild thing, dripping down in heavy rivulets. The man-thing snapped its jaws; teeth that would normally be brushed daily after meals of pasta or pizza clacked together menacingly, flesh and skin stuck in the cracks between. Jessica instinctively jerked back a step or two. The man twisted and threateningly thrust forward toward the shattered passenger window, toward Jessica. She stuttered back a further couple of paces and the man-thing turned back to his Sunday feast. Blood spurted from a newly torn rent in the woman's neck, coating the remaining glass shards in the driver's window. She gurgled her screams and started to choke. She was still buckled in to her seat and did not have the wherewithal to fight off her assailant and undo the belt, still dazed from the crash and looking none too fit and healthy herself.

Both Jessica and Jean were frozen to their spots as they saw the life ebb from the woman who vainly hit the man around the face, her blows becoming ever more weak until she lay there slumped. The man was literally *eating* her. The ravenous creature jettisoned blood and skin and flesh as he snapped and tore and ripped and rented. He turned once more to Jessica and bared his teeth, like a rabid and snarling dog, producing a guttural growl. Both Jean and Jessica turned and fled back into their properties.

Jessica slammed the door behind her, double locking it and pulling across the tiny chain. She turned, backing her frame against the door, and slid down to sit in a heap on the carpet.

Holding her head in her hands, she screamed and cried and slammed her feet up and down, every emotional ounce of energy expelled forcefully from the core of her very being.

In another room, her torment was echoed by the wails of a hungry baby.

13
Jason

"Okay, so, leaving a mentally disturbed and epileptically fitting man is morally all right, yeah?" Jason asked, sitting in the cabin of the campervan, looking in the rear-view mirror, back up the road towards the jolting body.

"Well, if the phones aren't working, not even for emergency calls, and the man is not showing you his appreciation for your help, then yeah," Bevan explained.

Jason looked concerned. "Mate, do you think this is all connected? Do you actually think the world is going to hell in a handcart?"

"Well, if it is, Jason, I'm pretty pissed off that I have to spend my last mental days on Earth with you, you miserable wanker."

"Bevan, for Christ's sake, be serious! I mean, what are we going to do?"

The men were huddled in the van, eagerly focused on their rear-view mirrors, Bevan in the driver's seat on the right. Their heart rates were soaring, and in their panic, they had run back to the van and locked themselves in, trying to phone any of the emergency services. Still no network service available. Jason was tapping the dashboard nervously. Considering Bevan was a bit of a mess of a man, generally speaking, he kept his pride and joy remarkably spotless. The dash was sparse, belying its age, and clean. There was no junk on the floor, in the footwell, no rubbish floating around the main compartment of the van. If dogs are like their owners, then on this evidence, campervans were the antithesis.

Jason's brain raced with random thoughts, procrastinating from actually acting towards achieving anything.

And then, out of the corner of his eye, Jason could make out the old man lurching unsteadily to his feet.

"He's up, Jason! He might be all right!" Bevan said, a tone of hope and excitement in his voice.

"Okay. You stay here, Bevan, I'll check him out."

With that, Jason opened the door and alighted from Annie. Bevan followed suit, paying scant attention to Jason's words.

The two men, some twenty metres away and next to the van, which had not been moved since the impact, slowly edged towards the old man. He was stumbling about in little dolly steps, facing the other direction.

"Er...er...excuse me?" Jason faltered.

The man's head twisted round at breakneck speed, almost literally. Body still facing away, but eyes intently focused on the men, the head lowered, just perceptibly, as if calculating something. With that bloody and perhaps even worse-than-earlier looking skull remaining still, the rest of the body twisted around to fully face the men. Then it lifted as a wolf might lift its head to howl at the moon, and let out a guttural "Gackkk!" before returning to stare at them, flesh and bloody spittle dribbling from its mouth.

The two friends had stopped their slow movement towards this badly injured old man. Something intuitive was controlling their movements now, their subconscious brains clicking into flight or fight mode. They edged backwards.

"Er, old man! The ambulance... It's on its way..." stuttered Bevan, putting his hand out on the van to steady himself as he retreated as calmly as he could. The old man, on the other hand, was in no mood to retreat, head lowering again, ever so slightly, and tilting somewhat to the side. The man's left leg was badly broken, but this didn't stop him from half-dragging and half-throwing it out in front of him as he set about trying catch his quarry. The ungainly action with his leg gave him a twisted, jolting gait as he lumbered, snarling, ever closer to Jason and Bevan.

And then the flight mode kicked in. Both men turned and ran the few steps back to their doors, scrabbling in panic to open them. They jumped in and frantically pushed the locks down.

Suddenly, a hand slapped the rear passenger side of the van. Jason looked into the rear-view mirror and saw the stretched facial skin of the old man contort and grimace back from his teeth.

"Start the van, Bevan! Start the bloody van!" Jason screamed, eyes engrossed in the figure shuffling down the side of the van. The van wheezed and then cut out.

"Start the van!"

"No shit, Sherlock!"

The old man levelled with Jason, snapping at the closed window mere inches away. Jason recoiled across the handbrake area towards Bevan.

Bevan shouted at Annie, who had wheezed twice now, "Come on, you bitch!"

She listened, and purred into life. The old man was clawing at the glass, as if he was unaware of what glass was or did, not quite figuring out how he could see Jason, but not touch him, claw him. His face, all of a sudden, slammed against the window, lips pulled back to reveal what were predominantly, on closer inspection, false teeth. Pearly white false teeth, surrounded by bloody saliva, and gnashing at Jason.

Annie lurched forward, tyres screeching, the edge of the window, where it met the door seal, hitting the old man and sending him spinning about and falling to the ground.

"Yes Annie! Woo hoo! You beaut!" Bevan gleefully shouted and accelerated off down the road. They drove on for a mile or so and then stopped at a gateway to a field, out in more open countryside.

Bevan cut the engine, though the fan remained whirring, cooling it down from its unexpected race down the windy roads.

"What. The. Fuck," Jason said. "I need to go home. I need to get home."

"Well, that's kind of where we are going," Bevan replied.

Jason shook his head, "No, I mean home home. I need to get back to Winchester to see if my parents and my sister are all right."

Winchester, he calculated, would be some four hours' drive, perhaps. His sister Sally was, at the age of thirty-two, living back with his parents, and had been for some six months since the bitter end of her marriage. With no house, and having lost her job as a result of her not being in a good mental space, she had opted for the failsafe.

The two siblings had always got on fairly well, probably helped by the six-year gap. As a result, Jason had taken her under his wing when he could, and treated her as an opportunity to show how 'cool' older brothers could be. He doubted whether he had always, or even often, succeeded but they remained pretty close. In fact, he had been hoping that she would visit him in his midlife-crisis retreat in the late summer, after this July had been and gone.

"Well, I think we need to get back to Olding to see what the hell is going on, and then we can take it from there. You can jump on the train, or borrow Danny's van or something."

Jason had sold his car in an attempt to rid himself of all the things which had reminded him so much of his city life and existence. His Mercedes had had to go.

"Right, we'll get back to Olding first. How are we doing for fuel?" Jason looked over at the gauge. "Switch on the ignition." Bevan switched it on and the gauge registered a distinct lack of fuel. "Bugger."

The two men sat for about half an hour, discussing what they should do and what they thought had happened before finally agreeing to their original plan, which was to return to the village shop and petrol station a mile or so up the road. Before they could realistically achieve anything, they needed fuel.

Bevan started Annie up again, and she obliged first time.

Bevan scolded her: "Bitch! Never there when you need her!" before feeling sorry for her slighted emotions. "Sorry, my lover!" The West Country twang stretched out the words with their beguiling lilt. He pulled out and continued down the road, driving carefully and vigilantly, taking on board their last encounter. Usually the roadkill that he hit on the country roads didn't get back up and try to attack them. This was a first. Whilst Bevan was driving, Jason cycled through the FM and AM frequencies to be met with the same radio message that they had previously heard.

"Jason? You know what? This is like my favourite films and TV shows wrapped up with my favourite thing to think about while I'm in the shower."

"You what?" said Jason, confused.

"Well, you know I like zombie films—"

"They're not bloody zombies, you idiot!" Jason interrupted.

"Well, okay then, Mr I've-got-a-degree-in-being-a-knob, what *was* that guy?"

"Economics."

"Eh?"

Jason explained. "I've got a degree in Economics. From Bristol. Thank you very much."

"Yeah, not a lot of use if you can't tell a zombie from an old man! Look, what do you think he was?" Bevan jibed.

Jason thought for a short moment, and said, "Well, it's clearly a virus, isn't it. It's clearly what everyone's getting. And we don't want it. We've got to think about how not to get it. And the virus, well it makes you go mental. Makes you turn into someone who you're not. "

Bevan continued his questioning. "Do you think he was trying to eat you? You know, actually trying to get food from you? Out of you?"

Jason paused again. Suddenly a sign appeared ahead. "Catlington, mate. We're here."

Bevan slowed the van down to about twenty miles an hour as they rounded a bend to the small straight road which housed the shop on the left and the petrol station opposite. It was a local petrol station, not franchised to one of the big companies, and all the rarer for it. The old white sign along the roof cover read "J. Ayers and Sons" in red writing, outlined in black. The van pulled under it and next to one of the two pumps. The men warily got out of the van, Bevan moving to the pump and retrieving it from its cradle. He opened the petrol cap with his keys and placed the pump inside, pulling the handle lever. Nothing. No sign of life in it.

"Is this one of those old-school places where they have to come out and serve you? Didn't think they still existed!" Bevan asked, looking over towards the attached petrol station shop. There was no sign of it being open, or anyone being inside. "Mate, do you want to go have a look?" he asked Jason.

"Sure." Jason took a couple of looks around, to get his bearings, and to be just careful. The small petrol station courtyard was clean and free of any cars. The shop, with its large glass window over empty newspaper stands and buckets of rather withered flowers, was in relative darkness. Jason walked up to the wooden-framed door, with its "CLOSED" sign showing, and pushed it. To no avail; the shop was clearly shut.

Bevan had put the pump back on the cradle and pulled up beside Jason. "What should we do?" he asked.

"Jesus, Bevan! You scared the life out of me! Well, there's clearly no one here. And we need petrol. There are no police about. In fact, I have no idea where anyone is. One simple solution would be to nick it. Break in and turn the pumps on."

"Check you out, Mr. degree-in-Economics turned petty criminal!"

"Well, what options do we have? Annie's running dry!"

Jason moved off to see what was around the right hand side of the shop.

Round the side was a short concrete driveway ending in a white garage door. Behind the shop, attached to it, seemed to be the owner's house. There was a short, beige, bristled mat with the word "Welcome" dyed into it in black, which sat under a white door. The two men walked around, looking from side to side, to face the door and its brass knocker. Jason lifted the knocker and rapped it several times. The sound appeared deafening in the silent early afternoon stillness, cracking and reverberating around the empty courtyard and surrounding houses. Opposite the door was the wall of the next house, whose short garden ended abruptly in a low brick wall and the road which they came in on. There was no answer at the door.

Jason looked across the road to the small village shop where they had visited some days before. It looked equally closed and uninviting.

METAMORPHOSIS

"Where the hell is everybody?" he asked no one in particular. Moving to the side of the door, towards the large garage, and stood beside a big window. He turned to see where it looked out to. "Hmm, nice view of that house's side wall. You come and live out here in the country, and *that's* your view?"

Jason cupped his hands and peered in through the window.

"What are you doing?" Bevan asked.

"Well, we need petrol, and I don't see you helping."

Bevan walked over to the door and banged on it impatiently. Nothing.

"Hang on! What's that?" Jason called out as he peered through his cupped hands into the darkened living room behind the wall of the petrol station shop. Past a dark brown sofa, which was placed diagonally in front of the window, he could make out what looked like a woman's legs covered in a patterned white dress, visible from upper thigh down to her black pumps. Bevan joined him at the window.

"What do you reckon, Jason?" he asked.

"Well, it could be another 'old man' situation. Or she might need some help. If we bash her door down and anyone asks, we are saving her life. If we get some fuel out of it too, then all the better," Jason replied. "Question is, how do we get in? This door and the window are double glazed."

"I think the front might actually be single glazed. Let's bust that in," suggested Bevan.

The pair took to looking around for some tools to break the petrol shop window with. Eventually, they set eyes upon the red metal fire bucket, two-thirds full of sand.

"Ooh, bit heavy, this!" said Bevan as he heaved the bucket up from next to the petrol pump. "Help me with it."

Between them, they decided to hurl the bucket over the newspaper stands and into the large window. The door was reinforced with thin steel wire, so that had been discarded as an idea. After a count of three, the pair launched the bucket, sending it soaring through the air like a lead balloon. It hit the glass with a solid crack and fell back on to the newspaper stands, spilling its sandy contents, including cigarette ends and bits of rubbish, over the now empty racks. The glass was tougher than they had anticipated but they had done enough to have it almost shatter, webs of lightning cracks spreading out from the epicentre to the edges.

"Looks like she's gonna go!" Bevan announced.

Jason picked up the now mostly empty bucket, took it by the handle, and launched it with all his might at the point from whence the cracks spread. The result was strangely pleasing. What was it about destruction which was so enjoyable? Jason remembered a popular science documentary he had watched once about the universe, one where presenter Brian Cox stared wistfully at nothing in particular whilst standing on mountains. He remembered the one about order always devolving to disorder, with some fleeting images of a derelict house succumbing to the powers of nature. *What was it, e-en...entropy, that was it! Well entropy that, window!*

The window now had a gaping hole about a metre in diameter, with vicious looking shards thrusting into it.

"That's not very nice glass is it?" mused Bevan. "Ah, Jesus, if only we had a bucket or something to smash it out of the way..."

"Very good, Bevan. Very good," replied Jason, glancing about to see if any of the houses around had been roused by the noise, and to look for something to clear the dangerous-looking glass with. Walking round the other side of the garage building, Jason came across a wooden broom propped against the wall. *Perfect!*

"You see, Bevan, there is a god!" Jason proposed.

"Sure, because he gives more of a shit about you finding a brush than this country falling apart at the bloody seams, and old men going mental and getting hit by beautiful campervans!"

Jason stared at Bevan.

"You know what, Bev? You might just be cleverer than all of humanity give you credit for."

Holding the broom at the brush end, at length, Jason began to prod and push large shards of glass into the interior of the garage shop. After a few minutes, the garage window appeared safe to enter.

"Well, I wouldn't have thought we'd be doing this a few days ago," Jason admitted thoughtfully. "This feels like some alternate reality, just like a dream, you know?"

"For sure," Bevan agreed, and clambered up on to the newspaper units. Jason held them steady as they started to wobble and move on their wheels. Carefully placing his hands over on to the chocolate bar shelves which were propped up on the other side, Bevan was trying to be careful not to get too near to the window and its potentially hazardous jagged edges.

However, the chocolate bar shelves on the other side of the window were not designed to hold the slightly overweight frame of a would-be thief-cum-do-gooder, balancing precariously in an attempt to defy basic physics.

The shelf gave way.

The quiet late summer afternoon air was again broken by the loud sounds of a garage being maligned.

"You all right mate?" inquired Jason.

"Nothing a Biscuit Boost couldn't help with," Bevan answered, head eventually popping into view, mouth chewing gleefully on a chocolate bar.

"Give us a hand, mate."

Bevan helped Jason over the threshold of the window and into the rather small, slightly old-fashioned garage shop. Jason glanced around, scanning the interior. Everything seemed pretty normal: shelves were stacked neatly, full of all of the normal garage paraphernalia, the aisles were clean, the counter was clear. He looked about the shop for a light switch since it was a little on the dark side. Sighting the white switch by the front door, he moved over and flicked it on. The fluorescent bulbs above glimmered at the starter end and then gave up. Jason flicked the switch a few times to see if he could bring about an alternative outcome, but to no avail.

"Er, that's not a good sign."

Bevan turned around, realised what Jason was implying, and gave a puzzled look.

"What, so there's no power here?"

Jason shook his head, bending his mouth to show a sort of hopeless look. "I guess it's worse than that, mate. I reckon the power might be out everywhere.

Suddenly, the lights flicked into life.

"Ha! Have some faith, Jason, me old codger!" Bevan's Cockney accent left a lot to be desired. "Right, we need to turn these pumps on, and we need to see if that person on the floor next door is weird or not... So, any idea how to turn on petrol station pumps? Any idea where the switch would be?"

Jason paused to think. "Well, whenever you fill up, you have to wait a bit until they press a button on the till to allow your pump to work. So we need one of us out there, and the other in here on the till. And we need to switch everything on."

"Nice one, Brains." Bevan vaulted the spilled chocolate bars and ran around the counter, switching on every switch and turning every key.

The computerised till hummed into life, and lights switched on here and there. "Woo hoo, Houston, we have power!"

Suddenly, there was a noise through the door at the back of the small shop. Both men turned in immediate silence, hearts giving a long and nervous pulse. Bevan looked at Jason, caught his eye, and pointed towards the door vigorously. Jason furrowed his brow and made a face that said *of course the noise came from there, you idiot!* Both men slowly moved towards the grey door which stood between them and the faint noise. As they moved closer, Bevan looked around for something that resembled a defensive weapon, without thought as to why. He grabbed a bottle of Rioja.

Jason was the closer to the door, and reached out and took the handle, twisting it as slowly as possible so as not to make any noise. The sound of each of their breathing was all they could hear. Slowly, so very slowly, Jason turned the handle and eased the door back. It squeaked loudly, like a baby in a quiet campsite. Both men instinctively winced. The door opened outward into the bright, sunlit corridor behind, through which they could see the lounge where they had seen the body.

"Nnnnggg..."

"Aaaaahhhh!" Jason let out a startled cry as, from the right of the doorway and out of sight, a tall, thin frame appeared; a man in his late sixties dressed in grey trousers and an off-white shirt, now somewhat dirty. His face, Jason could see, was a mess. Blotchy and yet wan, the skin was haggard, punctured by deep eye sockets, deep due to the dark skin and bags surrounding them; but in their centres were bloodshot eyes, terribly discoloured so as to draw a further flinch from Jason as he looked on.

"Nnnngggg!"

The man stumbled into the doorway, looking at Bevan and then snapping toward Jason, an inhuman movement if ever he had seen one. With his right arm remaining down by his side, his left lifted and stretched towards Jason, fingers bent and warped, barbed and twitching. He stumbled and then stopped, and lifted his hand onto his forehead. "Felisht...nnnnggg..." he uttered, as if trying to say something intelligible.

"Er, sorry about this, mate," Bevan rambled. "It's just that, you know, we saw a body and we were just sort of, you know, like, coming to see if..."

The man's head snapped up from what appeared to be struggled thought processes.

"Nnnnnggg...aaarrgghh," the man gargled as he lurched forward, stretching out in the direction of Jason, who was keeping a metre's distance.

"Er, excuse me, but are you okay?" mustered Jason as he shuffled backwards down the very short car accessories aisle. The man grunted in return and shambled on in Jason's direction. His lips peeled back to reveal his perfect teeth, more dentures, over which strands of saliva stretched menacingly. "Um, please stop. If you keep coming towards me, mate, I'll have to, er, clock you," Jason informed the lurching man, sounding something less than truly threatening.

Meanwhile, Bevan was tentatively following proceedings at his own safe distance, bottle in raised hand. "Mate, if he's got that illness, you don't want to let him get near you!"

Jason took heed, and turned to his left once he had reached the end of the aisle, and backed into the next aisle, containing magazines, maps and other non-perishables.

The crazed man followed him, grunting.

"What is it with old men today?" Jason shouted.

"Mate, I think we need to do something about this guy—"

But just as Bevan was explaining that they needed to take the law into their own hands, the man's attention switched to him. Staggering, gargling and spraying spittle, the garage owner launched himself at Bevan, surprising him, managing to clutch Bevan's face with his contorted right hand.

Bevan moved by instinct, even with his face in a vice-like grip. The bottle of Rioja hit the man on the side of the neck as he seemed to be lurching forward towards Bevan's own neck, false teeth arrayed in open-mouth frenzy. The dull thud pushed the man down marginally, the impact causing him to stagger sideways, before his arm grasped the shelf of tin cans and he righted himself.

"Fsssshhhhttaa!" he exclaimed, though the onlooking Jason was unable to tell whether there was any anger or emotion in the outburst. The man convulsed forward, thrusting his arm out at Bevan menacingly. Heart pulsing with adrenalin and self-preservation, Bevan, though shorter than his attacker, swung the bottle as hard as he could over the man's shoulder and into the side of his skull. The bottle broke off just below the neck which Bevan had been holding, shattering over the man's head and shoulders. Wine exploded everywhere, instantly filling the air with its pungent aromas and tannins, gushing down the attacker's shirt, and splattering Bevan liberally.

The impact of the wine bottle threw the man against the shelf, and he half collapsed onto his right knee. The vinaceous attack had left several daggers of glass protruding from the more than nasty wound in the side of his head, though it was hard to tell what was blood and what was red wine.

However, the man seemed unperturbed by the weeping wound in his head which had been inflicted with not a little brutal force. Clawing himself up to his feet again, he threw out his grasping hand and made towards Bevan. All Bevan could think to do was to grab anything which came to hand, in this case a 2.5 litre plastic bottle of diesel oil. He duly swung the oil at the man's head, throwing him back a pace, and repeated his first oil-based step again.

"Jesus, Jason, fucking help me, man! I swear he's trying to EAT ME!!"

Jason had been somewhat incapacitated by shock, staring at the unfolding crisis in static silence. The last time this had happened was when he had been involved in a hit and run car accident when he was fifteen, as a friend's mother was giving him and his friend a lift back from a concert. It had been late and raining, streetlights reflecting off wet puddles on the dark tarmac roads. His friend's mother was a slightly nervous driver, and the junction in the city had been confusing for her. That said, the car which hit them had been travelling over the speed limit, and the driver, who was later caught, was somewhat over the legal drink driving limit. Jason had sat frozen in that back seat for what seemed like an age, the mother dead in the front, his friend hysterical in the passenger seat. Jason's senses had phased everything out but a blurred vision. Ever since that moment, he had been trying to tease out the causality involved in that whole incident: who was to blame? Was it the drunk driver? Was it the people who designed the junction? His friend's mother and her driving abilities? Or his own fault, as he had been insistent on the pair going to the concert? And to this date, he had found no satisfactory answer. Perhaps, he often thought, there was no satisfactory answer, that the question was somehow wrong. At other times, he just blamed the universe, building up to that moment with inexorable inevitability.

Back in the garage shop, he looked around for something, anything, which could be used as a weapon to try and make sure that this inevitability didn't end badly. The best bet was more wine. He ran to the wine shelf and availed himself of two further bottles of red wine, then dashed back down the aisle to surprise the staggering man from behind. Jason pulled his right arm back and brought his first bottle down with a mighty swipe, crashing it into the back of the man's head. Wine cascaded through the attacker's hair as the glass broke, the impact causing the damage as opposed to the glass, which fell about rather impotently. Jason switched the other bottle to his right hand.

And then suddenly, the realisation of what they had done hit the men.

"Jesus, Bev, what are we doing?" breathed Jason, astonished at the scene, which only now seemed to be unfolding itself before him, letting itself finally be known.

Bevan exhaled a slow "Shiiiiit!" Jason looked over at Bevan to see emotion and rage being perceptibly released in his expiration.

The man's head had two large contusions on each side, oozing dark blood, which mixed liberally with the copious body of red wine. He lay flat on his back, twitching and gargling inhuman noises.

"Um…what have we done? I mean, what have we done? What have we done?" was all that Jason could manage under the circumstances, repeating himself again and again.

"I'm phoning the police," said Bevan, pulling his mobile phone from his pocket, and dialling 999. Of course, there was no response; the phone lines were dead, communication down.

Jason looked down at their handiwork. "Shall we help this guy? I mean, he still seems alive. Shall we put him next door, in his house?"

Suddenly concerned, equally for themselves in the ramifications of what they had done, as well as for the person whom they had battered, the two stared in consternation at the mumbling man.

Jason bent down, and then dropped to one knee. He let the bottle that he still grasped tinkle to the floor. The man was half lying on the bottom shelf in the aisle, packets of noodles and other dried foods scattered around, swimming in wine and the viscous claret of congealing blood. Pulling his spattered plain navy hoodie over the bottom half of his face with his left hand, Jason reached out and grabbed the left shoulder of their attacker. Suddenly, with a grunt, the man's head and neck swivelled with menacing speed to reveal a gore-framed face with even more drawn features than but ten minutes prior. The thin lips retracted to bear still pearly false teeth, and he lurched toward Jason. His mouth latched on to Jason's arm, whilst his right arm circled round to grab Jason's left arm.

"What the—!" screamed Jason, pulling back.

Before Jason could even compute fully what was going on, the loose and heavy combat boot of Bevan's right foot connected with surprising force with the side of the gnarling face. Two things happened: the man's neck could be heard breaking, and Bevan's boot came off as his follow-through connected awkwardly with the shelving unit. The boot flopped on to the man's chest.

Amazingly, the man was still grunting. His body had been thrown back into the shelf of dried food, his neck at an awkward angle, head between the first and second shelf, facing down. Blood from the wounds on his head had been flicked off as a result of the forceful kick, droplets spraying the foodstuffs, tiny specks of flesh from the gashes in his head speckling the floor and shelves.

"My God," muttered Jason. "He tried to bloody bite me!"

The man's body still moved and convulsed. His hands grabbed the shelves as he seemed to be trying to pull himself up, despite his broken neck.

Bevan stared, mouth agape. "Is this guy for real? What do we do? We've sort of killed this guy, except he isn't dying easily...I mean, what are the police going to do?"

"I'm not sure the police are going to do anything. I'm not sure the police are even, you know, policing," added Jason. He was starting to shake with shock and confusion, all the while the broken man was trying to claw his way upwards, his head sagging to one side.

"Look mate, we need to get some fuel and get the hell outta here," said Bevan, staring in awe at the scene in front of him. "We tried the police. This guy attacked us. It was self-defence. Simple."

But as they were discussing what they should and shouldn't do, the man was gaining his feet.

Distraught and drained, Jason suggested, "Let's get to the van, Bev." And with that, the men left their assailant-cum-victim and helped each other back out, over the confectionary counter and through the broken window. Bevan helped himself to some chocolate bars on the way.

Heading straight to the pumps, Bevan checked them. "They're on, Jace!" he chimed as he lifted the nozzle from the cradle.

Jason had run to the road, looking up and then down, not really sure what he was searching for—witnesses or help? Pausing, he then jogged back to Bevan.

"I was just thinking, we need to fill up on fuel."

"What do you think I am doing?" Bevan asked.

"No," Jason said, "I mean *really* fill up. You know, get some jerry cans and that..."

"Um, I think there might have been some back in there. Not a hundred percent sure, mind." Bevan thumbed in the direction of the broken window. Jason walked around the van and was greeted by the lolling and distorted head of the man whom they had set upon, bordered with a jagged frame of broken glass, trying his level best to negotiate his way over the confectionary stand with the look of an adult who had never gone through the necessary childhood processes of learning basic coordination. His flailing arms were knocking chocolate bars this way and that.

"Do…do you think this guy wants to…like…eat us?" Jason enquired of Bevan.

Bevan finished filling the van and, replacing the cap and nozzle, returned to Jason's side.

"If he does, I can safely say that your meat is of much higher quality than mine, so if you want to get these cans, be so good as to go first. You know, for his benefit," Bevan said, offering the space in front of them with his hand in a gesture of generosity.

"What should we do? I mean, do we really need these cans now? Can we get them from anywhere else? Shit man, I mean, what's going on. What the FUCK is going on? One minute we're camping, the next we're in the midst of a fricking apocalypse! Jesus, Bev, what are we doing?" Jason's voice rose until it reached a fever pitch of hysteria, confusion and panic.

They stood for a short while, watching the old garage owner thrashing at the chocolate bars, head flopped to the side.

"Two things, Jace: First, how is that man still alive? Second, what is that man, because I don't really think that's the same guy who was last week running this garage?"

Jason thought for a while. "I'm not sure I'm the same person I was yesterday, Bevan. What does that mean? Shit, I think I've just entirely changed in the last hour. I've done things totally out of character. I mean…I mean…Who am *I*?" He paused, gathering himself. "Look, this thing is mental. No one's answering the phones. I have no idea what has happened to my family, and we're stranded in a petrol station considering attacking a diseased mentalist so we can get some jerry cans to fill with petrol just in case we really are stuck in an apocalypse. Personally, I think we're actually trapped in some weird West Country Bermuda Triangle, and if we just made it to the other side of Exeter, things would actually be fine. But as it is, I figure, well, I figure we are going to have to neutralise this…this…thingy person."

"Er, thingy person?" Bevan was a little incredulous. "Seriously? *Thingy person*? Mate, don't ever make a movie. 'Out now, *The Day of Thingy Persons*'!" Jason was amazed that Bevan could manage a laugh, that there was humour here for him, like blood from a stone oddly extracted with success. Bevan continued. "Look, this man is proper diseased. He's a biting machine. Reminds me of *Dawn of the Dead* or something—"

"Don't say it. Don't bloody say it. We are not living in a movie. These are not... not... *zombies*. I mean, that other guy, he was just ill and stuff. This guy is just ill, too."

Bevan laughed. "Mate, I broke his freaking neck! That's not *ill*, that's *crazy*! Right...let's do something. I'm not standing here and chatting all day!" Bevan sauntered back to the campervan and rummaged in the boot (at the front) and retrieved a wheel jack handle, before returning to stand next to Jason. "Right, Jace, are we doing this, or what?"

"I'm not sure we have talked in detail about *what* we are doing, but if you mean staving this guy's head in just to get some jerry cans, I'm not sure I can."

"Look, Jason, if this shit is really happening, then we just don't know how long the power is going to be on. So, let's assume the worst and make sure we get as much as we can now. And, after all, it *was* your idea."

"No. No. Let's go back to Olding, see what's going on. We've gone naught to sixty in three seconds flat. Let's get in the van and shoot home. We've done enough here, and I can't help but think we're going to get into a whole heap of trouble as a result." Jason was now a good deal calmer than he had been, even though the two men were still confronted with a grunting human windmill doing his very best to upset what was left of the confectionary.

Bevan was not convinced and added, "Look, you were right: we need to be thinking ahead a bit here, mate. This might be our best chance to get ourselves some fuel. You know, more than just a few days' worth."

Jason was still not happy. "Bevan, you realise you are advocating killing this man. How else are we going to get in there? I've got a better idea, I think. How about trying some sheds in the back gardens of some of these houses? How about ringing on some doorbells?"

Bevan looked at some of the houses over the road, and then back at the snapping dentures of the old man behind broken window of the petrol station. "Your second plan seems a little more appealing. I *advocate* doing that... Don't try and use big words, Jace. Remember, *I'm* your audience."

They two men turned and jogged over to a house across the road from the petrol station. A typical West Country stone cottage several hundreds of years old, it was decked in a covering of flowering wisteria and ivy, cleared around the windows and main front porch area. The late afternoon sun cast a glorious glow on the front of the house, glinting off the window panes between the lattice metalwork which criss-crossed them. The men pushed through the short front gate and up the quaint pathway which ran the length of the tiny front garden.

Jason took the initiative and rang the front doorbell, which could be heard through the thick wooden door, its sonorous tones sounding much louder in the afternoon stillness. He rang again and put his head against the door.

A number of rings later, Jason and Bevan wandered around the side of the house, to be met by a head-height wooden gate apparently locked from the other side. After furtively looking around for any sign of a witness (other than the now drooling face appearing from the broken garage window, across the road), they measured up their route.

One last glance, and the men vaulted the gate, with not a little difficulty, and a good deal of help. The gate separated the house from a stone garage, with a thin concrete corridor leading to the enclosed garden; a slightly dark affair, with a variety of mature trees and shrubs curving their way around a compact lawn. And at the far end, tucked away to one side under a willow tree, sat a shed.

"Well, if there ain't any cans in there, then there's always the garage," suggested Bevan, thumbing toward the garage they had just passed.

They walked to the end of the garden. About half-way down, Jason turned to look back at the house. The back of the house mirrored the front in its verdant décor. Jason instantly flashed back to his parents' house on the outskirts of Winchester, where he and his sister had spent a happy childhood. The garden, though bigger, had provided a lush and organic surrounding for much of their play and time spent together. Both his parents had been outdoor types, and the children had been encouraged to play outside no matter what the weather. It had been a surprise to his parents, then, that he had chosen a career which was the antithesis of this. Perhaps, Jason had thought in his self-imposed rural exile, his midlife crisis had been a chance, or a wish, to get back in touch with nature and the outdoors.

The house even looked similar, though smaller, though the lattice windows were different, and—

"Wha...wait a minute." Jason was standing in the garden, looking back at the house, whilst Bevan had arrived at the shed. "I swear a curtain just moved. I bloody swear it!"

Bevan turned to stare back at the house. "You reckon someone's in there?

"I *know*."

"Look, if they didn't answer the door, then they don't want to talk to us. I guess they'd be scared, and all. Let's just check in here," Bevan said, motioning towards the shed, "and then do one," he reasoned.

"Okay. You check in the shed, and I'll just keep watch. Then yeah, let's 'do one' and get the hell outta Dodge."

Luckily, the shed was unlocked, and Bevan took less than a minute to find a plastic jerry can which was a third-full of petrol.

"Always good when people have petrol-driven lawnmowers. Nice!" And then, when he was outside, standing next to Jason, Bevan lifted the can into the air and shouted towards the house, "We're not bad people really! We just need to, er, borrow your jerry can! Is that okay?" He turned to Jason. "It's polite to ask, you know." And he strolled back off up the garden towards the gate.

Jason stared at that same window, with its curtains drawn, checking for further twitching. In a sense, he really wanted there to be someone alive and well, compos mentis, inside the house. He wanted to talk to someone, wanted to confirm, or better, deny, this whole state of affairs. He wanted to know whether this was reality, or not. But then he figured that speaking to anyone would not necessarily confirm this reality; that person might just be part of this crazy reality. Maybe this was a computer simulation, maybe he was in *The Matrix*, maybe he was the main character in a computer game, and he would have to work his way to safety. Jason remembered a film he had seen years before, a film with Emma Thompson and someone else (Will Ferrell? Someone else? Did it matter in this melting world?) where the main character heard voices in his head, voices which turned out to be an author writing his life, dictating his future. And this is how he felt, some protagonist lacking control in what was happening to him, living his life out in the imagination of some author, some Emma Thompson sitting in an alternate reality.

She'd better get me out of this shit, he thought.

With that, Jason jogged off to rejoin Bevan, who was happily entering the unlocked garage side door.

"Mate, what now?" Jason asked, exasperated.

"Strike while the iron's hot!"

"Yeah, but there's someone in this house!" Jason protested.

"Well, if they mind, they'll let us know," Bevan answered, an air of reason about him.

Jason wondered whether their moral codes had just taken a left turn, deviating from the A-road, and hitting some country lane, and quickly on to an unmetalled road, bumpy and full of jarring gravel. Before Jason could offer further protest, Bevan was in the garage and rooting around for what he could find to fulfil the criteria of carrying fuel safely. In a few minutes, with Jason standing guard outside armed with nothing but his wits, Bevan reappeared like the prodigal son, but this time equipped with the original plastic jerry can and a large old metal oil container.

Bevan looked happy. "This'll do!"

"Let's get the hell outta here."

The two newbie burglars bundled themselves over the gate with the combined grace of a pair of dancing water buffalo and gathered themselves on the other side. Brushing themselves down, they tried to look as nonchalant as possible (as if every day was full of these sorts of challenges and successes, irrespective of the moral dimensions) and carried their bounty across the road to the waiting campervan.

Just as they got to the van, Jason noticed that something was not quite right, that something was amiss.

"Bev, mate, where's that bloke? The garage guy?" Jason stood next to the van and glared wide-eyed at the gaping hole in the side of the petrol station. There was no old man, no misshapen garage owner.

"Um..." Bevan stood next to his campervan, half way through throwing the cans in the back.

"Stay here." Jason grabbed the jack handle from the front seat of the van where his friend had set it down, and walked slowly towards the petrol station window. Each step brought on a higher heart rate, and more laboured breath. As he edged closer, more and more of the confectionary counter came into view. But the closer Jason got, the more evident it became that the man was no longer there. Jason caught site of a Mars bar on the ground, a metre or so from the window. Arriving at the newspaper stand, he could now see fully into the little shop. There was no one to be seen.

Jason stepped back and turned to Bevan. "Hey, there's no—BEVAN!"

Some could five metres behind Bevan, the distorted figure of the dishevelled and broken man lumbered towards Jason's partner-in-crime, one arm outstretched, head sideways on its broken neck.

Bevan turned and backed away quickly in the direction of Jason.

"Bloody hell, how did he get there?" Bevan shouted.

Armed to the teeth with the jack handle, the pair looked at each other as the man drew level with the van. There was nothing right about the scene. The man was not incapacitated, when by rights he should have been dead; he was a mangled mess, from oozing wounds to broken bones. To the two friends, intuitively, this *thing* was barely, if at all, human.

"Do we do this?" Jason asked.

"We do, mate. We do."

Bevan grabbed the discarded broom they had used earlier to clear the glass shards from the edge of the window. He felt the handle—it was solid wood, an old and thick broom. He clutched it near the brush end and swung it back, ready. Jason drew his own jack handle back, also ready for action. Then the two split sideways, like circling jackals. The old man, with his lolling head attached to its broken neck somehow managing to navigate the body, moved left towards Bevan.

As the man shambled after Bevan, Jason instinctively took the initiative and made a rear-guard action, attacking the back of the pursuer's head with the jack handle. The first impact did a good deal of damage. But it was the further four in quick succession which sent the old man irreversibly to the ground. Blood and gore flew with every retraction of the metal handle. The man's skull was cracked and crushed, and all Bevan could do was stare in shocked disbelief, broom raised in defensive readiness.

The man slumped, crumpled and forsaken, to the concrete, blood running freely from the horrific remains of his head, dented brain exposed to the elements.

His teeth had finally stopped chattering.

Jason's weapon clattered to the floor. He looked at himself to find his hoodie generously sprayed with blood and bits of sinew or brain or whatever—he wasn't sure. Looking down at the body, he again wondered what the hell had happened to them over the past day. The two men stood there, silently surveying their workmanship—the remains of an old man.

METAMORPHOSIS

"I wonder if that's him in there. You know, *him*," said Bevan, pointing at the man's open, gaping head. "Whether, you know, if he was, like, *thinking*, at the end. Whether his mind just floated out of that hole and into, like, the air? What d'you reckon?"

Jason pondered. "Jesus, mate, I have no idea what I reckon now. I've just fucking killed someone. You know, actually *killed* someone."

Jason's mind flashed back to his parents' house again, near Winchester. They had kept chickens for several years, in the hope of becoming more ethical consumers and members of society. It had gone pretty well. They had originally got three chicks off a friend's farm, and luckily only one had been male. Chickens were difficult to sex, unless (he had later learnt) you were a Japanese chicken sexer who could do it intuitively. His father had told him how they learnt to sex chickens without being taught, per se: the knowledge was intuitive and in some way unfathomable. They just *knew it*. Well, none of Jason's family had the time or need to just *learn it* through trial and error; instead, with the next batch they received, they had to accept that some could be cockerels; and indeed, two were. Which meant three cockerels in total amongst a clutch of eight. Not too bad, but something would have to be done about the cockerels because in such a small area, too many males would cause too much noise, and too much sexual aggression with the hens. Partly for this reason, and partly for ethical reasons, two had to go; the ethical reason being, so his father told him, that if one willingly eats meat, and buys it to devour it, then one should have some idea of where that meat comes from. By this, he meant, the process of killing and preparing it. To eat chicken, in other words, one should have the experience of killing and preparing it.

So Jason did. He followed the example of his father next to him, who took the cockerel under his arm, dispatched the animal with a quick, sharp twist and pull of the neck.

On the other hand, Jason's pull and twist was amateur. Essentially, in having these chickens in order to look after them ethically, he was finding himself failing to kill the chicken, but succeeding in breaking its neck quite severely. Jason remembered the eye of the chicken, with its upside-down head, looking at him as if to say, "You know, this shitting hurts!" The situation worsened when his father ordered Jason to lay a broom handle on the floor, across the chicken's head and neck, and then to grab the chicken's legs whilst standing on the handle. By jerking the chicken's legs backward, Jason would finally break the neck properly and kill the chicken for sure.

Except, life (and death) is never that simple. Jason pulled whilst standing on the handle, which was pinning the neck down. That all worked just fine. However, the pull was a little enthusiastic and the chicken's head and neck remained jammed under the broom handle whilst Jason held a convulsing chicken body, flapping and spraying blood. His father had grabbed the dying body off of him and stuck it, open neck wound down, in a nearby bucket. Ethically killing things had not started off as Jason had hoped, but he had gotten over it to dispatch another couple of Sunday roasts-to-be.

But caving in a man's head was a different kettle of fish.

"I mean," he continued, pulling himself from his reverie, "I've killed a *chicken* before. But nothing like this."

"No shit, Sherlock. You've killed a bloke. A human. Well, yeah, a human," replied Bevan.

"But is it? You know, was it?" Jason pleaded.

"*It*? Jesus, mate, he had a name and everything. I presume."

Jason shook his head. "No, no, no. This guy had, like, *changed*. He wasn't a human, surely. Or not like we know humanity. You saw him. He had a bloody broken neck and a smashed up head! He didn't speak. His skin's a weird colour. His eyes! Man, his eyes! Anyway, your tune's changed from earlier."

"Look, mate. Maybe who you are here, now, isn't who you *really* are. Normally. Who we *need* to be now, that's changed," said Bevan.

Jason looked him in the eye. "This *is* 'normally'. Who I need to be is who I *am*. I didn't pull this shit out of thin air. This...*this*..." Jason motioned to the lifeless body, to what they had done. "...is inside me. *This* is me."

"Look, all I knows is, we'd better get outta here." Bevan's West Country accent seemed stronger than ever, as if this whole episode had sent his brain into a default shock mode whereby he was operating with his core Devonian being.

The two men slowly stood up, still entranced by the oozing body, the blood seeping ever closer to their feet. Jason looked down again at his hoodie and grimaced. Pulling it off, he threw it over the man's head, covering the indignity.

The sun was starting to get lower in the sky as the summer hours dwindled in advance of the encroaching evening. Nocturnal Delilah was inevitably cutting away at the rays of Samson's golden-haired sunshine.

The men retreated to the van, and loaded everything up that they needed. But just before Bevan fired the engine up, he hopped out and ran to the smashed window-entrance to the garage shop. And helped himself to the chocolate bars which were spread around on the concrete.

"It'd be rude not to," Bevan said with inappropriate cheer, on returning to Annie. He started the campervan, and guided it out of the petrol station forecourt, picking up the journey back to Olding.

***

Some five minutes down the road from the village with the petrol station, the two men in their campervan passed a car speeding in the other direction.

Bevan turned back to look through the rear window at the car speeding away. "What do you reckon they're up to? Shooting back home? Do you think they're holiday-makers?"

"Guess so. They're going somewhere in a hurry. I figure we need to be careful who we stop and talk to if this virus is all around. I'm pretty worried about the blood from that guy. Do you think it went in our mouths? And if it did, would we catch it? Man, I've got sooo many questions." Jason's right leg had been nervously bouncing up and down for the five minutes they had been on the road.

After chatting over the ramifications of what they thought was going on, the pair were still nonplussed. Some twenty minutes later the trees receded and the rolling Devon countryside of farms and fields hinted that they might soon be approaching the coast.

"I've been thinking, Jason—"

"There's a first!" Jason automatically reeled off the empty-feeling joke.

"Ha. Look, I reckon that Olding will be deserted. Well, not deserted, just no one out of their houses. You heard the radio messages. Anyone with any sense will be waiting it out indoors until the authorities kick into action or until this thing naturally goes its course. I think people will either have it or will be hiding from it."

Jason thought about Bevan's reasoning and felt a rare sense of agreement. "I think you're probably spot on. Let's head for mine and then reassess. We can check out town from the van."

Feeling more secure about their rather short-term plan, they continued their drive towards Olding and the setting sun.

14
Fran

Fran slammed the phone down in angry frustration. The phone lines were dead. Neither her mobile phone nor her landline were registering a signal. Suddenly, she was hit with a sense of isolation that she had not felt before, even given her self-imposed apartment sanction. No, this severed connection to the outside world, which she could plainly see from her windows, which she could walk to and almost touch outside her French doors, was terrible. She felt nothing less than being stuck in an ice cave in the Antarctic. All her life she had grown to accept, without ever having thought of it, that help was on the end of a telephone line; whether her family, friends or the emergency services, they were there and she was not alone. And now she was alone.

Fran had kept abreast of everything that was going on via the internet up until the servers seemed to drop, one by one, around the world. Now her internet browser returned the alert "…cannot display the webpage" followed by the pointless button "Diagnose Connection Problems". Of course she had tried that, but at no point did it give the option "It appears society has quickly deconstructed after a pandemic, causing the loss of basic services locally and internationally. Try rebooting or upgrade to Homo Sapiens 2.0."

Fran returned to the TV, which was dwindling in its ability to perform perfunctorily. She switched it on. Networks were showing what news they could. But over the days, workers of all shades, journalists to IT technicians, managers to HR, had all been calling in sick or refusing to come in out of self-preservation. The channels were either dead or running on skeleton staff and relaying news feeds. The BBC News channel flicked on.

"As you surely know, we are struggling to keep broadcasting here at the BBC. We think something like ninety percent of our staff are ill at home, and I can vouch for many colleagues being very, very ill indeed, perhaps near death. It is that serious, but something which you all must be experiencing too. The problem seems to be that all the government offices who we are turning to for answers are suffering in exactly the same way. The speed with which this has happened is breath-taking. In less than a week, the world seems to have fallen apart. The hope is that Public Health England or someone, somewhere, some

government representative, will come forward and explain what is happening and offer some sort of a cure, or at least direction.

"However, even the armed forces and police have disintegrated as their ranks have split. People, understandably I suppose, have put their families and loved ones over and above their duty to their jobs and their countries. In these times of need, people are retreating to what is most important to them. And that has left a big hole as far as authority and organisation are concerned.

"The last we heard of the Prime Minister was two days ago, and suspicions were raised that he did not look like he had escaped catching the virus.

"But what is the most worrying of all is this: it appears, and I say this with the utmost seriousness...it appears that this virus does not end with death. Or at least death does not end the virus. Damned if I know. What I do know is that this is the stuff of fiction, of horror films. Not only are the streets being looted in the absence of any proper semblance of law and order, but we are also facing a new threat. What do I mean? Well, I can only show you this..."

The newsreader, for want of a better word, took a mobile phone from the news desk and held it for the cameraman to focus on. It seemed they either did not have the capability or the knowledge to transfer the data from the phone to the feed. The camera zoomed in on the man's slightly jittery hands as he played a video on his phone.

"This is what I saw on the way here..."

The short video played out through the driver's open window of a car, phone held aloft. There were looters all over the place. It must have been a street near Broadcasting House. Windows were being smashed, mainly of grocery shops, and people were hauling all sorts of goods out. It was as if the London riots had been nothing but a playground fight, Fran thought. She remembered well the London riots, having been up in London visiting her family. It still amazed her how, over such a very short time, parts of London had degenerated to such strife and violent confusion; how communities suddenly imploded or watched as members started thinking as individuals and not as collectives; not ants, but mosquitoes preying on the lifeblood of society, drinking from its social and economic veins.

But this, this was something else. Those who weren't ill were doing much the same as those on the streets of the riot, but they were targeting very different places: supermarkets, hardware stores and the like.

Suddenly, in the forefront of the video, a woman jolted clumsily into view. In the grainy third-hand footage, Fran perceived someone who looked very ill indeed. She could just about make out a pallid face but there was something wrong with the eyes. Definitely the eyes. The woman half-stumbled, half-jogged toward the car that the man with the phone, presumably the newsreader, was in.

"*Shit!*"

The driver pulled his hand into the car, perhaps getting a better idea in real life of the woman lumbering his way. The phone jittered all over the place, as he quickly put the window up, and then returned to the same view from within the closed car window, safely behind its glass. The deranged-looking woman slammed against the driver's window, with force and with what must have been scant regard for her own wellbeing. Her face, to one side, squashed against the glass, was inches away from the camera phone. The face was much more visible now, and it was not a good sight. The eye pressed against the glass, bulging, was heavily dilated, bordering on milky in the middle, and it was very bloodshot, though the colour was not easy to gauge. The face was slightly drawn and very pale. But what was truly horrific, and Fran felt she would never forget this, was how the mouth started opening and closing as if trying to bite through the glass.

"Jesus Christ!" Fran felt herself tense enough to snap.

The saliva, mixed with partially clotted blood by the looks of it, smeared across the window, distorting the grim view. Then the woman started licking the window, the dull and swollen tongue impotently trying to taste the driver's face from the other side of the saliva-tinted glass.

"*What the hell are you doing? Are you fucking mental?*" screamed the driver. The image spun as the camera was dropped on to the passenger seat.

The newsreader in the studio pulled his phone back, and turned it off before setting it down on the desk.

"*What does this mean? I don't know. I don't know if this woman was trying to…to…get me but I can pretty much guess that this was a result of her illness, of the virus, and I can pretty much guess she was contagious and I can pretty much guess I didn't want to be anywhere near her. Given that no one seems to be forthcoming with any kind of official information since, I imagine, most people in power or in key positions appear to have this thing, I don't know what to do. There are a number of us here at Broadcasting House who know a thing or two about TV, but we've got families to get to, and we don't know how long power is going to keep going. My guess is that, if there are any decisions being made, that power will be redirected to where it is most needed. Fewer and fewer BBC workers are returning with each passing hour.*"

METAMORPHOSIS

Fran heard a loud booming crash and the sound of glass shattering, through her open French doors. She stood up from her sofa and slowly moved towards the doors, as if she herself was in danger from something going on outside, below her. She edged to the opening, and peered over the wall of her balcony, still remaining inside her apartment. Standing on her tiptoes to get a better angle, she caught sight of the source of the noise, across the lawn and over the hedges, across the road, and embedded in the convenience store. Someone had ram-raided the store with a silver car. The alarm was sounding. It was the first time she had seen any looting, since there were few shops in her line of sight. However, she had heard things, both from her apartment, and over the internet while it was still properly or partially functioning. In fact, she was fairly surprised that it had taken this long for her local Tesco store to be broken into. And broken into it now was. The alarm had the feeling, Fran imagined, of some modern *Titanic*'s PA system as the ship went down, falling on deaf ears, no help forthcoming.

Fran was unsure what to think about the looting taking place in front of her. Her mother, now on her own, no doubt, in a hospital in a quickly degenerating society, was a very religious woman, and Fran had been brought up in Bristol in that context. She had never felt the urge to get involved with any even remotely dubious members of her peers at school or college. She had decided not to go to university, instead working at a local newspaper. But neither in her work, nor at school, had she been particularly involved with anything untoward. Yes, the odd case of under-aged drinking and pot-smoking like most everybody else in this day and age. Fran had reported on the London riots and how they affected Bristol, especially with regard to the "ethnicity dimension" as her editor liked to call it. Or "you're black, and this story involves things to do with black people," as she translated it, since she was the only woman of colour in the offices until she left to cope with her agoraphobia. Freelancing from home was tough when you only had the internet and your own experiences to draw on. You could only get so many Skype interviews…

No, Fran had been, and still was, very respectful of the law. She had thought about this recently, wondering whether this was something she had rationally arrived at, or whether it had rubbed off on her from her parental influences over the years. Or, indeed, whether she was just the sort of person, with just that sort of personality (given to her by her parents) who respected rules. Nature/nurture. The endless quarrel. Or were they just bedfellows, Fran had thought, a Richard Burton and

Elizabeth Taylor? True co-dependent lovers who often drunkenly fought. In fact, Fran had come to question much about herself, her life, society and her place in it, ever since she had been cooped up in her flat. Which itself was an idea she had questioned. Had she been cooped up here by external forces, or was she the one who was doing the cooping?

Fran refocused. There must have been one or more people already out of the car and inside, helping themselves to whatever they wanted. Then, sprinting across the lawn and running under the balcony vista toward the car, were two men. Neighbours, maybe. And then a woman joined in, running from up the street and past the apartment to the left of Fran's. A few more from here and there, bags in hand, joined in. The floodgates were open and the Tesco store was being emptied. Visions from the London riots revisited her mind. Fran was reminded of a piece she had written on large supermarket chains insidiously milking the hearts out of communities, preying on small independent stores. Now this convenience store victim was being mercilessly set upon by those it supposedly served, in a bizarre reversal of fortune.

Among the variety of looters, from the direction of her own apartment block, there shambled the man whom she had seen a few days before, looking worse for wear, even more so than before. His clothes appeared to be the same, though dirtier; his skin paler. In his ill state, it appeared that he wanted a piece of the looting action, his own groceries for survival. Perhaps he was getting better, thought Fran.

After he had worked his way across the lawn, through the open gate and towards the wailing shop, he started to pick up his shuffling speed. Someone with a backpack full of stolen goods, emerged from the shop and vaulted the car which was blocking the broken entrance. As he landed on the other side of the car he set off running past the ill-looking person whom Fran had been analysing. Just as the looter passed the scruffy figure, the figure lurched to the right toward the looter, his right arm outstretched as if to grab at the newly minted criminal. The looter dodged, but stopped, turned to the lurching person and starting saying something, one arm flailing as to remonstrate, "Hey! What are you doing?" The lurcher, as if he were some deranged security guard, made for the looter; the looter backed off and shouted something, turning on his heels and sprinting away.

The lurcher made as if to follow him, but then halted and turned, looking at Tescos emitting the loud alarm, a true Siren. He stumbled toward the car. Fran watched without being able to tear her eyes away as the lurcher attempted, at first in vain, to navigate the car bonnet in order to get into the shop. After scrabbling for some thirty seconds, he managed to get purchase on the shiny surface and half-crawled, half-slid, over the car and into the shop through the smashed entrance.

Fran pulled nervously at the braids which ran down to the middle of her back, occasionally interrupted with colourful beads. A couple of other opportunist looters joined in, vaulting the car, coming out of the urban woodwork like cockroaches, Fran thought. And then, a minute or two later, one, two, three…the looters exited the store, jumping the car frantically, casting panicky looks back at the store front. Fran could hear from the distance shouts like "What the fuck is going on?" and "What the hell is he doing?" And then the looters seemed to pour out, the last one just getting on to the bonnet when the hand and dishevelled arm of the lurching man followed him, trying to grab his leg. Failing, the chasing, shambling thing again tried to negotiate the car bonnet with some eventual success as the looters looked on, some with their hands on their heads. This, this…*thing* seemed intent on attacking these onlookers. As it stumbled forward, seeming to arbitrarily focus on one of the looters, the looters scattered, like woodlice after a brick had been lifted from behind the shed. And then, to Fran's fascination and following shock, another body came into view, falling through the shop opening and against the silver car. It looked like one of the first looters who had entered, a man in his late thirties, perhaps, dressed in a white t-shirt and jeans. Except the T-shirt was no longer white, being drenched in blood streaming from wounds both on his back and his neck. His right hand was trying to clasp the wound while his left was outstretched over the far side of the bonnet as if beckoning for help.

The man slumped down, out of Fran's view, behind the car. Fran turned her attention to the rest of the looters, who had all but disappeared, with the lurching person chasing them off down the road.

What the hell was going on? What *was* this?

Things were buzzing around Fran's head: snippets of film, ideas, confusion. Her mind was agog with all of the sensory stimuli she had borne witness to, all playing out to the music of that penetrating alarm. And yet there was no response from anything that resembled authority. Had everything broken down *this* fast? Was it *really* too much to ask that anyone who gave a toss could come to the assistance of these people, of Tesco, of society? By now Fran was at the edge of the balcony gripping the railing, a part of this big open space before her. Her brain was busy computing, too engaged to worry about where she was and how *she* was feeling. She stood there, entranced, for some five or ten minutes until she broke herself out of it and went to retrieve some binoculars from the cupboard. The pair had been her father's, though she never quite knew why he had owned them as she had never seen him use them. There was not much call for a retired railway engineer with a keen interest in playing dominoes with his friends, and little interest in the outdoors, to have owned them. Fran had kept them anyway, sure that binoculars would at some point come in handy. Fran focused the them on the car behind which the injured man had disappeared.

And then she saw it. A hand reached up and over the bonnet, gripping at the edge where it met the panel. Another hand came up, gripping onto metal in what she could make out, or perhaps half-imagine, was a twisted spider-like contortion of bones and joints.

And then Fran's known world fell apart.

In the background, the television warbled.

"...What more can I say? There is no leadership. Everyone seems to be out for themselves... From winter, plague and pestilence, somebody, something, somewhere, deliver us!"

METAMORPHOSIS

15
Greg

The bad weather had passed; it was just the edge of a weather front, which came and went. This boded well for the start of their run ashore, Greg thought. They had been sailing alongside the northern coast of Cornwall, the western- and southernmost edge of mainland Britain, for some hours, on the final leg of their inbound journey to Olding Bay.

The three men were certainly ready to alight, since it had been tiring navigating the Atlantic, though the weather had been kind, which was a blessing. It was mid-afternoon now and they were hoping to be able to moor a little way off the main beach at Olding Bay, in the mooring area which was protected at least a little by the western rocky edge of the bay.

Dale was now at the helm, relaxed and even smiling. He took in a long sniff of the sea air. "I'll be damned if you can't smell the coast, Greg."

Greg followed suit and replied, "Yup. Smells different to me!" Greg smiled a broad and warm smile. "It's been good, Dale."

"What, the trip?"

"Everything. Us, the sailing, the weather. It's all felt right. I feel fresh and alive. Alive with the Holy Spirit," Greg said.

"I'm with you there, Greg," Dale agreed, looking at Greg. Dale had told Greg how much he thought Greg had come alive on this trip, how he had let go of any residual stress he had had before setting off from the States.

Not that Greg needed much lightening up—he was a fairly jovial man in many ways, happy with his lot in life. He had been married once, though he had no children from his marriage, and this had preyed on his mind. Eventually, he had come to terms with the extreme unlikelihood of having any children. The marriage had ended well over a decade earlier, for one reason and another, and it was after this, when he had been feeling very low and depressed, that Greg had really found God, had become *born again*. Now, all these years later, Greg was surer in his belief than anything else in his life. He had spent the best part of the last decade learning about his chosen religion, or the God who chose him, as he liked to frame it. Hours a day, days a week, weeks a month and year, Greg had studied apologetics and arguments to defend his faith. He had even, recently, taken to finding himself online and arguing with unbelievers around the world, half to fortify his own belief, and half to do his duty to convert those without the Christian faith.

Greg, himself, had sometimes wondered whether such a pursuit had made him lose an edge of light-heartedness that he had once been renowned for amongst his friends. His single-minded aim of defining his life in terms of his faith had had a corollary effect of making him more serious than he used to be.

Peter climbed up from the cabin to seat himself next to Dale. "Gentlemen, just a few hours to go and we should be there. Perhaps mid to late evening?"

Dale agreed. "Yes. I think that sounds about right, Peter. My plan would be to moor up in Olding Bay for the night, settle the boat down, get prepared, and then go ashore early the next morning. What say you?"

Greg and Peter both nodded in approval. Greg took a sip from his coffee and looked over the side towards the coast. "Perhaps we can drop in and see your cousin Bill in the hotel and grab some breakfast. I hear the British do a calorific breakfast!"

Peter added, "That may be, but I don't think it will be any more calorific than Denny's!"

"Point taken," Greg affirmed, and patted his belly, thankful that he had been able to shed some superfluous weight on this trip, an added aim of the venture for them all.

The wind was favourable, if a little light, and the yacht was making a fast enough parallel course with the coast such that the crew were, indeed, likely to make Olding Bay by evening. The men passed a pleasant half hour discussing what they were expecting of their stay in Olding, and what they might get up to. Devon and neighbouring Cornwall had a lot to offer in terms of tourist destinations and points of historical interest. All three men were at least a little interested in history, Peter more so, which had coincided with his genealogical research, mapping his family back to its Anglo-Irish ancestry. The men were looking forward to visiting the Eden Project, with its bio-domes containing rich flora.

The men were hoping to borrow a car from Bill, Dale's cousin and hotel-owner, or hiring a car to get about. Of course, they were looking forward to driving on the "wrong side of the road".

"So, Dale, what have you most enjoyed about this journey?" Greg had a habit of starting sentences off with "so". His ex-wife had been an English teacher at the first school he had worked at, which is where they had met. With her traditionalist view on the rules and regulations of the language, she had always reprimanded him for using "so" as a sentence starter, especially given the sentences not particularly being connected to anything previous. Many of the times Greg started his sentences with "so", an image, or feeling, of his ex-wife flashed through him.

Even after all of this time, he had mixed feelings about her. They had been married for eleven years, but the last few years had been difficult as the relationship had become something of a power struggle rather than a partnership, each trying to get one up on the other as if it had some kind of importance of meaning. In all of his reflections over the years since the eventual break-up, Greg had come to realise the futility of such behaviour. The instinctive characteristics of each of them led them to behave in such ways, whether in "competing" over hobbies, and everyday activities like cooking, or over things connected to work and their professional lives; the two had had a tempestuous relationship at times. Greg often remembered sitting with his wife, Julie, and watching the movie *The War of the Roses* with Kathleen Turner and Michael Douglas, which portrayed a pugnacious marital relationship. It had been an embarrassing time as he felt certain the both of them were thinking reflectively about it as they watched, knowing that there were elements of the film which were deeply biographical.

Things had admittedly run their course within the context of their relationship, but that had not meant that he was ready and willing to give it all up; he still deeply loved Julie. Or at least the idea of loving her. Julie, on the other hand, was not so sentimental, and ended the marriage, to him, abruptly and with scant regard for his emotional wellbeing. Well, this was *his* interpretation of events. In any case, he had been left in a bad way, with a hole in his heart and a hole in his life. A hole that was amply filled with and by God.

Dale took a moment to reply to Greg's question of enjoyment. "Well, I guess it is getting to know you guys better. I think that has been really fulfilling and I think it bodes well for the future back in Charleston, don't you think?"

Peter chipped in, "Sure, we've done well. I've really enjoyed the sailing side of things. I'd sure love to keep it up. May this be the first of many trips, gentlemen! Though perhaps the next few will be considerably shorter. As in, day trips!" To which the three men laughed.

With the sun on its downward descent towards the horizon, the men continued their coastal leg, their home run, in the knowledge that life was good.

***

It was twilight when *Grace* pulled into the bay. The sailors tacked around the Western headland and sailed in to the westerly end of the bay, which offered protection from prevailing winds. There was enough light for Dale, as Peter took helm under motor, to hook up the pennant with a boat hook and attach the line, which led to the mooring buoy, to the bow cleat on the yacht. The yacht was moored, and courtesy flag raised, as the three men busily went about securing lines and tidying away sails. After some time making sure that the boat was well secured and ready (they hadn't had much practice at this on the open seas), the men sat on deck with a mug of coffee in hand looking toward the small town of Olding Bay.

"Seems quaint enough, from what I can just about make out," said Peter, peering across the water to the town in the dim, late evening light.

"Doesn't seem to be many lights on, to be honest," remarked Greg. "I guess it's not got much of a nightlife! Still, does seem pretty quiet."

Peter took a swig from his coffee, wiped his beard, and added, "Perfect. A nice, rural, English village. Just what the doctor ordered. I suggest we get cooking, turn in early, and get ashore for an early start."

In agreement, the men finished their coffees and settled themselves into the labour-specialized routine of preparing and cooking their evening meal. Some forty minutes later, they were sitting in front of a pasta meal (not the first they had had) and said grace.

"...thank you for providing us with the strength of mind and wherewithal to land us safely here in England; and may God, through his Holy Spirit, grant us a truly memorable stay," Greg finished.

"Amen!"

16
Fran

The twilight had set in and Fran continued to stand where she had been, watching the horror unfold, though now with a green fleece to keep her warm. What had unfolded had catapulted her into a tumultuous disposition. She had seen people come and go to the Tesco as the alarm continued. She had seen a number of strange figures straggling their way up and down the road, including the bloodied man from the store. She had seen these same people appear to chase others, albeit rather unsuccessfully.

However, she had also seen something which had made her vomit.

Again, it happened at the shattered entrance to the store, where later opportunistic looters had turned up to see what they could get. That same injured man had returned to the shop, but was unable to jump the car bonnet, though through no lack of trying. Some looters had entered the shop and as one young woman, equipped with her fill in bags and backpack, had tried herself to manage the jump over the bonnet with all her acquired belongings, the nightmare truly started.

Fran recalled it vividly as she stood.

The woman, in her mid-twenties and not the most agile, half-threw her bags to the other side of the car and readied herself to jump and land her backside on the bonnet to slide over like some very bad Dukes of Hazzard interpretation. She never made it. She never saw him coming.

From the right side of the smashed entrance, a pair of outstretched hands, followed by the bloodied figure of a man, set upon the woman. There seemed to be only one thing on his mind, that being to bite the woman. *He's trying to bite her! Jee, he is actually biting her! What the…?*

The woman, utterly taken off guard, had no time to react as his hands literally grabbed her face and hair, yanking her upper torso towards him. His gnashing jaws set into her neck and ear. Unbalanced and shocked, the woman fell to the floor and the man fell on top of her, disappearing from Fran's sight. At that moment, a man in a blue sports hoodie and grey jogging pants, running from up the road to the left with looting bag in hand, rounded the car, cautiously glancing about him. Arriving at the bonnet, he jumped up on the car and was then able to see an unfolding nightmare accompanied by some horrific screaming. Fran could now hear her over the persistent alarm bells which continued to sound. Swearing, he jumped down and kicked the injured man in the face, sending him backwards and off of the victim's body.

Fran could just make out the gashed face and neck of the woman, gnawed rapidly in places by human teeth. The erstwhile rescuer bent down and laid his hands on the screaming lady who had turned to face her prostrate attacker. Despite the kick to the face, the attacker rallied almost immediately; on all fours, like a child pretending to be a dog, he scampered towards the pair, face stretched in frenzied ferocity.

The rescuer stood up off his haunches and levelled another kick at the bizarrely acting man on all fours, which again sent him backwards to the floor.

The woman, holding a hand to her wounds, levered herself up from the ground and backed up to the car. As another kick was levelled at the attacker, the woman joined in, and together the two people set upon the blood-spattered man in the white T-shirt who was acting so crazily. In the mêlée, though, the attacker turned victim caught one of the woman's kicks, and like a cheetah sensing a weak wildebeest, this was the opportunity he wanted. Losing balance as her ankle was grabbed through her jeans, she toppled to her right, knocking into her helper, and together they both fell. The attacker was acting as if he hadn't even felt the volley of kicks he had received and promptly fell on to the woman, burying his face in her midriff, as if he could sense that it would be too tough to bite through the jeans of his victim.

C'mon man, get her out of there!

The rescuer regained his feet and grabbed the attacker off the woman, swinging him off to the side with adrenalin-fuelled strength. In the scant seconds he had, he pulled the screaming woman to her feet. She was bleeding from her face and neck, and a little from her stomach as the assailant had bitten her under her black T-shirt. Shielding her from the crazed man, the rescuer backed them towards the car and the woman managed to haul herself over the bonnet whilst the man sent some useful kicks into the psychotic attacker.

Get out of there! Get out of there, for God's sake!

The blue-hoodied man timed a soundly-connecting kick well before leaping athletically over the car bonnet and out on to the pavement. The woman was standing a few metres from the car, looking back at the entrance. Glancing behind him to see the attacker struggle at the car, the rescuer ran over and, speaking to the woman, helped her back up the road and eventually out of sight.

All the while, the alarm wailed.

With a sense of resignation to the predicted outcome, Fran nonetheless retrieved her telephone and again tried to call the police. Through that resignation shone a sense of hope which always seemed to surface, like a dim torch in a fog. It was as if her mind couldn't compute the unfairness of it all, that there must be some kind of just world in which equity and justice prevailed. This must all be happening for a reason, she thought; the books must be balanced. Things which are just crazily unfair don't *just happen*. The universe is Ying and Yang, not just one without the other.

This was the basis of her dalliance with some of the Eastern religions over the past few years, settling on her own kind of Buddhism, where some sort of karma prevailed. And yet, here she was staring at what looked like a nightmare in full swing, and she was speechless and idea-less at how such a state of affairs could come to pass. Fran had felt that her meditation had been coming on well in recent months, and yet, with her heart thumping and in need of calming, she couldn't bring herself to even contemplate contemplation.

Fran's mind was awash with the debris of thoughts that this conceptual storm had brought in. Confusion and mental turmoil prevailed.

Fran had stayed at her balcony, both riveted and perturbed. She had seen the deranged psychopath eventually escape from behind the car to wander the street, up and down, lolloping after looters, until he disappeared underneath her field of view, perhaps escaping between the apartment blocks. There were those about looting, the odd car driving up or down the roads, on its way out of Bristol, or across town to visit incapacitated loved ones, no doubt.

And occasionally, some ungainly figure staggered about, under the influence of the virus, following people or noises. Luckily, to Fran's relief, there had been no other cases of a passer-by being set upon by anyone else. And yet Fran felt it was only a matter of time, since it appeared that there were just a few more examples of such people jolting about the theatre stage that was the view in front of her.

Eventually, Fran turned in and shut the French doors behind her, closing the curtains as if to symbolise an end to the horrific play which she had witnessed. She fell into her sofa, its soft corduroy cushions sucking her frame into them.

METAMORPHOSIS

As she lay there, images of her mother came to her, stuck as she thought she would be, in a hospital bed, with no one to really care for her. Her dad had had an affair over five years previously, running off and living with his new partner, leaving her mum to survive on her own. She had been seriously toying with the idea of coming back to Bristol to live with her daughter, helping her through her mental health problems.

Fran's parents had moved to London a decade earlier due to her father's job, engineering on the railways. Mum worked in admin, doing secretarial work, and was able to get a job working for a cardboard manufacturer in Hackney. Fran had never had a great relationship with her father, and had always been closer to her mother, though her religious convictions, which bordered on fervour, often meant that she had been a more authoritarian mother than she had ever really needed to be. Fran was in no way a handful as a child, and would have been plenty manageable with a softer approach, she had often thought to herself. That being the case, Fran still missed her mother from time to time, and longed for her to return to Bristol to rekindle the flickering familial bond.

Fran pulled the beige throw liberally draped over the back of the sofa on top of her, and drifted off, images of her mother lying solitary and sick in a hospital bed, unloved, flittering through her mind.

17

Jason

"Jason, mate, we need to drop by mine, first. In fact, I reckon we should stay the night, and head back to Olding tomorrow when it's light. We can make some plans tonight to work out what the hell to do," Bevan suggested as they neared his own village of Galston, which sat a mile or so from the outskirts of Olding.

"Yup, I was thinking that myself. We can check the TV, radio and whatever from yours."

The van followed the winding country roads into Galston, where Bevan took it off into a cul-de-sac to park on the driveway to a small tiled cottage. In the dusky evening, Jason could see that the cottage was a far quainter and more impressive set-up than he would ordinarily have given Bevan credit for. It was almost a typical chocolate box scene, although somewhat dark in the evening light. But still Jason could make out the leadlight in the windows, giving it a rustic air, a wisteria growing up and around the front of the house, cut away from the windows, and a well-tended garden.

"Wow, you've got a lovely house, Bevan. Kept that quiet. You're useful with a trowel!" said Jason, genuinely impressed.

It was at that time that Jason noticed that there were no street lights on in the cul-de-sac, or, indeed, anywhere on the way into the village. Other than two cars they had passed, the men had seen nothing signifying human life on the way, and they talked about how it seemed that the desire for self-preservation had actually kept people inside.

The two men were still sitting in the cabin, looking around at their surroundings, when Bevan broke the silence. "I wouldn't mind going round to see if Jacqui and Jim are okay," he said. "They're my neighbours. A bit old, but we get on all right. They were good friends of my folks. I guess I wanted to keep that going. Y'know, in respect to my parents." Jason thought that Bevan must be tired as he was becoming more Devonian again. The "i"s became "oi"s, as if he was a much smaller and decidedly less hairy *Hagrid* from the *Harry Potter* movies. Jason particularly liked it when Bevan referred to everyone around him as "my lover" with that accentuated ending as if he was caricaturing himself, except that Bevan didn't have the wits to be that ironic.

"Let's go inside yours first and think how we can get prepared," Jason added, reverting to his default mode of cautiousness.

The two men alighted from Annie and made their way through the low, wooden front gate and up the short garden path, past several thorny yet well-manicured rose bushes, to the front door. The sound of Bevan's keys jangling and unlocking the Yale lock seemed deafening in the eerie silence of the still summer night. Jason looked edgily behind him. Everything that had happened today had put his world upside down; every reaction to every stimulus was now different as his body was in survival mode.

And still he had no sufficient idea how his family were, or anyone close to him. He was isolated on this inland island world, clouded as it was in panic and confusion.

Bevan proceeded to let them in and switch on the lights. They flicked into life. Jason exhaled a long breath, full of relief, unaware that he had been holding his breath tentatively up until then. The small hallway came into view, its old carpets colour-worn. Some old pictures remained on the walls, remnants of Bevan's parents.

"How long have you lived here, Bev?"

"A few years now," Bevan replied.

Jason looked about the ground floor, moving from room to room. There was a small kitchen, dining room and lounge, all with outdated furniture and furnishings. And in contrast to the well-maintained outside, the interior of the house was messier and in better keeping with Bevan's exterior persona. The kitchen was the worst of the rooms, with evidence that it was shown as much contempt as the fire and beans of their recent campsite. Having thought that, Jason did then recall his third-year university house and its complete lack of cleanliness, organisation and general sanity.

"Fancy a beer, mate?" Bevan chirped. There was some oddity to this, Jason pondered, since it was a serious time, requiring some serious thought, and Bevan appeared to be as indifferent to regular emotions as if it were a normal evening before setting off down the pub.

"Umm…noo?" Jason was unsure of his convictions.

On the other hand, Bevan held no uncertainty. He retrieved a can of cider from the fridge and cracked it open. Jason filled the kettle and put it on, hoping that there was some milk that was still within the realms of taste and health acceptability. Looking into the rather pungent fridge, Jason's hopes were dashed, only to be revived by finding some UHT milk.

The two men settled into the lounge and immediately turned on the television. Scouring the channels, they were met with static screens or messages for almost every channel. The Sky and BBC News channels offered a little more, and the men watched avidly, as they took in some clips, news bites, or visuals with a tickertape of commentary below it, which were on rotation. It looked to be a day old, detailing the evolution of the crisis to that point, where everyone was self-quarantined. There had been rioting in some cities, but even that was surprisingly muted; there was not a great show of force from police or armed forces as it appeared that most members of those organisations had put their families and homes in order of priority above that of country, and duty to society. Those in the forces who continued to act for the greater good were used to support key installations and places of strategic significance: nuclear power stations, bases, supply points, key hubs and so on.

The challenge was that no single position had afforded immunity to the outbreak. From Prime Minister to Commissioner of Police, the illness had struck, and this played merry havoc with chains of command.

"Surely it's impossible for this much to have happened so quickly? Surely..." murmured Jason pleadingly.

Bevan replied, "Yeah, it's only just over a week since the flu started getting on the news. That is super-quick. It must be proper contagious, like."

And then the piece of news that really shocked them rotated into use. It was the recording documenting the BBC reporter's experience out on the roads, followed by some other equally amateur pieces, showing sick and seemingly demented ill people out and about, attacking others. It was not live, but still sent shockwaves right through the two men who watched avidly. There were recorded scenes of people ill in bed, looking like death not particularly warmed up, moaning and groaning. Then one scene of similar people in hospital beds trying to attack the health workers, but being restrained; clawing for the camera crews, looking into the lens with their milky eyes set in sunken sockets.

One piece showed a camera man actually being attacked and injured by someone on the street. He received scratches up and down his arm as the assailant looked to try and attack him with her mouth.

A variety of scenes from different places around the UK and world played out similar stories before finally cycling back to where they first started.

"What happened to us must have happened up and down the country. This is freaking mental, man," said Bevan, a strange mixture of fear, shock and excitement in his voice.

"My family. What the hell will have happened to them? All of my friends. Are they ill? Are they...dying, or dead? My sister..." Jason lost himself in thought, anxiety etched across his face, furrowing his brow. "Is this a dream?"

"Sadly not, mate. Look!" Bevan lifted his arm and pinched himself above the wrist. "See, I felt that."

"Yeah, but that could be in the dream. I mean, I could be experiencing all of this in a dream, right. Because this shit ain't real. This doesn't happen. It must be a dream."

Bevan stood up and walked over to where Jason sat, and before Jason could react, he slapped him round the face. Not softly, either.

"Ow! Sod off, Bev!" Jason snapped.

"Wouldn't have felt like that in a dream," Bevan stated, as he returned to his own seat. "That stinging, that isn't a dream sting, that's a flesh and blood sting. And don't tell me you're in *The Matrix* either, or I'll slap your other cheek, you loser."

"That's quite a practical approach to thinking," said Jason, delicately rubbing his cheek.

The television went on cycling through images and videos which appeared to have been hastily uploaded to the BBC network. The two men saw various people interviewed, but no one particularly high in the government. There were some reports speculating that the Prime Minister and much of the government were themselves too ill to act in their proper capacities. But still, those images and scenes of the walking ill haunted the men, visual echoes resonating in their minds.

"This stuff is a day or so old, right? I mean, this epidemic has just taken out the TV networks, and most of the organisations we rely on, right?" Jason asked no one in particular. "It's like it's just gathered pace and momentum. Maybe it's, you know, evolving, and getting more virulent, or something."

"Everyone's been hit so quick and hard, like, that they couldn't put anything in place quick enough."

"Yeah," Jason agreed, "it's like the very people who are needed to put stuff in place have been equally victim, if not more so, to this thing. The country's been crippled."

"What d'you reckon we do?" asked Bevan, turning his head to look directly at Jason.

And then the lights went out, and the TV flicked off. Their world suddenly became silent.

METAMORPHOSIS

18
Vince

Okay, so things had really gone tits up. Really. He wasn't stupid enough, either, to think that life was going to be the same again, at least not in the next half a year. So, what was he supposed to do now?

Vince was sitting in his lounge, in his armchair, decked in sky-blue hoodie and grey jogging pants. In fact, he hadn't changed in days other than his underwear.

In all his pondering about what to do next, Vince had actually made up his mind to go round to his parents. He had a funny way of putting things off that he knew he had to do, things that he didn't want to do. A selective procrastination.

It was getting late, around nine o'clock, and Vince had decided to find out whether his parents were properly ill, as was his suspicion by the fact that they were no longer answering their phones. He picked up his phone and gave them one more try. However, after quickly dialling his parent's number, he put the phone to his ear to be greeted with a dead tone.

"You're kidding me," he muttered as he tried to redial several times, to no avail. Vince chucked the phone onto the other armchair with disdain. He stood up and walked through to the kitchenette, picking up his keys from the side.

Vince was going to take no chances, though. Walking back through into his lounge, sparse as it was with nothing on the magnolia cream walls, he picked his motorbike helmet up from the beige, slightly tatty carpet and squeezed it over his head. He grabbed his thick, dark jacket off a hook by the door and zipped it up. Having opened the front door, Vince paused.

"Fuck it."

He turned around and walked through into his tidy bedroom. Vince had always been tidy, looking after his body, his clothes and anything else he owned. Through school he had always been well-presented, particular about his appearance. This extended to any room he had inhabited. He walked past his bed to the only other item of furniture in the small room other than his tiny bedside cabinet—his wardrobe. Opening the flimsy door to the cheap, flat-packed cupboard, he pulled the hanging clothes aside to reveal a plain wooden baseball bat. He gave it a few practise swings, imagining some hypothetical combatants in his way.

With a newfound swagger, Vince returned to the door to the maisonette and walked out on to the street, pausing to fix his shiny black helmet on his head after locking his door. It was getting toward being a dim twilight now and he peered about to see what was going on. A car sped down the road past him, laden with baggage. The local shop had been well and truly looted by now. The street was eerily silent, bar the sound of a few shuffling sets of feet. There were some pretty ill people moving about on unknown business. Surely there would be people taking advantage of this situation, thought Vince. There was, it seemed, a very strong sense of self-preservation that was keeping an entire nation inside their houses. Those who were well clearly wanted to stay that way. After all, that was precisely what Vince had been doing. Marvelling to himself that Britain had become like a ghost town in less than a week, he trotted past the launderette attached to his maisonette and round the corner to the back of the building. The launderette was the last building on the main street, with another small road making the washing facility a corner building. There, at the back and under the stairwell to the upper flat, was his scooter. He hadn't used his moped since the virus had hit, and was looking forward to getting out and about. His tag would surely fall on deaf ears, alerting no one in the present context of law and order.

His motor scooter was a black Honda, something which he was pretty happy with. Cheap to run and useful. He slotted the keys in, sat down whilst kicking it off the stand and fired it up, placing the baseball bat between his legs. The engine seemed louder than usual in the quiet environment. He pushed it backwards with his feet, in order to drive off and onto the main street. Just as he turned his head to face forward, he was met with another face.

"Jesus!"

It was a woman, probably in her mid-forties. Probably, because it was so hard to tell. She was drawn, looking terribly ill. Her face was so pale it was almost grey, and her lips were cracked, whilst her shoulder-length brown hair hung lank and lifeless. The woman's eyes were dark pits, bags sitting heavily under the discoloured scleras. She was wearing a dark blue dressing gown, tightly wrapped around her, and matching slippers.

"Ex-excuse me, you-young man," she rasped and went to put her hand on his shoulder as if to steady herself. She looked weak. "Help me. I-I'm so weak and I don't remember... remember where..."

"I'm sorry love, but I've got to go. Get yourself to a hospital is my advice," replied Vince with a distinct lack of sympathy or care, struggling to be heard through his helmet.

"But...but they aren't taking anyone in and...and...I don't remember where it is..."

"Sorry, but I've got to go."

With that, he revved up the engine and rode onto the main street, moving away from the centre of town.

As he drove on, a number of things stuck out. There were the odd burnt-out car or smashed shop or broken windows to some houses. It looked like there might have been some genuine burglaries here and there, which remained in need of being cleared up. *Well at least some things are normal, like I was expecting.* Further up the street, as the houses started becoming larger and more middle-class, typical Bristol townhouses, he spotted a few more burgled properties, but also a number of ill-looking people on the road, perhaps in the same state of confusion as the woman who spoke to him. One man even shuffled into the road, disorientated, and Vince had to have his wits about him to swerve in avoidance. It was night time. What were they doing?

After a bizarre and bewildering five-minute ride, and a couple of turns, Vince arrived in a residential area of smaller roads of council houses. Turning off into Laurence Road, he slowed down and came to a stop outside a pebble-dashed terraced house with a discoloured, old looking UPVC double-glazed door. The small postage-stamp front garden was overgrown. Nothing unusual there, as the weeds and grass were asserting their authority over the will of man, fighting with each other for light and nutrients, approaching the height of the chest-high brick wall running down the length of the road, interspersed with gates and gate spaces where gates had once been, some stolen for scrap, others ditched for being cumbersome annoyances.

Vince got off his bike and stood it up, his bat in his right hand. He looked about the dark street with its last remnant of summer daylight creating a gloom which would normally be interrupted every twenty metres by streetlights. It was only now that Vince realised what had made the journey here strangely different. There had been no streetlights. He couldn't believe he had not noticed it.

In the gloom he started to pick up the sounds of the Bristol evening. House alarms could be heard, several of them, in the distance (though none too nearby), as well as a few vehicles somewhere vaguely close. Suddenly, though his helmet, he heard the smashing of a window a few streets away. He turned, unable to make too much out. On the opposite side of the road, some twenty metres away, a door opened. Vince took his house keys out of his jogging pants and cursed in his realisation that he had forgotten his gloves. He didn't always wear them, but should have done today in an attempt to quarantine himself from any unwanted germs. Vince located the key quickly and inserted it into the lock and opened up. The door swung lightly inwards to reveal nothing more than a few metres or so of the thin hall, the width of the door. Vince lifted the visor to his helmet, paused in giving the decision another thought, and then closed it again. He was taking few chances.

Concerned that there were no lights on and that there didn't appear to be anyone at home, Vince flicked the light switch in the hall by the front door. He closed the door behind him and moved down the small hall corridor with its faded flower-designed wallpaper, marginally peeling at its edges, past the small lounge, until he reached the dining room. After flicking on the dining room lights, Vince could see that all wasn't particularly normal. The room was in a bit of a state. Despite their lack of money, and despite his father's slobbish habits, Vince's mother had always tried to keep the house tidy, no matter which council house they had lived in. Vince had always figured that this was where he had picked up his own tidy habits.

Vince moved past the simple sideboard and up to the dark-wood dining table. He shuffled various dirty bowls and paperwork around to look for anything of interest. Nothing.

"Mum! Dad!" His voice deafeningly reverberated in a muffled manner around the interior of his helmet.

There were a few sounds he could just about pick up, coming from upstairs. The floorboards creaked as the noise of footsteps emanated from the ceiling.

"Thank God for that," Vince murmured to himself.

He moved back out of the dining room and into the hallway and the bottom of the straight stairs which led to the dark gloom of upstairs.

"Mum?"

Small padded and uneven footsteps scuffed along the short landing to the top of the stairs. Vince could make out the socks on the feet at the bottom of some bare, chubby legs which must have belonged to his mother. Slowly, they descended the stairs, and out of the darkness appeared at first those chubby bare legs, eventually revealing an overweight midriff clothed in some pale underwear. Each step was laboured and difficult. His mother's legs, as they were illuminated by the downstairs lighting, were discoloured and veiny. Dark purple streaks of lightning broke up the otherwise deathly pale skin. She was wearing her underwear and a thick, green jumper. She must have just got out of bed, Vince thought.

"Mum, are you oka—"

And then he could see her face.

"Shit."

His mother's hair hung shoulder-length, lank and dank around her pale and swollen face. In fact, her face differed little in complexion from her legs. Her eyes had dark, almost purple sockets, and the eyeballs themselves were looking terrible, bloodshot and, well, very ill.

Vince felt to make sure that his helmet visor was still down.

"Fshhhh...I'm...siiii...fshhhhh..." His mother was mumbling nonsense, making low and garbled sounds.

"Mum, are you okay? I mean... Mum?"

Step by step her large body approached Vince before half-sitting, half-falling onto the bottom step. She stared up at Vince, a look of confusion and absence on her face. A small rivulet of saliva escaped from her mouth and dribbled a grim path across the sallow skin to pool at the bottom of her chin. "Fshhhh..."

"Um...Mum, answer me, what's going on? Where's Dad?" Vince was worried, but not really sure what to do. He wanted to help and yet realised that his mother was most probably highly contagious with some kind of virus that he did not want to get. He was immobilised.

Suddenly, the sound of a door, the back door, crashing open against the back porch wall, could be heard through the kitchen beyond the dining room. Vince looked through the doorway to see his father, in dirty, baggy jogging bottoms and a large T-shirt. The bulky man, overweight from decades of sedentary lifestyle, was stomping his six-foot-one body through the kitchen and towards Vince.

"Dad? Hey, what's—" But as his father joltingly careered through the kitchen, Vince could make out that there was something seriously wrong with him. Though his father's face was similar to his mother's, discoloured and veined, it was a good deal worse. His lips were dark purple and his eyes were unseeing, as if they had milky cataracts covering them.

And Vince realised that there was intent in the movement of his father: intent directed at him. The man's arms were outstretched, fingers distorted, twitching and grabbing. The jerking manner of walking made

METAMORPHOSIS

the hulk of a man look like he had something wrong with his legs, like his muscles weren't working as fluidly as they could and should.

Vince backed up, stepping back down the short corridor towards the front door, raising the baseball bat to a poised position. However, the narrow width of the corridor meant that he would not be able to do much with it, not easily. As his father stumbled through the dining room, he started making noises, a mixture of gurgling and growling. Whether it was attempted communication, or just an outpouring of anger, triumph or some other emotion, Vince couldn't tell. His mind was awash with myriad instantaneous thoughts, wondering at once what was going on, what he needed to do, and whether these representations of his parents were, indeed, his parents.

"Dad! What the hell are you doin'?"

His father grunted into the short corridor, obliviously past his mother. In the dim hall light, Vince looked on in amazement as his father's face came fully into view. The skin was pallid, starting to grey, and dark, heavy veins were beginning to show through the seemingly translucent skin over his balding head, and down his cheeks. His lips were purplish-blue and were surrounded with caked dirty saliva. As he came within a couple of metres of Vince, his eyes bulged, grotesque discoloured eyeballs pushing themselves out of their sockets. Worse was what his lips revealed: their parched edges stretched back to uncover teeth which were grimy and starting to darken in what was either rot or actual dirt. Or perhaps both.

Vince had no time to consider any of this given that his father appeared to be about to launch himself his way.

"For shit's sake, Dad! Wha—"

Vince had time to lift the baseball bat up as a pole to keep his father at a safe distance. But his father had come at him with an unexpected force, arms outstretched in front of him as if to grab Vince's very face. The impact of his father's body on the defensively placed bat pushed Vince back onto the closed front door. With some strength, Vince managed to keep his father at bat's length. In a cacophony of grunts, his father's right arm gave a short swipe at him (with little backswing given the tight hall walls) from which Vince pulled his head away. The hand slapped harmlessly against the tastelessly decorated wall, leaving a grubby mark. Then the left hand came at him, followed again by the right. With all his might, and using the door as a springboard for his right foot, Vince surged forward, pushing his flailing father back with the bat.

"Aaarrggh!" Vince's exertion exploded out of him. He thrust at his father, and the bulky frame stumbled backward, falling with a heavy slapping thud. The sound was the bodily impact of Vince's father on his dazed mother's body at the bottom of the stairs.

"Fsshhaaarrgghh! Gerroffsshh!" came the grated warble from underneath his father's body. The push hadn't seemed to dampen his father's crazed disposition. His face stretched out towards Vince, eyes bulging more than before, teeth bared as his arms felt behind him, trying to get purchase on his wife's body.

Vince turned to the door, then turned back to look at his father. "God, man! I mean, what the...!" He swivelled to open the front door and get himself outside. The noises behind him made him twist back to see his father's bloated form stagger towards him along the tiny corridor, grunting with some kind of emotion, or reaction. Vince raised his bat.

The massive downwards swing landed plumb on Vince's father's right shoulder, which exited the threshold first. The impact, delivered with all the strength and precision he could muster, sent his father to the ground. However, no reaction of pain seemed to come from him, and he raised himself unsteadily to his feet, arm hanging, a little more uncontrolled. Vince slammed the bat down on the other shoulder. The same reaction took place. Vince was surprisingly calm, but when his father staggered to his feet, seething with what could easily be interpreted as anger or frustration, as if nothing particularly problematic had happened other than being obstructed from getting something he really wanted, Vince's stomach fluttered with nervous butterflies. The last time he had felt like this was on his first day in prison; he had felt like a big fish in his little pond, his own bubble, the day before. But experiences like that bring you back down to earth.

Vince didn't want to go for the head. He didn't know why, but he didn't. He had no particular love for his father, but smashing his skull in with a baseball bat had never been a priority of his when visiting the family (though he had no doubt threatened him with such an eventuality on occasion). And yet his father, face spitting and bulging, arose again, like a determined boxer on the wrong side of a beating. Vince knew that repeating this odd little dance would not give him enough time to start up the scooter and get away. The next blow was aimed for his father's left kneecap. The bat connected with a sickening crack and his father's leg buckled, biology giving way to sheer physics. But he did not instantly fall. Instead his heavy frame staggered forward and he half-collapsed, half-launched his broad frame onto his son. Vince had no time to pull the bat back for another go. Before he knew it, he was lying on the short concrete path, his father, or what appeared to have recently been his father, scrabbling about on his legs.

Just then, the older man's head lolled up from around Vince's waist and the look changed, as if suddenly recognising his son, or at least clouding with confusion.

Whilst those bulging, dilated eyes were staring toward Vince's face, Vince, grasping the bat handle with his left hand, brought the handle across from the right and slammed it into the side of his father's head. The head cracked to the side, and then returned to its position, teeth bared, its crazed demeanour now fully mastering its features.

Vince slammed the bat handle a second time into the side of the head. And a third. And again and again. Blood started flying out as his defence mechanisms morphed into rage. Soon, Vince's midriff was drenched in dark blood and his father's skull was nothing but a pummelled nightmarish watermelon, as if Tim Burton had taken up fruit selling. His father's body lay limp, pinning his legs down.

The night-time silence was punctuated with gasping breaths as Vince surveyed the scene. He hauled his legs out from under the body but could not bring himself to roll his father over to see his head and face. Instead, Vince pulled his own legs up to his body, holding them tucked in. He lifted his visor up since it was now misted with exertion, and gasped the cool evening air. He looked at his hands: his hoodie and hands were covered in blood. His father's blood dripped freely from them. White-knuckled, he still held onto the bat. The bat with which he had killed his father.

"Fsshhhhttt... garrgggh..."

Vince looked up to see his mother stumbling down the short corridor.

"Oh shitting hell!"

Standing up and grabbing his keys out of his pocket, Vince ran a few short steps to his scooter and managed to get the keys in with little trouble. *Thank fuck for that!* He glanced over to his mother who was still, it seemed, confused. She was looking down at the carcass in front of her, and then switched her view to Vince. By which time, Vince had got the engine going. Sitting on the seat, and jamming the bat between his legs so it rested on the foot area, he revved the engine. Driving off the stand, Vince wheeled the moped around and started to motor off. He glanced back at the confused and deteriorating look on his mother's face with the full realisation that he would probably never see his family again.

Over to his left, a front door slammed open, almost coming off its hinges. A woman ran screaming down her front path. Behind her, a dishevelled figure lumbered on, grunting.

METAMORPHOSIS

19
Jessica

It was now nine o'clock at night and the summer sun had faded to what would normally have been an enjoyable twilight. Cloudy, but warm enough to sit outside for an alfresco dinner.

Nothing could be further from Jessica's mind. For the third time since the early afternoon events, she checked every window and door in the house with an obsessive sense of anxiety. She had pulled the thick curtains on every window tightly shut. Only the lounge light was on, enough to give her at least some sense of warmth and security. It would have been just too eerie to have sat in the house in shades of twilight. That man was still out there and Jessica was not leaving anything to chance. He wasn't getting in, she was sure of that.

Galen had gone down easily tonight, which was a real blessing. It had been hard enough to feed him after what she had seen, let alone comfort him to sleep. There had not been his usual nightly bath, as routines suffered with the most un-routine set of circumstances.

Jessica had spent a few frantic hours moving from one room to another, only sitting down for a short while for a nervous cup of tea. Her mind had been reeling, considering all manner of things, even whether she was living in a simulation. Was she a brain in a vat, a victim to Descartes' evil demon? Was she in a *Matrix*-type world with all sorts of stimuli being pumped into her brain? Because this surely couldn't be real life, it was too…well, bizarre and twisted. It was like a goddamn movie! But after slapping herself around the face a number of times, Jessica concluded that this Bedlam of horror was, indeed, reality, as much as she wished it wasn't so. There was something inside her that sought to click her heels together and magic off back "home". But this *was* home. And she didn't want to be here. But where, then? Her parents? With Mike?

Jessica sat down on the sofa to think what she should do, what she *could* do. Tutting to herself in annoyance, she picked up the phone from the small wooden table to the side of the sofa and stood up to walk over to the desk in the corner of the room. She searched around the random collection of things which had been dumped there over the last couple of days and retrieved her address book. Fingering through the pages, she found Jean's number. She needed to talk to someone and that someone would logically be the other person who had experienced the same ordeal as she had and who seemed *normal*.

Returning to the sofa, Jessica dialled the number and waited. She was not all that confident that the phone lines would still be working. Earlier in the day she had phoned 999 to get hold of the police, or someone, but to no avail (and, indeed, meeting her lowly expectations). She was greeted with the aural delights of a recorded message imploring everyone to stay inside, that the authorities will be helping to keep order, and that everyone was working to their optimal capabilities to remedy the situation.

Now, however, she was hoping to discuss with Jean, well, anything. In fact, she was fairly annoyed that the idea hadn't occurred to her before, although her brain was clearly not working as well as it normally did, she was aware. Jessica and Mike had only moved to the little village of Stanton some six months earlier, in the cold January weather. With the warm summer blossoming, Jessica and Mike were hoping to enjoy picnics in the open air, experiencing their large garden with their newborn son. Mike had even put his hand to gardening to get it ready for the summer months. Perhaps it would never bear witness to a smiling Jessica and giggling son.

The phone connected and sounded for a number of rings. Eventually, and to the vast relief of Jessica's heavily beating heart, someone picked up.

"H-hello? Jean sp-speaking,"

Jessica had probably only spoken to Jean a handful of times and had her number in case of emergencies (something she always liked to do with neighbours).

"Jean? Thank God. It's Jess, from across the way. I didn't think I would be able to get hold of you. Are you okay?"

"Oh Jess, I can't tell you how happy I am to hear your voice. What's going on?" Jean sounded worried and tired and not a little old.

"I don't know exactly, but I'm guessing that the virus is making people ill, and then changing them to whatever we saw out in that car. I've been thinking about it for hours. My husband…" Jessica paused and her bottom lip quivered. She tried desperately to hold herself together. Taking a deep breath, she continued, "My husband works at the hospital, as you know, and he caught the virus and…"

"Oh, my dear, I'm so sorry—"

"…and he told me it's bad. I mean, really bad. And I think this might be a terrible development. I guess that the woman driving was attacked just before your house by her passenger. Maybe they were getting away to somewhere, though she looked pretty ill, too. And whoever that was must have, I don't know, changed, or something. Have...have you seen him since, since, you know...?"

Jean's well-spoken, soft tones answered, beginning to calm, "Well, dear, I haven't. I have locked myself in here and have been too afraid to *look* outside, let alone go outside to see where that thing is. I think I'm safe in here, but you never know. People are good at getting in places they shouldn't, you know."

"Have you got it? Are you ill?" Jessica asked, working out whether the plan she had been rapidly concocting was viable or not.

"I seem to be fine. I hardly get out these days, just to church once a week, and as soon as I heard what was happening on the news," Jean explained, "I battened down the hatches."

Jessica started to explain the plan she was quickly configuring in her head, "I've been thinking, do you want to come over to mine? The place is safe and we can work out what to do. There's food and, I don't know, other people! Well, one of them's a baby..."

"Oh Jessica, that's a wonderful offer. I think—"

An unpredicted pause followed.

"Jean? Jean?"

There was nothing but a dead ringtone. The line returned nothing but a dull beep. Jessica pressed the 'end call' button and redialled Jean's number. She was met with the same monotone. After several more attempts she dialled a few other numbers that she knew and was similarly disappointed.

The phones were down. Was that just her phone, or everyone's? An inundation of a feeling overcame her, a mixture of helplessness and doom.

Instinctively, Jessica stood up and went to the lounge window, drew back the curtains the minutest bit, and peered through the crack into the gathering dark of her drive. She could see nothing much with the added glare coming from behind her.

She needed to get to Jean, to help the older lady back to her house, but it was too late tonight. There was no chance she would be leaving the safety of her own castle. Jean would have to wait until tomorrow.

SLAM!

"AAAHH!" Jessica screamed.

Literally inches from her face was one grotesque, inhuman eyeball, pale grey-white in the middle suffused with capillaries, lacking a deep-red colour in the evening dark, radiating outwards haphazardly to reach the pulpy corners of the eye. The face that had thrust itself onto the window in front of her was that of the man in the car, and the intervening hours had done it no aesthetic good. The blood had dried and caked down the side of the face, which was squashed against her pane. The blood of another human. Well, of *a* human. This thing looked anything but, its skin distorted and splayed terrifyingly on the outside of the window.

Jessica almost fell backwards, but managed to let the curtains fall back together. She stood there, motionless, listening. There was a horrible sound of flesh squeaking across the glass as the face was dragged from the middle of the pane to the edge. And then silence. Deafening silence.

20
Vince

Vince's thoughts reeled through his mind at lightning speed as he raced up street and down road, winding his way around Bristol, taking in the evening sights. His internal monologue was accompanied by a string of unusual and often violent images. People running, others shambling about; cars diving at high speeds, often erratically; windows being smashed; shops being looted.

Chaos reigned supreme.

Driving in amongst these fearful scenes, Vince was acutely reminded of his awesome, engrossing and generally epic video games. But this was a less-than-epic reality. His brain, however, was starting to distort and blur those lines, though his adrenalin and fresh memories of his parents kept him just about anchored in the here and now.

Vince, though he was experiencing the world as a kaleidoscope of (albeit rare) emotions, synthesising the data piecemeal as it was thrust onto his radar screen, was not feeling remorse over the scene at his parents' house. A cold and murky bubble of feelings formed by a mottled history of poor parenting and a disaffected youth had just been popped with shock and violence to reveal nothing but formless vapours, hints of what could have been, but which never came to pass, and which dissipated, unable to be caught, even had he wanted to do so. What was left was the here and the now and the yet to come.

Some ten minutes of driving had passed before Vince admitted to himself that he didn't really know where he was going or what he was doing. He pulled the moped over to the side of the road, next to a small park equipped with children's play equipment. Around him there were otherwise perturbing sounds emanating from a strange blanket of silence as though the night couldn't decide what it was trying to be.

Vince's mind fizzed. *Col. Man, Col. You're fucking ill, mate, aren't you?*

Unfortunately for Vince, there were only a couple of people whom he could count on in life as good friends, Col being the only properly local one. He had come to really rely on Col in recent years in a way that made him feel like his friend was his family. The two of them were like brothers, both of them giving each other what they lacked in blood relatives.

METAMORPHOSIS

It was now that Vince was hit with a wave of nausea; it was now that the pit of his stomach moved in waves of angst, each swell knotting cords of unrecognisable feelings and emotions. These were emotions which he had never remotely felt before, and he was rocked, like a toy boat tossed and thrown in a storm coastal wash.

He knew, he simply knew, that Col had whatever disease this thing was, whatever was crumbling the country around him to its very foundations. The pit in his stomach stirred itself into a cauldron of pain which bubbled and frothed until it boiled into something new. *Anger*. Anger at what, he didn't have the present wherewithal to know. He started hitting his forehead with his palm. The maelstrom was whipping itself into a fury of hormones and chemicals speeding about his veins and body.

"Fshaaarrrghhh."

The sound came from his left, on the other side of the park. Vince turned his head and looked over towards the source. There was what looked to be, in the moonlit gloom, a teenager, perhaps seventeen, in black clothes.

Without properly realising it, Vince's world morphed into a rage-filled computer game. Managing to put the moped on its stand, he swung his head left and right, checking for hazards. His immediate vicinity appeared safe enough. Vince picked up his bat from between his legs and took it in two white-knuckled hands. Stepping off the moped, he immediately picked a purposeful and hurried pace through the gate to the park and in the direction of the oncoming youngster.

The young man was wearing a *Damned* T-shirt above some skinny black jeans. His floppy and unkempt hair fell over some glasses and what Vince could make out was pale skin; Goth pale or sick pale, this boy-becoming-man was in the wrong place at the wrong time, as far as he was concerned. Marching with the hurried pace of a very angry person being driven by his raw emotions, Vince stormed past a horse on a spring, some baby swings, and a domed climbing frame, to raise his baseball bat high over his right shoulder. This was no time to play. The adolescent stared at him with inhuman eyes, mouth parted in a grim snarl. There was an element of incongruity which flashed briefly into Vince's mind, filtered through the fuzzy haze of rage and adrenalin: the mouth, the teeth. This young man, whilst his skin was somewhat discoloured, and his behaviour certainly far from being normal (even for an "emo" teenager), had lovely gleaming white teeth and a good clean mouth. Vince had subconsciously joined dots in his head, founded on a diet of popular culture—movies, TV and video games—and had a preloaded image of what was going on in the quickly devolving environs of the city he knew. However, this kid seemed not too dissimilar from the kid he must have been but a day or two before; a kid with good dental hygiene, and less than 20/20 vision.

The incongruent elements of his thoughts dissipated in an instant as the bat sung through the still air to land a mighty dull-thudding impact on the side of the teenager's skull, sending his glasses flying several yards to land beneath a baby swing, the sensation feeding Vince's already overloaded endocrine system. It was rush hour on Rage Highway, and the traffic was free-flowing, feeding his automatic impulse to repeat the blow a second time. The subsequent contact of wood on skull sprayed thick spots of scarlet, over the nearby swing frame, caving in the skull to the sound of a floorboard cracking under a carpet. The bright red on garish yellow paintwork looked black on white in the evening gloom.

The two blows had reduced the adolescent to a crumpled mess on the ground, flinching and twitching.

There followed a third and final blow to the same destination. Vince looked down at his violent achievement.

"That was self-defence, motherfucker."

METAMORPHOSIS

21
Jason

"Holy shit," Bevan stated, matter-of-factly.

"The power's gone. It's bloody gone. Can you see any light? Is there anything on?" Jason asked hopefully.

"Nothing mate. Nothing," replied Bevan, swinging his head around in the darkness. It was very dark, all of a sudden, with not even the smallest of man-made lights casting their glow on to the world. No DVD player light, no TV standby light, no cable box light. Nothing. When the men's eyes had become accustomed to the unnerving darkness, the faint light of a crescent moon managed to reflect but the merest of glows through the window and off some of the furniture.

"Hang on," said Bevan, as he arose and felt his way around the room, into the small hall and then the kitchen. He managed to negotiate himself to the drawer with the torch in it.

"Let there be light!" announced Bevan, enthusiastically, before walking back into the lounge to shine the torch directly into Jason's eyes.

"Yeah, thanks for that," moaned Jason. "Mate, we need torches, batteries and candles."

"I think there are some emergency candles in the kitchen. We've had them for decades."

Together, the two men gathered some lighting essentials and set a couple of candles up on the dining room table where they sat themselves down for an organisational meeting. There was a lot to talk about

"Okay, so Bevan, what do you think our priorities are? I mean, things are just starting to properly fall apart. We have no power, no phone signal. It seems that the emergency services have gone AWOL, though we might want to check that. We *do* have our basic possessions or access to them. However, we have no idea who of all of our friends and family are ill, and whether for sure everyone who gets ill turns into a mentalist, and whether you die as a result." Jason gesticulated into the darkness with each point.

"Well," added Bevan, "what we need to *get* next and *do* next is, like, what our big goal is. Let's start big and zone in." Jason was impressed with Bevan at rare times, this being an example.

"Alright," said Jason, "I guess we need to work out what is happening officially. You know, what the situation is on the ground.

Then, for me, I'm getting back to Winchester to see my family. That's what's important. I haven't been able to contact them since the other day."

Jason had been distraught at not being able to contact his family since the phones had gone down, having had to bury the emotions deep within the recesses of his mind. He had concerned himself more with the immediate stimuli and associated problems, rather than having to deal with the idea that his family were far away, possibly ill, and (dare he think it) on their way to becoming dead or worse. That being so, he had taken comfort in the fact that they had been apparently fit and well the last time he had spoken to them, though a lot can happen in a few days with the walking ill lumbering around.

Sitting in the near-darkness with his elbows resting on the dark wooden dining table, and with his head in his hands, Jason thought. Ideas, images and words mixed together to form a confusing synaesthetic thought-stew in his mind.

"Okay, Jace, I can see we need to get to Winchester—"

"Look, Bev, you don't need to come..."

"I've got no real reason to bother hanging around here, really. I've got no family left any more, and my mates. Well, they're mates 'n' all, but, well...we gotta stick together, like," reasoned Bevan, looking at Jason over the top of his cider can.

"Have you got the internet—no, that's stupid. We're too late, of course. We have no power... I guess we need to get some stuff together. I wouldn't mind getting back to my pad in Olding, grabbing my things and then shooting all the way to Winchester. It's difficult to know what to need, though. I mean, is this just a temporary thing? I can't get my head around what's going on. It's insane. We've been away and the whole country, the world, has fallen to pieces, and we're not even sure how much it has fallen to pieces, or whether it's going to get back to normal next week!"

Bevan thought a little. "Maybe we'll just have to wing it, you know. Keep pinching ourselves and take every day as it comes."

"I guess our lives have changed. Life has changed. Our environment. And we have to survive it. We have to work out what we need to do to adapt and survive, what this illness does, what we need to do to *not* catch it. *We've* got to evolve. Change our ways. We evolve, or we die." Jason lost himself in thought, his face flickering in the candlelight, Bevan staring at him intently. The gravity of the moment hit them, and silence prevailed.

Suddenly, from somewhere in the village, they heard something like a wheelie bin being knocked over, followed short moments later by a car starting, revving and screeching away down a near street.

As if reading Bevan's thoughts, Jason continued, "And we need to stick to being safe. I reckon we don't react hastily to things and sounds like *that*, right? I mean, I've seen enough horror movies in my time to know we need to make sure we're not overstretching ourselves. We need to stay safe."

Bevan had his final swig and added, "I'm no hero, Jace. I'll be staying indoors tonight, for sure."

"Agreed. You're the most unlikely looking hero I've ever seen," said Jason, looking over Bevan in his Doctor Marten boots, combat pants and bomber jacket, with his balding, bespectacled head poking out.

The two men stayed up for another drink, discussing what they would need, and what they thought was and had been happening. They hypothesised, guessed, reasoned, reckoned and planned. Every so often, the quiet evening was interrupted by odd sounds from the world outside.

Around them, they figured, the world that they knew was quickly disintegrating; order was melting away into disorder. The first act was well under way in this global entropic play in the New World Theatre.

Just before they retired for the night, they set about looking for something, anything, which would give them a sense of safety within the confines of their rooms. Their armoury included a hammer, a crowbar and a hand axe, retrieved quietly from the shed in the back garden.

The day had been long and tiring for the two men. Jason took himself to the spare bedroom and settled into bed after brushing his teeth. He mused that the world was falling apart around him, but it was still vital to make sure he achieved good dental hygiene.

As he lay in bed, random thoughts flashed through Jason's mind before an image took hold. Never too far from his thoughts, his thoughts returned to his previous partner, Catherine. Six years the relationship had lasted. He had wanted children, a house, a secure job. The whole cosy package.

She hadn't.

He first found out about her affair through a friend, who had done the honourable thing, and conveyed his suspicions. After a little investigation, his worries turned out to be warranted. Catherine had started to see a workmate on the side. But rather than confront her, Jason had set about on a warped mission of revenge. *If she can do it, then so can I,* he had told himself. He was never sure whether this was just an excuse to see if he could get together with someone he knew from work, and whom he had for some time admired. As his relationship with Catherine worsened over those months, his mind had erred.

Jason's face contorted as the memories, so different from the terrible things he had seen throughout the day, had just as bad an effect. The relationship had got seriously messy, his plan backfiring spectacularly. The end result remained to this day. He had realised that he had loved Catherine with much more vigour than he had known, had really wanted to make things work.

"But you fucked it up. You fucked it up big time." His whispered voice cut through the quiet with surprising power.

He was here, now because of that decision. His life had changed. He had opted out of everything that was associated with Catherine. Everything. And he was now shacked up with a balding numpty, surrounded by God knew who, with nothing but a crowbar and an axe for good company.

But he was alive.

Maybe, just maybe, that decision, all those months ago, had saved his life. Catherine had done him the biggest favour of all. He was not in London. He was virus-free and Devon-alive.

Jason eventually drifted into a fitful sleep punctuated with uncomfortable dreams as the noises outside invaded his slumberous thoughts, sound effects to an inner horror movie. Gruesome entities with ghoulish grimaces stumbled around his mind uninvited.

22
Vince

Vince sat on the lowest rung of the domed climbing frame. Head in his hands, bat at his feet. His adrenalin had slowly seeped away over a twenty-minute period. Some short distance from where he sat, across the soft-surfaced playground, lay the distorted body of Vince's victim.

Man, what've I done? What the hell have I done? Have I murdered someone? I mean, this is a person, so... He would've attacked me, no doubt about that.

Vince had stood there for some time looking over the body as he felt its life force ebb away with every rivulet of blood which seeped out of the crushed head and into the foam-like surface underfoot.

I did that, he thought, mind a maelstrom of confusion. *But if he hadn't been, hadn't been a fucking zombie, then it wouldn't have happened. So it's his fucking fault. Some government boffin's been pissing about with viruses and shit and made a mistake.*

Vince felt like he had seen this a thousand times before. Of course, he had, in popular culture everywhere. He was continuing to blur those lines between reality and fantasy.

But this was very much for real, this dead body, nefarious government activity or not. Vince returned his thoughts to Col, and he immediately felt a pang, a mixture of grief and anger. Of all things, he suddenly had images of playing on the console, shooting up bad guys, with Col; of a simple existence which had been so rapidly dismantled. Vince was in a bad dream in which he was a protagonist in a violent video game.

Still, he was alive and had racked up a few points already.

What now? Where should he go? Who should he see?

The anger he felt earlier formed a wave of reprisal. His mind quickly cycled through people he cared about, and those he wouldn't normally think about past Christmases and seeing occasionally down the pub. There really were few people that Vince actually cared much about.

Shit shit shit... There is Lou though. She might be alright. Yeah, Lou.

Vince sat there with his moped ticking over, considering the ex-girlfriend whom he had not seen for some time. They had moved on. She had found someone else when he was inside, much to his annoyance. It had felt like an affront to his image. He followed her on Facebook on his phone every now and again, more out of boredom than any real intent. They had never had any major falling out, though the eight-month relationship wasn't the most serious and consistent relationship one could imagine. She was attractive, thought Vince, and thus, without so much as realising it, he wore her well and often. The relationship was, then, a veneer—shallow and for show—and he knew it.

And yet, in prison, Vince had found himself a lot of time to think. Too much for him, as he wasn't quite used to such introspection. Lou often wound her way along the memory pathways of the outside world which he held something like dear. He came to appreciate much more what he had had, and more so when he came out and found he didn't have it any more. There were fireworks, then. Vince was not one to hold back his anger, especially in such an important social scenario.

Still, things had calmed fairly quickly as he soon came to realise, begrudgingly, that she had found herself in a better place with someone else (though clearly not a better someone else, in his eyes).

So whilst she may have been a "bitch" to his friends and closest allies, she was still someone to whom he paid a lot of attention. For him.

Wheeling his moped around, Vince fired it into action and motored off in the other direction. She lived a good twenty minutes across town in Bedminster on the southern side of the city.

She was not his primary concern just yet, however. First, he had to get his freedom back.

23
Jessica

The carriage clock inherited from Mike's parents, much to Jessica's chagrin (it didn't remotely fit the modern style of the lounge), ticked and tocked its way from one time to another; how much time had passed, Jessica didn't know. She had been sitting in silence with the light turned off, up against the wall in the hall outside Galen's room. The only noise she had heard for perhaps five minutes (maybe ten, who knew) other than the infernal clock was Galen's soft breathing.

Jessica looked out at the clock from her seating position. The bottom floor of the house on which Galen's room was situated was fairly open plan, so the lounge morphed into the dining room, which turned into the kitchen in one smooth transition. Where one started and the other ended was open to some philosophical debate, as she had joked one late evening with Mike.

***

"You see, Mike, it's called the Sorites Paradox, of the theory of the heap or beard. Take that scrotty little beard you're trying to grow," Jessica joked, toying with his latest attempts at "metrosexuality" and his being a big fan of male grooming (which didn't always work with his long doctor hours), "If I was to pluck a hair out of your beard, would it still be a beard?"

"Well, I guess so," Mike replied, before taking a sip of pinot noir from a thin red wine glass. He insisted on only having decent wine glasses, fancying himself as some kind of wine connoisseur.

"And if I took one more hair, plucked from your chinny chin chin, would that make any difference?" she continued.

"I guess not."

"So," Jessica went on, "if I continued to do this, there would be no real point at which the beard would definitely stop being a beard. This would continue until your face was nice and bare and we could have a nice kiss. Instead of this bristly insult to my senses!" and she leant over and gave him a lingering, wine-soaked kiss on the lips. "And the paradox is that you get down to a bare face and still apparently have a beard, because at no real point does it stop visibly and definitely being a beard. This is the same for a heap of grain, or with ages."

"Uh-huh. I think I get it. What do you mean with ages?" asked Mike, a little interested.

"Well, imagine an adolescent. At sixteen they can have sex; at eighteen they can vote, right? Well, what's the difference between a kid at seventeen years, three hundred and sixty-four days, twenty-three hours, fifty-nine minutes and fifty-nine seconds, and that same kid one second later?"

"Not a lot."

Jessica's eyes gleamed, as they often did when explaining such philosophical nuances, at which Mike sometimes glazed over (apart from when concerning bioethics and medicine). "There is no difference. But humans need to have rules, and a workable society, so we draw arbitrary lines and label them, but they don't really exist, those labels. The lines and properties are fuzzy. There is no difference between the kid and the adult one second later, but now they have the ability to legally vote! At some point you get a beard—it's fuzzy… Ha! That's a joke! Get it?"

"Hmm?"

"You know, fuzzy logic with no definite yes or no, here and there, and fuzzy. Like a beard! Dammit, I'm hilarious."

"It's why I love you, sweetheart," Mike added, matter-of-factly.

"It's also why there is no such thing as a species in evolutionary terms. Just a long line of transitions which morph slowly and surely. We just draw arbitrary lines here and there and say, 'Look, that's a homo sapiens, and that's not'. But a homo heidelbergensis didn't give birth to a homo sapiens just like that. Dogs don't give birth to non-dogs! And lounges don't have a real border when they turn into dining rooms and kitchens! It's all in our heads."

"Okay, you've officially lost me there. Anyway, I thought only doctors knew long and complicated words. I have also lost the will to live, sooooo…take me to bed and lose me forever."

***

She considered going through to the lounge and putting the clock underneath a cushion, but then thought better of it. The repetitive sound provided some semblance of sonorous civility to what was a pretty terrifying experience.

And then a bang came. Jessica let out a small and involuntary yelp and jolted her head towards the wooden front door. Bang, again. A dull, thudding bang, as if someone was just walking into the door from the outside.

Then silence.

On all fours, Jessica crawled over one of the hall door thresholds and into the kitchen. She scrambled over tiles to the main kitchen counter and reached up to grab a large kitchen knife from the knife block. An image of Mike cutting onions with it flashed through her mind. He would only use the big knife, swearing blind that you should never use "small, crappy knives" to cut things. There was a chef in him somewhere.

Sitting with her back against the kitchen cupboard, and clutching the knife to her chest, Jessica tried to control her breathing, which seemed so loud and desperate.

Tick tock tick tock. Slowly, from the lounge.

As she sat and listened to the ticks and tocks, Jessica wondered whether the intonation raised for one and lowered for the other, such that the tick went up and the tock went down, just as people say it. *Yes, they do go up and down...no, hang on, that's my brain priming me. They're the same pitch...*

Jessica caught herself. *What the hell are you doing thinking about that, for chrissake! God, I'm tired.*

Putting the knife on the white tiled floor, Jessica put her head in her hands, ruffled her hair and rubbed her eyes. *Come on! Sort it out, Jessica.* Though she hated it when people talked to themselves in the third person, particularly when she used to play friends at tennis at school, she occasionally couldn't help it in her own mind. It was like her mind did things to taunt her just because; like when, she often thought, you make a pledge not to think something in your head and your mind breaks the pledge just to spite...your mind.

In a whirl of fuzzy thought, Jessica picked up the knife and walked to Galen's room. All of a sudden, she was startled by the sounds of hands slapping on the lounge window where she had earlier seen the face at such close and horrifying proximity. The squeaking of skin on hard glazed panes was torturously unnerving.

Setting the knife down by Galen's cot, she carefully picked her son up in trembling arms, and bent down to retrieve the knife in a barely free hand. With her family in her hands, Jessica walked upstairs to the master bedroom, each slow step at a painfully slow time, listening for every sound form outdoors. She set Galen down on her bed, put the knife on the bedside table, and went about moving her larger, more manageable pieces of furniture in front of the bedroom door. If that thing did get in, he'd have a job on his hands getting to her boy.

24
Vince

Vince had driven back off to his maisonette for one reason and one reason only: he still had his ankle bracelet on and was more than keen to remove it. It wasn't as if he was naïve enough to think that some outsourced private security company were still active enough and cared that a petty criminal was untagged. It was symbolic. This, in some bizarre way, could be a new start, a rebirth. He really did sense that in a matter of less than a week, Bristol, the UK, and the World At Large had fundamentally changed. It had rather quickly broken.

But he was still here, and appeared to be one of the few people around who had nothing wrong with them. This was his chance to remove what was left of his life that was only a week removed. He accepted that this was rushing things a bit, but in driving through the night scenes of Bristol, with sporadic outbursts of violence, some looting, and a fundamental lack of authority anywhere to be seen, and no doubt more people stuck inside (whether ill or not), Vince just *felt* like things were irreversibly different. There was no quick coming back from this. Even if everyone woke up tomorrow absolutely fine, reordering society and sorting everything out would take months. And no one would remotely care about his ankle bracelet for a good long time. He had nothing to lose and everything to gain.

He felt he had *everything* to gain.

This was a resurrection moment, a phoenix from the flames. His mind was flooded with ideas and plans and things he needed to do. But strangely enough, he had realised that he couldn't do it alone. In many ways, Vince had strong aspects of being a loner. He was outgoing, loud and obnoxious, even, but his refusal to form many close bonds meant that, often, he would enjoy and prefer his own company. But the pull of human cooperation and interaction was suddenly strong. He didn't fancy starting this new adventure, as he saw it, on his own. Bracelet off, and then to Lou's, in the hope that she was free from whatever it was that was rocking the city and society.

Vince pulled up right outside his door, mounting the moped on to the pavement. With a few glances around to make sure that no one was immediately close to him, he dismounted and unlocked the door, shutting it and locking it back up again straight away. He felt along the wall for the light switch and flicked it.

Nothing.

He flicked it again, and then again.

"Shhhhhhhhhiiii…" he exhaled, exasperated.

It was dark inside. Very dark. The night sky was in full pitch darkness, and with no street lights or light sources from any other house or vehicle, there was nothing to illuminate his small abode, especially given the scarcity of exterior windows.

Scissors. Bracelet. Wash hands. Food. Gloves.

Vince felt and stumbled blindly around the room, getting a proper sense of what it was really like to be blind. He remembered when he had been at school, for the Comic Relief annual charity days that many of the schools participated in, one of his classmates, Simon Moores, had blindfolded himself for the whole day. He had required constant help to operate as normally as possible. Vince didn't like Simon as he was one of the clever ones with whom he never had the urge to mix; whether that dislike was resentment for being someone Vince could never be, he was unsure. That said, he had always had respect for Simon doing that, as he, Vince, tried it for a few minutes that day, and it was incredibly difficult. Simon had professed to the class how difficulty and need to rely on those around him had shifted the way he viewed blindness. Now in his flat, Vince remembered his own few moments blindfolded in the class, falling on people for comedy effect, but really knowing how challenging it actually was. Here he was, stumbling on this and that, grappling on to walls, swearing and utterly disorientated.

Vince ticked off his mental list, with eating food being the most bizarre thing to try to do in almost complete darkness; the night-time light through the few windows was about as weak as could be. He had felt his way around the newly stocked fridge, which had a random assortment of looted goods from the shop. He struggled to open and peel back the plastic- and foil-wrapped salami snack before eating it in roughly two bites. The strong aromas and flavours of spices and garlic made him feel nauseous, but he continued working his way through a variety of refrigerated snacks, and gulping down a can of Coke. It was the finest arrangement of food he had had in the fridge for quite some time, and yet he couldn't see any of it.

Vince left the ankle bracelet removal to last. Stumbling to his sofa with a pair of scissors in hand, he slumped back. He carefully inserted one of the blades down the inside of the strap and gnawed away at the thick plastic. They were not designed to be impregnable, since that would become a safety hazard to the wearer. The idea was that, with some circuitry in the strap, if it was removed, or tampered with, it would open the circuit, which would send a signal, via the box, to a control centre, somewhere.

After a few minutes, the plastic unit fell away from his leg. Being free of his virtual shackles, he lay back on the sofa with his head resting on his interlocked fingers in a moment of internal elation.

Memories flooded back to Vince, memories of being released from prison, of that feeling of freedom, of an invisible leaden weight being lifted from his shoulders. It was tainted by the fact that his parents didn't bother coming to pick him up. He had to call his friend Col to drive out of his way to get him. It wasn't wholly unsurprising, but it still hurt, and fostered that growing sense of resentment for his parents that he had nurtured over the months. It had been blossoming right up until that terrible moment earlier in the evening.

Sitting there in the dark, on the tatty sofa, Vince recalled the vicious scenes with bat in hand and winced involuntarily. He had, in his darker moments, envisaged committing violent acts against his father. They had never been close. Vince had grown to realise more explicitly during his time in prison, and long hours lying on his bunk at night, that his parents had neglected him. Yes, he was more similar to his father than he had previously believed, and this realisation had hit him hard. A conversation with an older inmate in prison clawed its way to his conscious movie theatre.

***

Vince picked up the chalk and dusted the end of his cue. "It's just that he wasn't there. He was *there*, but he wasn't...*there*."

Bending down, he took a shot, smacking the cue ball into a group of colours, scattering them about.

"It's the way it is, my friend," said the tall, thin man, tattoos running down the side of his neck. "I had no idea who my father was. None. Just this big absence in my life. My mother couldn't cope, you know. I went off the rails. Same as anyone else in this place. Nothing unusual, you know. Sayin' that, it takes some thinking at times like this to realise what's what. Turns out, talking to me mum, that he was just like me. Or I was just like him. The apple don't fall far from the tree." The man took his own shot, potting a red.

"Eh? Apples and trees?"

"You know, the apple don't fall far from the tree. Me and me dad, we were two peas in a pod. The same. Apparently. An' I never met him. It's, you know, biology an' stuff."

Vince stood with the cue in his hand and thought. He thought about what he knew about his own father, and it was only at that moment that he really made the connections. They were the same. His dad was fatter and balder, but essentially the same. His life, his whole life, he had been doing what he wanted. School had come and gone; jobs had occasionally, for brief periods, featured; a few interests—football and motorbikes—had, at times, been important. And yet, in following what he had liked, in doing what he had wanted, he had still ended up being like his dad.

"Hello! Your shot, mate!"

"Oh! Yeah, sure, Neil."

Neil looked at Vince. "Penny for your thoughts, mate. Me mum used to say that when I was little."

"I was just thinking that you might be right. But then I think of the times I have spent with my dad, long time ago now, and all we ever do is argue. So we must be different." This was more of a plea than anything else.

"That's not difference, mate. That's because you're so similar! I bet that's the case."

Vince miscued and the cue ball hit a red. "Shit, two shots to you." Vince stood back up and dusted his cue again, out of habit.

Neil potted another few reds, pacing about the pool table as he talked. "You know, the way I see it, you know your parents well and you spend your whole life trying not to be like them. You don't know them at all, you end up not being able to do anything about *not* being like them. Either way, we've got a lot to thank our parents for!"

"Thank them? You're shitting me! I ain't gonna thank them. If it wasn't for them, I wouldn't be in here, that's for sure!"

Neil stood up and looked at his cue tip. He walked over to Vince and took the chalk from the side of the table, dusting the tip. "You telling me you haven't got here by doing what you wanted? That your parents made you do the shit you've done?"

Vince furrowed his brow. "Yeah, but…but…" He struggled to think his way out of this impasse. No one likes to take the blame for wrongdoing, least of all Vince. No, this was in some way his parents' doing.

"Maybe..." Vince stammered, "maybe what I *want—that's* because of my parents? I mean, I'm *me*, right, because of *them*!"

Neil was still looking intently at Vince. He shrugged his shoulders and upturned his mouth, turned, and took another shot. "Maybe. If you wanna pass the buck. Your shot."

Vince moved to where the cue ball sat and lined up a simple yellow pot, before moving on to his next shot. "You said it, Neil: the apple don't fall far from the tree. Like father like son."

"The trick is, mate, trying not to be. Look at him. Everything about him," Neil said, "and do your best to get away from that. If you blame your parents for being in here, for not taking you to football practice enough, for not giving you a clever brain, then you need to use that knowledge. You need to recognise when you're being your dad. And stop. You wanna make something of your life, don't give in to it."

"Fat lot of good it did you, Neil. You're here, too," Vince quipped.

"That's my challenge, mate. I might not win, but fucked if I'm gonna give in to it. I ain't coming back here again, if I've got anything to do with it."

***

Vince sat a while longer. *The apple don't fall far from the tree.*

"Screw you, bracelet. Screw you," he said aloud to the unlistening darkness that enshrouded him.

I'm free! Fricking free to do what I want! No one's gonna get in my way. I can be who I want to be, go wherever I want. I am free!

As if some yin was needed to balance his yang, Vince suddenly saw an image in his mind of his father's body. A rush of nausea overcame him, and he grabbed the arm of the sofa. He shook his head as if to physically dislodge the image from its place.

"That was your doing, Dad, *you* attacked *me*. If you'd just stayed upstairs. If you hadn't been ill..."

And then an image of his mother's confused and stricken face barged its way in. "Mum" was all he could muster with a low murmur. In the darkness, an invisible tear edged its way into the corner of one of his eyes. With a wipe of his sleeve, it was gone.

Feeling the sides of the sofa, Vince found purchase to thrust himself up. With his arms outstretched like a zombie, he moved towards the TV, bumping it with his thighs until he felt the comfort of the wall. There was something reassuring and solid about the walls, as if they were his sight, his frames of reference for creating mental images. They were the roads of his internal satnav.

Slowly, but surely, he moved back towards the door to where his assorted gear awaited him.

I'm fucking free!

25
Callum

Bang.
Thud.
Shuffle, shuffle, thud.
Bang, thud.

The awkward discordant musical manoeuvres played out by limb, body and toilet door still retained a terrifying tension in the air, even after an hour.

Go away, go away, go away, go away.

The door was locked, but locked only with the small bolt that most toilet doors have. And sooner or later, Callum reckoned, his mum and dad would be able to work out how to get in. They would rip the door backwards. Luckily it opened outwards and not inwards, he had soon realised, otherwise their combined body weight would probably have broken the bolt, and his parents would have fallen in on top of him.

Callum loved his parents, but right now he wished they would puff away in a moment of unexplained magic. He had even tried to will them away with the power of his mind. It turned out that the claims of some of his books of the unexplained were bogus. Or he had the wrong technique. No, he probably had the wrong technique. Telekinesis worked. Somewhere. Somehow. And with someone.

His parents' murderous intents had developed over the afternoon, culminating this evening in trying to attack him in his bedroom and following him down to the ground floor toilet. He was at least safe for now. His tears were drying, having exhausted their reservoirs.

He had previously thought that being twelve sucked for a whole host of reasons, primarily as a result of being overweight. Callum had got used to being called "Chunk" at school, after one kid had come back from seeing *The Goonies*, where a young fat kid hilariously did the "truffle shuffle", exposing his belly, jiggling about and making silly noises. Callum had not found it hilarious when his classmates shared video clips of the scene and taunted him to stand on a chair and do it himself.

He knew he had let himself down by doing it, too.

That was a year ago, and life had been one annoyance after another.

Callum had spent the last twenty minutes reflecting on the year and had come to realise that he would swap doing the truffle shuffle for this any day, in the blink of an eye.

Sniffing up the last of the evidence of being upset, Callum resolved to being as quiet as he possibly could. He wanted to get out. He wanted to live. This much was clear. He also realised that there was probably nothing he could do now for his parents, who appeared to want to get in, and wanted him to die. At least, if what he had seen earlier that day on the street beyond his bedroom window could be trusted.

Old Duncan from up the road had meandered up the street and tried to attack his neighbour, Peter, as he was loading up his car to go somewhere. Peter had managed to get in, just, but Duncan was a horrible sight as he tried to bite through Peter's coat.

Callum could still see it, as clearly as he the first time, playing in his mind like a viral video on repeat.

No, he needed his parents to be distracted, or to give up their siege. He couldn't stay in this pathetic excuse for a castle forever. He had water from the tap, but presently no light and no food. But he also couldn't trust himself to bust out of the door and past his parents whilst they were banging relentlessly on his exit route.

A waiting game, Callum figured. He had to bide his time, and strike whilst the odds were good.

They'd better get good, or better. Because right now, the odds must be crazy, he thought. Yup, they sucked.

26
Vince

The first part of the trip to Lou's house had been fairly uneventful bar the odd swerve to evade obstacles and hazards, like some three-dimensional Donkey Kong or Frogger. What was distinct was the *feeling* of the place. It was like Bristol had become a foreign or even alien city. It was as if Vince was a third party travelling through the streets; that his vision and interpretation was like a video camera being watched on a TV somewhere else. His brain, for the first time, had become more obviously an experience machine: observing, interpreting and relaying back to the conscious recognition.

In one of the streets a fire had broken out and was ripping through a semi-detached house. But short of a few people looking out of their windows, no one seemed to care as a small, shuffling posse of onlookers gazed, mesmerised by the flames thrusting out their light and heat from the house's orifices. Vince took a wide route around the group, staring at the bizarre congregation of beings as they huddled next to each other. This was the first time that he had seen more than one of these viral victims in the same place, together. It was quite an unnerving sight. He wondered just how many people were huddled inside their houses, scared and yet perfectly fit. Or was it a case of not realising they had contracted this contagious virus? Or, indeed, how many were sitting in their houses knowing they were ill, and seeing those shuffling outside, thinking they would be like that soon enough?

And then, as if by some uncanny coincidence, someone stumbled out of a house. She careered down the few steps, which led to a townhouse sitting pretty above the pavement, and out on to the road and into his path. Hands outstretched, a bedraggled forty-something woman, slender and blonde, struggled out some faint cries: "Help, please help me! For God's sake, what is going wrong? What is going on?"

Vince had enough time to take a similarly wide route around her, staring into her sallow face soaked in sweat and despair, all hopes drained out like coloured sand from a broken sand picture.

As he revved past the distraught woman, she turned her body to face his moving stare, eyes locked on his visored head, pleading…begging.

He drove on, passing some shambling figures moving in her general direction. Vince had a plan and he was sticking to it.

Someone mattered. No one else did.

Lou worked part-time in a hair salon, cutting hair. She had always had intentions of running her own salon, but this was really a pipe dream, the sort of hope most people have—in running their own business—without necessarily knowing how to go about it or having the required skills. The two had known each other since school, which both had left at sixteen, both part of a behaviourally challenging group who were routinely in trouble. "The council just doesn't do enough to occupy us young people" was a common trope which bounced around their peers as authorities questioned why they were doing this or had done that. Whilst there was undoubtedly a large element of boredom thrown into the melting pot of adolescent archetypes, that boredom was often self-inflicted. Finding their own solutions to the boredom of inactivity was not on their agenda. The easy option was always to free-ride on society's goodwill, and face the consequences when they were caught. For them, that calculation paid off.

It did end up, eventually, with Vince in prison, where he had wondered whether he would find himself on the path to career criminality like so many of those around him. Prison appeared to work in one of two ways: it was correctional or it amplified already worrying behaviour. With the confusing social landscape now presenting itself to him, with the rapid, dreamlike, gamelike, movielike crumbling of the structures of society on which he relied or predated, Vince was unsure whether he would need to make that decision in the coming days.

As Vince drove along, he thought again about his predicament, about how long this *thing* would last and whether he would wake up tomorrow and find out it was a drug- and video-game-induced psychoactive dream, where he had advanced through levels for dispatching zombies and had eventually got the girl. And then he had a sudden thought which hit him with not a little force, an urge of overwhelming doubt. Doubt that he really knew anything: what was going on, what he was doing, what he was *supposed* to be doing. This realisation overcame Vince to the point of forcing him to stop at the side of the road and gather himself. He was next to another park, which sat alongside Bristol South Swimming Pool. His moped engine ticked over as he gathered himself from this unique feeling in his repertoire of experiences.

Come on, mate, pull yourself together!

At that point, two men ran past him, with bags and rucksacks packed with things, loot from somewhere. They were shadows, fleet feet slapping and echoing on the road surface as they ran from somewhere to somewhere else.

Suddenly, even through the aural insulation of his helmet, sounds hit him: small ones, loud ones, surprising ones. Vince's senses strangely came alive to the locale and the disturbing orchestra of reality—the brass, wind and percussion sections creating an awkward, fairly distant, cacophony of jarring din.

Vince's alertness translated quickly into a sort of edgy panic, head swinging this way and that to see who or what was advancing. Not wanting to take his chances by sitting still on his metal pony, Vince revved the ticking engine into life and continued on his way past the swimming pool.

There wasn't far to go. God, he hoped she was there, that she was okay.

On the final section of his journey, Vince even passed several cars which appeared to be racing out of the city in obvious haste. To where, who knew; this crisis seemed not to recognise geographical boundaries. He had seen a number of vehicles that hadn't fared so well, crashed here, abandoned there.

Eventually, and without too much threat to his safety, Vince turned up at Lou's house—a tiny terraced affair not too dissimilar to his parents' house. It was a council house provided by the local authority on account of the benefits that she was on, not earning over the threshold with her part-time hairdressing. She shared it with her current boyfriend, Gary. Vince knew little about Gary, but what he did know, he didn't like, informed by his biases that sought to paint Gary negatively as a competitor and a threat. Whenever Gary came up in conversation, Vince turned into the archetypal alpha male, chest puffed, peacock feathers bristling. Even as Vince presently thought of Gary, his heart-beat raised a tad, supplying some extra adrenalin, as if he needed any more.

Vince stopped the moped in front of the house, squeezing it between two cars parked against the kerb. Unsurprisingly, there were no street lights here or lights coming from inside people's houses. There was a variety of noise coming from up and down the street, within houses, often as if someone was walking around throwing things on the floor. In the distance, in the darkened gloom, Vince could make out a figure half-walking, half-propped up by the cars parked along the road in a line, stumbling down the length of the cars, knocking the wing mirrors as it went.

Vince stood up, grabbing the bat from between his legs and putting it over his shoulder, hands now safely covered in thick motorbike gloves. Col had given them to him, though where they originally came from, Vince could only guess. Having walked up the short path, Vince banged a gloved hand on the paint-peeled wood of the front door. The sound seemed deafening, like a pneumatic drill operating in a museum.

Nothing.

Vince banged again. He looked at the downstairs and upstairs windows on the front of the house. There! There was a small twitch in the upstairs curtain, he was sure. Vince banged again.

Nothing. Not wanting to attract too much attention to himself, he lifted up his visor and hoarsely whisper-shouted "Lou! Lou!" There was no response.

The house was an end-of-terrace with a side gate that went into the pokey back garden, overgrown and neglected as it was. The gate, over head-height, was locked from the other side, meaning Vince had to negotiate its height using the wall and the gate post as leverage, whilst holding on to his baseball bat.

She had be better be there, and not just that weaselshit Gary...

Already, Vince's anger was starting to bubble like a sulphurous geyser, ready to blow. Successfully defeating the gate, he moved round to the back of the house. He banged on the kitchen window and the back door, again to no avail.

He knew Gary was in there.

Feeling around on the stone patio slabs under the kitchen window, in the dim, echoey night, Vince searched for something hard, like... *a brick...you beauty!*

With the brick in his hand, Vince looked at the kitchen window at the back of the house, only just able to make it out in the starlit sky, with only a sliver of moon.

Here goes...

There came a resounding, thudding crack as Vince launched an attack on the window. The brick broke in two as the double glazing just about withstood the impact, though a large dented spiderweb of cracks snaked out from the epicentre. The two brick halves fell to the floor. Retrieving the bigger one, Vince gave it a second go. And a third, and a fourth in quick succession, until the glass fully gave way. Leaving jagged glass around the outside, Vince had to call on his trusty bat to finish the job, quickly clearing away the shards with jolting snatches of the bat.

Facing him past the kitchen sink, which was full of unwashed crockery, was a figure dressed in grey jogging bottoms and a black Nike hoodie, not too unlike Vince himself. Vince had met Gary a number of times, always an uneasy and tense affair, and here he was, staring back at him through a perfectly well-broken window devoid of all its glass.

Holding a kitchen knife.

"What…the fuck…are you doing?" snarled the man. He was in his early twenties, with short spiky black hair and a pockmarked face, victim to childhood acne (without which he would have been a fairly handsome man, but with which there was an edge to him).

"You didn't answer the door, Gary," Vince replied matter-of-factly.

"You don't just fucking smash someone's window when they don't answer the shitting door!" Gary seethed in whispered exclamation.

"I do… I did."

The two stood and stared for a few long seconds, bat and knife separated by a wall and some dirty crockery. A duel at twelve o'clock in the South West. The Wild West for the modern times, saloon bar replaced by council house, cowboy boots by Nike trainers, steed by moped. But Bessie, who ran the bar and whorehouse on the side, was nowhere to be seen.

"Where's Lou, Gary?"

"Why the hell do you care?" Gary replied indignantly.

"That didn't answer my question. Where's Lou?"

"Why the hell do you care? She's not here, alright, so just fuck off!" Gary spat.

Vince looked at Gary intently, visor lifted up, just about making out some detail of his face. He looked wan, but that could just have been the lack of decent light. Were his eye sockets dark and sunken? That could be the light, too.

Vince's brain was making some calculations. His heart rate increased. A surge of adrenalin came over him in a tidal wave of energy and anger. Moving a step to his right, Vince slammed his foot, with his full body weight and leg muscle capability, into the back door by the lock. He repeated this again and again until the lock and plastic framing gave way and the door swung in. Gary was standing in the threshold of the doorway into the lounge behind, a murky silhouette against the dark opaque of the front lounge window some way behind him.

"What the hell are you doing, Vince? Have you lost the plot? Do you think this will help you get Lou? Do you? Do you really, you *idiot!*" Gary frothed, seeming to muster up all the defensive anger he could, standing staunchly with knife poised. Vince felt like he was in control; he had a physical advantage, being more toned, a height advantage, and the reach of the bat.

Gary was expecting a reply, but he didn't get one. This offered Vince the advantage he needed as he rapidly swung the bat in the most economic way, given the confined space, towards Gary. The arm holding the knife instinctively lifted to block the swing; the bat cracked violently on to it from Vince's left to his right, sending it sideways against the wall, and the knife flying. Almost immediately, without even a hint of hesitation, the bat came down several more times to leave Gary on the floor, arms protecting his head, body in the foetal position.

"No, Vince, don't! Please don't! She went out to see her parents and I ain't seen her since then! I promise! I can't contact her as there ain't no phones workin'!"

Vince looked down contemptuously. "What's she doing with a prick like you?" he asked, rhetorically, and levelled two more crunching blows of the bat at Gary's protected head. He would have continued the assault, but something clicked inside his head, something which had failed to click the last time he was in a similar situation with a normal human and which had caused him to end up in prison. There was some kind of veto mechanism at work that pulled him back from the brink of continued violence towards this unarmed, broken-armed, badly harmed man.

That veto mechanism didn't stop Vince from the final insult of spitting on him, before stepping over and moving to the front door on the right hand side of the lounge. Luckily, the key was in the lock and he was able let himself out with ease.

Outside again, Vince gathered himself a little and allowed the hormones and enzymes and chemicals racing around his body to chill out. He took his helmet off and sucked in a lungful of evening air, letting it out in a controlled and deliberate manner. Slowly, his heart rate normalised. He stood there listening to Gary, behind him in the house, whimper and move. However, he also heard something not too far away, a stone's throw down the road.

A wing mirror folded back in on itself as the same figure Vince had seen earlier slid along a silver Volkswagen Golf.

"Mmmggh!" It sounded as if someone was gagged and was trying to get out, trying to communicate, as if there was something properly sentient trying to break through. But as he looked over toward the dark figure over the rooftops of the cars, all Vince could see was a man in his forties in a round-necked jumper, an ordinary looking man, lollop along, his right arm sliding over the car roofs. He didn't look all that together and as he caught sight of Vince, Vince looked as closely as he could into his face to try to work out exactly what it was he was looking at. Was this a man? Was it someone who was ill but who might well get better in a few days? Were the authorities going to find a cure?

What the hell was he to do now, the bloke was right next to his moped!

Vince quickly repositioned his helmet on his head and snapped shut the visor. The man was standing behind his moped uttering grotesque mixtures of mumbles, throaty yawns, spits and convulsing snarls. Looking Vince full in the helmet, the man tried to move toward him, without really taking care to move around the tightly parked vehicle. He stumbled and fell over the front wheel of the scooter and both man and vehicle tumbled to the ground.

"Holy shit, where're your pants, man?" Vince shouted from within his protective headgear.

The man below was indeed trouserless and pantless. He was naked from waist down, bare feet and all, and he was sprawling, uncoordinatedly, over Vince's front wheel.

Vince tapped the baseball bat in front of the man's downturned head to get his attention. The man looked up from his prone position. He knew nothing about the swinging violence of the bat-pendulum as Vince's golf swing connected perfectly.

The sight that followed was thankfully largely blurred by the dark night. But the sound managed to travel through Vince's helmet, and was not one he would quickly forget.

METAMORPHOSIS

27
Greg

Dawn broke summer-early, placid and quiet, save for the occasional ravenous cacophony of some soaring gulls, looking to break their fast.

The 6:30 alarm sounded in Dale's forecabin and he sleepily leant over and hit the off button. As was usually the case, Peter was woken by this and stirred himself to his feet to move from his tiny cabin to the toilet. Greg, on the other hand, contentedly slept on, rocking gently in his equally small cabin directly opposite Peter's, his large frame squeezed into the small bed within. Greg had struggled to sleep well, as had Peter, during the first three or four days and nights, before tiredness and necessity had led their bodies to adapt to the new and uncomfortable surroundings. In sailing across the Atlantic, the men had had to work in watches, especially through the night. The Atlantic was a dangerous place and someone had to be in charge. As Dale always said, "Boats don't sail themselves!"

After such a good and long night's sleep, the longest they had all had since leaving the US, Dale managed to kick his legs over the side of the double bunk he was entitled to, and pulled his clothes on. Today was special, though, since he was not putting on his waterproofs and sailing paraphernalia, but some half-decent clothes, choosing some khaki slacks and a thin blue jumper over a white cotton short-sleeved shirt in which to go ashore. The same went for Peter, who knocked on Greg's door with a loud rat-a-tat-tat, before returning to dress himself finally in a pair of jeans and a blue and red checked shirt.

Greg only arose from his slumber properly when he was greeted with the smell of freshly brewed (albeit instant) coffee, delivered to his cabin by an efficient Peter.

"C'mon Greg! Time and tide wait for no man!" bellowed Peter.

Greg muffled a reply from the covers: "They that go down to the sea in ships, that do business in great waters; These see the works of the Lord, and his wonders in the deep."

Peter laughed. "Have you been saving that one up all these weeks? What is it, Psalm...114?"

Greg feigned shock as he sat upright. "You heathen! Psalm 107, verse twenty-three to twenty-four. I think...Thanks for the coffee, I'll be out in a minute."

"Right, and I'm going to check your quote!" returned Peter, as he made his way back to the galley to concern himself with making the breakfast for the crew.

Dale was up on deck, undoing the ropes and lines that had safely fastened the dinghy to the deck of the yacht, just beyond the mast. After efficiently freeing the dinghy from its voyage-long incarceration, Dale flipped it onto its bottom, grabbed the foot pump he had taken out with him, and proceeded to inflate the dinghy to seaworthiness. It wouldn't be long until they set ashore for the first time in some weeks. Once the dinghy was prepared, the coffee had been made, and Greg was dressed and ready, the three men sat down to their morning bowls of cereal and coffee refills.

"All things said and done, gentlemen, I think it has been pretty tough. We've had some interesting encounters with large ships in taking the Northern route," declared Peter.

"It was certainly a tough choice," said Dale, between mouthfuls, "but I think it paid off in terms of time. We were incredibly lucky with weather. Hardly a stormy day, really."

"The end of the first week was pretty hairy, with that weather, but otherwise, sure," added Greg.

"Yeah. I'd forgotten that. Seems like so long ago. In fact, it seems like we've been at sea for months! Well, I suppose it's not too far off two months as it is," said Peter.

"So," Greg said, considering the day ahead, "I suggest we get in the dinghy (without falling in!) and scoot on to shore. I guess there will be somewhere to park the dinghy up? Anyway, shall we have a little wander around before heading up to the hotel?"

The other two nodded, and Dale added, "I've got the printed map so we know where to go. I think, as we've discussed, we should moor up at the marina tonight, over in Dawlend, once we've met Bill and his family and sorted ourselves out here."

"You mean after we've had a darned good lunch!" laughed Peter.

The men finished their rather meagre breakfasts and gathered some belongings into their rucksacks: cameras, wallets and general tourist paraphernalia. Greg pulled on his cargo pants and a navy blue collared sailing sweater over his black T-shirt, with its small ichthus fish emblem on the chest. Small enough not to be overpowering to people whom he would come across, and yet noticeable enough to garner the attention of fellow believers.

Greg had thought at length during the voyage how he would fit God into their foray across the pond. He, as had the others, had done a few days here and there of witnessing on street corners on behalf of his church, but that wasn't entirely his style. He was more into his books, now, and preferred to sit down with people at length, either to discuss theology with them (if they were *on his side*) or to spar with them (if they weren't). He was proud of his faith, and to some degree he wore it on his sleeve (or T-shirt), but he also knew there was a time and a place; he wasn't so much obsessed in an external way, but more so in an internal sense.

The internal/external element to his belief was something he had also been grappling with on his trip. Though he didn't believe in the literal, body-boiling notion of hell (a recent transition of belief), he did feel as though people needed to be shown the way of Jesus to save their souls from eternal annihilation in favour of union with the all-loving God. What he was questioning himself about was how much should he be trying to convince others about this? Where should he stop? And how many others? Everyone? Questions, questions.

Before long, they were all ready to go, and clambered down on to the small boat to row to shore. Dale picked up the oars and positioned them in the rollocks. He felt no need to use the small engine. Today was for rowing.

Dale's two passengers looked at the destination bobbing ever closer ahead of them. Olding's many white buildings were starting to shine in the early morning hazy sun. Peter twisted around and clicked pictures with his digital SLR, pressing buttons and adjusting settings to get his perfect holiday scenes committed to electronic memory.

On the other hand, Greg relied on his eyes. He wasn't a big fan of photographs because, he felt, they constrained your memories falsely to those photos that you took. He preferred to write a diary to document his feelings and emotions associated with whatever he was recounting. He had kept a voluminous account of the last ten years of his life and had been writing up his sailing experiences in the same manner, dedicating a good half hour a night or day, depending on his watches, to the task. His diary, indeed, was packed with his other daytrip belongings in his rucksack.

"The town seems pretty quiet," commented Peter from the bow, whilst looking through his viewfinder, scanning for appropriate snatches of digital inspiration.

Greg glanced at his watch. It was almost eight o'clock. "Well, if I have my time zones right, then I figure it is has only just gone eight, so perhaps the other tourists haven't got up yet." He placed his hand over his eyes and took a good look at the village. The beach and bay were quite open, providing a decent panorama. From east to west it was about half a mile, with a craggy headland out to the right-hand, westerly side, near where the boat was moored, and a lazy sloping headland of flatter rocks curving round to the east and the next set of bays and crags.

"It's more of a village than a town, to be fair," Peter observed as he looked over the mixture of houses and shops and eating and drinking establishments which were arrayed on the front behind the promenade, receding up the rise of the land.

"A pretty place, for sure," added Greg, which Dale took as a good excuse to pause and look over his shoulder at his slowly approaching destination. There didn't seem to be anyone around other than a man taking a walk along the beach.

"Well, I hope the cafés will be open soon!" said Greg. The dinghy was some eighty metres out from the shore still, sitting calmly on the millpond sea. Dale took up his oars again for the final push.

"Would you like me to take over, Dale?" asked Greg, looking to share the work.

"I'm in my stride, Greg, thanks," Dale puffed between strokes, his voice ever so slightly raspy from the decades of smoking he had done before finally giving up a half dozen years previously.

The boat soon came to rest on the shallow sands and a barefooted Peter, camera safely packed in its carry-case, jumped into the cold and gently lapping Devon water. Grabbing the rope attached to the bow in one hand and the dinghy in the other, he tried to haul it up.

"It's a bit difficult with you two Behemoths inside!"

"Patience is a virtue, my friend!" replied Dale as he set the oars inside, careful not to bash Greg's leg. The two inside the boat dipped their bare feet into the water and grimaced.

"It's not the Caribbean, that's for certain!" Greg noted accurately. They all pushed and shoved the dinghy up until it was clear of the high tide mark.

"Are you sure it'll be safe?" Peter asked.

"I guess so. There's nothing inside but a coupla oars. I wouldn't have thought this was the place to worry about things like that," Dale responded, gathering his bag and belongings.

They looked about themselves. The beach was long and unbroken from end to end, the gentle sea lapping lackadaisically close to the high-tide mark. They had brought the inflatable up at the midpoint of the beach, opposite a large café which they were unable to see due to the rising sand and the fairly wide promenade with its reddish tarmac, which extended the length of the beach. The promenade dropped on the other side at various points along the beach to descend in short flights of steps to the pavement and adjacent road, with shops and small streets leading off from the inland side. Near where the men were gathered stood a sign which announced to the world that the promenade was erected in 2011 with the assistance of National Lottery funding.

The men took themselves to the edge of the promenade, lined with large wooden sleepers bolted into the side of the walkway, and sat facing the sea. Peter, like the others, took his shoes and socks out of his bag, dabbing his feet dry and brushing the sand off with his socks, before getting himself ready for walking about the village.

"Are you ready, gentlemen?" he asked, turning to face the buildings which sat on the other side of the promenade, and over the silent road.

Greg, twisting his legs up and over the edge of the promenade, stood up to survey their destination from up close. "Certainly is as quiet as a church mouse here. Lazy Europeans!"

They were standing opposite the café, named "The Happy Starfish", which acted as a corner to a street that took itself off at forty-five degrees to the beach road.

Peter scanned the seafront, and the road with its shopfronts and cafés. "Well, I suggest, my good men, that we walk up there," he said, pointing up to their right, "and check out some of these quaint shops. Maybe there's a place we can grab another coffee in. Would be nice to get a fresh one!"

"It's a plan, Peter, lead the way! You are our rock, after all; now be a rolling stone!" chimed Greg, chirpily.

The men, shoes and socks in place, rucksacks and cameras at the ready, wandered slowly towards some steps down from the walkway leading to the pavement below.

Behind them, some hundred yards down the beach, a figure lumbered, kicking sand awkwardly, in their general direction.

METAMORPHOSIS

28
Fran

Fran slept only fitfully, her slumber interspersed with the scary sounds of reality reminding her of the nightmare which inhabited her waking hours. She tried to sleep to inoculate herself against its dark pull.

Eventually, morning came and Fran was unable to do anything but get up as soon as she properly came to. There were things to do; she was just unsure of what those things were. This was new territory for her, for anyone, she guessed.

She went to make herself a cup of tea. Filling the kettle enough for her cup, she sat it back on its powered base and flicked the switch.

Nothing happened.

She flicked it again.

Nothing happened. Again.

Flick. Flick. Flick flick flick. "Fuck!"

The power had gone sometime in the night while she had been sleeping. That changed everything. Absolutely everything. And yet she knew it was going to happen, like a tsunami following an earthquake. Just to make sure, though, Fran moved about the flat switching on electric and gas appliances to see if there was any reaction, all in vain.

"Goddammit!"

Resigning herself to a lack of power, Fran made herself a blackcurrant squash and sat down with a notepad and pencil to write herself a list entitled "Options". There was something about the scratch of lead against paper which made writing with a pencil so much more gratifying for her, as against the slippery lack of friction of a ballpoint pen. This randomly mundane thought seemed odd to her in the present context, as if she shouldn't be allowed to think of such ordinary things. She turned her thoughts to what she should do in the coming hours and days:

1) *Stay here, wait it out, things get better—NO POWER!!*
2) *Go to London to see Mum*
3) *Find others around here to seek safety with*
4) *Get to police station*

METAMORPHOSIS

Fran quickly realised that she needed to find power, either in terms of energy or authority. She would struggle here on her own, though it could be worth waiting it out for a while. Her pencil tapped nervously at the end of the uninspiring list. Thinking for a moment, she added underneath:

Stay or Go?

Letting out a tired sigh, Fran pushed her chair back with her slippered feet. It scraped across the laminate flooring loudly in the silence of her apartment. Needing to clear her head so that her decision might come to her unfettered, she stood and walked to her bedroom.

Meditation, for Fran, had become a daily occurrence, and a ritual had formed. Fran pulled off her dressing gown and slippers and donned her loose jogging bottoms and a sleeveless T-shirt. She had tried lycra shorts because she had thought that minimal clothing would mean minimal sensitivity to the environment around her. However, she continually felt the touch of her skin on the often colder yoga mat, so she had opted for warmer, more comfortable clothing on her legs. There was a particular order that she did things in before she could get herself comfortable and ready. She had had to work on her flexibility and core strength a little before being comfortable with her seating meditation posture, and now used a small, shaped cushion to make those long periods sitting cross-legged more unnoticeable, with two smaller cushions supporting her knees.

Once in position, with her cushions, on her mat laid out on the lounge floor, and with the coffee table moved, Fran gently swayed from side to side to loosen her back. She brought a soft focus to her half-closed eyes as she laid her tongue in its usual position, resting against her front teeth at its tip. Her breath naturally lengthened as she relaxed, and soon Fran found herself in a more meditative state, tranquil and regular.

And then the disfigured man from across the road flashed into her mind like a drunk in a library. This involuntary addition to her lack of thoughts threw her mentally sideways and in very little time her window of opportunity for meditative clarity had passed. Visions of such dystopian marauders continued until she swore silently to herself and got up.

Putting on her ankle-high slipper-boots, Fran went to the kitchen to grab a glass of water. Just as she finished taking the final gulp, the doorbell rang and a hammering at the door resounded through the apartment.

Fran's heart leapt.

There was no one she really knew these days in Bristol who either knew where she lived or would have the desire to come round and visit her. That was the sad result of her mental health predicament. As she had retreated, so too had the vast majority of her friends and colleagues. For a year or two before the onset of her agoraphobia, Fran had been suffering from fairly regular panic attacks. She went through a progressively worsening stage where her own fears of her panic attacks brought on panic attacks themselves. This cycle eventually debilitated her to the point of not wanting to leave her apartment, and this metamorphosed into having an irrational fear of leaving, and of the places beyond. As she ventured out less and less, the places she did occasionally visit became less familiar and this accentuated her burgeoning problem.

Eventually, she confined herself to her apartment and a small number of relatively nearby places. She got rid of her car when she started panicking on longer journeys, which shrank the radius of her travels to the point that her car was gathering dust and rust.

Over the last six months, Fran had been seeking the help of a psychiatrist on the National Health Service who had felt she was making progress.

However, as the banging at the door continued, no amount of cognitive behaviour therapy could have stopped her from having a panic attack.

Fran's body obliged.

Her breathing rapidly shallowed as the feeling of control left her. Muscles tensing, she slid down the hall corridor, peering at the door, dread washing over her.

"Please, open the door!"

Fran heard the words like they were fighting their way through an aural fog.

Breathing, breathing, breathing...

Fran fought with herself to regain control of her body. The voice from outside her door, a female voice, was oddly penetrating her fog of despair, and within a minute or so, she was able to regulate her breathing to a greater degree.

Breathing...sort out my breathing...

"I know you're there! I heard your TV!"

"Wh-, wh-..." But Fran couldn't quite get her words out.

Bloody breathe properly!

Breathing through her nose, and closing her eyes, Fran fought to normalise her body, and to some degree it worked. Pushing up through her thighs, Fran was able to thrust her body upwards, her back sliding up the wall.

"I can't go in my flat, I can't...and there's someone coming up the stairs! Please!" The voice outside was desperate, pitch rising in tandem with her own panic.

Fran tentatively edged down the corridor towards the door, her back still pressed against the wall, sweat creating a reflective sheen on her dark forehead.

"C-, c-, coming," she managed, low and unsteady.

After what seemed like a small age, Fran managed to calm herself enough to get to her apartment door, a heavy, dark wood-veneer piece from the seventies, equipped with a small peephole. Fran grasped the doorframe on either side of the door and supported herself to look through the peephole.

"Help, he's coming!" shouted the blonde woman, strangely rounded from the fish-eye lens. Fran released the bolt that sat above the door lock and then swore as she realised that the key, which she needed for the main lock, was in the key box at the end of the short corridor.

Shuffling back up the corridor, Fran reached the small white box, and flung open the little door so hard that the box came off its small screw holder in the wall and rattled its way to the floor, scattering its contents.

"Shit!"

Fran scrabbled around and managed to grab the key. She had had a thing about locking the door and returning the key to the box. She was a person of habit. Running back to the front door, she fumbled the key into the lock and twisted, whilst unbolting a further lock. As she pulled the door back, a woman, her neighbour, fell in. The woman, in her twenties and wearing a grey tracksuit, was someone whom Fran had barely got to know in her time in the flat. Her brown ponytailed hair and large hoop earrings swung about as she fell through the threshold and on to the floor. Turning her head to Fran, she shouted, "Close the bloody door, he's com—!"

But before the woman could finish, another body fell through the door and on top of her as she lay prostrate on the parquet flooring. Fran, behind the door, jumped back into the corner, next to the door hinges, horrified at the unfolding spectacle.

The fallen man turned his head to look into Fran's corner. He had greying bushy hair on top of a rough-skinned face, which once might have been blotchy with eczema and weathered through heavy smoking, and was now gaunt through illness, yet coloured with blotches of pallid purples and spidery veins. He wore a loose-fitting white T-shirt with what looked like pyjama bottoms, barely elasticated around his generous waistline, revealing the top of some equally generous buttocks.

Turning back to his prey who was pinned down and shouting, the uninvited guest tried to bite the woman's face.

"Get off me!" she shouted, fighting desperately to keep his face and snapping jaws, with their dropping blobs of saliva, away from her.

Fran stood rooted to the spot, traumatically frozen, though whether in self-defence like a rabbit under the gaze of a fox, or in numbing shock, she would never know.

The woman was struggling, as the man's weight was too much for her; she had no purchase on him, as she only had grasp of his forearms to try to hold him back. With each successive jab of his jaws, the man's face drew closer to hers until he was mere inches from her chin.

Fran's heart was pounding like a gorilla trying to break out of her chest, and her lungs were forcing the air in and out, causing her to pant loudly. She stared as the woman shouted "Help me, for God's sake, help me!" But there appeared to be nothing that she could do.

The man's face eventually fell into striking distance of his victim's, and he gnashed at her chin. The woman screamed, but he had not broken the skin; his teeth were not in the best of shape—brown and crooked where they still poked out from the abscess-ridden gums.

Suddenly, the middle-aged hulk managed to force one of his arms free and his dirty, veined fingers grasped the side of his victim's face. The fingers of his right hand clenched around their purchase, his index finger poking first into her eye socket, and then pushing harder into the eyeball. The woman shrieked with pain and managed to turn her head sideways. The shift in weight caused the attacker to fall forward, smacking the front of his face into the woman's newly offered cheek. Amongst cries and shouts of pain and terror, the man sank his rotting teeth into the smooth skin of the hapless woman, unsuccessfully at first. But as the petrified Fran stared on, hopelessly rooted, his thrashing face and jaws finally managed to break through, loosing a flow of blood from a tear to the woman's skin.

Perhaps it was the blood, perhaps the screams had reached a tipping point, but whatever it was, Fran's body kicked into action from its shocked hibernation. She shuffled the couple of steps between them and raised her right leg, slamming her foot diagonally down onto the man's side, near his kidneys. The body, unsuspecting of the flanking attack, slumped off the woman, who took the opportunity to pump her legs and feet and slide her body away.

The man, however, had other ideas. He grabbed at her legs, encircling her ankle with one of his hands.

"Get off me, you bastard!" the woman shouted, with vitriol in every syllable. Fran stomped her foot down another couple of times and the man's grip was lost. Turning his head slowly, he rested his eyes on Fran, above him, and it was only then that Fran got a full view of the festival of horrors that was his face. And not all of it was due to his present illness and injuries, though his skin pigmentation and the blood dripping from his mouth was enough to give Fran nightmares. The attacker had clearly never had much regard for personal hygiene and oral health, his skin having several sickening looking sores that seemed well-established.

He snarled, and Fran jumped back against the wall, suddenly aware of her own vulnerable position. Scrabbling at the walls, the man raised himself unsteadily to his feet.

Just as he did so, he took a huge impact from the side. The woman with the earrings had taken the chance to run at him with all her remaining strength and rugby-tackle him around the midriff. The man, not expecting yet another broadside, was smashed back through the door and into the hall where he was stopped abruptly by the railings of the stairwell at the centre of the block.

He crumpled to the floor, still entangled with his victim.

Feeling much more in control of her body and surroundings, Fran knew she had to help her neighbour disentangle herself from the crazed attacker, so she ran through the threshold and stomped her foot into the man's chest. This allowed the other woman a split second to get herself on her feet. The two women glanced intensely at one another and tumbled back into the flat, Fran slamming the door shut and locking it as quickly as her panicked hands would allow.

29
Jason

Jason and Bevan both awoke early to the sounds of birds twittering innocently in the gardens around them. Reality soon overcame the sounds from outside, and Jason stretched his still-tired body. There was much to do today, and no real need or desire for procrastination, no daytime television to while away those hours.

Jason was amazed at the number of times he wanted to use electricity: light for the dim bathroom, shower, tea, TV, radio. All of his desires were thwarted. Bevan was already downstairs when Jason got down. The two men sat down to a breakfast of cereal and tea boiled from a pan on the gas stove, which still seemed to work.

"Okay, so…communication is still down since power's out," reasoned Bevan. "But we can see if the radio in the van's working. We need to tool up, get in Annie, and shoot to yours in Olding."

"Do you think we need a new vehicle? No offence to Annie, but she's thirsty and we need to drive a long way later." Jason was unsure that a forty-year-old campervan would be the best transport in a national emergency.

"Well, Mr Newton, I challenge you to be able to make a cup of tea in a fucking Mercedes!"

"All right, Colville. Point taken. But we need to make sure we are stocked up on fuel at all times," said Jason.

"What the hell?" Bevan was sitting opposite the lead-inlaid window which looked out onto the front garden and over and down the road. Towards the end of the road, before it curved round to join the main road, a plume of smoke billowed from a ground-floor window of one of the houses. "Fire," he said calmly.

Jason leaned over to see.

"Let's try the phone again," he suggested, as he retrieved his mobile phone from his pocket and looked to see if it had any signal. It didn't. "Shit."

Flames started to lick the sides of the window across the road. The two men sat watching the house, eating their cereal in silence, frozen, as the fire quickly took hold, and became audible through the window. This reaction intuitively made Jason feel uneasy.

"We can't just sit here!" he said.

"Mate, that would have happened because one of those ill people will have left the gas on or something. If we go and help, you never know what might be over there," Bevan replied.

"Bollocks. I'm going to check it out," said Jason firmly. He stood up, grabbed his nearby crowbar and hammer for good measure, and walked to the front door.

Outside, Jason was met with an otherwise typical summer morning, tainted with the acrid smell of a burning house, wafted on the gentle wind in the cottage's general direction. He trotted to the end of the path and stepped over the low gate, looking cautiously around him as he made his way down the road. There didn't seem to be anyone around. As Jason approached the house, the noise of the crackling fire became louder. The fire was coming from the right-hand side of the house, with the main door towards the left. There were flames erupting out of that first window, which had been left ajar, and he could see them licking at the inside of more windows further back.

Jason ran up to the front door, banging and ringing There was no reply. The wooden door had some misted privacy windows arrayed in a fan at around head height. He peered through them, and was surprised to see movement from someone just behind the door.

Jason tried the door handle. It turned! Pushing the door back, he was buffeted with heat, and then a huge suck of air whooshed past him as the fire demanded its oxygen. His eyes tried to take everything in as he was bombarded with visual stimuli. The acrid smoke was belching from various doorways into the hallway, passing out of the house at the top of the front door, forcing him to bend down. That is when he caught sight of a dog on the floor a few metres away.

"Hey, dog!" Jason called to it, before his eyes reached the back of the dog. Or what was left of it. Just in front of the hind legs, a rent had been torn in the mongrel's rear quarter, bloodily spilling guts onto the wooden floor. Patches of flesh were missing on its sides and back. The dog's fur was blotched red with its own blood, its eyes lifeless, frozen in a stare of disbelief and terror.

"Holy shit!" shouted Jason as he jumped back on to his haunches and raised his hammer. The dog was motionless as smoke distorted the view momentarily.

And then the door budged. From behind it emerged two thin, blotchy legs, intricately veiny and mottled with purple bruising. Jason's eyes lifted to take in the full sight. He wished they hadn't. What he saw was haunting. A half-naked woman in her fifties, with a printed T-shirt sporting various dogs, stuttered into view. She stood there, head rocking, smoke cushioning her wispy body, a veritable angel of hell floating on Satanic clouds. Blood was dribbling off her chin, dropping in thick tears onto her T-shirt, disfiguring a Yorkshire terrier. Her eyes were a mixture of listless milkiness and wild rage, as if there was some fight going on behind them between two diametrically opposed adversaries. The skin of her cheeks was the same colour as her legs, capillaries shooting their purplish venom liberally about. Jason was momentarily rooted to the spot, looking directly at the discoloured genitals of someone who had just half-eaten her own dog. His brain could not compute his world.

As if in slow motion the woman stumbled forward, with half-collapsing and half-jumping on top of Jason. He let out a muffled cry as he fell onto his back, dropping the hammer from his left hand. Deftly, he managed to grab the crowbar with two hands, holding it horizontally against the woman's neck as she fell. The sound of the fire within the house grew louder, but became somehow almost otherworldly, as if it were just background noise.

The woman's ghastly face was a mere foot from his own. She was languidly snapping at him in a vacant manner, as if the lights weren't on and no one was home. With all his might, Jason twisted and threw her sideways so that her back slammed into the doorframe to his right.

This seemed to wake the woman from whatever daze she was in. It was as if a switch was flicked in her brain. Eyes widening, her head turned with a little more momentum and she stretched out an arm to grab Jason's with a vice-like grip.

It was at that moment that a spade hit the woman square in the face, making a loud thwacking sound. Dark viscous blood spattered out and flicked onto the wooden doorframe and wall as her nose was broken and flattened against her face. Jason looked over and was astounded that the impact elicited no reaction from the woman, though she looked like the victim of a bar-room brawl. Jason, on his backside, skittered backwards on his hands and feet away from the intensifying inferno complete with deranged virus victim, past the legs of Bevan, who was standing with spade in hands, ready and more than willing.

The woman looked at Bevan with her strange eyes and pulled her lips back. Blood from her nose dribbled slowly down and pooled in her mouth, coating her teeth and gums. She made a lunge from her distorted position against the door. For a second time, she met the wrath of Bevan's garden weapon, the spade making a hollow clunk as it sailed through the air and struck her on the forehead. She reeled backwards.

"Let's do one, Jace!" shouted Bevan, over the sounds of the burning, crackling fire developing within the house.

"Thanks, Bevan. I mean, I had it covered," said Jason as they jogged back to Bevan's house, glancing now and again over their shoulders.

"Well, we said we needed to, er, tool up!"

"Jeez, Bev, give it up," replied Jason, looking back again. "Shite. She's up and coming."

The two men stopped and turned to see the woman stumbling, bloodied, down her path towards the road.

"Let's get our shit together and get out of here," Jason said, thumbing back towards Bevan's house.

They ran back and flung themselves inside, being careful to lock the door once inside.

"Do you think these ill people can turn door handles and stuff like that?" asked Bevan.

"I'm not sure we want to take the risk. Better be safe than sorry," Jason replied.

They set about collecting a rather random assortment of things, ranging from food to tools-as-weapons; torches, batteries and candles to clothes; bottles for water and everything from the bathroom cabinet to the *SAS Survival Handbook*. It was a veritable camping holiday in the making. Boxes and rucksacks were hastily packed and left in the hallway. All the while, the men ignored the banging at the door. The woman from the burning house had followed them.

Initially, the two had stopped. "Do you think she'll be able to get in?" Bevan had asked, as they peered through the small frosted window.

"No, it seems like she has no real clue about what's going on. It's like she's not really conscious, just a sort of meaty machine following some pretty simple orders. A moist robot. I reckon we can finish packing and work out what to do in a minute," Jason had advised.

It took some twenty minutes for them to organise what they needed. Then they assembled next to their collected belongings to formulate a plan. They weren't, however, expecting the woman pestering their door to be joined by another figure, with a louder thud.

The two men sidled into the dining room and peered through the curtains. The window was a small bay one which allowed them a good view, almost sideways, of the front door. There, next to the half-naked woman with the battered face, was a man in his forties in khaki shorts and working boots, sporting a dark blue T-shirt. His bronzed body had become sallow with the virus, mottled with purplish undertones; his brown bearded face was oddly similar to that of the woman next to whom he was scrabbling, scratching and pushing the door with his veiny arms.

"Um. What now? The van's out the front, so we need to get past them somehow. We can nip out the back and round the side. But then we've got all this stuff to move," said Jason, pointing at the assembled bags and boxes in the hall.

"Right, we have two choices: do them over, or leave the stuff and get more at yours. You wanna be a hero?"

"Bev, I've got as much hero in me as the 'great' England defender, Carlton Palmer."

"Is that a football reference?" asked Bevan.

"Yes."

"No idea what you're talking about." Bevan had never been one for sport. Football or cricket, racket sports or team games, Bevan had been next to useless or uninterested at school, and this had continued to the present day. The nearest Bevan had got to strenuous exercise in the last few years was when Jason, in a moment of charity, had convinced Bevan, a weak swimmer at best, to accompany him surfing. This had been like the one-eyed man leading the blind into a washing machine. Jason, at least, had found the whole enterprise entertaining. Bevan had never been friends with the sporty types at school, dropping out at sixteen and taking up an apprenticeship as a painter/decorator and whiling away the days off smoking weed and drinking cider. Again, this scenario hadn't particularly changed in the intervening decades. Only a hairline recession and small belly boom had changed matters, the core threads of his life remaining constant. Some might say, flatlining.

Bev turned to the assorted luggage and announced, "Grab what you can, mate, and let's run."

The two men grabbed some small rucksacks and jammed them with what they saw as essentials, which entailed an odd collection of tools, implements, clothing, batteries and random electrical goods.

"We'd better fill ourselves some water bottles. We have no idea what is going on with the mains water supplies," advised Jason.

"Good thinking, Batman. We could also fill some things and leave them here, just in case."

Jason thought a little: "Yeah, but I don't think there will be any lack of water, to be honest. But sure, let's fill a few things." And they set about finding what they could: a few empty Coke bottles, even a jerry can from the shed, filling them and leaving them in the kitchen for some potential later use.

"Better to be safe than sorry, Jason!" said Bevan chirpily.

"Listen to you, you forward-thinker!" said the incredulous Jason.

The pair took to the back door to the rear garden and readied themselves. Jason armed himself with a hammer, Bevan with a crowbar. Looking out of the glass pane of the back door, Jason glanced about the garden. It was small, and was surrounded by large shrubs and small trees, such that it was not overlooked. This made the garden a little dark, as the sun was partly blocked by the house and verdant border. Other than the trees and shrubs, there was little to maintain, which no doubt suited Bevan. Like a flash, with complex ideas flickering through his mind's eye instantaneously, Jason thought about the garden; how long it would be before either of them returned here; the uncertainty of the world around them; the idea that there wasn't a great amount of light getting to the garden being irrelevant in the big scheme of things. Indeed, Jason realised, the only relevant consideration for him was running twenty metres successfully to a campervan without being attacked by some viral abnormality. This was the summation of his life. If he couldn't make it to that van in good time, it could all be for nought. It really wasn't important that the garden wasn't overlooked.

"You ready, mate?" asked Bevan, turning to look straight into Jason's eyes, the seriousness of the situation hitting them both hard.

Jason looked back at Bevan. "This feels a bit *Butch Cassidy and the Sundance Kid*-y, don't you think?"

And then the two men ran out of the door, tools and bags in hands, round the side of the house, unlocking the head-height side gate, and quietly running through. The van was parked in the driveway which was on the other side of the house, past the two figures clasping, clutching and scratching at the front door. Jason and Bevan sprinted past the two at the door by a matter of a few metres and got to the van. Bevan had to run around the other side to unlock the driver's door, leaving Jason on the near side, turned with his back to the van so as to be able to deal with trouble.

Bevan threw his bag to the ground and fumbled with his keys. The monstrosities at the door turned around and focused their milky eyes on the escapees. Jason's heart accelerated in his chest and his knuckles turned white on the shaft of his hammer.

"Hurry up, Bevan, you bastard!" he shouted.

Bevan finally got the key into the door and let out a short cry of delight. Meanwhile, Jason had dropped his bag to the ground and stood, legs askance, hammer held sturdily, fist moving ever so slightly back and forth in anticipation. The half-naked woman and the man in shorts were making sounds that were a mix of growl, spit and guttural gargling.

"Hurry the hell up!" Jason shouted as Bevan leaned over and unlocked the passenger door. Jason yanked the door open, caught up his bag and threw it at Bevan. The two figures had already stumbled within a couple of metres. Jason, by the skin of his teeth, jumped in and slammed the door shut behind him as the two viral figures ploughed into the side of the van, into his door. Their fingers, with harshly angled knuckles, scratched and clawed at the window. Then, thud! The woman mashed her face up against the glass, like a bird flying into a window, unaware of the invisible forcefield, not understanding the physics. Her mouth snapped open and closed as she attempted to bite Jason's face from the short distance. Her face and head were squashed further by the weight of the man behind, who was almost trying to get through the woman in front of him, to Jason, as if she didn't exist.

Jason pressed the lock shut on the door.

"Drive the fricking van, Bev!"

Bevan had put the key in and was turning the ignition. The engine turned and died. This was nothing particularly unusual, as Annie was often a slow starter, but for Jason, it added to the panic. He was usually fairly calm in panic-warranting situations. However, this was on the more unusual end of the panic spectrum and he had no frame of reference for being attacked by virally deranged apparent subhumans.

"C'mon, man!" he shouted, slapping his leg with his spare hand in heightened frustration.

"Don't worry, she's fine!" assured Bevan, remarkably nonchalantly given the scenario at hand. And as if in total control of the situation, the air-cooled engine chugged drily to life, her rasping mechanical voice sounding akin to a choir of angels singing "Hallelujah!" to Jason's blood-pumped ears.

The van reversed as quickly as the old engine would allow it and the two assailants fell to the ground as the object of their support spun backwards and away. Jason saw the arms of the two stretching up and towards them as if trying to snatch the van out of their view. To Jason, the sight of a semi-naked woman in her fifties and this other man, dressed and ready to do some building, was wholly bizarre.

Everything about the last few days had been wholly bizarre.

METAMORPHOSIS

30
Callum

Light seeped through the crack under the toilet door. The gates of heaven had opened. All Callum had to do was open his own door to be welcomed into the light of salvation.

Only, he knew this was not the case. Callum was acutely aware that the gentle thudding on the door was indicative of a twelve-hour-long threat. A few minutes of stretching in the confined space had eased some of the muscular pains he had collected after an exceptionally uncomfortable night's sleep, with nothing but a toilet bowl and a basin for immediate company.

The familial company on the other side of the door was somewhat more worrying. He had resigned himself to having to bulldoze them out of the way with the door. If he took them unawares, and they were more to the right of the door as it opened, hinges on the right, then he could push them both behind the door, towards the front entrance to the house. This entrance would ordinarily have been his exit goal; however, the door opening out to the right meant that he would block himself from getting there.

No, upstairs would be his only viable option. He had a plan, concocted during his overnight sojourn in the water closet. Blocking his parents behind the door, he would run as fast as possible up the stairs and into his room. He knew, as a result of an argument he had with his parents several years before, that if he moved his bed over from the wall to sit behind the inward opening door to his bedroom, the door could not be opened. It pushed the bed back against the chest of drawers which rested against an internal chimney stack.

The challenge was being able to move the bed quickly enough, as he had to lift one whole end over the chest of drawers to slot it into place, all the while hoping his parents wouldn't make it up the stairs quickly enough to thwart his plan.

The final stage was getting out of his bedroom window. There was a slanting slate roof from the lounge extension below to negotiate and then he could hopefully lower himself down to the front lawn. He had often dreamed of doing this whilst imagining being a teenager and falling in love with a beautiful girl from school. He had Gemma in mind. She looked so pretty now, and he was sure she could and would only get prettier over the next few years. He often dreamt at night, lying in bed and trying to get to sleep, of crawling out his window to escape the house for a clandestine meeting of romance and mutual appreciation with Gemma.

Of course, Gemma had been one of the classmates who had urged him to do the truffle shuffle, too. There were always difficult odds and obstacles to surmount in finding love. It was in all of the films. And there must be elements of truth to films, right? He had romped his way through his mum's collection of eighties films. She called them *Brat Pack* movies, but he didn't really understand why. There was *Pretty In Pink, The Breakfast Club, Mannequin, Weird Science* and others, too. Each time, there seemed to be unlikely romances which came about after people saw the true qualities in the protagonists. Gemma would see through to his heart of gold.

Or so he *had* thought until yesterday, when his life started turning upside down. He had resigned himself to possibly never seeing Gemma or his classmates again. Not that, on the whole, that was a bad thing. Most of them were people with whom he had little affinity.

Callum erased any thoughts from his mind that didn't affect his immediate situation. He took a long drink of water from the basin tap and readied himself.

"Here goes," he whispered to himself and gently put his ear against the door to listen for his parents.

Without any sounds from outside the house during the night, his parents seemed to have had no need to leave the toilet door and what they knew was behind it. The thudding had subsided to a gentle scraping which had led Callum to question whether they were sleeping, or in a sort of sleep trance. Surely they would still need to sleep? They were human after all.

Listening carefully, he guessed that now was as good a time as any. If banging open the door revealed anyone to the left, then he would quickly close it again and wait for another opportunity.

Counting down from three in his head, Callum took in a big breath and slammed open the door. No one. There was no one in front of him. And there was clearly someone behind the now opened door. He heard, over temples surging with blood, a body collapse to the floor behind the toilet door.

Instinctively, Callum charged out of the toilet to the left. Everything was working perfectly!

That thought lasted about a second. Callum was reaching the bottom of the bannisters leading upstairs when he saw his father in the entrance to the dining room, on the other side of the stairs. His father's face was a grotesquerie of illness and menace. A happy and genial man had turned into a predator. And his own son was the prey. Callum's heart almost exploded. He was caught between the two threats. In a split second, his mind was made up, though his body appeared to be one step ahead; he grabbed the wooden sphere at the bottom of the bannisters, swung himself with perhaps the greatest agility he had ever shown, and launched himself up the stairs.

His father's reactions were not the quickest, as Callum's escape was a surprise. With flailing arms, he fell out of the doorway in an attempt to grab his son. Callum had flung himself up the stairs, rather than running up them, and he was prostrate and scrabbling from the fourth step up.

"Ahhh!" Callum screamed as he felt his father's chubby hand dig into his calf. The boy kicked and kicked with all his panicked determination, causing his father to lose balance and fall against the bannisters. Callum twisted back and used his knees to propel himself up to his feet and up the stairs, his father's hands scraping his trainers as they pumped up to the landing.

He had no time to lose.

Turning at the top of the stairs, Callum bolted along the railings of the short landing to his room at the end, slamming his door open. Once inside, he slammed the door shut again, and set about lifting the wooden bed. With Herculean strength that came from nowhere, he lifted and swung the bottom of the bed, and threw it over the corner of the chest of drawers. It scraped the walls and chest and fell awkwardly at a diagonal.

Damn!

A second or two later, the door buffeted the bed with force, opening as far as the diagonal would let it. This was not perfect. Far from. He would have to do something.

Callum's father's chubby face appeared, grimacing through the door, which could open only so far. Spittle flew in globules.

He could only think of one thing. As if in a P.E. lesson at school in the dying moments of a basketball game, Callum jumped with all his collected might. But instead of slam dunking a basketball in the hoop, he brought his legs into a tuck and, as he came down, extended them both with full force on the near side of the bed. He then fell unceremoniously on his backside, sprawling in the middle of his bedroom floor.

Dazed, it took him a second or two to come around, and when he did, he was utterly relieved to see his jump had slammed the bed into position, sitting neatly along the wall and past the door, jammed between them and the chest of drawers on the other side. Callum stood up and patted the chimney breast that was stopping the chest from moving, as if to say, "Thanks, mate, for being built just there."

The door continued to batter ineffectually at the bed.

It had worked.

Before he set about gathering a rucksack of belongings, Callum took time out of his manic day to congratulate himself by giving his upper left arm a gentle punch with his right fist.

"Well done, mate."

31
Jessica

The chattering birds in the countryside village appeared unaffected by the goings-on both around the houses and cottages of Stanton, and in the wider world. There were worms to get, other birds to talk to, and a busy day ahead full of all the things that they had done the day before, and the day before that, and indeed the many thousands of years before that. A bird's life was nothing if not routine, driven by the consistent waves of time which lapped against the landscape, eroding winter to show the newly formed headlands of spring and summer, before they themselves collapsed, weakened by the tides, into the autumnal sea of the past.

For Jessica, though, nothing was routine, nothing was consistent. Change was well afoot, causing nothing but panic and raised blood pressure. After barely sleeping through the long and tense night, she had resigned herself to getting up with the birdsong and packing bags. What for, she only had half an idea, but pack she did. She packed her old backpack, requisitioned from the loft, an heirloom from happy times spent travelling the world after university; and she packed a suitcase that was mainly clothing and equipment for Galen. Solemnly, she took out her favourite pair of Mike's jeans, his own favourite green Superdry logo-emblazoned T-shirt, underwear and trainers, as well as the jumper she had bought him for Christmas. Before packing them, she smelled each piece. Her heart ached with the painful reminders of her husband. One recollection hit her hard.

***

Jessica looked hard at Mike, studying him. This was her way, and she was aware of it. It was her shortfall, that she had an overly analytical mind. Her friends at university often quipped that she had a mind like a man, which riled her with its over-simplistic and rash generalisation. Now she studied him trying to select something from the menu, wondering what was going through his brain. He always took a long time to decide on his food, not unlike herself. She suffered from this same issue of Burridan's Ass, often stuck equally between two options, whether jeans or a meal or something more important, and being unable to choose through endless deliberation about the consequences. This happened when the ramifications were a close call. Unable to choose from the equidistant foods, her donkey form would starve. Knowing this, though, over the years she had trained herself to be able, in those more equal of options, to lump for one on an intuitive basis, but this had been hard. Indeed, she sometimes tortured herself with the "what if...?" questions which followed those decisions.

Mike only had this with food. He loved his food and would engage in his own torturous decision-making to find his optimal outcome. And she loved him for it. Though he loved his food, he seemed to be able to hide it in his ankles, because the man was on the rake side of skinny.

That was working hard as a doctor for you. Always on the go.

His new green T-shirt, bought only yesterday, fit him well. It was his colour and somehow brought out well the pale hues of his face and his strong, angular jawline. Even though he had to pay a hefty premium for the logo, she could tell he was pleased.

Sometimes, Jessica had to catch herself as she became lost in the throes of analysis. It had been difficult for Mike to open her up emotionally during the early days of their relationship. Despite his medical background and profession, he was the intuitive and emotional half of the duo, Jessica often losing herself to abstract reverie. In fact, Jessica's life had become very much a series of philosophical decisions. *Do this because this is the most rational option.* Mike balanced her beautifully. *No, let's do this because, well, it's bloody awesome.* And yet, when he did get through her conceptual armour, she would often melt like a hard lozenge with a soft and gooey centre.

"What are you thinking, mister?"

"Well," Mike said, as if about to relay an important medical theory, "I was wondering about the ribs, but given the fact that we are going to the musical tonight, I don't want to have smelly, sticky hands."

"They do have basins in the toilet. You are aware of the concept of *soap*?"

"As I was saying, there are the ribs. But also the paella. Now, you know how cosmopolitan I am. Well, I'm feeling a little Spanish today. A little Español, don't you know." His accent left a lot to be desired. Languages were not his forte. "Speaking of Spain and paella, any thoughts on having a baby?"

Jessica was just taking a sip of water, and almost spat her mouthful back into the glass. "Paella's not a good name. I prefer Tagliatelle. Sounds like an Italian Renaissance painter. Anyway, that was random."

"Just thought I'd read your face when I caught you off guard," said Mike.

"And? Did I give anything away? Was it good reading?"

"To be honest, it was a bit spitty," Mike replied. Jessica chuckled.

Babies had been on the agenda for few months now. Jessica was just getting comfortable teaching A-Level philosophy to seventeen- and eighteen year-olds. Mike was very keen to start a family, Jessica was adamant that it wasn't the right time. Mike was always quick to point out that it was never the right time, but thinking like that would lead to species extinction.

Mike looked into Jessica's eyes. "I just think that it'd be lovely to move into the country a bit, to have a few kids. You could be a full-time mum for a bit, and I'd work my socks off. But we'd be together. As a unit. A bigger unit. You. Me. Some small people. I want to start writing the next chapter of our lives together, baby."

Jessica's outer coating melted away to reveal its gooey heart.

***

I love you Mike Russell. Please be alive. Please. Come on cosmos, conspire it to be so! Jessica had spent so many years arguing about the existence of God and gods that even the most unwieldy of phrases were second nature to her. She had always spent an awful lot of time in her own head, effectively talking to herself, having contrived internal monologues, or dialogues and debates with other, often imaginary, people. Her favourite internet meme was of a pie chart which depicted what took place in the shower. It had a tiny sliver of about five percent labelled "washing hair and body" and a large ninety-five percent segment labelled "winning imaginary debates with other people". That always made her chuckle for its aptness in describing her shower reality. Which made her unusual amongst all of her female friends.

Jessica had never been too bothered about things often considered by society as stereotypically female—something which was a result of her challenging every concept, opinion and idea that she thought she had held dear. She had been on a psychological and intellectual journey since beginning her immersion in philosophy, and it had sent her in many a strange and unforeseen direction. Not only did she pride herself on following the evidence to whatever intellectual conclusion was necessitated by the bricks that she mentally constructed out of the raw materials of ideas and concepts, but she followed those same directions in her life, in a pragmatic and very real sense. Intellectually, her philosophy was driving her thoughts and worldviews, but also directing her in her obstacle-ridden traverse through the rigours of life.

However, as a victim to society, she remained, to all intents and purposes from the everyday onlooker's perspective, "feminine" in how she dressed and looked. She often internally challenged herself in her acquiescence to the conformity of society and admonished herself in this light. Whilst continuing to do and dress and act, in many ways, as expected.

This was all paralleled with her approach to eating meat. Jessica had prided herself in trying to be as moral as possible in her daily life. As a philosopher (as she genuinely labelled herself, as opposed to presently being a stay-at-home mum), this was important as it was the bread and butter of her trade. What she ate had a strong moral dimension, and the provenance of her food was important. This included whether it was organic, local, or reared with compassion. Jessica had started eating responsibly farmed meat, and though brought up on a societal and familial diet of meat-eating, she made the eventual move to vegetarianism. She had stopped short of veganism only on account of it being "too damned difficult". This had prompted her to write a paper on the intersection of psychology and philosophy in owning up to being morally imperfect. So often, she had met people who defended eating meat with this argument or that, without realising that they were mainly arguing from an intuitive desire to eat meat (because they liked it) and rationalising their reasons after arriving at that previously found intuitive conclusion. This "dishonesty" annoyed Jessica, and she had promised herself not to go through the dissonance and tension in her mind that created the scenario whereby people effectively lied to themselves, and invented reasons that allowed them to sleep easily.

Whether indeed she was or not, Jessica prided herself on being intellectually honest, though she was well aware that everyone probably did this. Humans' capability to lie to themselves to create harmonious minds, filled as they always are with bias and nebulous mechanisms involved in decision-making and problem-solving, was staggering in its prevalence, she often mused. Evolution had developed the most complex structure in the known universe: the human brain. But the corollary of all that complexity (or the result of millions of years of evolutionary forces) was an extraordinary ability to fool itself before fooling others. Jessica swore by the famous maxim: the first principle is that you must not fool yourself—and you are the easiest person to fool.

With bags packed and placed by the front door, and Galen sorted, Jessica secured some cardboard boxes from under the stairs, and went about gathering food and utensils. She ended with a rather eclectic mix of things that she thought would come in handy: penknives, a hammer, matches, some travel washing liquid left over from a distant holiday.

Now what? Did she have to get all of this stuff and Galen into the car? She needed to get to Jean's and pick her up. Did she leave Galen here whilst doing that? He was safer in there, but if anything happened to her, he would be stuck. Then again, if anything happened to Jessica and he was with her, he would still be stuck. Would it have been easier to get him afterwards, after getting Jean? Two people were better than one.

So she decided to get Jean first.

Jessica had moved into her default logical mode where she worked things through fairly methodically towards the best course of action. She had decided that getting to the car and getting Jean was the primary objective, so she put Galen in his cot.

"You stay here while Mummy goes outside for a little while. Which toys would you like, baba?" Picking up a few teddies and a shape-sorting toy that Galen wasn't yet sure of, short of dribbling over it and putting the corners in his mouth, Jessica left Galen with hopefully enough stimuli to keep him occupied and happy. She also left some halved grapes and a baby cup of very weak juice. She had no idea how long she would be away. Even though Jean's was just across the road, there was no telling what might take place outside her own castle doors.

Jessica stood near the front door in a pair of khaki cargo pants, hiking boots and a faded green hoodie, the knife from the night before in her right hand and her car keys in her left hand.

Knife or hammer…knife or hammer?

Hammer.

She slotted the knife safely in a cardboard box, blade sandwiched between tins of baked beans and tuna. She located the hammer in another box and removed it, waggling it about in her hands to get used to the weight of it. She took a couple of swipes at an imaginary boogieman, then swapped the keys for the hammer and tried swiping with her left hand, before settling back to the former.

Right, where was that freaky bastard?

Jessica walked around the house pulling back the curtains, finishing off in the lounge. There, across the window, were smears of dried blood, blurring her view. Darkened to a rusty brown, the smear seemed to stare at her tauntingly.

METAMORPHOSIS

Jessica's face contorted in disgust.

Putting that out of her mind, Jessica looked about. She couldn't see anything untoward, and so settled in front of the lounge window to inspect the surroundings. Her plan was to run out to the large red VW. It was a fairly new acquisition, moving to having an estate car with its large boot as they now had a child; Mike had claimed this heralded a new era in their lives. *Mike...Mike...*

She needed to get in it as fast as possible and lock the doors. Jessica unlocked it with the remote key from her lounge thus saving her time. Next, she would see if they were safe, and then pack the car with everything but Galen. He would be safest in the cot. After that, she would drive to Jean's house. The problem was that the crashed car was blocking the drive entrance, so she would have to pull up only a stone's throw from her own drive. However, the car was safer than walking, of that she was sure. She figured, unless Jean was looking out of the window for her, that she would have to run in and pound on Jean's door, opening herself up to danger. Hence the hammer. Jessica reasoned that beeping the car horn would probably not be the best course of action.

Much to Jessica's surprise, all sorts of images and ideas had been pumping into her thoughts, collected from years of stored memories of movies and TV series and books and popular culture references. Of zombies.

"Zombies. Zom...bies. Zombies." No, that was silly. Stupid, even. But hang on, what the hell was that person? What the hell was going on? That label made sense to her, because that's what that thing looked like, to Jessica. Yes, he was ill and had a virus and was walking around in dire need of medicine or something. But he bloody *looked* like a zombie. That reference had truth for *her*! Jessica was in danger of losing herself, as was often her wont, in philosophical reverie. Pulling herself back, she thought about something which had irked her when she had watched series like *The Walking Dead* (which she had appreciated for the moral conundrums the characters were drawn into): that they never even mentioned the word "zombie", or even referenced and talked about zombie movies they all would have seen, from George R. Romero to any other number of shared experiences. It was as if none of the characters had existed in the same world as the audience, full of popular culture reference points and ideas.

But at the same time, just mumbling the word felt strange, as if she were in one of the shows she was thinking about, in some alternate universe which fundamentally lacked a coherent reality. It felt silly; not real.

Reality. Back to reality.

Where are you, you bastard? Of course, she thought, the thing could simply have wondered off down the road into the distance, never to return. In which case, she could sit here all day like someone in a ticket office at the beachside Ferris wheel in gale-force, horizontal rain, waiting for a customer who would never turn up.

Right, that's it. Jessica gave Galen a hug and asked him to hush, before moving to the door, unlocking all the latches as quietly as possible and stepping outside. She peered quickly around and then closed the door gently, with latch lifted so as not to click loudly in the windless morning quiet. She released the latch for protection for Galen, after tapping her pocket to make sure she had remembered the house keys.

Jessica's heart was thumping, bombarding her chest cavity in an anatomical assault. Her breathing rapidly shortened and her muscles tensed visibly. Still throwing glances left and right, back and forth, she tiptoed to the car making hardly a sound. Almost there...

Suddenly, and to the detriment of her heart, blood pressure and nervous excitement, a blackbird flew out from under the car, a mere metre or two away.

"Aah!" Jessica let out a curt, high-pitched yelp which sounded to her much louder than it probably was. With that, she charged the last few steps, yanked open the door to the car, and almost threw herself inside. Fumbling with the key, she eventually found the lock button, but accidentally pressed the unlock button straight away, necessitating the re-pressing of the lock button. The clunking sound of the locking mechanism of her car sounding three times again felt more than it was, like boulders of an earthquake falling on the car roof.

"Shit, shit, shit!"

She looked about her, through all the windows of the car, to see if anyone was about, but still nothing. Not a sound apart from the birdsong, the twittering of the sparrow, the chattering of the finches and the delicate whistling of the other songbirds. But no crazed figure lurking in the shadows.

Yet.

After sitting for a while, with thumping heart beating against her ribs, Jessica guessed that the crazed car passenger from yesterday was not in the vicinity. She carefully left the car, and went about quickly, yet quietly, packing the boot with the bags and boxes. The baby car seat was set up in the rear for Galen. He had not quite outgrown it—still a few months for that. At present, leisurely trips to local upmarket shops to buy her groceries with Galen safely strapped into his seat were far from Jessica's mind.

Eventually Jessica, with trembling fingers, stutteringly inserted the key into the ignition and fired up the engine, which roared into life, producing yet more looks about her, through every window.

Get a grip, woman. Get a grip!

Tense and with heart pounding, Jessica found herself thinking about every movement and finding everything feeling strange and clumsy. In another context, she would have said, "Thus conscience does make cowards of us all" quoting Hamlet, which she had always taken to mean that overthinking of things led to the erosion of your resolve.

Now, though, her mind was full of nervous panic. She edged the car to the entrance of her driveway and slowly pulled it out on to the road. There was still no one in sight. Inching along in first gear, Jessica brought the car forward to sit alongside the vehicle that sat broken in front of Jean's crumbling dry-stone wall. Turning her engine off, she tried to control her erratic breathing, whilst looking intently at Jean's house. She didn't even allow herself a glance at the broken car until she realised that he could be in there with the body he had ruined.

Jessica made herself look into the vehicle and stared at the human wreckage. The body gaped, open and spilled, lacerated and torn. Blood had been spattered everywhere. Jessica could make out remnants of internal organs displayed in ways which her medical husband had probably never seen. It was as if a pack of wolves had taken to this woman's body in a survival-fraught frenzy of gnashing and ripping. The woman's face had been chewed off her skull, leaving jaw and teeth glaring from remaining flesh and skin. Her nose had been entirely removed: easy pickings. The blood-spattered forehead framed the cold eyes with pallid melancholy. Swarms of flies, attracted to the carnage to feast and lay their eggs, were seizing the opportunity with excited buzzing. The car had become a mortuary of fetid gore.

Nature went on about her business, undeterred.

Jessica wretched and forced her eyes away from the body. Looking back toward the house in all its normalcy, she saw nothing moving. There was no sign of anything—no sign of life, no movement, no distorted figures lumbering about. Just Jean's house. Jessica unlocked the doors. Every sound impacted on her consciousness with echoing reverberation. She opened the door and stepped out, feet crunching on nuggets of broken glass scattered like diamonds on the grey tarmac, and closed the door gently behind her. With a nervous sense of self-preservation, she moved her head from side to side, glancing and peering. In her right hand she grasped the hammer, knuckles whitened with fear, nobbly joints of bone pressing against her translucent skin. Step after quiet step, she stole slow yards towards Jean's front door.

After what seemed like an eternity, Jessica faced the burgundy-coloured wooden door and rang the bell. The euphonious chiming felt deeply out of place. She rang it again, and was sure she could hear something inside. Something…somewhere. Perhaps to the back of the house…

Without warning, the door flung open and Jean stood there aghast.

"Oh Jessica!" she exclaimed, eyes bright with relief. "Quick, that man's at the back. He's been there all morning." Jean glanced backward, before shuffling out.

"Have you got anything? Anything to bring?" Jessica asked.

"Yes, but…have I got time to get it?"

"Where is it? Quick."

Jean flapped her wrist in the direction of the hall indoors. "In there, inside the door."

"Just get in the car. It's open. Go!" Jessica barked.

Jessica could see through the hall and into the lounge where, pressed against the French doors with their curtains oddly thrown open, was the figure, its skin stretched menacingly back as its face was pushed along the glass, revealing snapping teeth and gums. One eye was nearest the glass as the right cheek was forced against the pane. It bulged and stared and moved sideways as the body moved. Jessica stood still, entranced by this wicked and deathly hex.

And then the face slipped off the side of the French door as the body moved out of view.

"Shit!" exhaled Jessica, as she returned to panic mode. Grabbing a small overnight bag and a small knapsack, one in each hand, she turned and bolted out of the door. "Get in the car, Jean!" she exclaimed as she saw Jean awkwardly hurrying to the car in the way only an older person would, as if muscles and bones hadn't been rushed for the last decade or so.

Jessica overtook Jean out of the drive and rounded her parked car. Dropping the bags, she hurriedly opened the driver's door, and pitched the bags over the headrest onto the back seat. Plonking herself down onto the driver's seat, she slammed the door shut behind her, all in good enough time to be able to lean over and open the passenger door for Jean to drop herself in little more delicately, holding the roof and door seal for support.

Jean was, Jessica guessed, in her early seventies. She knew nothing about this older companion, really, having never spoken at any great length. She had hoped to get to know the neighbours over the summer, but that had not really happened as yet, what with pandemics and whatnot... Jean's husband had died a decade previously: that was something which Jean had previously communicated, obviously still feeling her identity entwined with that of her husband of some forty years.

Jean managed to get the door slammed shut before Jessica sighted the lumbering figure, his curtains of lank black hair crusted with matted dried blood, swinging back and forth. Precious seconds ebbed away as Jessica sat transfixed.

"Come on dear, we've got to go," said Jean, rather calmly Jessica realised Jean could not see the apparition behind the car, as she was looking forwards, hands clutching each other with white-boned tension, belying her voice.

Thud. Slap. Skin and flesh and bone sounding on car bodywork.

Jessica was still staring, but now the man's darkly smeared face was staring right back at her from a very short distance, separated only by a metre of air and a suddenly paper-thin pane of car window. The face peering back, eyes wide, was squashed, as earlier in the house, onto the window. Even his teeth made contact with the glass, tapping softly noise against it.

Jessica remained motionless, as if under a spell. Her fight, flight or freeze mechanisms were switched firmly to freeze. It took Jean grabbing Jessica by her arm to break her from her trance.

"Come on Jessica! Drive!"

Jessica broke the madman's gaze. She fumbled the key into the ignition barrel and revved the car into life. The car accelerated away in first gear until its revs were so high it felt as if the engine might burst, and finally Jessica geared down.

"Where are we going, my dear?" asked Jean. "I thought you had a little boy..."

"I do," Jessica replied, staring into her rear-view mirror to see the dreaded figure awkwardly attempt to regain its balance with the support of the car suddenly removed. "We're going to drive through the village and out and round, to come back down School Lane and get in from the other side. I didn't want that thing following me to the house where I have to get out and get Galen. Too much risk."

"Oh, I see. Yes, good idea." Jean paused. "And then where are we going?"

"We'll stop and talk about that when we're safe, and we've got Galen."

The main village centre was down the road some couple of hundred metres, a right turn at a roundabout and past a dozen houses. It consisted of a number of typically countrified houses dotted around a small green, with a fading old red phone box kept for posterity and heritage reasons at one corner of the triangle. A healthy ash tree was the focal point on one side of the green, adding ample shade when in full foliage, as it was now.

There was road all the way around the green, offering access to all the houses, and to the shop and post office and village pub, which nestled together like a comfortable old couple, delighting in the memories of yesteryear. The post office had, against all odds, remained open, despite years of smaller post office closures, supported by the shop which did fairly good business in monopolising trade for the surrounding area. Jessica slowed to a crawl so that she could get a good idea of what was going on.

Both were closed, which was no surprise to her. *What day is it?* What with staying at home to look after Galen, and her husband on random shift patterns, Jessica had a poor grasp of time and the days. Her week was stabilised and landmarked by a rhyme-time session for babies and toddlers at the library in Street, once a week. Now, though, with her absence from the session in the last week or so, she had little grasp on the day of the week.

The closure of the shop and pub was ratified by the notices on the doors. Jessica drove around the green to stop opposite the shop for a better look. Glancing about the area and the vicinity of the car, she opened the door, leaving the car running, and walked to the shop door, fashioned in outdated wooden framing and glass.

DUE TO ILLNESS AND GOVERNMENT WARNINGS, THE SHOP AND POST OFFICE WILL REMAIN CLOSED UNTIL FURTHER NOTICE. THANK YOU FOR YOUR PATIENCE, OLIVER AND MARGARET

Jessica peered in thought the window into the dim shop interior. There looked to be a few tins and packets of crisps spilled on to the floor in front of the shop counter. She cupped her hands over her eyes to block out the light coming from the hazy day that was developing behind her.

There was an all-encompassing silence which permeated every corner of the green and village centre. Not a breath of wind caressed the plants and leaves of the village focal point.

Without warning, something crashed across Jessica's view, from left to right. She jumped back with fright, letting out a small, muted shriek.

Postcards and greetings cards littered the floor as the tall, thin unit on wheels which contained them had toppled over. Where there is effect, there is cause. And true to Newtonian physics...

"Shhhshhh faschhhhhhh!" came the faint sound from behind the glass. An arm came into view and suddenly Jessica realised that she had been standing so very close to someone who was remarkably similar to the person from whom they had run away. It was Margaret, she could just make her out, hidden from view behind the boards hung in the window to display personal adverts on postcards for locals to see. Jessica had had a number of encounters with the wife of the postmaster in the shop. She had been helpful and welcoming to Jessica and her family in the first few months of them setting up in their new home and village. A couple in their early sixties, the pair had run the store for a good thirty years, witnessing the slow change of English country village life.

Now the change was more than social, it was physical, and there was no better example of this than Margaret herself.

But before Jessica could get a good look at Margaret's transformed face, the woman, in a dressing gown and slippers, toppled in equal ungainly fashion on top of the mobile postcard rack to a chorus of crashes, bangs, arms and legs. Her foot had become entangled with the white-mesh card holder, and she had tumbled like a felled pine tree.

There was no hint of pain, no indication of discomfort; there was merely a flailing of arms and legs and a spitting and rasping oral expulsion. Her neck was craned upwards, whilst suspended above the ground courtesy of her cushion of cards and white plastic-sheathed metal wire, eyes boring into Jessica's own, into her mind.

Jessica stumbled backwards, losing her footing, and falling to the pavement painfully on to her coccyx, pain shooting up her spine. She let out a cry of shock. Meanwhile, Margaret's arms and splayed fingers banged on the window, attempting to reach Jessica's face, as if the shopkeeper couldn't conceptualise the window in front of her, and was imagining she could just reach out and grab the prostrate woman on the ground several metres in front of her.

Scampering on her behind, Jessica managed to get herself to her feet and run the few short steps back to the car.

Slam. Safe.

"What...what is going on, Jessica? Dear God, is this all a dream?"

"Um...er...I guess this is the virus. The virus has changed people, maybe even mutated itself. I don't really know. I mean, you've been watching the news, right? Well, everyone's been staying inside, frightened of the risk of getting this. Although, I gather there's been some looting. There're always opportunists. But I guess this virus changes you into something which makes you like...a...zombie..." Again, just saying that word made Jessica feel awkward, silly and not a little uneasy

"A what?"

"You know, like in those films. You must have seen them. They're like they're dead, and just seem to crave to eat things which they see are easy pickings for food. In other words, us. You and me. Welcome to Nature, Jean. We're back in the food chain."

METAMORPHOSIS

32
Vince

The morning sun broke only as dull grey curtain-filtered haze through the bedroom window which faced the concrete delivery driveway at the back of the shops, away from the solar source. Vince lay in his bed on his back, eyes open, body perfectly still, hands behind head. Staring at the ceiling in this way was a normal early morning position, though his fitful night's sleep was anything but normal, broken by the sounds outside the safety of his small maisonette. It was as if Bristol was suddenly coming alive after a winter hibernation. Except that these didn't sound like the melodies of happy and new spring life. Things sounded a lot more…heinous.

Vince had taken, over the last few years, to waking up early and lying, thinking. Not that he was Rodin's The Thinker, but this was his time to organise his thoughts and his actions for the day ahead.

He was still trying to come to terms with exactly what was going on, what had happened to his parents, and what he was to do with the day. With the latter, he was a lot clearer; but with the notions of what exactly was taking place in the screwed up world in which he found himself, he was less sure. His parents were dead. He had *killed* his father. Actually *killed* him. Something deep inside was telling him that this was okay, that he would never be prosecuted for what he had done there, because this was how the world had changed, almost overnight. Vince winced as he recollected the crushing blows he had delivered to his father. Ghastly scenes replayed themselves in the Cartesian theatre of his mind: *"Tonight's double bill! It's horror horror all the way! Get your popcorn quick, and settle in for Scream Screen!"*

Vince rubbed his eyes to erase the images in his mind, and returned his hands to behind his head. Whatever was going on was going on. He couldn't influence that now. What was important was what *he* did now. This was a mantra that had enabled Vince to cope with many a situation which he had himself created. It was the mechanism which enabled him to cope with prison, and with any number of misdemeanours. Though not quite a justification of his own actions, it did mean that Vince never lingered in the past, worrying about what he had done. Out of sight, out of mind, and this meant that his mental energies were more focused on the present and the future.

METAMORPHOSIS

The world was indeed going crazy; it was what he did about it that mattered. The whys and how were of no interest to him. They didn't help him get from A to B.

And today, A was his place, and B was Lou's parents. He knew that her parents lived in Devon, but wasn't really sure where. He'd probably remember it if he saw the name. This meant that Vince needed a map of Devon. A real paper map, with pages and a cover. They did still sell them, right?

Not being a car driver, and scooting around Bristol on his moped, following his nose and local knowledge, Vince had never really had use for maps, or even sat navs. But he needed one now. This meant that the list in his head read:

1) *Get bag and stuff together for trip on moped to Devon*
2) *Get map of Devon from petrol station*
3) *Make sure I've got enough petrol*
4) *Get more stuff that I might need from… anywhere*

And that was that. He needed to find where Lou's parents lived. *It's Great…Great something. Man, what is it! I think it's not too far from the sea.* Gary wasn't an option. He figured he'd played that card pretty badly. He could have got much more useful information from him instead of just attacking him. He had looked ill though. He was doing him a favour, right? *That was then, this is now. C'mon.*

Vince left the justifications and ruminations about what had taken place with Gary until another time. Or never. Swinging his legs out of bed, with his mind clear and intent on what he needed to do, Vince got himself ready.

33
Greg

Greg peered through a window at a sea-themed shop full of trinkets and thingamajigs aimed at passing tourists. He could get himself a lighthouse here. Greg had a thing for lighthouses, ever since his father died, and he had inherited his father's collection of ornamental lighthouses. He found it was important to carry on something of his father into his life, as though there was more than genetics that was passed from one generation to the next, that something of his father's soul lived with him.

Suddenly, in the quiet of the village, the three men heard the smashing of glass somewhere further back from the shops.

"Did you hear that?" asked Peter.

"Sure did," Greg replied. "Sounded like a window, maybe."

The men took a step back from the souvenir shop and scanned around. There barely seemed to be any hint of life in the village, which made the smashing of glass all the more startling. Staring back down the road towards where they had come from, Greg caught sight of the man that they had seen on the beach from afar, making his way up to the edge of the promenade.

A sound in front of Greg nudged his attention back to the souvenir shop.

"Sounds like someone's in!" Greg was hoping this could be the first bit of social interaction this side of the pond, long awaited as it was. He stepped back to the large glass shopfront and placed his face against the window, cupping his hands around his face to cut out the background light.

His eyes focused on the lighthouses directly on the window display in front of his, and then moved into the darker shop environs behind: a jumbled array of bits and pieces scattered and heaped around the shop in sensory overload, boats, keyrings, fridge magnets, mugs, ornaments—

From the back of the shop, over to the right, there was a sudden movement. A display of name stickers toppled to the floor with a clattering crash. Dale and Peter, peering into the art gallery next door, turned to look Greg's way. Greg took a step towards the door, continuing to peer into the window, hands cupped. He strained to look past the central till area, a large cubicle with two tills surrounded by a counter laden with bits and pieces designed to suck the tourist into a world of tat consumption. From behind the right-hand walled partition, a figure in a pink dressing gown stumbled into view.

"Looks like we have life in there," Greg mumbled, more to himself than anyone else.

Then he looked more closely. The woman's dressing gown was messy, as if she had spilled something down it, or vomited on it. His eyes travelled up her short figure and rested on her face.

He gasped.

She wasn't going to be selling him a hand-painted ceramic lighthouse any time soon, that was for sure. Her face was ashen, blotchy in places, and her eyes were sunk into dark-rimmed pits, seen even in the dark shadows of the unopened shop. Lank dark-brown hair fell about her slightly chubby cheeks, just short of shoulder-length. She was probably in her forties, but looked considerably older from whatever sickness had ravaged her body. One of her hands grabbed the counter by the till to steady herself. After all, she had already knocked over one of the display carousels.

"Guys, this lady does not look well."

Peter and Dale sauntered over to check out had grabbed Greg's attention so completely. They pressed their faces against the window.

"Jeeee..." involuntarily escaped Peter's lips.

Dale responded more caringly. "Is she okay? Do we need to get in and help her? She is not right!"

The movement of the men to the windows caught the shopkeeper's attention and her right arm swung awkwardly back to her side, brushing magnets and miniature ornaments off the counter to clatter on to the floor. The woman, eyes bulging as her head wobbled on her neck, like a frightening version of a nodding dashboard dog, shuffled forward, crunching over the disarrayed seaside-themed thimbles and whatnot scattered on the floor.

All the men could now clearly see the woman's milky eyes, and her inhuman face, lacking any sort of emotion beyond a determination to reach the window through which the men were staring. She was an object of fascination to them, a grotesque charade of humanity which, the men subconsciously felt, might just spin and twist only to reveal the normal shopkeeper in some perverse example of seaside circus antics.

Instead, in a display of distinct lack of smooth coordination, the woman jerked unevenly toward the window on the right of the shop door through which Peter and Dale were compulsively watching. There was a display table in the window covered with a table cloth embroidered with sailing boats, the sort that might be seen on boys' bed linen. Perhaps it was, and had been co-opted to provide nautical background for the plethora of boats, tankards, themed mugs, cushions, and small storage boxes with imprints of seaside scenes which adorned them. The woman stumbled the few last metres, banging up against the wide table as if it wasn't there. The force of the impact must have caught her off guard; she lost her footing and fell to the ground, her discoloured hands grabbing the sheet of sailboats on her way down, pulling it and most of the sale items down on top of her.

Greg finally moved and tried to open the front door, but it was locked. He rattled it until the "CLOSED" sign shook on its string.

"We've gotta help this lady!" Greg said. We need to phone a doctor or something."

From behind the table, a pink flannel-gowned arm stretched up and navy blue chipped and peeling nails scratched into the wooden surface. There was enough traction to allow the woman to regain her unsteady feet. As she looked down, Peter and Dale could see the roots of her greying hair on the top of her head and then they saw the most frightening thing they had ever witnessed. The woman's head snatched up, cloudy eyes fixing onto them, enraged, and her mouth snarled back, baring her teeth. With a spittle-clogged gravelly exhalation, the woman reached out her right hand and thrust it against the window as if to rip the skin from Peter's face, right down to his skull beneath.

Both Peter and Dale jumped back from the window with a cry.

Greg was still rattling the door and so the insane woman inside shifted her attention to him. Her head snapped towards him in the same fashion, and she adjusted her body like some badly programmed and constructed fleshy robot, and almost fell the rest of the distance into the door. Her face pressed right up against the glass of the door: lifeless skin, purplish capillaries and squashed nose and eye sockets.

The distorted face bore such little resemblance to what must have been its original form that Greg shouted, "What in God's name is going on?"

As Peter and Dale and stepped back a further pace or two, they both caught sight of movement above as a face appeared in the window of the apartment above the art gallery.

"Hey! Hey there! Help" shouted Peter, to what looked like a balding, spectacled man in his late fifties, himself not looking too well.

"This woman is really ill. Can you call an ambulance?" Dale called, but the man, simply shut his curtains, nodding quickly from side to side in a panicked fashion.

"What the heck is going on?" Peter demanded, unbelievingly.

Greg backed up to stand next to Peter, his heart beating like a kettle drum playing a symphony of fear and panic. "We...We..." was all he could manage.

"We need to call someone. I would advise not trying to open that door, either. It's like she's got rabies, or something," Peter added.

Dale was starting to get angry. "Where the heck *is* everyone around here? It's like a ghost town. I can't believe that man up there simply ignored us!"

All the while the woman in the shop flailed against the door, banging and rattling its frame, seething in its window.

"I think...I think she is trying to *attack* us," said Greg.

"That's what rabies does, right?" asked Peter.

At that moment, the men heard a noise behind them. The man from the beach had descended the steps to the road and was crossing towards the confused and alarmed trio. Then the woman in the shop slammed against the door with no inconsiderable force, which refocused their attention on the shop. Dale took some sideways steps behind the other two in the direction of the man from the beach, hoping that he might be able to help. Perhaps he had a mobile phone on him so that they could call for some assistance?

Then Dale turned to face the man moving towards them, and stopped in his tracks. The newcomer was dressed in jeans and a white T-shirt draped over his rather thin body, the body of probably a fifty-year-old. He wore no shoes, and his feet were planted, with each step he took towards Dale, with an uneasy lack of grace. His face had that same look: cloudy eyes embedded into sunken holes like dreadful pearls being sucked down by a hideous vortex; blotchy skin thinly scattered with scraggly grey hairs of a beard; a mouth which offered a grimace of saliva rather than a welcome and an offer to help.

Before Dale had time to properly react, even before his nonconscious brain kicked into automatic mode, the man grabbed at him, catching the camera strap around his neck. The man's scrawny fingers had an effective grip, curled around the strap like the talons of an eagle around the hind leg of a rabbit. The man's left hand swung round and tried to grab Dale's ear, but Dale finally reacted and parried it.

The barefoot man launched himself onto Dale. Not like a leopard onto its prey, but like a drunken lunatic in a bar-room brawl.

"Wha—!"

The others turned and saw what was going on. With cries of surprise, they rushed to help. Peter grabbed Dale from behind and yanked him backwards, but this only served to pull the crazed man on top of him. Greg used his not diminutive bulk, to hoist the man up and literally throw him backwards. The sight that met him gave his heart a feeling similar to both freezing and burning.

"My God!" Greg exclaimed as he saw Dale's face with a patch of cheek missing. Greg knelt down next to Dale as Dale himself pulled his hands up to his face in realisation that he had some searing pain, and not a little blood flowing freely.

"He damned well bit me!" shouted Dale incredulously.

Greg had already forgotten about the man he had disposed of behind him, but Peter moved round the prostrate Dale to confront the silver-haired psychopath, who had returned to his feet and was swinging himself around.

"Er, Greg, what are we going to do with—" was all Peter could manage before the man threw himself on Peter. Luckily, Peter was able to grab both of the man's arms as he launched, so that he almost caught him and cushioned the attack.

Greg leapt to his feet and again threw the attacker on to the pavement on the beach side of the road.

"Let's find a police station or something! These two are insane!" Greg called out.

All three men were on their feet and watching the assailant, who was slowly getting up, unperturbed at the blood dripping down his mouth from where he had torn part of Dale's cheek off. Dale pressed his hand against his wound in a fairly futile attempt to staunch the blood flow.

Just as the men were turning away from the rabid figure, they heard a screech from down the road as a car revved hard and skidded around the corner where The Happy Starfish was situated. The red estate car was headed straight for them, some thirty metres up the road. The men jogged to the inland side of the road away from their would-be attacker, who stumbled off the pavement and on to the road. Greg could see what was going to happen some seconds before it did. The car, accelerating all the time, over-accelerating in changing gears as if in a blind panic, was heading on a collision course for the shambling man, who was now in the middle of the road.

The vehicle was going at some thirty miles per hour when it reached them and took a sudden swerve as if the driver wasn't really paying too much attention and surveying the road for potential hazards. The driver must have seen the man too late and automatically swerved to avoid him, but then lost control and headed for the three.

Dale and Greg managed to anticipate the situation in split seconds and dived out of the way. The car careered off the road and lifted on to the pavement, catching Peter's left leg as he failed to get out of the way in time. The crash was deafening in the otherwise quiet village as the car broke through the art gallery window which fronted the premises from the ground up. Peter was thrown by the impact against the right side of the window before collapsing to the ground, screaming, glass falling down around him.

The driver of the car was not wearing a seatbelt, and the crash caused the young man of about twenty-five to slam into the wheel. The car was too old to have an airbag, so his face took most of the impact, knocking him clean out and appearing to break his nose.

Greg and the bleeding Dale were not quite sure what to do. The sensations of sight, sound, hormones, enzymes, emotions and touch cascaded around, in and through them in a vortex of experience.

Peter's screams of pain brought them out of their shocked trance.

The car had completely broken all the windows of the gallery and damaged the edge of the souvenir shop, breaking the narrow-sectioned pane of glass on its right side.

"Aaaaah! My leg's broken! It's damned well broken!" screamed Peter in a high-pitched fearful outpouring of hysteria.

"Okay, Peter. It's okay, we'll sort you out. We'll get you help," soothed Greg as he knelt down beside Peter, who was propped up against the metal strut that framed the window panes.

Greg heard a snuffling sound, followed by grunts of exertion, and looked up to see the woman from the souvenir shop trying to make her way through the thin gap in the window frames, from the display table onto the top corner of the bonnet of the car which was diagonally inserted into the adjacent gallery. Her chubby cheeks were less than endearing as they stretched back to reveal the woman's gnashing teeth, as if imagining she was eating Greg's face from halfway out of the window. As she clambered onto the bonnet of the car, she lacerated her wrist and one of her legs on the broken shards protruding from the narrow framed gap.

Dark red, viscous blood meandered its way down her limbs, rivulets of merlot on a blotchy and lifeless landscape.

The woman was not the only threat that Greg's fight-or-flight brain had picked up on. From the corner of his eye, he saw the unscathed barefooted man stumble his way around the car. Greg removed his rucksack and looked around to see Dale backing instinctively away. The art gallery was on the corner, and he backed into the road which joined the one they were on. Dale looked up the road.

"There's another one. Mother of God, Greg, there's another. Is no one normal around here?"

Greg's brain decided.

Fight.

Greg grabbed Peter's camera quickly from his around his neck, a large *Nikon* SLR, an expensive one that Peter had brought especially for this trip, and rose to meet the oncoming man who had taken a chunk out of his friend. Without really thinking what he was doing, since everything was now becoming a sensory blur, Greg drew his right arm back and, like an almighty shot-put, launched the camera-weapon into the man's face. The man staggered back, and tripped over his own feet to land with a dull thud on the tarmac of the road.

"Greg!" came a hysterical alarm, and Greg turned to see the woman from the shop, having navigated to the other edge of the car bonnet, reach down and grab Peter by the face. Some of her fingers found their way into his mouth, and she pulled back, grasping his cheek, gripping it from within. Her nails raked excruciatingly along the inside of Peter's cheek, taking chunks of tissue from his mouth. Like some monstrous beast, the woman licked her fingers, tasting the specks of blood and flesh she had scratched away.

Peter screamed.

The woman fell onto Peter from the bonnet above as Greg had turned and stepped back to deal with the grey-haired man. Greg had to act fast. He lifted her, as he had the man, from behind, arms cinched around her waist, and threw her back towards the first assailant, face *Nikon*-dented, returning yet again to his feet. As she was hoisted away like some two-bit amateur wrestler, her hand grabbed Peter's right ear. Her nails cut through the large lobes, and nearly tore the ear off. Blood trickled hot from the wounds, running down his neck. Peter felt a stinging pain from his ear, receptors sending signals, vying for notice in the chaos of injuries that he had suffered.

Peter felt for his ear, and pulled back his hand in horror.

"She's taken half my ear off, Greg!" he screeched, and started to panic He tried to stand up, but the pain in his leg was too much, and he crumpled back down.

Meanwhile, Dale had been edging further and further back towards the sea, away from the other figure stumbling maliciously in his direction.

Greg stared at Dale and then back to the brace of reprobates he had discarded, and then at the whimpering Peter, who was in a state of clear and blind hysteria, blood wetting the collar of his checked shirt. The man looked more diminutive than normal, grimacing with pain, propped up against the thin metal post. He tried to get up again, this time with greater success.

"Greg, help me," he implored and Greg paced backwards, standing over the hunched Peter. He put his arm around Peter and grabbed just under the man's arm. "I think my bone might be sticking out of my leg. You know, under my jeans."

"Just hold on, Peter, we'll get you out of here".

Greg guided Peter up to the corner and looked up the road to where Dale had been fixated, and sure enough, now only ten metres away, another similarly acting man, rotund, in a pair of sports shorts, belly poking out under an ill-fitting blue T-shirt, was wobbling their way. Behind him, further up the road, was what looked like an elderly lady in a dress gazing around, up to the sky, before eventually turning and setting eyes on the melee at the shore end of the road. Neck protruding as if to focus better, with scrawny head jutting out like a praying mantis, she started jolting down the road, walking as if she had had both hips replaced at different levels.

Thinking quickly, Greg decided the beach was the best option. The man and woman stood between them and the nearest steps up to the promenade. Greg didn't fancy their chances, and besides, they were only a matter of metres away. Dale had already had the same idea and was continuing along the coastal road which carried on for another hundred or so metres before ending in a car park providing access to some amusements, cafés and the western edge of the bay.

There were some steps about twenty metres down the road. Peter was in such a state that Greg didn't want to take any risks with bundling him over the promenade. The steps were the way to go. With Dale a few metres ahead, Greg half-carried the wincing Peter, whose face had gone utterly pale in shock, up the middle of the road. As he glanced behind him, he saw the woman from the shop and the silver-haired man, trundling after them, occasionally stretching out their arms as if they could touch their retreating prey from afar. Soon, when the men were some ten metres from the steps, the large-bellied man rounded the corner, and they were being followed by the bizarre sight of three crazed and assorted assailants.

"Dale, for God's sake man, help me lift Peter up the steps!"

"Yeah, yah, sure. Ah, sorry, I'm not too good with, er, blood. I just don't know what's, er, what's going on here. What *is* going on here?" he mumbled, turning around and coming to help Greg lift Peter.

"I dunno. Dale, grab his legs just below his butt, and I'll take him underneath the arms...There you go. Hold on Peter, we've gotta get you up these here steps," said Greg, trying to soothe the panicking man.

"A-ah-ahh!" Peter screamed, as the other two men manoeuvred his body past the handrails and up the steps to the promenade.

Behind them, the three people were about ten metres away, following towards the steps.

The men had now managed to get Peter to the top with only a few screams of pain. Blood seemed to be coming from a number of places, not least falling from the wound on Dale's face, and dropping all over Peter's crotch.

Dale carefully lowered Peter down so he could hobble with Greg's help. "We need to get to the dinghy, get on the water, and reassess what the hell we are going to do!" Greg mumbled agreement and looked back at the steps to which their followers had just arrived.

"Come on!" Greg insisted as he realised they had precious little time. With Dale running ahead to prepare the small tender about twenty metres away, Greg helped Peter move along the promenade. Up ahead, though, Greg saw something that made his heart sink. There was another person on the beach. Perhaps it was someone who could help them! He peered further into the distance, only to recognise the gait of the person, a young or teenaged girl, by the looks of her, as she lumbered across the sands.

In their direction.

"Come on Peter, we've got company. From both sides."

However, Peter barely had his eyes open, such was the pain that he was experiencing. He was unaware of the people behind him, at some ten metres or so, and the girl about equal distance the other side of the dinghy.

"Peter, you've got to stay with me. Give me something. You're going to need to walk yourself, maybe, in a bit."

"No, no…I can't. I…aah, aah!" was all Peter could return as his foot bounced off the red tarmac of the promenade, sending lightning strikes of pain up his leg and to his brain.

"Okay, rest on your good leg and hang on," and with that, Greg put his left arm under Peter's knee and hoisted him up to carry him. In all honesty, Greg still didn't know where the break in Peter's leg was, or whether it was multiply broken along its length, though he did now notice that there was blood soaking through the bottom half of his right leg, and quite lot of it. Greg was pretty fit considering his bulky size, and managed the lesser weight of Peter without too much difficulty, He could see that Dale had reached the boat and was trying to drag it down sideways, in his panic, but finding that less than efficient in the process. Greg was moving as rapidly as he could, a fast, yet bouncing and stumbling jog over the sands now, and to the boat. Peter was screaming in pain at every nudge and jolt.

To Greg's shock, he realised that Dale hadn't seen the girl advancing from the other side of the boat, so busy was he with yanking the dinghy down to the retreating water.

"Dale, watch out!" Greg called.

Dale looked up and then around to see the young girl, with dyed dark hair, and piercings through the lip and nose, once pale skin now even paler, though with large mottled patches of purple-beige. She lurched toward Dale, who looked for something to fight with and grabbed an oar from the middle of the dinghy. In the time it took him to pick up the thin aluminium oar, with its plastic blade, she was almost on him. Dale turned and beat her back with the oar held in both arms, like some sparring stick. He thrust both arms forward, outstretched, so that the centre of the oar smacked the girl square in the face and she fell backwards.

At the same time, Greg arrived at the boat which still remained about eight metres from the sea. He dumped Peter unceremoniously inside, and turned to realise that they were going to have to deal with these attackers. He was determined that it would not be Custer's Last Stand.

34
Fran

"God I'm so sorry, I'm so sorry. Are you all right? I mean, are you all right? How's your face? What the hell! I mean, what the hell is going on? Let me get you something for that..." Fran's panic and shock translated into a torrent of verbal outpouring. She ushered the woman into the kitchen and then went through to the bathroom to get some first aid equipment, which amounted to a bit of tape, bandage and some old and tatty plasters.

Fran returned to find the woman staunching the wound with some paper kitchen roll. The gash to her cheek, whilst cosmetically grimace-inducing, wasn't the worst of injuries, and they soon had it bandaged up in a rather amateur fashion.

That was when the muffled thuds started. The man outside appeared to be trying to get back into the flat. The bump, bump, bang was unsettling for the pair of them. Fran ushered the other woman into the lounge and sat her down on the sofa, closing the door behind her. The thudding continued unabated and hardly any quieter in the hush of the mid-morning.

"I'm Fran, by the way. I'm so sorry I was just, you know, stood there. I couldn't move. I was panicking. I've got these issues, you know, with panicking."

The woman looked at her, looked her in the eyes and said, "Yeah. Well, I don't know what to say. I think you could of bloody moved, you know. Your kicks were a bit late. You could of stopped me bloody face getting bitten!" There was not a little anger and frustration in her voice.

"I know, I know. I've got these problems, you know, which..." but it all sounded a bit pathetic in comparison to what had just gone on, and Fran gave up trying to explain her fears and her predicament, her inner turmoil.

The woman's face softened almost imperceptibly. "I figure you're not quite right. I've lived 'ere a year and seen you, what, once? You're a herman...no a hermit, aren't you? One of them people who hates coming out."

"Yeah. I'm agoraphobic and get...get...panic attacks." For some reason, Fran found it tough to actually tell this woman, like she was in some psychiatrist's chair, what had been inhibiting her actions earlier, and inhibiting her from being a normal and interacting neighbour. "Anyway, I've got issues, and I'm sorry." Fran paused. "What's going on? Have you been outside and on the streets? I only get what I can glean from the news."

"I've been out about a little, but had to come back. My husband's been ill, and, well, he's...he's...ill...he's not right, like that guy outside. I can't go back into my flat. I can't get back in there. I won't go. So I tried to get out and go and see my parents across town, but I didn't even get to the bottom of the block. That bloke out there, he tried to attack me downstairs and chased me up 'ere. I don't know what to do." The woman was openly and obviously disturbed and started to shake as the adrenalin began to ebb away from her system.

"So you can't go back into your apartment?" Fran asked, seeking confirmation for her suspicions.

"No. Dave's not right. I think...I think...he's like that bloke outside, you know? No, I *know* he is. He tried to attack me. That's why I ran. He'll still be in there."

And indeed Fran's suspicions were confirmed. "So what do you think we do now?" Fran asked, though there was an odd ring to the "we" as she took for granted that the two of them were somehow thrown together to deal with their present predicament as a pair.

"Do you think this is like *The Walking Dead* or those other films? You know *Day of the... Whatever it is*? Holy shit..." and as a sudden realisation hit her, the woman lifted her hand to the bandaged wound on her face. "Am I ill? Am I...like one of them? Am I? Oh shit!"

Fran had little idea about what she was referring to but got the gist. She was looking at the woman's face and could see it change in front of her, as the hormones and chemicals of panic revisited her face; the muscles and lines, eyes and nose reacted as she realised that she, too, could be ill.

"I'm sure you'll be fine," managed Fran, who herself realised that the woman could be right, and that Fran herself could be in danger.

Oh my goodness! What do I do?

The familiar vanguard of her own panic started to rush out from the core of her body.

Calm down, damn it, calm DOWN!

Fran managed, somehow, to maintain her heart rate at the already increased speed, and, struggling, got her body under some kind of control.

"Right, er, sorry, what was your name?"

"Tanya."

"Tanya. Okay, Tanya, what do you think we do?" Fran had thoughts and what ifs buzzing through her head as neurons lit up and synapses fired. Action stations in the brain.

Tanya sat herself up and got to her feet. Pacing up and down the corridor, she thought, muttering to no one in particular. "I…okay, I…or we…We need to get somewhere safe and I need to get me face looked at. I need to make sure this injury is safe, that I don't have that crazy disease. Because if I do, well, ya know…"

Fran looked Tanya deep in the face, searching for signs that she might be changing into the sort of person the man outside was, a harmless nymph into something far more sinister. Perhaps she was a little paler in the skin? No, come on, she was imagining things! But…

"Okay, so I need to get out. We need to get past that man," announced Tanya, stopping still. The man outside the door obliged with some more door-thumping.

"How the hell do we do that? Anyway, let's at least calm down and get prepared. I'm not leaving this place in my slippers, and I'm not leaving this place without everything I think will be handy. Who knows what the heck it's like out there? We don't even have a plan on where to go!" It was clearly Fran's turn to panic now as she managed to work herself up into a state of heavy breathing and racing, drumming heartbeats.

"Let's grab something to eat, get some stuff together and work out a plan," offered Tanya, diverting Fran's focus away from her panic.

The two agreed that Tanya should get some food prepared (a few sandwiches) whilst Fran prepared a rucksack with some clothes. Fran began wishing she had gone on a year abroad, travelling as a few of her friends had done. She needed a backpack now, rather than the diminutive green rucksack she had originally bought to go to the gym with, when she had been a little more outgoing than she presently was.

With the small bag in her left hand, she went about stuffing a selection of clothes into it: a jumper, some underwear, an anorak, a beanie hat, leggings, jeans, toothbrush, toothpaste… Very soon, her bag was bulging and she had to fight the zip closed.

Fran returned to the kitchen some ten minutes later, bag in hand, walking boots and jeans on, a lime green Nike hoodie over a black Lycra sports top. Tanya had prepared the ham and cheese sandwiches with some tortilla chips on the side.

"Thanks, Tanya," Fran said as she grabbed the plate from the kitchen side. Tanya was already sitting at the table and Fran came to sit opposite her. She looked at Tanya, and her heart raced a little. Munching through her food, Tanya had small beads of sweat on her forehead and the colour had drained a little from her skin.

Holy cow, I think she's actually getting worse. Maybe she's right, maybe she could have it...

"Um, how are you feeling, Tanya? Are you feeling Okay?" Fran asked, trying to feign her concern and internal panic.

"Well, I feel kind of shitty. My head is starting to hurt a bit. Well, a lot."

Oh no. Oh no. Oh no. What do I do? I need to get out of here. Can I help her? Is it too late? Is there anyone who could help? Can I just run off? No, don't think that. But if I don't get out of here, then two of us could get ill...

Fran put her sandwich back down on the plate.

"What's wrong?" Tanya asked, a distraught look on her face. "Jesus, mate, you think...you think I've got it, don't you? You think I'm frigging ill!" With every word, her voice raised and the anger etched itself on to her bandaged face with ever fiercer and deeper lines. Suddenly, in an outburst that shocked Fran, Tanya's arm swung out and swiped Fran's plate off the table and across the room, shattering on the wall and spilling sandwich on to the floor below. Tortillas sailed about like little cardboard kites, rattling and scattering windlessly to the floor.

Whitish spittle dotted Tanya's lips.

"Okay, okay, Tanya. Calm down. I'm just not taking any chances, all right?"

"Calm down? *Frigging calm down!* Me husband's a freak, you're a freak, I've been chased in here by a freak, *and I'm turning into a frigging freak!*" she screamed, forcing Fran to move her face and neck back to avoid the full force of the woman's exertion, wary as she was of germs spreading.

"What do you want me to do?" Fran shouted back, exasperated.

Tanya sat back down from where she had been half-stood up, hands on the sides of the table, her aggressive stance reflecting her anger at her predicament. "I...I...I'm sorry. Let's just get out of here and find some help. Now."

Tanya exhaled nervously. "Okay. But what about that man outside the front door?"

Tanya started looking around the kitchen. "What weapons can we get hold of? Broom? Knives? Got anything else?"

"That's about the size of it," Fran replied, thinking of what else in the flat could possibly be used to fend off the crazed man fumbling about her door.

"How about," suggested Tanya, "we open the door, and as he comes in, we stand each side of 'im and fling 'im down the corridor, and run out the door?"

Fran thought, and then said, "Sounds all right, but the corridor's hardly wide enough for the two of us in it, let alone throwing a bloke in between us." Fran paused as she thought some more. "No, I think we have to push him back and run past him and down the stairs. Maybe we get some duvets and pillows, or something else, and use it as a shield so he can't get to us, and then run him backwards?"

After discussing a few alternatives, they agreed upon this idea, and set about preparing themselves. Fran lent Tanya another small rucksack into which she packed a few things of Fran's that might come in handy (clothing and odds and ends). Tanya then grabbed herself a length of hollow aluminium piping, detached from the vacuum cleaner, and stood in the kitchen ready.

Fran, with rucksack on her back and hammer in hand, looked at Tanya, who had continued losing colour. "Do we need any food? I've packed a few snacks."

"Let's keep it light," Tanya answered.

The pair grabbed themselves Fran's double duvet, and the single duvet from the spare bed and, handling both, stood next to each other, squashed into the corridor, facing the door.

METAMORPHOSIS

35
Jessica

The car crept slowly along at less than ten miles per hour. Both women in the front were acutely aware of their surroundings, scouting and scoping for anything out of place. Nothing seemed to be amiss as they got closer and closer to the destination: namely, the driveway to Jessica's entrance. Banked on each side by ivy-covered walls, another job which had been saved for those summer weekends but which had yet to be done, the driveway opened up to the house with its layer of pea shingle. The car wheels crunched over it with nerve-grating noisiness. Why was everything so dammed noisy!

Jessica turned to her elderly neighbour, and said, "I'm leaving the door open so I can get in quickly. I'll likely throw Galen at you. Get ready. Shut the door if you see that bloke, and I'll have to stay inside."

Pulling the handbrake on with the car parked as close to the front door as possible, and leaving the engine ticking over, Jessica exited the car with her house keys in hand. She took the few steps to the front door, with a few covert glances over and about her shoulders.

Nothing.

So far, so good.

Her hands were trembling again as she offered up the key to the door lock. The store of adrenalin upon which she was drawing seemed inexhaustible. The key caught and entered, fitting like a glove as well-matched keys always do. The door was open, she was in, the door was closed.

So far, still good.

Now running, she could hear Galen screaming, obviously hungry, or having soiled his nappy. "I'm here, baby, I'm here!" she called as she rounded the corner to see Galen lying on his back in his cot, wailing away for his mother, but until now to nothing and no one.

"Baby, baby, baby," Jessica soothed as she picked him up and held him close to her. She lifted her top and unzipped her nursing bra, offering her breast milk to him. She had considered, along with a whole host of other things, trying to wean him over the summer months, but again, this had been shelved for the time being. Right now, it was perfect and was just what Galen needed, topped up often with formula milk. "There you go, baba. That's what you want," she purred, between pants, combing his short, downy hair with her fingers. The pull of baby on nipple was something she had come to really appreciate in a way which she found hard to put into words, even to herself. Although she couldn't feel the physical experience so much at this stage, now she had been regularly feeding Galen for seven months, there was still that persistent tug at her nipple which she often looked forward to. In some sense, she had analysed in herself, she even craved it. There was this idea, to her, that this was dependency in its most primal form; this little bundle of her love was utterly dependent on her to provide, from her own body, her own physicality, for him. Mixed with that was the feeling that her breasts were full and needing to be emptied; as her milk drained, she felt relief.

In the present situation, these ideas and many others were swimming around her panicked and perplexed mind. She remained in the seat in her son's room for a minute or so, feeding and regaining her composure.

Jean would be wondering what she was doing…This could wait. It would have to wait.

Standing up, she took Galen off her breast, re-arranged herself, and brought him over to rest upright in her left arm, hand through and under his bottom.

Galen squealed as only babies do. Interrupted. He wasn't happy in the slightest.

"Shhh, shh, shhhhhh…" Jessica whispered into his ear, to absolutely no avail. There was nothing like food to settle a little boy's hungry tantrum. "Okay, you and mummy are going to go for a drive. Yes we are! Yes we are!"

The car door slammed.

She definitely heard it. There was definitely a door shutting. She could hear it from where she was, only a few metres from the front door of the house. Jessica's heart murmured in that funny way again, as if drowning and panicking and struggling for breath in a dark, sinister ocean, whilst having a great white circle beneath, menacing.

She froze.

Is the door locked? Yes, yes it is. It bloody is.

She moved into the lounge, and up to the window where she had seen the man at all-too-close a range, smearing and squeaking and scaring. She peered round the edge of the window, inch by frightened inch. There, on the far side of the car, the passenger side, was the man, bent over and pressed up towards Jean, trying to get at her through the closed window.

"Shit. Damn."

Galen let out an almighty wail. Jessica ducked back round to the side of the window and out of sight. About fifteen seconds later, the now familiar sound of body slapping on glass came from the window only steps away.

Breathing hard, Jessica thought. She had to get him out of the way, she reasoned. She had to get access to the car. There was access to where he was from the back garden and round the side. If she could lure him to the garden, then surely she could outrun him back through the house to the car. She ran on down the hallway and into the kitchen, which backed on to the rear garden.

Weapon.

Jessica spun on her heels, reeling about the kitchen, until her eyes came to rest, once again, on the knife block. She retracted the longest knife left in the block and held it in her free hand, Galen still propped in her left. She wasn't letting him go. Not now.

Unlocking the large sliding patio door which offered entrance from the large open kitchen and into the back garden, Jessica set about trying to lure this *thing* around to the back of the house. She stepped carefully on to the rear decking which led out from the back of the house to the edge of the lawn. Carefully, because it was notoriously slippery, even in the hot weather. Her outdoor tap needed a washer replaced, or some such attention, and it dripped incessantly on to the worn decking boards near the back door, forming a green layer of slimy growth. Jessica had slipped a number of times whilst taking the washing out to be hung on the washing line, once doing the splits for the first time in her life. Not now, though. She was careful.

She ran left around the side of the house, and up to the side gate which separated the two. The key was stiff, but she was just about able to unlock the door. Although recently repainted in a rich, verdant green, the lock remained old and rusty and in serious need of attention. Jessica prised the door open ajar, and peered through. Nothing but the shady path that led to the front edge of the house, and her intended subject.

Although Jessica didn't need to shout, given a still-screaming Galen offering his opinions with unfaltering and unaltering clarity, to the world, she nevertheless did.

"Hey! Hey! Hey you freak. You freak of nature!" she yelled at the top of her voice, nervous excitement amplifying her calls. She walked slowly forwards, protecting Galen by holding him almost behind her, and advancing with knifed hand held aloft. "Come on you—"

She was cut off into silence as a vanguard of shadow advanced past the corner of the house to be followed inexorably by the obstacle to the sun's rays, spitting and exhaling, raking and rasping.

Fighting the freeze, Jessica forced herself to say, "Come on, you bastard! Come on, follow me!" She beckoned with her knife and then, getting a measure of his pace, she started backing away. As the man looked at her, Galen continued to wail, and this seemed to perceptibly heighten the man's arousal. One of his arms led out further than the other, at about chest height, as he stumbled on, intent on something that Jessica had to offer.

He moved a little quicker than she had been anticipating, at about a slow jogging pace. Realising this, Jessica turned and ran, with her infant burden, to the rear corner of the house. She turned back and realised that this *thing* was a little too close for comfort, and so she immediately turned to re-enter the sliding door, shouting at him to follow all the way. A few paces in the kitchen, she had second thoughts.

I'm not letting that fucker into my house. It's my house. It's Mike's house, and none of you freaks will experience it. EVER!

Jessica turned and threw the knife on the ground to shut the door, which was wide open. A heavy sliding door, it took some might in the present context, with her one hand, to close it; but close it she did.

Slam.

She stared, waiting for him to appear round the corner. She saw, without processing, hydrangeas, petunia, geranium and other bedding plants, all in need of a good water. She saw her experimental English wildflower beds, surviving well in the dry soil.

But she saw no man. No shambolic demon of a human being stuttering around the corner.

"You're kidding me!"

Setting Galen on the well-oiled oaken wooden table in the middle of the kitchen, Jessica turned back to the sliding door and opened it.

"Come on, you freak, where are you?!" she shouted, eyes on that rear corner. She glanced back inside. Galen had sat himself up on his legs and bottom and was perilously close to falling off the table, still red-faced and shrieking. *What the hell did I put him on the table for, for Christ's sake?*

As she turned back to look to the corner of the house again, the man appeared, attracted to her remonstrations.

"Fsshhhhhtarrrrrr!"

"Come on, you sicko!"

She backed slowly up to the door again, making sure he was following her, and stepped back into the kitchen with one foot.

Jessica's other foot, though, slipped right from under her. She landed heavily on her posterior on the back threshold of the white sliding door frame. Her already bruised coccyx took another painful blow, with her left leg folded underneath her and her right leg flat on the decking. She tried to lever herself up, using the door handle for support, but there wasn't going to be time.

Galen bawled as the shadow of the freakish man loomed over his mother. Galen wanted milk. His mother needed help.

She screamed.

METAMORPHOSIS

36
Greg

"C'mon fatso!"

Greg had more adrenalin coursing through his veins than he had ever had, like a drug, intoxicating him with heightened senses and channelled focus. It was like Communion wine giving him divine sustenance. *Please God. Thank you for this strength, now let me do your work. Let me save my friends.*

He had grabbed the other oar and held it two-handed towards the blade end so if felt like a baseball bat. Greg was no baseball player. He had dabbled at college, joining the club and playing for a month or so, using his rudimentary high-school skills to get by. He had joined for social reasons but had soon come to realise that he was, at heart, more of an academic. What his students would now call a geek. Well, that might have been a bit harsh. Greg had always been socially fairly adept, owing much success to his good-humoured nature.

Although he had never really kept up any particular sport as anything more than an occasional passing hobby, he had always been quite fit, liking walks in the open country, or doing home improvements and work in and around his home. Of course, with the sailing trip, he had been very active and had lost some of those pounds, converting fat to muscle.

He would need every ounce now.

Baseball oar poised, it was the large man whom they had not yet encountered who got to him first, somehow circumventing the other two. Greg took a swing back before smashing the oar across the side of the man's head. He barely moved. Greg had time to do it again, before retreating a step. The oar, light but fairly robust, was still intact. Greg glanced round and saw that Dale was still dealing with the girl. It was Peter who was the worry.

Luckily, Peter had come to his senses, to a degree, the importance of the moment possibly filling his body with strength and defiance, and dulling his pains. He had managed to prop himself up on the edge of the boat, sitting on one of the inflated sides, but he had no weapon. He had nothing to defend himself with.

In short, the man had little hope.

It was the woman from the souvenir shop who arrived first and came at him. He grabbed her around the waist from his sitting position, and tried to keep her at bay, at a safe distance. Peter wasn't, however, the biggest man, and his arms were not the longest of appendages in the defensive armoury that day. The woman's clawing hands grabbed the sides of his face and started raking and pulling, gripping and grasping, scraping and scratching, time after time after time. And all Peter could do was to keep his own arms straight for as long as possible. Those crooked, angular fingers, with knuckles bent and distorted in some kind of seething attack, made short meal of the skin on his face, which after the first few flails was lacerated and red with blood. Her sharp nails were too much for even his sun and sea-hardened skin.

To make matters worse, were that possible, the silver-haired man, last to arrive, fell onto Peter from the side, forcing him to lose balance and topple from his sitting position, propped on the dinghy's side. He landed on his face and side in the soft sand next to the small boat. And then his two tormenters overcame him. Peter tried to fight them off; they weren't the biggest of people who could have attacked him, but neither was he the most formidable of men.

Greg looked over, "Nooo! Peter!" But he himself had his own challenge, and one that seemed to be going nowhere but backwards. Greg was repeatedly backing up towards the sea, beating his big attacker around the head in the hope that, eventually, the damage he was doing would accumulate to a critical level. Unfortunately, that plan seemed to be ineffectual, and the man's head, though utterly bloodied and battered, was still sending commands to its limbs and curling the lips back in threat, as he advanced one-tracked and sense-free.

Greg took a mighty backswing with his right leg and gave the man the biggest damned kick he had ever given anything in his life, aiming for the area just above the ankle. The man's weight caused him to buckle as the supporting leg was swept away with the kick. Dale had forced his attacker to the ground, too, and was pummelling her about the head with the oar. But when Greg looked over at Peter, all he could see were two bodies writhing atop him, with no shortage of gore being thrown about.

Whilst the big man was still down on the sand and struggling to get his weighty mass up on both legs again, Greg ran and grabbed the tender at the bow and spun it toward the sea. Taking the attached rope, and quickly spinning his wrist so the rope wrapped around his hand several times, he yanked it with all the energy he had left, and as quickly as possible, until he manoeuvred the boat into the shallow water. Running back to the chaos, he took a huge swing at the fat man's head which sent him off balance, falling onto his back, buying Greg some more precious seconds.

"Dale, come on!"

Dale turned, and then looked at Peter.

***

Peter's last thoughts, as his arms finally ran out of energy trying to defend his ailing body, were of pain. The pain of his leg, his face, his ear, everything. So much pain that it all blurred into one. His left ear had been bitten off, and much of the skin and flesh of his face were missing. Eventually, bites were made into the soft tissue of his neck, and his arteries started spurting, though it took some three or four strong-jawed gnashes to get there.

As his consciousness ebbed away with each pulse of blood pumped from his still-beating heart, so the pain dulled bit by bit, pulse by pulse. And that felt good, like falling asleep after a terrible nightmare.

Finally, Peter's tide went out for the last time.

METAMORPHOSIS

37
Jason

The van accelerated past what had now become an awesome inferno. The dry weather had left thirsty grasses and shrubs around the cottage which provided perfect fuel for the burgeoning fire. The flames, which had started as hellish dancers prancing about the interior of the house, had now become powerful demonic elementals, ripping through the property, and hungrily lashing out at the surrounding foliage and outhouses.

The two men drove slowly past, staring in amazement at the unfolding village disaster. Jason stared intently at the blaze.

Man, the world is going crazy. I can't even phone the fire brigade. I'm just driving past a burning house, and I'm going to do nothing; absolutely nothing.

Bevan accelerated the van once they had passed the fire-enveloped house, and pulled up to the T-junction. He stopped the van, leaving it idling, and switched the radio on. Pressing buttons on a piece of equipment in the van which was vastly more current and technological than the van itself, Bevan heard nothing but dead air.

"The transmitting stations can't be getting any power. Power's the key. Without it, everything will fall apart. Just think how much we use power. I mean, we talked about this last night, but Jesus, mate, just think how totally fucked up life will be until they get the power back on," said Bevan.

"Well, that does beg the question, like, as to whether they *will* get it back on. I mean, who's the 'they'?" Jason responded.

As they sat there pondering their predicament, two figures were slowly plodding up the road behind them, having picked themselves up and stumbled past the burning house in pursuit of the van. Bevan glanced fortuitously in his rearview mirror.

"We've got company. We'd better do one. You listen out for some radio stations," said Bevan, pulling the van out on to the main road and driving left towards Olding.

On the road, after a hundred metres or so, they could see a car approaching them from the other direction. Bevan flashed it in an attempt to flag it down, but the car didn't stop. The two men peered at it as it drove on by and could see someone lying on the back seat, the driver sporting a bandana over their mouth.

"I reckon the person in the back seat was ill," suggested Bevan, to Jason's agreement. "Could've stopped to let us know what the hell is going on."

Some minutes later, another car could be seen approaching from the outskirts of Olding. Again Bevan flashed the car, a black BMW. This time the car slowed. The two vehicles braked and edged slowly closer until they were side-by-side. The driver of the BMW was in his forties with a dark beard flecked with grey sitting on a square jaw. He looked nervous as he wound his window down a fraction, enough to hear Bevan who had wound his own window almost to the bottom, peering at the other driver from above.

"Hi there, fella. We've been away for a bunch of time and we seem to have returned to a crazy world. What the hell's going on?" asked Bevan.

"You really don't know? Really?" The man looked at Bevan incredulously.

"Well, just what we got off the TV and radio before we lost power. It looks like a virus has ripped through, like, the world? We've been camping in the middle of the moor."

"This last week has been insane. Like a bad, bad dream. In a matter of days the virus has ripped through every town and city," replied the man, anxiety etched across his furrowed brow.

"We left to there being a flu going around, but that was it," Bevan explained.

"They say it's a mix of rabies and bird flu, or something. Problem is, *everyone* seems to have got it. I don't know how, but they have, and those who haven't have locked themselves away for self-preservation. The scientists and politicians sorting this thing out were caught unaware and seem to have got it before they could do anything about it!"

"So who's around? Who's doing anything about it?" Jason interjected, leaning over Bevan's lap.

"There's been minimal help from the police and army—only in the cities. Even then, most people deserted to help their families and friends. But again, most people had it before they knew it. I'd been ill in bed with my own health problems, so I didn't come into contact with anyone. I reckon I'm fine. But my kids and ex are in London, and I've got to see if they're okay. I'm duty-bound to get over to London and check them out. Last I heard my son was feeling lousy. I'm heartbroken to think he could be in trouble." The man was visibly struggling to hold back tears.

"I know, man. I have no idea whether my family in Winchester is alright or not. We'll be following you back up this road in an hour or so," Jason asserted.

The man made an odd face. "You've got to be careful, you two. People have changed—"

"We know. We've seen it," nodded Bevan.

"Well, I've seen it back in Olding. Just stay away from anyone. There are people wondering around Olding who, well, aren't really people any more. The virus has destroyed their brains, and I don't reckon there's any reversing it. I heard things last night that scared the life out of me. I know there are ships off of Portsmouth and elsewhere down south which are safe. They've got some kind of emergency group operating. But I guess they just don't have enough people or equipment to effectively deal with millions of people who are ill. I guess I'll head there after London, depending," the bearded man said, looking a little desperate.

The men said their farewells and good lucks before continuing their respective drives.

Jason turned to Bevan just as they were about to enter Olding and said, "What gets me, Bev, is that throughout life there's always been some authority, some knowledge base which we can refer to. The council, local government, police, central government. But one week, they've gone AWOL. We're like ants who've been separated from the nest. No direction, nothing to sort us out, no orders, no frame of reference. I've got no idea what to do other than find my family. But when I do that, what then?"

Bevan thought a while.

"Well, I guess, when it comes to it, survive?"

"That's a bit serious," said Jason. "A bit final. Do you really think that's what life has come to in *one week*?"

"Dude, that's what life has always been about. You just clutter it up with Playstations and iPhones, watching football and drinking tea. But really, it's about survival. Don't you remember this morning? You were almost bitten in the face by a mental woman with her muff out. If it wasn't for my spade, you'd be burning right now." Bevan had stopped the van to explain this.

"Yeah, I guess. But surely there's got be something more than survival?" said Jason.

"Really? I reckon there are those who do, and there are those who don't. Those who do, get to do other things, like shag and have babies.

That's like the World Cup. Woo hoo! Those who don't, fly into fires or get their faces bitten off. Which group do you want to be in?"

"Yeah, but life's more than just shagging and having babies," implored Jason.

"Only if you don't get your face bitten off. So survival first. That's number one. Then we can think about having babies, Jason. Me and you…"

"Um, no. Okay, mate. This is a new rule. Survival first. We have to make it to Winchester. No stupid decisions. No putting ourselves at risk. Playstations and iPhones aren't going to help us now. We need our wits and a bit of planning. I've got a few ideas… C'mon, Bev, get us to my flat."

Bevan looked at Jason with a mischievous smile. "Sure thing. And then can we shag?"

38
Fran

Fran had struggled immensely to suppress her panic. Leaving her flat was hard enough on a normal day when all she had to do was go to the hairdresser's, a five minute walk up the road.

But this involved a crazed potential killer outside her door and a world that was only several steps away from insanity.

It had taken some pills, and Tanya talking to her and calming her whilst sitting on the sofa and having a last cup of tea. Tanya had herself been panicked by her own predicament and had given a sterling effort to ease Fran's worries and palpitating heart. Whatever was to happen next, it wasn't going to be easy for Fran.

Grasping their respective tools in their white-knuckled clenches, the two women now stood buffered in stylish quilts.

"Er, how do we open the door?" asked Tanya, quizzically.

"Good point," said Fran as she wove her hand through the folds of the bedding to poke her stretched fingers out of the other side. Pulling the bolt to the side, she collected herself and took in a deep breath. "Okay, Tanya, on three, I'll open the other lock. He'll probably fall through into us, so we need to stand our ground. Better still, we need to give him a mighty push back. Take him unawares. Outside, we run around, maybe one each way, to the stairs on the other side, and get the hell outta here."

"Sounds good."

Fran looked over at Tanya, who had lost much of her colour now and was sweating herself to an unhealthy sheen. Damp strands of hair hung limply from around her ears. She did not look well. Not at all well to Fran's eyes.

"On three..." Fran said, looking at Tanya.

"You've said that."

"Okay. On three. Er, three...two...one!"

And with that, she clicked the lock open and the door budged inwards as the weight of the man on the other side pushed against it, until it hit the inner wall. The two women fumbled and staggered back until Fran shouted "Push!" and they rallied, heads down behind their wall of stuffing, and shoved. Legs pumping, the women drove their would-be attacker backwards, engulfed as he was in comfortable bedding. Letting out guttural stutters, the man was propelled back and out of the threshold to Fran's apartment. Once more, he was slammed into the railings opposite the apartment door, over which a drop to the ground floor and hallway below could be seen. The stairs to the block skirted all four sides of the large interior stairwell.

The two women had succeeded perfectly in the execution of their plan as the man lay crumpled under the bedding, arms flailing, muffled spitting and gasping emanating from beneath. Fran went left and Tanya went right as they ran, each grasping their weapon, which they had been holding under the duvets, rucksacks joggling on their backs.

Survival instincts had kicked in as Fran's thoughts were as far away from panicking about her current apartment-external predicament as possible. Her focus was on the floor, the stairs, the railing, and each floor as they descended the staircases until they reached the ground floor, unimpeded.

"Now where?" panted Fran as they arrived at the entrance to the block, suddenly blank of mind as to what they were doing.

"The hospital, you idiot! I need to get some help!"

Fran paused as they stood inside the wooden doors with reinforced glass panes at head height, which offered a finely grated view of the lawn outside the front of the block. As they both got their breath back, Fran studied Tanya and for the first time properly realised the situation she was in. Extrapolating the woman's deterioration, it wouldn't be too long until she was debilitated and too ill to run. Already Tanya seemed out of breath, and, well, sick.

Tanya turned her laboured eyes towards Fran and said, "We forgot to do our planning. Have you got a car? I don't."

"No. No, no I don't. I sold it when I started getting too...stuck in my flat," Fran admitted.

"Great. So we need to get to the hospital. There'll still be people driving about who can give us a lift. Let's just stick together and catch a lift off someone."

Fran was dubious. She didn't think there would be many people thinking straight because even if they weren't ill, they'd be panicking, or doing definite things without wanting to derail their own plans on behalf of these women. Fran, though, resigned herself to risking going outside with this woman.

And then she panicked.

Everything about the day, and the idea of going out onto the lawn outside, into the world outside, hit Fran like speeding train, literally knocking the wind out of her. Struggling, suddenly, to breathe appropriately, with her heart hammering at a phenomenal rate, she flattened herself against the wall to the side of the door. From further up the stairwell at the centre of the block, she could just about hear the shuffling of feet above the deafening pulsations of her blood flowing through her veins, thrumming in her ears.

"Oh my god, oh my god, oh my god," was all that she could manage as she became shrouded in a sensory overload.

Tanya grabbed Fran, grasping her upper arms in what was an ailing grip. "Sort it out, come…come on…" She turned her head to the side to let off a wheezing cough. "Let's get out there and get some help. There's bound to be heaps of people out there in the same position as us."

Speak for yourself. I'm fine. Fran admonished herself for her selfish thoughts, and then quickly questioned that very position. *I've got to look after myself, otherwise I've got nothing left. I'm just me. I'm no one else. If I get ill, and die, then I die. Everything I do has to be to protect me. Everything.* In a moment of clarity, Fran had separated her entirety from the oneness of the world which she usually strived towards, and focused her attention on the being that was Fran. She looked up the stairs to the third floor to see the shadowy form of the man whom they had pushed over, and she looked back to Tanya. Moving to the doors, she looked out at the deserted urban landscape, peppered with the odd shambling body, and the occasional car which sped past on some unknown mission.

Glancing around to Tanya again, she looked hard at her face.

And then ran.

Not out of the doors, but back through the entrance hall with its dirty linoleum flooring, past the entrance to the stairwell, and back to the rear door which led to the car park at the back of the building.

The sunlight hit her with unexpected force, as did the fresh air of the summer outdoors, albeit air having circulated about the city of Bristol to find itself gently idling about a concrete carpark. The doors slowly returned to their positions having been slammed open in a hurry. Fran had little idea of what she was doing as her conscious thoughts caught up with what her non-conscious brain had calculated was the best course of action.

She stopped.

Jesus, what the hell am I doing? What about that poor woman? Ah, she's surely got no chance of finding proper help… Damn I can't just leave her like that; I'll never be able to live with myself!

Standing, overlooking a lot full of parked cars, Fran's universe spun around in her mind, a phenomenal vortex of abstract thoughts. Who she had been, who she was, who she thought she had been and was, and every bit of sensory data, came together like a mental tumult such that she staggered a step sideways. *Is this who I will be?* She turned and stepped back to the rear doors, peering through the reinforced glass rectangles, through the hallway, to see Tanya, back against the wall, slumped with her head in her hands, sobbing. Letting out a long breath, she pushed the door open and walked back into the hallway to Tanya.

"Get up, come on! Let's go get a lift."

Behind her, the stumbling footsteps of the dishevelled man could be heard faltering their way down the final flight of stairs.

"Now."

39
Greg

The morning sunshine was warming the barnacle and limpet bedecked rocks on the eastern side of the bay, whilst spray struggled to cool the tops of the sprouting rocks as the waves yielded to the summer laziness. Rather than battering, the waves merely circled, and occasionally massaged their erstwhile nemeses.

There was barely a breath of moving air, rare for such coastal waters where warm air meets cooler sea. A different year, and the beach would be teaming with sunbathers, tourists, boaters and other assorted seaside activities and partakers.

Just not this year.

Further up, towards the middle of the beach, which sat between the two headlands embracing the town, the two men, Dale and Greg, were floating some twenty metres off the shore, exhausted and lying together in the dinghy. Equipped with one oar, the other falling victim to the pitched battle onshore, they looked back at the aftermath. Without relenting, the large fat man was repeatedly walking out of his depth and returning, then going of his depth, and returning again to breathable depth, like some animal with no memory being tested in some experiment. The sea lapped just as lackadaisically against his forehead.

There were still two bodies atop Peter, seemingly *devouring* him, with scant regard for anything else in the world, intent on only what was in front of them. Animal feeding in a frenzy of gore. The final body, that of the girl who had distracted Dale, lay twitching on the sand. Dale had done enough with his repeated aluminium oar-blows about the girl's head.

"Peter..." was all Greg could muster. There were scant few thoughts going through his confused mind; a morass of neurons, images, memories he might never forget, experiences, feelings, emotions. Yet they seemed to cancel each other out. The end result was a feeling of numbness, of blankness. Perhaps it was shock, but instead of feeling a sense of loss and sorrow in light of seeing Peter die, Greg felt confusion, like an equation which just didn't balance but he couldn't work out where or why.

"What in God's name just happened?" Dale asked, staring intensely at the beach scene horror.

"I...I...I don't know. I have no idea what is going on. Where is everybody?" Greg replied. "Is this the only town which is, I don't know, ill? There must be people here who aren't ill, wouldn't you say?"

"There was someone in the flat above the gallery. But he didn't seem to care or want to help."

"It's the plagues, Dale."

"Eh?"

"The plagues of Revelation. I can feel it." Greg was deadly serious, as serious as he had ever been. It had just come to him. In times past, he had been dismissive of the Book of Revelation in the New Testament, having argued in Bible Study that it was not supposed to be read literally. But something had changed. This experience had changed *him*. "'Then the fifth angel poured out his bowl on the throne of the beast, and his kingdom became darkened; and they gnawed their tongues because of pain, and they blasphemed the God of heaven because of their pains and their sores; and they did not repent of their deeds.' The pains and sores, Dale. The pains and sores."

Dale gave his own rejoinder, looking at the beast that sat atop Peter, blood coursing down her chin from the entrails of their friend, "She is Babylon, drunk with the blood of a saint, of a witness of Jesus. God rest his soul."

Greg's knuckles went white as he gripped the oar. "We are being punished. Surely we are. There is no other explanation." His speech, his usual rather slow drawl, sounded almost slurred with an edge of delirium.

"I can't believe that Peter is...gone. I'm not sure I know how to react." The weirdness of the situation was taking its toll on Dale. "Let's get back to the boat. I need to get my face sorted out. It's really painful, and I'm feeling pretty weak, Greg."

"What monster on God's Earth could do that?"

With that, he sat up, moved to the rear of the small boat, and worked the small engine down into the water on its hinge, pulling the cord to power it up. The sturdy inflatable carved its way effortlessly through the calm sea towards *Grace* accompanied by a distant background symphony of gnawing, guttural exultations and the muffled sputtering of a demonic beast whose head was breaking the surface like a lone beacon of insanity in a serene sea.

***

Back at the boat, the two men alighted with some difficulty, and Greg saw to Dale's injured face with the limited first aid kit stowed on board. Up until this point, the most action the kit had seen was providing small Band-Aids to the occasional cut fingers, and soothing and cleansing a bad knock to Peter's brow early in the first week of the trip. Booms are dangerous things in the hands of amateurs. Greg had apologised profusely, as it had been his fault. "It's all a learning curve," Dale had said, explaining that such an event had provided good training such that it wouldn't happen again, with worse possible consequences. And it hadn't; for given that crossing the Atlantic was an exceptionally dangerous thing to do for such an inexperienced crew, bar Dale's accumulated knowledge, they had gotten through the odyssey with nothing but good memories.

Until arriving at their destination, that was.

Greg inspected the wound on Dale's cheek. The patient had already swallowed a number of painkillers. A decidedly large chunk of skin and flesh was missing, with a smaller flap of skin at the bottom of the gouge hanging down ever so slightly. Greg was reminded of some of those video nasties, horror movies that he had momentarily shown an interest in during his younger years. Except this was so very real; Greg had Dale's blood on his hands.

He took a large gauze out of its protective wrapper and placed it squarely over Dale's gaping wound, where it stuck with its gory adhesive. Taking the tape and scissors from the red plastic box nestled on the bench at the stern of the boat, to the side of the helm, he pulled some tape out and snipped some pieces, attaching them to the gauze and Dale's face. The sun struck his face brightly, and there was some dissonance in Greg's head as if such a nice day with its shiny sun shouldn't be heralding such weird experiences, and such a nasty looking injury.

"Yuh, well, I'll never be a surgeon," he joked, trying to lighten the moment, inspecting what looked like some five-year-old's attempt at playing doctors and nurses.

Dale seemed a little dreamy. "It...hurts, Peter, it hurts."

Greg ignored the confusion. It had been a long day, after all, despite it only being mid-morning. He took one of the rolls of bandage out and snipped a generous length, winding it around Dale's head so that it kept the gauze neatly in place.

"Right, Dale, we need to work out what the heck to do next. We obviously need to get to shore, and we need to do it safely. And we need to contact someone. You know, the police, or anyone other than those...things." Greg was still struggling to comprehend exactly what those people, their beach assailants, were; exactly what was motivating them to behave in such a manner. "Maybe they were ill. Maybe this town has an outbreak." And with that a penny dropped. He took a look at his hands and walked off to the small galley sink, pumped himself some fresh water, and scrubbed his hands with soap.

"I'm feeling pretty...bad, Greg. Do you think you could check the radio? See if...if you could...can get hold of someone?" Dale laboured.

"Sure, Dale. Take it easy there."

Greg took himself over to the captain's desk by the galley, a small wooden table bedecked with maps and navigation equipment, and the all-important radio. Switching it on, he dialled through some frequencies to listen out for chatter and any kind of information that he could garner, but was met with grim silence. There was an FM/AM radio fixed to the desk which connected to the speakers around the cabin. Greg clicked it on, using the AM setting, and again dialled through the frequencies until he came across some sound.

"Thank goodness for that," he said as he listened in. What he heard froze his heart and stopped his lungs.

...take care to look after yourselves, and do not leave your houses until further notice. Live broadcasts are restricted to one hour from 21:00 tonight. This is a national emergency message. All listeners...

"Dale, are you listening?" asked Greg, looking over to his friend who was sitting up at the stern of the boat, through the cabin door.

"...Yeah. Sure," replied Dale, looking something like a post-operative patient sinking under sedation.

...indoors and refrain from coming into contact with anyone in the wider community. This should minimise the spread of this outbreak. We repeat, please do not leave your houses. The police 999 number is not presently working due to personnel shortages but will be up and running as and when possible...

Greg listened over and over, to the same message, as it looped around on itself.

"Is that it?" he asked himself as he came to the conclusion that it contained hardly any usable information, and yet explicitly communicated what seemed to him the most important message in his lifetime.

Greg slammed his fist down on the small desktop in frustration. Although he was a fairly jolly man, he also could be quick to temper, especially when under stress. He was under stress.

Most of all, though, Greg was confused. It was as though his brain could not compute the today's events, as though his memories and experiences were fragments of a jigsaw, but piecing them together formed no discernible pattern. Events were just happening without any obvious purpose.

There must have been a purpose. There must. God couldn't have let this happen for no reason. All evil was explicable.

All the rationality and arguments he had employed in his Bible study group and online were now coming to the fore; except those highfalutin' philosophical principles were now seeing the light of day in a *really real* context. This wasn't ten people sitting in a circle, or listening to a guest speaker, and throwing ideas back and forth. This was one dead friend, demons eating bodies on a beach, a village deserted as a result of some outbreak, and the two remaining friends quarantined on a yacht.

Greg returned his attention to the more pressing needs of the day. "Dale, I'm gonna pack my big bag, just in case."

"Okay… Just going to sit here a bit," Dale replied, sounding a little distant.

"You okay, Dale?"

"Sure. Sure."

Greg took himself to his own cabin and rummaged through his belongings, gathering a variety of things that he might need, mainly clothing. He took his pocket knife off the small shelf and put that in his pocket of his cargo pants. After packing a larger backpack, his main "travel suitcase", with his things, he moved across to Dale's quarters and slung together roughly the same sort of things. Maybe Dale was feeling pretty weak because…because he'd got what *they* had. If that radio broadcast was anything to go by, there was an outbreak of something. Hell, it might have gotten around the world! Greg had to make sure he was careful around Dale.

And then it struck him and again his heart froze.

What if he became like *them*. He had that injury, so whatever they had, Dale probably had!

Greg was immobilised. He couldn't move a muscle in his body, like a rabbit caught in the headlights. Then his heart crashed back into motion, hammering in his chest. Backing up to look towards the stern from the forecabin threshold, he could just about make out Dale's legs at the bench seat back aft. Greg's heart calmed to a more reasonable and regular beat. He finished tucking Dale's clothes into a large holdall bag that he had found in a wooden cupboard, and headed into the main cabin, or what Dale preferred to call *the saloon,* lifting his own backpack on the way.

"So, Dale, I've got our stuff. I think we need to get on that boat and find our way to a safe part of that beach and get ourselves to a car, or someone's house, like your cousin's hotel."

Greg had been going over and over the options and it was hard to know what to do without really knowing what was going on, onshore. There were just too many unknowns. Dumping the bags, he made the short few steps through the hatch and into the bright sunshine of the cockpit.

Dale was still sat in the same position, but his head was lolling back, resting on the deck behind.

"Hey Dale, you okay?"

Dale moved his head to look at Greg. However, his eyes were looking terribly bloodshot, whilst his skin was covered in a sheen of sweat. Altogether, he did not look well.

"Gee, Dale, you're looking a little peaky there. Do you want me to put you in your cabin? I'll go and find us some help."

Dale looked at Greg, appearing to try to decipher Greg's face. "Peter... I'm... not well...," Dale wheezed.

"You've taken a turn for the worse, my friend. I'll get you down below," Greg said, and hauled Dale up to his feet, placing his arm around his torso, grabbing Dale's left forearm and pulling it over his shoulders. Under Greg's guidance, they bumped their way down into the saloon, and then on through the short corridor to the forecabin where Dale was somewhat unceremoniously dumped on his thin mattress due to the constraints of space.

"Sheeeesh...," was all Dale could muster.

"Right, Dale, I'll be as quick as I can. I'll get to your cousin's place and I'll get you some help. We'll sort this mess out, Dale, I promise. Hold my hand, Dale, hold my hand," and Greg took Dale's hand in his own, dipping his head in prayer. "May God the Father bless you, God the Son heal you, God the Holy Spirit give you strength. May God the holy and undivided Trinity guard your body and save your soul, Amen."

Dale mumbled something. He seemed to be fading fast.

Greg knew that he'd better get a move on...

He stood, moved quickly to the galley and grabbed a water bottle from a cupboard, and pumped it full of water. Returning to Dale's side, he placed it in his right hand. Greg patted him on the arm, turned and walked back off aft. On his way to the cockpit, he grabbed what few snacks they had left and jammed them into the top and pockets of his backpack, which wasn't particularly full at any rate.

Up in the cockpit, with backpack in his hands, he looked out towards his destination, back towards the shore. He could see the figures of their attackers around what must be the mere skeletal remains of Peter.

"Bastards."

Greg hadn't, in general and since breaking through adolescence, been one to swear all that much, especially as his faith had grown. He had sat down one day and wondered why that was, and whether God would actually care one fig about such words. After researching the topic one rainy weekend afternoon, he was fascinated to find out that there was precedent within the Bible itself for bad language. That being said, he had thought, he had still come to feel that swearing was a reflection of a lack of respect, that God would value respect, and that overly rude words were markers of a lack of general respect, as well as being less aesthetically pleasing. As such, he just started swearing less.

Today warranted an outburst, but even so, he was restrained in his vocabulary. A younger Greg would have painted the aural surroundings somewhat bluer.

Putting the backpack on the rear deck by the stepladder, he manoeuvred his large frame down the steps, and onto the tender, which he had pulled close. Once on, he hauled the bag down, untied the line and sat carefully at the back. The engine sounded abnormally loud in the quiet backdrop of an otherwise serene panorama, if one forgot the events of the day so far. Greg had decided to head for the right hand side of the beach, almost where it started getting rocky, and to make a beeline for the road which seemed to lead up and out from the car park. He was hoping that the outboard motor was not going to be loud enough to garner the attention of the beachcombing beasts.

All was well, so far.

The tender motored along fairly innocuously. But not innocuously enough. Over where Peter's remains lay, there were now four devouring subhumans laying waste to what was once a close friend. The ticking of the motor had caused the younger girl who had tussled with Dale to lift her head up and look around like a meerkat in the savannah. She caught sight of Greg in the dinghy and immediately stood up as if Greg provided a more enticing distraction, that the latest craving was by default the most important one. To his dismay, his heart a stone sinking to the sandy depths, the young girl stood and started walking along the beach towards where he was heading. The other three looked up and around and, blood dripping from their faces, staining almost every piece of clothing, they stood and followed the lead.

Greg was some twenty metres from the shore when a thought hit him. He was going to need a weapon. Something. He had...a pocket knife, and that wouldn't do.

Making a split-second decision, he steered the boat around and made back for the yacht. He didn't fancy taking his chances, having to run through town with his backpack and nothing but a small selection of hinged tools for defence. As he pulled back away from the shore, the four shambolic figures turned and stumbled their way into the sea as if nothing should get in their way of their target. Greg stared back, mesmerized by the unfolding behaviour of what, days or even hours before, must have been normal enough people. His mind was fizzing with ideas of constructing different weapons from the items available on board. *Maybe I could attach a kitchen knife to a pole*, he thought, *or I could break the final oar in two and have two clubs*. Either way, his trip ashore needed to be slightly more carefully planned.

Greg pulled up alongside *Grace*, gliding the final few metres with motor off. Standing at the bow, he grabbed the stern of the yacht and tied the rope quickly around the ladder. He clumsily raced up the ladder and into the cockpit. Without really having formed a concrete idea of what he wanted, he stomped off up the deck of the yacht and up to some rope which ran from the rigging to be tied around a cleat. He untied and unwound the rope, and then removed the pocket knife from its rightful home and set about slicing through the splicing. It took him a little longer than anticipated; the rope was tough and the knife far from at its sharpest. The rope was too thick to be useful in its present form, so Greg started to unwind the threaded cords until he was left with several much thinner pieces that he could more easily tie around smaller objects. Scanning around to see if there was anything to hand on the deck that might come in handy, he found nothing, so stood up and returned to the cockpit.

Moving into the darker cabin below, it took his eyes some time to adjust from the exterior brightness to the interior shadows. He went straight to the galley drawers and started emptying them of the more useful of implements, namely sharp knives, accompanied with a call of, "Dale, I'm back and tooling myself up. It ain't pretty out there." He heard a muffled mumble in response.

Now, this is insane to think about, but do I need a slicing weapon or a clubbing weapon? Hey, maybe a sharp weapon isn't so useful unless it's the size of a machete?

Greg wasn't at all used to such thoughts. He wasn't a violent man, and in fact, sat in stark contrast to many of the people with whom he went to church, who were far more right-wing than he was. Greg was a fiscal conservative, and he had, without realising it overtly himself, become more socially conservative the longer he had been around the people in his church, and the longer he found solace and intellectual stimulus with those around him. But he had never been a gun owner. His father had made sure of that, as Ted, his father's own brother, had died when Greg was a child. Ted had been killed when his son, Greg's cousin, at the age of five, had accidentally fired off a shot from Ted's handgun, which had not been put away. The bullet went right into the side of Ted's forehead and he died instantly.

Greg's father took it very badly indeed, and was rare in the family and the community as, from that point forward, he was outspoken about his contempt for gun ownership, and associated lax care and control. This had been passed on to Greg, and though there was much that Greg intentionally rejected in and from his father, the disdain for widespread gun ownership was something that, for some reason, he held on to. He had pondered that this might have been as a result of his general lack of desire for or interest in violence. He didn't *need* violence.

Now, however, violence had come to him. It had invaded his morning and turned it, and his life, on their heads.

Greg realised that one of his best bets was utilising the oar in the little craft tied to the back of the yacht, and so quickly set himself down to get it. He could certainly take the oar blade off and attach a knife so that it could be used both as a long club, depending on how strong the aluminium remained, and a cutting weapon. When he had retrieved it, he returned down to the saloon to get to work on crafting himself a weapon worthy of taking on the strange beasts which had appeared to have come straight from the gates of hell.

Pulling out drawers, clattering around some tools and odds and ends, Greg failed to recognise the dull thudding of Dale, aroused by the sound, as he unsteadily got to his feet and fell against the wall.

"Tape, tape, we've got some tape," Greg muttered to himself, in the throes of creative thought and design.

"Ahh shavvvv...," Dale exhaled.

Greg paused.

"Chhhhhhaarrr..."

Greg turned.

What met him was shocking. In the relatively short time since Greg had looked in on Dale, he had morphed into a very disturbing rendition of his friend. Dale's skin was covered in a sheen of sweat and had changed colour, losing its living tint of sun-blushed sailor. Instead, there were hues of pallid grey interspersed with spindly threads of dark red veins. Dale stood, head bobbing, swaying, staring at Greg.

"Er, Dale, you okay?" Greg asked worriedly.

Dale merely stared, head held lower than it would normally have been, as if it were half-full of lead.

"Dale...Dale?" Greg didn't, however, make any move further towards his friend. Dale just stood there.

"Look, let me just get you back to your room."

Greg advanced slowly towards Dale, hands held up instinctively in self-defence, as if Dale might suddenly become, or already be, one of those attackers on the beach. He was taking no chances.

"Dale, can you hear me? You're not answering," said Greg. He moved to within half a metre of Dale. Dale's eyes fixed on Greg's; there was some remnant of recognition, as if Dale was looking through a glass, darkly, struggling to make sense of his visual stimuli.

Greg grabbed Dale's arms tightly around the biceps and said, "I'm gonna get you to your room. You need to lie down, Dale, you understand? You need to lie down."

Greg swung round behind Dale, and re-grabbed his arms before turning him and pushing him slowly back towards his room, talking calmly to him. "Just have a lie down and take it easy. Sleep, my friend, that's what you need."

"Fsshhhaaarrr...," Dale replied, drunkenly.

Good God, I think Dale really has got this thing. How long have I got?

Greg returned him to his room, and closed the door, all the time reassuring him that everything was going to be okay. Listening at the door to make sure that everything was in order, Greg finally returned hurriedly to the saloon.

How much time did he have? Had he lost Dale? Was Dale one of them? Questions whirled about Greg's head in a flurry of doubt and worry. *Please, dear God, give me some guidance.*

Greg sucked in a deep breath and took himself back to making his weapon. The last time he had done something like this was when he had been a twelve-year-old with a penchant for kicking about outdoors with friends, in the woods. There, they had often made their own bows and arrows, having been through the testing phases for each of the materials to find the best wood for the strongest, most flexible bows, and the straightest arrows. He often remembered those halcyon days of innocent youth on hot, balmy summer days, running around, shooting at bottles, pretending to be all sorts of good and bad.

Now he had an oar, a knife, some twine and a number of other innocuous items. He managed to break most of the blade off the oar so was left with an aluminium shaft with a jagged end. With some weak tape from the first aid kit, he attached the knife to the end as firmly he could, overlaying that with some twine, tied in rather inept knots. Twelve was a long time away!

Finishing his weapon, he propped it against the cooker, and moved up to the cockpit. He had remembered that there were some ropes and pieces of random sailing paraphernalia under one of the bench seats. Greg started to sort through the bits and pieces under the bench. He was being fairly liberal with the amount of noise he was making and this prompted and then covered up Dale's own movement as he struggled to push the slide door along.

Greg was trying to work out a way of getting the chain off the spare anchor thinking that perhaps he could use the chain as a swinging weapon to smite the unfortunate victims of his wrath.

He heard a bang.

Spinning to his right to look down into the saloon below, Greg could see Dale stumbling out of the corridor and into the larger space.

"Hey Dale, you okay?" called Greg through the cabin opening. He crawled over and looked through, adjusting his eyes. Dale, in the half an hour that had passed, had deteriorated demonstrably. His eyes were now jaded as though he were wearing ever so slightly milky cataracts, and his skin had further taken a journey away from its previous healthy state, criss-crossed, as it was, with bloody capillaries, disappearing under the once white gauze, blotched with dark blood.

"Dale…"

METAMORPHOSIS

40
Fran

The sun shone brightly onto the grass of the lawn in front of the apartment block, refracting summer to the casual onlooker. Of which there were none. Fran and Tanya jogged up the path which dissected the lawn, casting furtive glances in every direction, hopeful that they could see someone who could help them in any way, but also cognisant of the potential dangers lurking out of plain sight. They reached the road opposite the blocks and rested their eyes on the Tesco store with the car protruding from its frontage. There didn't seem to be anyone around it. Whether that was because people generally had food for the immediate future, or because almost everyone was ill, or because there were ill people stuck inside, Fran did not know nor care to find out. Instead, she led Tanya to the right and along the pavement to the corner of the lawned area with its privet hedge, to the T-junction. The road rose uphill after the T-junction, and provided the route towards the hospital that Fran figured they'd have to start on foot. The hospital was several miles away, but it appeared to be their only hope at the moment. Fran took a look back towards the apartment block, to see the unwanted neighbour wavering up the path in their direction, exhaling gasping exclamations.

"All we bloody need," said Fran.

Fran took Tanya's arm, whom she felt was weaker than even five minutes earlier, and led her jogging across the road at the junction, and up the inclining road in the general direction of the hospital. They jogged up the road for some fifty metres before the road started bending.

Fran's heart leapt.

She was amazed that they hadn't come across anyone else already. It was like this major city was asleep in a sequence from a twisted fairy tale. And yet, in front of her, some twenty metres or so, stood a pair of people wandering aimlessly about the middle of the road. One, a thin pale man, was in bare feet and pyjamas and looked to be about sixty; the other, a large Asian woman in a sari, bumped into the man and staggered off towards one side of the road. The two were standing between two short rows of local and rather dilapidated shops, equipped with a bus stop. Fran had used to get the occasional and emergency fruit and veg from the greengrocers there before he closed down to be replaced by another betting shop. There were three betting shops in a mile on this same road, a condemnation of high street shopping, as Fran saw it. A sign of the times. Now the shops were quiet, their clientele either ill or imposing quarantine on themselves.

"We're going to have to run past them. I hope they're as slow as the other few I've seen," said Fran, reviewing her options.

The air still seemed deathly quiet, mild and now breathless in the midmorning haze. Pigeons had taken advantage of the lack of traffic, both vehicular and pedestrian, and scattered themselves on parts of the road and pavement, pecking and scratching. The man made a clumsy and almost lackadaisical lunge at one group of pigeons, arms outstretched. The pigeons, unperturbed, simply half-flew, half-waddled out of the way to continue their grazing a step or two away. The man tried it again; this time the birds jumped towards the two woman walking up the road, and the man, turning to chase them, caught sight of the oncoming pair. He let out a strangled catarrh-laced exhalation which just about echoed off the terraced houses and occasional car parked on each side of the road. His throaty gasps alerted the Asian woman who had been side-tracked by the Perspex shelter of a bus stop and its protected poster advertising heavily discounted beer at a supermarket. She, too, turned her attention to the two women looking to navigate their way up the road.

Fran raised her hammer in early readiness and looked to Tanya, who held her vacuum pipe limply in her right hand. Fran took her by the arm again.

"Look, Tanya, we can easily outrun these two if they are anything like the man from earlier. Are you game?"

Tanya let out a weak sigh, "Yeah…yeah, sure."

In the distance, from further up the road, Fran could hear an engine. A spark of excitement piqued her heart a little more as the sound grew closer. Looking up the street past the two lumbering figures until the road finally bent out of sight, Fran could see nothing. And then, all of a sudden, a silver urban 4x4 sped into view. Fran, reacting without thinking, started waving from her position on the left hand pavement. Sun reflected with a sharp brightness off the windscreen as the vehicle drove down the road.

"Hey, hey!" Fran called out, trying to elicit a reaction from the driver, such as slowing down. Either way, the driver would have to negotiate the man in the road, though the woman remained hidden behind the bus stop. However, Fran's shouting encouraged the bus stop woman to make towards her. She stepped off the curb by the shelter, left arm outstretched towards Fran.

The driver of the car never saw her.

Blindly stepping off the kerb and out onto the road, the large woman was completely unseen until impact by the person driving the 4x4. Being higher than a normal car, the 4x4 made impact with the woman at chest level, to her side, whipping her neck in towards the bonnet before she was pulled under the hefty car, and driven over by one of the rear wheels. The shock of impact sent the driver swerving to their right, across the road and in Fran's direction, narrowly missing the thin man stumbling on the same route. Travelling at some thirty to forty miles per hour, the vehicle was now out of control, relinquished so suddenly by the driver.

"Noooo!" Fran screamed, pulling herself into a near-foetal position as the car careened over the road and on to the pavement where she was standing. There were double yellow lines and so no parked cars, enabling the 4x4 to bump up the kerb and drive unhindered past Fran, a hair's breadth in front of her. It crashed into the building next to her, a hair salon with poster-bedecked windows, models flaunting haircuts and styles no doubt hardly ever purchased from that establishment. There was a loud bang and crash of glass as the vehicle easily smashed through the front of the shop and hit the interior brick wall that separated the shop from the house next door.

Glass flew everywhere, though luckily for Fran her foetal position saved her from a few stray shards, which bounced off her hoodie harmlessly. The alarm on the car started sounding and Fran could see the radiator had been punctured, letting out some hissing steam from the bonnet. There was debris and destruction all around the vehicle as it had made short shrift of the equipment and accessories in the salon. Bottles of conditioner and shampoo littered the floor and a broken till spilled its petty cash. The car had slammed through two hairdressing chairs and into the wall, smashing two large mirrors, and throwing scissors, razors, combs and dyes all about.

Fran expanded back to her proper size like an armadillo free from a predator, and surveyed the mess.

"Oh my god, oh my god, oh my god."

Whichever god it was seemed not to be listening, or at least cared little for the scenario.

"Fschhhhhaarr!"

Fran turned to see the unharmed shambling man in his pyjamas scrape uneasily towards her.

Where was Tanya? Fran had forgotten what she was actually supposed to be doing as all of these sensory inputs were hitting her brain at once causing a synaptic pile up and resulting traffic jam. She turned to look and saw Tanya, thoroughly disorientated and having her own brain malfunction, stumbling backwards and way from the crash scene. She buckled and fell, falling off the kerb and onto the road. There was a dull thud as her head impacted on the tarmac. Fran winced.

However, with all of the sound and focus on the outcome of the crashed 4x4, Fran had failed to hear the highly revved motor of a moped that was driving up the hill, ridden by a man in blue clothing topped with a motorbike helmet. Tanya had fallen at just the wrong moment for the driver, collapsing onto the road and into his path. He swerved, but his only option to the right was driving into the pale man wandering his way to the crash site.

Fran watched as the moped driver pulled to the right to avoid Tanya and then tried to avoid the other man, clipping him with the left handle on the handle bar. This sent the man spinning and falling to the ground, whilst the impact made the driver lose control and topple. The moped skidded on its side, throwing the man off. Most of the impact was on his side and he took a few rolls before coming to a stop. Fortunately, he was wearing gloves, and so there seemed to be minimal damage. He lay there for a short while before sitting up, to survey the scene. Then, seeing Tanya on the ground, he stood up, and started to walk quickly towards her, shouting muffled expletives from inside his helmet. Tanya lay there unresponsively.

The other man, who had been spun into a heap on the ground, regained his own feet, with some uncoordinated effort. Meanwhile, the moped driver had reached Tanya, and flicked up his visor to get a clearer look at her. He raised his head to look over at Fran, who was standing there wild-eyed and panic-stricken.

His eyes narrowed as he aggressively asked, "What you lookin' at, you black bitch?"

What the...? Fran's brain failed to grasp what was going on. She was suddenly confused as to what decade this was. Twitter aside, she hadn't been taunted in any such racial way since she had been at school, by kids who didn't really know their posteriors from their elbows. *Are you serious? Now? With this situation going on?*

Fran literally didn't know what to say.

The pale figure behind the moped driver had edged even closer to the point where the driver could hear the grunts clearly, and turned to see the advancing spindly frame.

"Oh, fuck off granddad!" He jogged around him in a wide circle back to his moped. About five metres away lay a wooden pole. *No, that's a baseball bat.* Fran suddenly realised she had to do something because either the ill man was going to come for her, or Tanya. And then there was whoever was driving the 4x4! Indeed, the pale man had caught sight of Tanya on the ground. He crouched down, grunting.

"Get away from her, you evil bastard!" was all the eloquence that Fran could muster.

And to her very great surprise, he did. The man straightened up, and ignored the woman on the ground, the easy prey. No, he had eyes for someone else. Fran stepped back in the direction of the house behind her, raising her hammer as a warning, shaking it a little as if to say *c'mon, try me out!*

But it didn't look like she would enter into any kind of fray with this bizarre entity snarling away at her, blotchy skin pocked with daubs of purplish bruising under a thin grey beard and a mop of grey straw. For behind this crazed man jogged the moped driver, baseball bat in hand. When he was within a few metres, he picked up the pace, bat, held back, and gave a mighty horizontal swing, connecting with the older man's kidney, the force of which sent the man sprawling to his left. He rolled once and then immediately started to get to his feet, amazingly, as if nothing had happened.

"You stubborn tool!" came the muffled voice from the helmet, as the driver took aim at the man again, and swung. For his head.

Crack.

Thud.

Blood.

Fran fell back and on to the wall behind her, bringing her free hand to her mouth in shock and disgust.

"You...you...can't do that. That's murder!"

"Arrest me, then."

"Jesus, what's going on? What is *happening*?"

"Each for their own, now," replied the man, bloodied bat in hand, standing, looking at her through his visor.

"I need to get this woman to the hospital; I need to get her some help," Fran explained.

"Are you nuts? Have you not seen the news? The country's gone mental. There's nothing left, I bet. And *she*," he said, looking down at Tanya's face, "looks like she'll be just like *him* pretty soon. She's ill. And there's no cure. And the hospital's a warzone. I drove past there last night. You do whatever you like though. I'm outta here."

Another engine sounded from back down the road, from behind Fran's block of flats. The two of them turned to see a car driving at high speed. Again, Fran's heart vaulted as she saw twin flashing lights twinkling on top, though no siren to accompany.

"Thank god!" she said in relief and started waving. The car didn't seem to slow down or take much notice, continuing past the junction. Seeming to catch sight of the two at the side of the road, the moped driver with a baseball bat standing over a pulped head that Fran dared not look at, the car edged towards the far side of road. She could see that there were two men in the front, both in protective police clothing giving them a bulky look. They were both wearing gas masks, which sat on top of their heads. One, the shorter and stockier passenger, sporting a large, bushy beard, stared blankly at Fran as if lost and confused and in a different world. Unfortunately, whilst focusing on Fran and her new friend, the driver failed to take note of the stricken moped on the side of the road. With certain finality, the police car drove over the rear wheel of the bike to the music of crunching mechanical parts.

"You're kidding me! That's my bike you fucking pigs!" but the police car took no notice and carried on its hurried way to wherever it was going, undoubtedly on a more important errand the helping out this disparate, desperate couple.

A sound broke Fran's focus, a scratching sound. Where was that coming from? She glanced about, and eventually looked up to be find a face pressed against the glass window of the flat above the hair salon. A young woman with streaked make-up, once plastered and now left to its own demise, had her face pushed up to the glass like a deranged mannequin at a Halloween window display. She was snapping at Fran, and then licking the window, and then snapping again. Fran wondered, out of all the things she had seen today, whether this was the most haunting. Fingernails scratched to the side of the woman's face, trying to get purchase on the flat, slippery glass.

"We've got to get away from here. We've got to get somewhere safe," Fran implored the man.

"We? *We*? Who the hell said anything about *we*? I'm nothing to do with *you*" he replied, nigh on spitting the last word. And then he thought for a few seconds. "Hey, you. Can you drive?"

"Yes, of course."

"Good. You might be useful. Let's get in here and see if it still works," he said indicating the steaming 4x4 which sat, bonnet crumpled, in the hair salon.

"We haven't even checked to see if the driver's alright yet!" replied Fran, concerned about her own lack of concern.

"Go on then."

"What about Tanya?" asked Fran, looking down at Tanya, who was still lying there, a thin rivulet of claret seeping away from underneath her head, giving an odd sense of colour to the dull grey of the tarmac.

"She's ill. *You* know that, *I* know that. Leave her."

"I…I…I can't leave her. That's just wrong!" Fran spurted, incensed at the man's lack of humanity, though forgetting her own attempted flight earlier on.

"It's wrong not to do something pointless? When it's gonna probably lead to you getting ill too? Bullshit. And you know it. Quickly, check the car." The young man was in no mood to hang about, clearly.

Fran stepped through the broken window to the right of the car, pieces of glass crunching under her feet as from a violent ice storm. She carefully picked her way through the debris to the front door of the vehicle. The airbag had been deployed, but had deflated.

"Oh, great, here comes another!" said the moped man.

Fran sighed. *It must be the guy from the apartment block. Damn, I forgot about him!*

She pulled open the door of the 4x4 to reveal a woman in her forties, blonde and still fairly well made up. She looked to have lost consciousness, but was stirring. Worse was the fact that she did not look altogether well. Her face had the same tint as Tanya's, with blossoming flourishes of purple starting to faintly show underneath layers of foundation, like mould beneath a Rembrandt.

Fran hastily closed the door again, and staggered unevenly back outside.

"She's got it and she's just coming to," Fran announced to the man who was standing there with bat poised. Some ten metres down the road, the large dishevelled man who had besieged her flat was stumbling towards them, gnashing his broken gums.

Fran looked at the moped driver. "Can you hotwire a car?"

"I can't drive the bastards, but I can start them. I've got skills, you know."

"I do now. Look, my block of flats is there," she said pointing back down the hill, past the oncoming threat, "and behind it is a car park. There are lots of cars there."

"As long as there are some old ones as immobiliser's suck. I need an old car and a screwdriver."

Fran had a strange feeling inside, as she was agreeing to work in partnership with someone to whom she had developed an instant dislike. She resigned herself to taking the moral hit in order for the greater good to come about; that being better odds for survival. But the sooner she could go her own way, the better. Although, could he help her? Did she have a better chance of surviving...with *him*. She still had her flat, and that was fairly well stocked. There was some thinking to do, but not a lot of time to do it. Perhaps a healthy scepticism of working with someone else right now was wise.

"Arrsshhhhh..." This emanated not from the oncoming man, but from the ground nearby. Fran and her unlikely colleague twisted their heads to look down. Tanya's eyes had opened to reveal a slightly milky colour with some fine deep red capillaries striking out from the centre. Her face, like the approaching man, had discoloured as those deeper hues fought to come through. Blood had oozed through her hastily assembled bandage. Her left hand clutched at the kerbside, nails scraping along the dry concrete. A modern rendition of John Hurt in *Alien*, Tanya's stomach thrust up from the ground and her shoulders contorted. Neck arching back, her mouth spat out some globules of spittle into the air to spray about her own face. "Kassshhhaarrr!"

"Time to go," said the moped man, and with that he set off, making a wide circle around the large man who was almost upon them, to jog off down the hill. With bat in hand, he turned his head back to survey what was going on behind him.

Fran reluctantly followed.

The two made it back to the apartment block in quick time. Unfortunately, the city seemed to be waking, its demons reviving to wander about looking for food. One such figure was trying to exit Tesco via the crashed car, another was ambling crookedly down the road past the convenience store.

Fran ran to her own apartment whilst the moped driver stood guard in the front entrance. She quickly returned unhindered (though there was some banging emanating from several flats that she passed) carrying a small tool pouch with several screwdrivers.

"Here you go. Hopefully it's got what you need. Oh, and what's your name?"

"Vince," came the mumble from within his protective headgear.

METAMORPHOSIS

41
Greg

Before Greg had a chance to think about what Dale might be up to, his friend drew his mouth back in strings of saliva and launched himself towards him. Dale slammed into the steps up from the cabin as Greg recoiled quickly. There was no time for Greg to even think as his animalistic brain took over. There was instant recognition of danger, and that Dale was after him. All he could do was to grab the spare anchor he had been toying with, and throw it with great force at Dale. The anchor hit him on the shoulder and face, the thudding impact sending him reeling back down below. Greg hurried through the cabin to look at Dale, who was sprawled on the floor below, a bloody gash taken out of his other cheek to reflect its twin injury, now with gauze hanging by tape revealing the oozing cheek flesh. Dale seemed unfazed by the large chunk of metal which had been launched at him, and started to stand.

Damn! Greg caught sight of his oar propped up in the galley below, impotently leaning on the cooker.

Seeing Dale get back to his feet, Greg realised that he had little option. He sprang to his feet, and turned, negotiating the helm, to approach the ladder.

Now he had nothing! He grabbed the top of the ladder and quickly started to reverse himself down it, seeing the emerging disfigured face of Dale appear through the frame of the cabin door. Greg's heart hammered in its osseous cage, seeming to want to break out and make it into the cool summer water. He was starting to panic as Dale might well be over to him before he had a chance to untie the rope and start the engine.

Hands shaking with adrenalin, Greg sought to pull the rope end through the knot. He could hear the exertions of Dale over and above his pulsating blood-flow. In that short time his body was breaking out in cold sweat.

There, he'd done it!

Greg almost fell backwards to sit down hard on the edge of the boat, so that he could see to starting the engine. He pulled the cord. Nothing. Standing to get more purchase, he pulled the cord and the engine kicked into life. With his hand on the throttle, Greg briefly glanced upwards to the edge of the yacht, to see Dale throw himself off the boat and down onto the tender below.

METAMORPHOSIS

Greg couldn't help but jump back towards the front of the dinghy, defensively. Dale landed with a splash as his legs fell into the water; but his body landed plumb on top of the outboard motor, arms outstretched, grabbing the rear of the boat and the motor itself. If Greg's heavy weight had not been counterbalancing at the front of the boat, the dinghy would have lifted clear into the air at the front.

Greg was immobile in shock. Dale, with his crazed face, missing patches of skin and flesh, mouth agape in snapping rage, teeth coated with glistening saliva, stared at him through glazed eyes. Thankfully, the motor was still ticking over.

Without thinking, Greg moved forward and grabbed the throttle handle, poking out from beneath Dale's enraged face, with his left hand. Dale tried to snap at Greg's hand, but could not get close enough, so he attempted to pull himself closer with his arms. Greg twisted the throttle and the small motor kicked into action. The boat, under duress, edged forward through the sea.

As the dinghy moved none too quickly away from the yacht, a trail of bloody froth emerged from the small wake. The propeller was cutting at Dale's legs, churning through his khakis, spitting his flesh out, pumping his blood into the sea.

The look on Dale's face was utterly unchanged. None of what was taking place beneath the surface was registering at all with Dale or his brain. His eyes remained locked either on Greg's face, or on the hand attached to the throttle.

Greg put the throttle on full, and moved the handle left and right, trying to cut through Dale's legs as much as he could. He didn't want to use his other hand if he could avoid it, as it was a risk. Being bitten was not an option. It simply wasn't. As long as Dale's mouth couldn't get to his hand, he would be alright. His friend's legs were disintegrating in the sea as metal sliced effortlessly through arteries and veins, flesh and sinew. The propeller stuttered somewhat as it gnawed at bone. Twice it stopped as it become clogged with grinding resistance, but twice Greg was able to wiggle the motor back into action before it stalled.

However, despite the profound loss of blood, Dale seemed unperturbed. Moreover, his arms were starting to pull his face closer to Greg's hand, snapping and gnashing. It was now or never. Greg swung his right arm, fist clenched, into Dale's temple. The blow was ineffective as it barely appeared to register in Dale's attention to getting towards Greg's hand. A second and third punch followed, before a volley of rapid beats caused Dale to lose grip with his left hand. His face slopped back as he continued to grab on to the boat with his right arm. Greg stamped with his left foot, crushing Dale's fingers, repeating time and again until Dale's other hand was mashed against the wooden backboard and rendered useless.

Dale fell away from the boat, final guttural sounds emanating from his torn face. Greg caught sight, below the surface, of bone and flesh surrounded by spreading redness. As the boat, with its tiny engine on full throttle, bumped away, Greg's last view of his friend, whom he had killed, was a haunting image of his shredded body sinking below a tattered and soulless face receding into the depths, surrounded by a stew of blood, bits of fabric and flesh.

Greg had little time to feel anything from remorse to revulsion as the dinghy jerked sideways, and Greg, unprepared and imbalanced, was thrown out.

A barnacled rock dashed the side of his face as he was catapulted off the side of the dinghy, pain searing through him like a strike of lightning. The shock of the impact and the cold water reflexively forced him to gulp. Only it wasn't air, but the salty brine of the rocky Devon coast.

METAMORPHOSIS

42
Jessica

The man seemed like a hulk. He had no great frame, but any-sized man lying thrashing on top of someone was a challenge. Especially one who seemed to have lost his mind and was intent on scraping, scratching, gnashing and gnawing that person.

That person, Jessica, had her hands grasped tight with terror around his shoulder blades, holding him at arms' length. The man's head jerked from side to side, teeth clacking with something approaching excited anticipation. Sputum flew out in malevolent globules. His arms managed to grab painfully on Jessica's upper arms with vicelike knuckles. His eyes, though... his eyes. That's what she would remember. Even as his head jerked about epileptically, his eyes remained focused with unerring accuracy on his prey. One dribble of saliva dripped with an expectancy of acidic lava, from his blanched chin still daubed with remnants of violence. As it fell, as if in slow motion, Jessica's head turned instinctively to the side. The large droplet fell on her cheek, rolling towards her ear.

And then she saw it, glinting.

The knife she had dropped.

There.

On the floor.

In spitting distance.

Jessica gritted her teeth, behind closed lips (something in her brain had decided that she, even in this perilous situation, did not want any of this thing's saliva in her mouth) and summoned all of her energy to shift her weight to the left whilst pulling him down to the right. It worked, and his body thumped on to the kitchen floor next to her, giving her only a split second with which to grasp her opportunity. She took it.

Jessica's right hand shot out like a darting viper seizing a mouse. Except this was no mouse. Grappling the handle with almost too much speed, she picked up the knife as if it was a dagger, blade pointing down, and with a downward swipe whilst lying on her back, thrust the blade into the side of the man's head.

She hadn't expected the first strike to be so ineffective. The blade struck the man just above the temple and its seven inch blade viciously sliced his skin up into his hairline, jarring off the skull. One of the man's arms shot out and grabbed Jessica's hair, yanking her head back so that the view was from the corner of her eyes.

This was her chance. A very fleeting realisation was that this would be her only chance.

Jessica gave it everything. And her everything resulted in the blade finding its target: the weakness of the temple. The blade met with some resistance to begin with, but then sunk in, deeper and deeper and deeper still. The handle met the skull. She wasn't sure whether it was the skull the other side, or the floor through the other temple which stopped the knife.

And yet, the man's grip barely faltered.

Rather than pull the knife out and do it again, Jessica wiggled it violently in its cranial sheath. She twisted it and rammed it up and down in small but rapid movements. Finally, she let go of the handle, and pulling her fingers back to expose her open palm, she effectively punched the handle away from her which slammed the blade back towards her, inside the man's skull.

This appeared to do the trick.

The man's head jerked a little as his grip entirely loosened. Jessica flopped backwards, eyes fixed on what she had done. The knife protruded from this man's head like a baseball bat lodged in a vandalised computer, hardware destroyed, components in pieces, connections and connectors severed and lost, power ebbing.

Who this man was, what this entity was, drained away with his blood. Who was this man who had irrevocably changed, before *this*? Before her *knife*. His brain was nothing but organic soup; lacerated and mixed with a seven inch knife at the hands of the most amateur of neuroscientific chefs.

Blood was oozing out all over Jessica's floor. Dark, rivulets amassing in a lake of claret, thick and sickening. It inched its way slowly towards the kitchen table, upon which sat a boy whose screams had become whimpers as something inside him realised that what was taking place wasn't just his mother ignoring him out of spite. Danger and death spoke in universal languages.

"Mmmummna…"

And that was Galen's first word.

43
Greg

Greg lay on the large flat rock, whose millions of years of material evolution had formed into a more comfortable slab for convalescence than the other options around.

He was exhausted. Emotionally and physically. Having been beaten around by the sea, powerful yet mercifully fairly calm, and with his head dashed on a rock, and with arms and legs slashed and cut by barnacles and limpets, he had managed to struggle up and out of the water. Splashed faintly by the spray of the muted surf, he was up a little and onto a drier platform above the lower, sharper rocks. Blood seeped down the side of his face as he lay there, gasping, staring up into the fields of blue with its occasional sheep-cloud, slowly grazing from one side to the other.

Greg had suffered a large gash to the left side of his head, dangerously close to his temple, and again on the other side, also in his hairline. Both seeped blood down his head to pool on the cool, smooth granite rock. He wriggled his toes in the realisation that he no longer had both shoes, his right foot being clad in only a wet sock.

His thoughts were wide-ranging, full of questions as he tried to piece together the events of the day, and, more importantly, the reasons why such things could have happened. And why they could have happened to him and his friends. *Why have you forsaken me, God? Why? What have I done? And Dale? Peter? What is the reason for this madness? Are you punishing us? Are you punishing others? What are you revealing? What is the message? Was there no other, better way that you could communicate this? Why? Why! Why!*

"Why! Why!! Fucking why!"

There was no question, no expecting a response, just seething anger; a post-traumatic explosion of incomprehension and anger. And yet, oddly, he still felt a pang of guilt for swearing *at* God.

Okay, so there's a reason. Don't be foolish, Greg, you've argued this before, this...problem of evil. And you know the answers. Why is there this evil in the world, and is it gratuitous? No. It is the by-product of free will and punishment for being fallen. But this, this doesn't look like the repercussions of human actions. This, this is...natural...So, why? We brought it on ourselves on account of our sinfulness. That's it. We are wicked. But Peter...Dale...? Do they...deserve this punishment? Dear God, you stepped in to change things in biblical times. Well, show yourself now. Why can't you step in now and change things? What is the use of this madness? Are you using us as instruments? Are we your tools to grind away in crafting some sculpture, some end result? Are you just using us? Pawns in a global, universal chess game?

His mind was whizzing, fizzing, and somersaulting; effervescing with ideas, accusations, thoughts and counter-thoughts.

But I am here. I survived. Why? Am I an instrument? Your instrument? Hey, perhaps I have some role to play?!

Greg had a pretty good memory for Bible verses, such was the need or outcome when one argued so much about biblical issues. There was one quote, one verse which bubbled near the surface of his consciousness.

What was it...? 2 Timothy..."Now in a large house there are not only gold and silver vessels, but also vessels of wood and of earthenware, and some to honour and some to dishonour. Therefore, if anyone cleanses himself from these things, he will be a vessel for honour, sanctified, useful to the Master, prepared for every good work." Am I now a vessel for your use, and what do you want of me? Am I the new John the Baptist, paving the way for the second coming?

And so it went on. Flitting from one idea to the next, Greg lay there, bleeding and soaking wet, for some half an hour searching for some lateral truth.

Eventually, and with an inkling of a resolution forming in his dissonant mind, he stood up. Looking towards the town from the rocky outcrop, he could see that it was approaching low tide on the beach. The town looked almost resplendent in the summer sun, though dimming from time to time in the shadows of the occasional high clouds. To the right of the town, the rocks merged into the beach, being swallowed piece by piece by the Devonian sand. And there, in the middle distance, he could see a brace of figures, struggling at the beginning of the rocks, scrambling like geriatric blind people, as they almost randomly negotiated the rocky outcrops and ledges.

"Are you kidding me?" Greg said aloud, recognising that the two figures were the fat man and the silver-haired man from earlier. Had they heard him screaming? Had they caught sight of him? Greg surveyed his options. The two didn't seem to be the most nimble of people, especially in their present states. That said, the rocks weren't that wide of a route onto the beach, and the two of them blocked the way fairly well. Surely he could chance his way past them? He was quicker and more agile. Suddenly, Greg spotted something intriguing. It was the dark opening of a small cave, about his height, some halfway between himself and his followers. Making his move forward, he started concocting a plan in his mind. After a step, he realised that he needed to even his feet out, and so kicked off his other deck shoe and hurriedly took both socks off.

The rocks were cold and sharp on his bare feet, but Greg barely noticed, grappling over limpet-covered rocks and stamping through what would otherwise be beautiful little rock pools. Some part of his mind registered pain here and there when his hands and feet were cut open on the sharp rocky outcrops. He didn't have time to consider this, or anything else. He had to get to that cave before the two men did, come hell or high water.

Greg could hear the animalistic sounds from the two, feeling that they had lost all ability to communicate meaningfully; that the very cornerstone of humanity, as a social species, had been lost at the drop of a hat; that the vagaries or nuances of Proust, Hemingway or Dostoyevsky had been irrevocably locked away from them, and by being locked away so, had ceased to exist.

The sounds of the two men grew louder and closer still as Greg made his way towards the rock face in which the small cave was set. Finally, Greg was able to climb a half-step up to a flat, dry outcrop, worn perhaps by decades of teenagers and beachgoers lured by the seductive pull of the unknown and the discreet. He ducked his head and waited a few seconds whilst his eyes adjusted. The cave was open enough inside, and with enough outcrops and rocks for seats, to allow the cave to qualify for a good party spot, indeed, for the local teenagers; and there were the remnants of some charred logs, visible in the sunlight which reached the front section. The cave obviously did not get much sea water in it anymore, except at the higher tides.

Greg grabbed up a hand-sized sooty rock into his bloodied hand from the old campfire and a smaller stone into his left hand, and hid around the entrance of the cave. The two victims of whatever outbreak had taken place were, by the sounds of it, close now, yet struggling to overcome their rocky hurdles.

Don't let them touch you. There was no doubt in Greg's mind that this outbreak, this disease, was dangerously contagious. Dale was evidence of that, as much as the would-be townspeople he had so far come across. He needed to lure them in, in order to slip past them from behind and have a clear run at the rest of the rocks. It was a risk, but he felt safe in assuming that their eyes would struggle as much as his did to adjust to the darkness, allowing him the element of surprise, and he could come out of the cave when their guards were down.

It seemed like an age before the two men, luckily close together, had finally scrambled their way to the cave entrance. The bright light of the sun at the entrance dimmed as they blocked it, casting their squat and grotesque shadows within, since the sun was coming from behind and above the headland in which the cave was nestled. Greg had a clear view of their profiles as they stumbled one step over the threshold. *This has gotta work.* Hoping that the two wouldn't see the stone whizz past them, Greg threw the smaller pebble with his left hand to the far side of the small cave, past their grunting faces.

The pebble did its job, landing with an invisible clatter on the damp rocks beyond any of their sights. Save for the immediate entrance area, the cave remained dark and obscure.

The two men blindly moved towards the sound, the silver-topped man almost tripping over on the charred remains of the fire.

Now!

Greg seized his opportunity. With two steps over to the men, his rock-clenching fist with all the might he could muster. The dull cracking thudding sound would ordinarily have been sickening to Greg, and in fact, there was a part of his brain which registered a moment of disgust (at himself and at the sound). The sheer force of the impact sent the thin man crumpling down on to the floor of the cave, his face crashing down into the cold and sodden ashes. The larger man, even more harrowing an image in the faint, weak light, turned grunting to Greg. His mouth opened into its own dangerous cave of disgust. He started to bring his arms up to attack Greg.

"Don't you *touch* me, you beast!" Greg screamed, as he swung the rock square onto the man's left check, splitting skin, shattering jaw, and sending teeth flying out of the entrance of the cave where they tinkled to the rock floor, gory pearls left to the fate of a high tide. Part of his cheek had been ripped away, revealing the jaw which had just been decimated. Bloody pulp, cheek and bone mixed to form a nightmarish image.

However, the impact didn't drop the second man to the floor, and Greg knew he had to grab this opportunity to run. With adrenalin pumping, filling his body with alertness and energy, Greg dropped the rock and ran out of the cave. The light dazzled, and he almost fell off the flat ledge of granite leading down from the cave entrance. Luckily, he managed to maintain his balance, and jumped down onto a flat rock below. He could barely hear the horrific combination of sounds coming from the big man with the shattered face as he came out of the cave in pursuit. Greg was away. Legs and arms pumping, not caring a fig about the punishment his hands and feet were receiving, he danced over rocks, through pools, until eventually his feet met with soft wet sand where rock met beach.

He afforded himself a glance back to see his follower back almost at the cave, suffering in his lack of energetic co-ordination.

It was then that the thought hit him. He'd just killed *another* man.

No, he thought, that was no man.

METAMORPHOSIS

44
Jason

The van entered Olding at the westerly side, from on high. There was a great view of the settlement and the bay which sporadically opened up between the houses. The green-blue seas could be seen to lap against the sandy shores with a single yacht moored towards the nearer end of the bay. Ordinarily, this was a thoroughly pleasant drive and entrance to a picturesque town. However, the aesthetics of the drive and the view were of little concern to Jason and Bevan.

Indeed, as they drove past the first rows of houses, they could see an old woman with lank grey hair standing in the middle of the road, adopting a stance that was starting to become a marker for them.

"I'm going to try to stay out of trouble. Best if I take evasive action when considering these *virals*. On the other hand, if she comes near me, I'm not gonna swerve. She's fair game," Bevan stated.

"Bev, we can't be sure of the state of these people. You know, they might get better. There is no way we can know the future like that, despite what that other bloke said. We can't...no, we *shouldn't* go around conducting vigilante guerrilla euthanasia!" Jason said forcefully, indicating the woman in the road ahead.

Bevan pulled the van over to idle on the side of the street. The women up ahead hadn't yet heard or seen the vehicle and just staggered around, waiting for something to come onto her radar.

"I'm pretty sure there's no way back for them. If that's the case, then if we do hit them, we are doing them and us a favour! Though poor Annie might not like it." Bevan patted the dashboard of his beloved campervan.

"But is 'pretty sure' enough? We've had a couple of days experience of all this and have *no idea* what is going on. We might end up killing these virals and then finding out that a cure has been found. It's like the death penalty and hanging someone who's later found to be innocent. It's just too dodgy," Jason reasoned.

"Dodgy! Would you describe that bird with her muff out, attacking you after eating her dog, '*dodgy*'? Put it this way, Jason, if one jumps into Annie, I'm not going to be too worried. It's their choice, I'm not swerving around to avoid hitting them and ending up crashing myself," Bevan replied. "I had a mate who used to drive *utes* in Australia; you know, with the big roo bars. He said it was safer not to swerve, to just hit the kangaroos head on when they jumped into the road."

"Mate, you *do* realise that these are not kangaroos? These are people?" Jason asked in reply.

"If I'm honest, Jason, I'm not really sure," said Bevan earnestly.

"And I don't think choice comes into it," said Jason.

"Okay then, have it your way. They're just like insects, waiting for something to come into their senses, you know, and then attacking *without* choice. Like that moth we saw flying into the fire, with its sense misfiring." Bevan indicated the woman ahead as he spoke. "*She's* like a malfunctioning robot. Her circuits are fucked... Look, imagine I had a pot of paint, and one night, something went wrong, and the paint turned to, I dunno, cheese. It's now not a pot of paint. It might look *to you* like a pot of paint. Really, though, it's just a paint pot, not a pot of paint. It's a paint pot, and it's full of cheese."

Jason looked at Bevan. "You get weirder by the day."

"*I* know what I mean. Anyway, *she's* a paint pot full of cheese, and I ain't treating her like a pot of paint. I ain't gonna try and paint my house with her. More likely to throw her in the bin. That said, I don't want cheese on my van."

And to Jason's most quizzical of looks, Bevan smiled, turned and took off the handbrake, pulling the van back out on to the road. With careful precision, he steered clearly around the viral person who stood motionless as the van ticked past her.

"This could be like that old game, you know, *Frogger*, but instead of avoiding cars as a frog, we're a car avoiding zombies. I wonder how many points—"

"You're kidding me. Seriously, Bev, shut up. You're making me feel sick."

From where they were, on the western side of Olding, they had to drive down through town and across to the eastern side, where Jason's flat was situated. Bevan drove through the quiet streets, eventually getting to the steep road which led down to the The Crab Shack.

As the houses blurred past them on the downward route, the café-restaurant on the westerly edge of the beach came into view. Just as they were nearing the car park and the corner which sent the road at right angles, a figure jolted into the middle of the road—a man with bare and lacerated feet, sodden clothes and hair, and with bloody arms flailing aimlessly in front of him. The two men in the car made their flash judgements.

"Watch out, there's a fucking viral there!" Jason shouted.

Bevan was driving, at the time, in the middle of the road, not anticipating any other traffic. However, and despite his earlier claims, something animalistic and perhaps violent in Bevan took over and instinctively made him swerve to the left so as to actually hit the man in the road, and then at the last minute, he pulled the wheel back a small margin, as if his subconscious mind was having a debate with itself, in mere instants, pulling him one way and then the next.

"What the fricking hell are you doing!" screamed Jason as Bevan swerved to the left, and then marginally right again.

The end result was that the van clipped the shoddy-looking (though in no way diminutive) grey-haired man. He was hit by the edge of the van and its wing mirror, which was bent back in the process, throwing him brutishly to the road. Jason glanced through his window to see the viral hit the ground and almost bounce.

"Take that" Bevan called back.

"What the hell are you doing? What were we just talking about? You can't go around running these people over! It's not just some kind of weird computer game. You don't get points by doing *that* to them, by running them over!"

"Look, it's a dog-eat-dog world now," explained Bevan.

"Bevan," said Jason, "you move from the sublime to the ridiculous at the flip of a coin. Jesus, *I'm* not a dog, and nor was *he*! And there could be a cure!"

"Mate, I'm not sure *he* was really a *he*," said Bevan as he steered the campervan past a car which had crashed into the front of the art gallery. "Wow. What have we come back to? Check *that* out!"

"I suggest we get the hell back to mine as quickly as possible. I wanna be on the first bus outta here."

Jason looked left, and from the raised position in the van, could just about make something out on the beach as the van slowly moved past the car-inserted gallery.

"Sweet bejesus," said Jason, a look of horror descending over his face.

"Oh my God," replied Bevan, looking at the car which protruded from the glass frontage of the gallery. More particularly, he was looking at the gore, liberally spray painted like some piece of caustic modern art on very public show, around the car and on the shards of broken windows.

Then everything properly came into view. Bevan stopped the van and his left arm reached out to grab Jason and attract his attention away from whatever he was trying to look at on the beach.

There, before the two men, was a scene right from the very horror movies that Bevan had so often whiled away his drink or drug-induced slumberous Friday nights watching, in post-pub dazes. What was once the driver of the old car was now a food bag for two ravenous freaks of nature as they tore into the flesh and sinews of his body, teeth grazing bone to make awful scraping sounds. Jason realised that the two infected people were no longer the people they once were, concerned with running a shop, or perusing the local tourist attractions. To him, they were animals, intent on one thing and one thing only. The body took all of their attention, bar a marginally snarling glance round at the campervan as it stood there idling, carrying two onlookers, ashen-faced with horrified astonishment. One of the pair who were tearing the body apart was a woman in her late teens.

Jason recognised her as she turned and dismissively half-snarled.

"Jesus. That's Ella, from the pub," Jason exhaled.

Ella worked at the local pub and often served both Jason and Bevan after a day's work. She was nice enough, and they often saw her about town, with her friends. Bevan had often tried to ingratiate himself amongst them to little or, in reality, to *no* avail. Bevan's track record with the ladies of Olding was notoriously poor, but it wasn't for the lack of trying. He was very trying.

But now the men didn't know what or how to think. This person whom they had once known was now *devouring* another human being in broad daylight.

"What do we...do?" asked Jason, unsure, confused and shocked.

"Er..."

The other infected person was a pony-tailed man in his thirties whom neither of the men recognised. His hair was dishevelled, mostly out of the hairband, and his brown T-shirt and jeans had soaked up an inordinate amount of human blood as he gorged himself on flesh and guts and skin and ligaments. All parts of the body seemed to be fair game. His face was covered in blood as he dipped his head and dived into the open carcass as it lay half out of the car. Perhaps the victim had been trying to escape when he was set upon, the men did not know. What they *did* know was that the world was now a very different pace full of new and shocking stimuli, which their brains had not gathered the experience to deal with. Their powers of induction were impotent as the file-drawers in their memory offices were empty of reference.

"Let's get out of here. Now." Jason felt like his world had closed in and around him; that only the immediate stimuli had any influence; that his actions were simple *re*actions to them—a sort of survival mode of pure cause and effect. That *he* was a mere insect, a moth.

And this, *here*—this, *now*—*this* was the fire. Jason's eyes were burning with the wretched horror of it all.

"Let's get to my flat and... Let's get to my flat."

Bevan slipped Annie into gear and accelerated off, leaving the decimated body in the car to be fed upon by the vulturous brace of virulent beasts.

METAMORPHOSIS

45
Jessica

It was a little past noon. A few clouds had gathered and were threatening an otherwise perfect summer's day, leaving the lounge alternating between too bright and just right. The two women were sitting drinking mugs of tea and sharing some biscuits; a period of recollecting themselves after the incident in the house. With gloves and hastily concocted masks, they had cleaned the kitchen up and left the body in the garden, leaving the room in as good a condition as it had originally been, before cleaning themselves up.

"I figure we have several options. Given that my parents live in London and I *think* that they are okay, we could: one) go to London; two) go somewhere else; and three) stay here." Jessica was counting on her fingers as she explained. "We could go to Bristol. My husband's working in a hospital there, but I haven't heard from him in a few days…" Jessica's eyes started welling.

"Dear," Jean moved up the sofa to put her hand on Jessica's for comfort, "I'm sure he's fine. We…we could maybe go to Bristol…"

"No. No, though I appreciate your kindness. I think I'm realistic enough to know that… that he…that he was ill when I spoke to him last. He admitted it. And if he gets well, he'll make it back here. He's not stupid. But I don't think I should go looking for him. If we go anywhere, I'll leave him a note." She paused. "God, it's hard to think like that!"

"Well, I don't think London is a good idea. Did you see some of the images on the news? It looked terrible," Jean responded, face etched with worry.

"You know, I think I agree with you. The thing is, things could change really easily. It might be worth staying here. We're safe, we have some food. I guess the question is what do we want to leave *for*?" Jessica had already thought a good deal about their potential options the previous night, so much of this was for the benefit of Jean, though sounding it out loudly gave her some clarity.

"Well, my husband's son from his first marriage still owns a farm down in Devon. We haven't spoken in a few years. We had a family argument, you see. I was going to phone him on the day that the phone lines went down. We could go there. Bill, my husband, grew up a farmer. It could be a good place to go. It'll be away from everything. Is that a good idea, or do we want to be closer to everything? What about the police and army?"

Jessica sank into her own thoughts. She hadn't expected a viable option from Jean, and it was a pretty decent suggestion. Jessica had packed her bags. She had been fairly confident that they would be leaving, though had not really properly concluded where. She had reasoned that London and Bristol were decent options, but they were also fraught with issues.

"I am beginning to think that any major town or city is well out of the picture. There are just too many people, and if they are all getting like that bloke, and Margaret, then it would be far too dangerous for us. As for what we need to leave *for*... I think safety. Where will we be safest until this thing blows over?"

"Will it blow over? How long will the virus last? Will people get better?" Jean asked, desperate for some knowledge and answers. "*Someone* must be working on a cure!"

Jessica shrugged, unapologetically. "I have no idea. Absolutely none. The news, when it was on, wasn't a great fount of knowledge and advice other than to stay inside. I think they had a good idea where this was going from some of the early cases. By then, it was too late. Essentially, this has been a complete disaster. Obviously. And I don't have any faith that it'll get better any time soon. So the sooner we can make some good decisions, the better."

Jean's hand squeezed Jessica's more firmly, reassuringly. "This is where faith, for me, is carrying me through. I was praying so hard for some help, and here you are. Here *we* are."

"Seriously? God thought an atheist would be your saviour figure to save you from something that he allowed to happen? Or created?" Jessica's emotions got the better of her, and she kicked into mental action, something which was second nature to her. "I could think of a few better options. Like not allowing this virus to mutate. That would get my vote. No, I don't see the hallmarks of God here, unless she's an evil bastard." *Don't start, Jessica, don't start. She's an old woman looking for answers, certainty and reassurance. Don't burst her bubble.*

Some things were like red rags to a bull for Jessica, and debating God was one of them. She couldn't ever resist, like being drawn into a black hole whilst holding on to the light of reason, as she saw it. She was also a fan of playing around with gender pronouns to poke fun at what she called "the anthropomorphic picture of God", made in the image of *man*. God made in man's image was more accurate in its reversal of the Genesis account, in her eyes.

Jean withdrew her hand and straightened her wavy grey hair, taken aback by this spiked assault. "Yes, well dear, we've all got our demons. This, for me, seems like another flood, and that's something I'd never taken seriously before. Like a flood of evil monsters... So, er, what do you think we should do?"

Jessica ignored the Noah's global flood temptation, like the devil on Jesus' shoulder in the wilderness (*Go on, Jessica, argue! The Flood is hilarious! Don't miss this opportunity!*), and said, "I'm liking your idea. I was going to suggest Wales for a number of reasons, but I guess a farm in Devon is pretty good, and not as far. Well done, Jean, you get my vote!"

With so many years spent arguing with people and writing journal papers concerning these subjects, it was hard to stave off the urge to argue about there not being enough molecules of water, about bio-geographical distribution of animals around the world, about carnivores and defecation on a boat full of creatures, about boat dimensions and about an all-loving God killing the world's population (including unborn babies) bar eight. Even in this strange and warped present reality, old habits died hard and needed quashing for a greater good under a flood of humanity.

"So why do we need to leave, exactly? Why don't we just stay here? I do believe it is safe. And speaking of safe, what's going on; what are the government up to? Can we turn on the television and see what the news has to say?" Jean reasoned.

Jessica grabbed the controller from the large IKEA coffee table to switch the TV on from standby.

Nothing happened.

There was no red light.

Standing up and moving over to the appliance, she switched the mains switch, to no avail. There were no lights on the Blu-Ray player. No lights on the cable box. She crossed the room to the main light switch for the lounge light.

Nothing again.

"Aaaand we have no power. Nothing. Nada."

"Oh my goodness, Jessica. How...how do we find out what is going on? We need to listen to a radio. Yes, switch on the...oh no. How about we listen to the radio in the car?" suggested Jean, eyes and face brightening with her idea.

Galen made a gurgling noise whilst waving his arms and slapping one of his shape toys on his play mat. Jessica looked at him and smiled, but the smile was devoid of any real warmth, just becoming a matter of habit. Her mind was elsewhere.

"Do we have to start considering things as if the world really is a disaster movie? A zombie apocalypse?" Again, saying that word felt ridiculous to Jessica, but the thought seemed entirely sensible and obvious.

"I've never even remotely considered anything like this in all my life," Jean declared, forehead rising in disbelief.

"Lesson number one: watch more TV. You might have been more prepared for an international viral apocalypse. Yup, the End of Days." Jessica lowered her hand to offer a finger to Galen to play with.

"You say that, but we haven't really seen much of what is going on. I feel I need to see this to really believe it. It's all so unbelievable!"

Unable to resist, Jessica gave in. "Of course, you were never there to see a global flood, right? I mean, you're not *that* old! And yet, you believe that." Immediately, seeing Jean's shocked face, Jessica realised she had overshot the mark and this was neither the time nor the place for his debate. "You've seen a man eat a woman's face off, and seen what was left of that man after he attacked me, so...Anyway, enough nonsense. Let's go and listen to the radio."

Jessica picked up her child and the car keys from the coffee table and the two women made their way to the car by the front door. Settling Galen on her lap to play with the car steering wheel, Jessica turned on the radio. It went straight to Radio 4. She had, for some years, been far more appreciative of talk radio than music-playing stations. The voice coming from the speakers sounded different. It appeared to be official and serious but she was sure there was an edge of something...of panic.

...The pandemic is still an unknown quantity and there is no known cure or relief from the symptoms. Victims are advised in the event of a death to please call 101 which has been co-opted as the new national line for reporting flu deaths...

The two women hung on every word as even Galen's baby sounds became as silence. The prognosis was bleak, at least for the time being.

Jessica broke Jean's concentration as the message went on to repeat itself. "How can this all have happened so damned quickly? I mean, it's been, what, two weeks since this started off, perhaps less. And then this. I mean, wow."

Jean sat still with her hands on her lap, staring out in front of her, through the windscreen into the mid distance. "And yet, if we are sitting here right as rain, don't you think lots and lots of others will be too? And then there are people who are fine and who will no doubt be out causing trouble and looting."

"Luckily, I don't think we'll get that here."

Jean turned to Jessica. "Yes, but what *about* here, in Stanton? There must *surely* be other people who aren't ill, who haven't caught it? We probably haven't caught it because we haven't been out much. Well I haven't, at any rate. But who is to say we're not immune? Who is to say there aren't lots of other people who are immune? Here, too, in the village!"

Jessica thought for a short while. "Hmm. I guess we could check the village. Or even our road. What about your neighbours?"

"Well, the Mann's place is up for sale and no one's living in it now, as I'm sure you know. David and Penny went on holiday to the Algarve just before this whole ordeal started. But we could check on the others."

BEEP!

Galen had pressed the car horn button on the steering wheel.

"Shhhh, baba! You can't do that!" Jessica took his hands in her own and rubbed them, turning to the older woman. "I haven't even thought to check on Derek as we don't really bother him." Derek was a quiet man in his sixties, who still played badminton in the local village hall amongst other things. Even so, he didn't seem overly social and so Jessica and Mike had paid him little heed in their busy schedule of moving in, expecting relationships like that to develop over time. Given that the properties were fairly spacious with well-hedged grounds in the village, and on this road in particular, the neighbours didn't need to interact if they didn't want to. To the other side of Jessica's, and to the back, through the hedges and trees, were a farmer's, fields, which had been part of the attraction of the property. This left Derek as their only neighbour.

"Well, perhaps we should see if he's alright?"

"Hmm. I don't want to be selfish or anything, but might it be better and safer to just sit things out for a few days. You know, don't put ourselves at risk?" Jessica looked intently at Jean, noticing at greater detail the mole on her right cheek out of which protruded several grey hairs. *What happens when people get past seventy? Do they just forget to look in mirrors? I mean, come on, they're like trees! Get a grip! Just five seconds of plucking, surely.* And then she admonished herself for such shallow musings, which ran against much of what she usually thought. Jessica had often wondered about thoughts just popping into people's heads with no control or intent from the conscious brain, which just seemed to be an innocent bystander more often than not. As she often wrote about in philosophical contexts, "Does the conscious mind drive human action like a jockey driving a horse, or does it sit back and observe the action driven by the nonconscious brain, like a passenger sitting in a cart drawn by that horse? Does the passenger, hoodwinked, think it is actually controlling the horse?" In the abstract distance, Jean's voice sounded through her thoughts.

"…if you think it's a good idea."

"I'm sorry, what was that? Sorry, Galen put me off," claimed Jessica, losing herself for a short while.

"I said, if you think it's a good idea to knock on Derek's door, then maybe we should do it."

"What, now?"

"Better late than never, my dear."

46
Greg

The beachfront café ahead would normally have looked thoroughly inviting. There would usually be tables and chairs set on the beach in front of the large establishment, welcoming tourists to take in the summer sun whilst sipping their drinks. The Crab Shack, now, stood with doors shut, shutters down, and tables stacked and padlocked as though it were mid-winter.

There was an irony that Greg himself had grown up near his own Crab Shack on the American East Coast, a far cry in style and size from this Devonian piece of modern commercialism. Greg's Crab Shack entertained, almost exclusively, the notion of actually selling crabs and crab-based delights.

None of which was remotely of any concern to Greg, as he made his way up the edge of the beach, alongside the sheer, shaded rock face, interspersed with plants. Life clinging on against all the odds, surviving in spite of the most difficult of challenges, exposed to the elements, unconcerned with the height, living despite the lack of food, the vagaries of the weather and anything else nature could throw at herself.

Greg was starting to feel the stinging pains in his feet and hands. All four extremities were damaged and bleeding, and neither the salt nor sand were helping.

Around the side of the café, through a small wooden gate, was a patio area with permanent tables and chairs. Greg moved through them to the car park behind. He hadn't really considered what to do next. He looked up the beach, and then moved into the car park to look down the road upon which, earlier, he had stood surveying the shop wares. He could see the odd figure stumbling about at the far end of the road. Luckily, no one seemed to have noticed him, crouched behind a blue Volvo left in the car park.

The car park stood on the corner of the coastal road which ran along the front of the bay town. As it cornered at the car park, the road veered round to incline up the slope to eventually meet the height of the bluff. Olding sat cosily between the two headlands, rising from the sea to a fairly sharp incline as the land retreated. The road, as it ascended up the slope from the car park, had houses and the occasional tea room, art gallery, or other retail establishment, huddled over it such that it struggled to accommodate cars side-by-side. Some fifty metres or so up the hill, the road veered left following the rocky outline of the headland as it narrowed the settlement to a rough U-shape.

Greg contemplated his options. He had the hotel to look for, but he simply didn't know where to start, standing as he was with bloodied hands and bloodied bare feet and nothing else to his name but the wet clothes on his back. He clearly didn't want to shout for help, but had to find it as safely as possible. Perhaps he could look for a car, or break into a house. Maybe there was a police station nearby. Or better still, he could find a public telephone box and phone the emergency services.

The town was deathly quiet, but that serenity was broken by distant shouting and a thudding crash, coming from what seemed like the far side of town. He heard the engine of a car, perhaps from the same place, perhaps not, starting up and accelerating through the gears. The sound trailed off as the car moved further into the distance. He thought he heard another vehicle a few seconds later, and then that died away.

Crouching behind the Volvo, eyes scanning, Greg found that his senses were heightened, listening and watching for any movement, sound, or sign of danger (or, indeed, help). After a minute or two, Greg heard the sound of another engine in the distance. The sound grew gradually louder until, rounding the corner up the hill, an aquamarine VW camper came into view.

"Thank you, God," Greg muttered to himself.

The van was not exactly taking a Sunday morning stroll in the country, screeching as it was around the last corner. Greg removed himself from his hiding place and staggered painfully to the side of the road, arm outstretched to flag the vehicle down. Whoever was inside would be able to help him, surely.

The van was navigating down the centre of the road.

"Hey!" Greg shouted, throat hurting and voice croaky from sea water.

The van was only ten metres away when Greg, bloodied and barefooted, called with both arms outstretched, hoping that his remonstrations would stop the van and, from what he could see, its driver and passenger.

To Greg's crashing disappointment, the van shifted left on to his side of the road, as if to knock him down! He could now clearly see the passenger mouthing something at him angrily. His instincts took over and he tried to jump back, but the wing mirror and part of the door slammed into his arm and side, throwing him violently backwards, where he landed awkwardly on the roadside, hitting his head on the tarmac. The van continued on its way, motoring down the seafront road, eventually up to the car jutting out of the gallery frontage. He could just make it out stopping. Perhaps they would come back and help him.

Greg's world was now a world of agony. Acute sensations ran up from his arms and ribs to his brain, messengers of bad news, angels of doom. His brain was in shock mode, and the full force of the pain was being somewhat held back. Still, Greg was momentarily paralysed, prostrate on his side, nerves throbbing furiously. Slowly, he rolled onto his back, though doing so seemed to open up his ribs and stretch his diaphragm, something which entirely aggravated his current predicament.

"Arrrgghh!" Greg surrendered, involuntarily, to an outpouring of noise, the pain requiring some kind of relieving outburst.

And then silence, save for the sound of blood pulsating about his temples.

And then "Fssshhhhhht" and the soft scrape of dragging feet.

Greg turned his head to look along and up the road from where the campervan had come. His world had shifted ninety degrees. His eyes took a few seconds to focus properly.

And then the sight of two legs came into view, fumbling and stumbling: a puppet on a string, handled by a blind amateur puppeteer.

And then Greg's lights went out.

METAMORPHOSIS

47
Callum

Callum loved playing games. Throughout his childhood, they had always been something that gave him joy and allowed him to compete as an equal with anyone. Sports had never been his forte. He was overweight, that much was obvious. His parents were both overweight and he had always felt he was fighting his biology *and* his home environment to overcome the challenge of eating.

Besides, he loved eating. It was that simple. He was savvy enough to realise a compromise when he was involved in one. Doing exercise and getting trim was not enough of a gain to giving up food and the lifestyle he was used to. Yes, it was a close call. He was teased, perhaps even bullied for it.

But he loved eating. And doing things which didn't require an awful lot of movement. Board games. Computer games. Movies.

There was no longer any electricity, and that sucked. He had a computer console and a television in his room, both now obsolete. Every so often Callum tried them, just in case the government had got things working again.

Nope.

So board games it was. He was playing Risk with himself. He had arranged three players to participate. All of them were him. But he favoured red. Red was *really* him. The other two were other hims. It depended on the dice as to who would win this, probably. Or probably not, Callum mused. He had positioned all the armies at the start of the game and had in mind that reds would win Australasia. Yes, the key to the game. With that continent only accessible from one place, the two armies it received per turn were a dead cert.

Reds would probably win.

One packet of biscuits and a can of Coke later (sequestered from his dwindled "secret stock"), the game was almost over. Reds had invaded each country, spreading their power such that their presence was almost ubiquitous. Blues had held out in North America before perishing before the growing, exponential might of the reds. Yellows held on to South America, the last bastion of hope under the seemingly inevitable and perilous threat of the reds.

That inevitability hit Callum. He had a sudden realisation that the fun in these contests, what kept the game alive, was the constant battling. The jostling for superiority. But when the superiority became established, the fun dissipated. As one supreme player got the upper hand, and the tide was so firmly in their favour, the joy for everyone was diminished.

In some sense, it was in everyone's favour that there was a constant battling, vying for resources. In this case, land. Then again, could you simply battle on forever? What were the chances of that happening? Eventually, *someone* had to win, surely! That was simple probability (which he was presently learning in maths class).

Callum looked at the board. The status quo had been broken. Reds were winning. There was no way back for the yellows. There was no defence. The reds had the whole world, for goodness sake. Callum started to resent the reds. He liked the yellows now. Always a fan of the underdog, he thought.

He picked the board up and all the pieces fell into the fold in the middle. Moving it over to the box, he tipped the pieces inside, and threw the board on top.

I've got to get out of here. But where to? Where?... That's it! Gemma!

The muffled banging continued at the door, unendingly.

Not that he didn't love him, because he did. But Callum said something he had been wanting to say for some years now, at one time or another, but had never had the guts.

"Oh, just fuck off, Dad!"

48
Jessica

With Galen safely back in the house, Jessica and Jean, equipped with a spade and a hammer respectively, took a slow and cautious walk out of the driveway and right along the road towards Derek's house. They had agreed that given any sign of issue of threatening behaviour, they were to return back to Jessica's house.

Just as the two rounded the well-maintained leylandii hedgerow, a sound could be heard: a soft scraping along stone. Hackles raised along with their weapons, they edged their way round so that the house came slowly into view up the purplish-brown paved driveway.

"He-hello, Derek?" called Jean in her most middle-classed and neighbourly voice, as if she were from the Women's Institute on her rounds to sell some pickle. Jessica stared hammers at her and mimed being quiet. Then there, strangely shuffling along the nearside leylandii hedging, was Derek, his thin frame dressed in blue striped pyjamas and topped off with an apt brown dressing gown. The sound was from his slippers as they scraped over the small paving bricks.

Surveying this man, the two women could see that he didn't look well; his skin was pale and covered in a heavy sheen of sweat, his thinning grey-brown hair was thrusting in various directions, and he simply looked weak. Jean's voice captured his attention.

"J-Jean...I-I'm...I'm not feeling very well. Can you, can you help me?"

Jessica and Jean were both taken aback. They had been expecting him, in their pessimistic worst case scenario, to be similar to the previous man they had encountered. Instead, this weak old fellow recognised Jean and appeared compos mentis enough to communicate normally.

"Oh Derek, dear, are you alright?" Jean responded, lowering her weapon and motioning towards him.

"He's not well, Jean. He told you that and just look at him. Don't go near him. You don't know how contagious this virus is," Jessica warned, worried at the sight of this man. An eel flipped and writhed in Jessica's stomach, supplanting what might have been mere butterflies. Her nerves had been soundly and roundly assaulted over the last week and she felt like she lacked control of her biology to a much greater degree than normal. On Derek's driveway, the whole scene played itself out to Jessica like she was a third party sitting in a late-night cinema watching some foreign film, *Jessica et Jeanne*, and not really understanding what was going on.

"I'm so...so...hot... I need fresh air. Must get outside... Help me...Angela..."

A good ten metres of drive and tall hedgerow separated Derek from the two women. Jean, a step behind Jessica, nervously advised her that Angela was Derek's wife who had been dead many years. He was evidently in some fevered delusory state, fumbling and stumbling both mentally and physically through his immediate surroundings without much conscious control.

"I...shhhh...I...fshhh...help... Yes, help, that's what...fshhhh..." and Derek's left arm came out, stretching towards the two onlookers. However, his right knee seemed to give way, and the dressing-gowned man fell abruptly to his knees. Beads of sweat dripped off his hawkish nose as he stared up at them, through them. Jessica could feel the state of chaos in him just by looking at his face and into his slightly glazed and discoloured eyes. She could sense a bodily invasion. She could feel, through heightened empathy, a loss of control.

With a staccato lack of fluidity, Derek's arms hit the floor and supported his now bent frame. The man was on all fours and twitching his awkward way forward. His head swung downwards but his body jerked on, like a prototype robot which hadn't yet been graced with the artificial intelligence to learn how to move like an animal, its joints jutting and jarring this way and that.

With alarming suddenness, Derek's head snapped up to lock eyes with Jean, perhaps in some distant recollection, perhaps for no recognisable reason, or perhaps spotting her as the older and weaker of the pair. In that short time his eyes had transformed, metamorphosed into something different and more corrupt.

"Hnnnngg...nngggg sshhhhaaaghhh..." To Jessica, in this internal struggle for control which was taking place, Derek was on the losing side. *Who* was winning was anyone's guess.

"Um, Jean...let's just, er, get the hell out of here?"

***

The car was packed. They had decided to go to Devon. The only problem was that between the two women and a baby, and the car, was Derek. A menace of spittle and jaw chomping.

Jean and Jessica, with Galen in her arms, were standing at the front lounge window looking at their neighbour. They were less than a metre from him and yet had gauged that he was in effect harmless, with the door, walls and window blocking him from getting to them.

"I guess," observed Jessica, "that these ill people can't use door knobs and handles and whatnot. They don't seem to have that sort of aggression that tries to break windows. If I was him and wanted to get at us now, with all my faculties, I would be using my brain to problem-solve. That includes turning a handle; that's just a mini-problem, right? Which means that they probably can't predict the future and rationalise in this state. You know, use all the faculties of personhood that we associate with being human."

"It appears that way, my dear. It certainly does. And lucky for us, too!"

"Well," Jessica continued, "luckily, *we* can. We can use our brains to get ourselves out of this mess. We just need to get into that car. That's all. Can you drive?"

"Yeeeesss, yes, I can. But I haven't for years. And nothing so great as your car. I...I don't...I wouldn't feel comfortable driving that. Especially in my state of mind."

"Hmm. I think we need bait. I would be happy enough to be bait, again, and lure him away so that you can drive after me and pick me up. But I guess it'll have to be round two of getting one of these people round the back of the house. I'm getting serious déjà vu."

The two homebound prisoners concocted a plan that looked remarkably like the previous one, with Jean taking Galen and the car keys, whilst Jessica looked to lure the now spasmodic and deteriorated Derek round the back of the house, before locking the door and running through the house to reunite with Jean.

As it happened, it all went to plan, though this didn't stop Jessica from almost having a heart attack with the sheer volume of adrenalin searing through her veins, pumping her body full of nervous energy.

Now sitting next to Jean, who had Galen on her lap, Jessica turned the key to hear the car's engine purr into life like an oversized lion. And she felt safe. Safe in the confines of this thing of metal and glass and plastic and locks.

Pulling out of the drive, she turned to Jean and said, "I've got the satnav if you've got the post code. This had better be a good idea. I'm leaving behind my house, my life and my husband."

And she burst into uncontrollable fits of tears, racking sobs of distraught and angry sorrow that shook her body like a rag doll.

EPILOGUE

The calm silvery surface of the Solent reflected the setting sun, which was slowly disappearing, in a pink-red haze behind the distant chimneys of the Fawley oil refinery by the port of Southampton. The tall, thin towers gave off no exhaust fumes; they stood silently to attention, waiting expectantly. Seagulls wheeled and screeched in the near distance, still searching for food in the quickly dimming embers of the day.

Alistair held on to the railing on the side of the ship, looking off into the westerly direction, wondering when normality would return. *If* normality would return. And how much would *he* have to play in that? He looked over to the coast of the Isle of Wight, the one hundred and fifty square miles of island facing the harbour entrances of Portsmouth and Southampton. It was his idea that the island had quickly become a serious factor in their plans. Maybe not right away, but at some point. The natural marine barrier presented a very real option for the Armed Forces to use, though it was still a very large expanse of land to deal with.

Looking back to Portsmouth, the Captain surveyed the stark reality of various plumes of smoke where fires had started, and had not been stopped. Portsmouth was reflective of every town and city that Alistair had heard from. And the situation was dire. The Prime Minister and most of the cabinet were dead, dying or reborn. Some were safe, here and there, or had taken themselves to their families. A few were on board HMS Daring with him, moored at the entrance to Portsmouth Harbour.

The Queen was dead. Or at least dying with no known cure, along with her husband. This much he knew, though he was under strict instructions not to share this with anyone for reasons of morale. Prince Charles and his son, Prince Harry, remained alive and quarantined in Balmoral, isolated in rural Scotland. He was unsure of any other royals.

A number of remaining cabinet members and some higher ranking Armed Forces personnel had been positioned at the Victorian follies which remained obstinately set in the water of the Solent: Spitbank Fort, No Man's Land Fort and Horse Sand Fort. These three squat concrete and granite squat turrets were built in the waters between Portsmouth and the Isle of Wight to defend the naval port from the threat of seaborne attack. They now served to immunise its personnel from airborne viral attack from the mainland.

METAMORPHOSIS

Commodore Alistair Connaught had just returned from a meeting with some of these decision makers at Spitbank Fort and was collating and filing his thoughts at the bow of the destroyer. The primary goal was to gather important personnel from around the country whom they knew were safe; gather them, quarantine them, and get them assembled in the two forts. Without a test to see who was safe, though, the importance came in quarantining them. An auxiliary vessel had been set up as a quarantine location, but unfortunately, two virulent guests had seriously set their plans back, and many people had had to be neutralised. Now they were back to square one. They had so far assembled a few scientists, a couple of top medical professionals, some cabinet and other government personnel, some high-ranking officers of the three military arms, and some (indeed, not many) of their family members on the two forts. Though a Captain was on board HMS Daring and was logistically in charge of the vessel, Alistair, as Commodore, and a young one at that at forty-four, was the senior officer stationed on the ship.

The extent of the chaos was huge. Alistair still marvelled at the rapid disintegration of the lines of communication and the structures of the Armed Forces and other forms of societal authority. The illness had spread with virulent speed, an exponential growth, which had pulled that rug from under society without warning. And society had nothing to hold on to. It had come tumbling down, and was only now gaining a sense of what was happening. Without news outlets and media to tell it anything, Alistair had mused, society was blind. Nature was fighting back and exacting her revenge, like a scorned and neglected lover.

"Sir?"

Alistair shook his head, breaking from thought and realising he had not heard the lieutenant walk up behind him. The ship was not exactly shy of people on board, but the front deck was devoid of anyone but him, and now his lieutenant.

"Yes, what can I do for you?"

His eyes were worried. Bloody hell, what now?

"Sir, we've had word from D-group over in the dockyard and...and it's not exactly good news."

"I'm not really sure how things could get a whole lot worse, Jeremy."

News had not been good on any day, ranging from someone releasing the animals at Longleat Safari Park to two Islamic fundamentalists blowing themselves up at the entrance to the Houses of

Parliament. As if there wasn't enough to be dealing with, without lions and religious dogma vying for attention. Perhaps this *was* the End Days.

"Well...we've had reports that some of the *subjects* in Portsmouth, well two to be precise, have been observed to move, er, quickly."

The Captain's brow furrowed. "'Er, quickly'?"

"Yes, sir, quickly."

"I know what you said. I heard you clearly. What do you mean, lieutenant?"

The lieutenant nervously rocked on his feet, hands still behind his back. "I mean that there have been two subjects which have run. Every other subject, sir, has sort of walked, or at very best half-jogged. Now two have been seen to run. Apparently not *really* fast, but a good deal faster."

Captain Connaught stared intently at his subordinate, mind clicking, whirring and making connections. "I see. Are you saying that this thing, this virus, has changed? Is this a new strain? Is it...getting worse?"

"I don't know, sir. All I know are the observations made from D-group. Also, sir, they saw one get someone else, someone whom D-group was trying to help. We've got Charteris from D-group on the radio in the Bridge, sir."

"Thank you. I'll be in momentarily." The lieutenant saluted, turned and walked back up the deck. Alistair turned and grabbed the railing one more time.

And thought of home. Of Samantha. Of George and Katie.

Inner turmoil came over him, a tsunami of conflict, guilt and indecision. He had his duty, to Queen and country. But also to family and loved ones. He had seen so many of his own men and women desert their posts. So many. There was something so visceral and yearning, deep inside him, which wanted to follow suit.

Queen and Country. So meaningful to him in his training, and in everything he had done for the Royal Navy. What did it mean now? Was it now King and Country? Was Charles still alive for sure? Was it just this nebulous idea of monarchy and country? Did he have a country left? This land mass, and this sea he was set upon? Was *he* in some important sense a vital piece in the jigsaw that was his country? Was he now appealing to *himself* and his country, *as* his country?

Alistair's mind was a flurry of confusion, set against the calm backdrop of the Solent; a maelstrom of consternation.

What, what is it all for? Why am I doing this? What is the most important thing to me? To me now?

METAMORPHOSIS

Samantha. George. Katie.
Katie. Samantha. George.
George. Katie. Samantha.

His mind was set. He had a new queen, and a very small country. Just one thing remained to be sorted out.

How?